# THE HEIR
## HUNTER

# CHRIS LARSGAARD

# THE HEIR HUNTER

DELACORTE PRESS

Published by
Delacorte Press
Random House, Inc.
1540 Broadway
New York, New York 10036

Library of Congress Cataloging-in-Publication Data

Larsgaard, Chris.
  The heir hunter / Chris Larsgaard.
    p.  cm.
  ISBN 0-385-33363-3
    1. Private investigators—California—San Francisco—Fiction.
2. Inheritance and succession—New York (State)—Fiction. 3. San Francisco
(Calif.)—Fiction. 4. New York (State)—Fiction. I. Title.
PS3562.A746 H45 2000
813'.54—dc21                                                    99-056185
                                                                CIP

Manufactured in the United States of America

Published simultaneously in Canada

February 2000

10 9 8 7 6 5 4 3 2 1

BVG

To my father and mother, Bill and Carla Larsgaard, for everything

# ACKNOWLEDGMENTS

Many people are deserving of thanks for this book, but the following individuals were absolutely vital.

To my fantastic literary agent, Matt Bialer of the William Morris Agency, for his patience, wisdom, humor, and common sense. Thanks, buddy—only you know what we went through for this one. Also, thanks to Maya Perez for her great feedback and for being there from the start.

To my fabulous editor, Jackie Cantor, whose thoughtful guidance was crucial to literally everything. Thanks for making the work fun, Jackie.

To my brothers Bill and Matt for their essential critiques. To my cousin Tim for his support.

To my earliest readers, Ed Wells, Danielle Wells, Paul "Pat" Nacario, Dave Garcia, and Elisa.

Lastly, my sincerest gratitude to the most important person of all: the amazing heir-hunting private investigator who, not surprisingly, wants to remain . . .

in the shadows.

# THE HEIR HUNTER

# PROLOGUE

THEY HAD DECIDED that the old man was crazy. Whether it was the onset of neurological disease or simply the inevitable effect of advancing years mattered little. Gerald Raymond Jacobs was eighty-seven years old and losing touch with his sensibilities. He was starting to talk, and talk too much, and they were very alarmed by this. They had instructed him several years ago on his final obligation—he was to remain silent until death. It was the simplest of instructions, but the old man was now refusing to abide by the rules, and this made him extremely dangerous.

The visitor sat patiently on the plush living room couch and tried to show a facade of attentiveness. He was thirty-eight years old with pale skin and reddish-brown hair, and his name was Malloy. For ten minutes straight, he had endured the old man's ranting, but his patience had now run its course. Jacobs was speaking from his recliner, barely taking time to breathe as he delivered his latest rambling diatribe. It was clear he was dissatisfied with everything. His carrying on only confirmed what Malloy had been told: his mind was gone. At this point it was just as well.

"I have serious grievances," said Jacobs once again, finally pausing to draw a noticeable breath. "And I'm tired of being lied to."

"Well, that's why we're here, Mr. Jacobs," replied Malloy soothingly, as if he were speaking to a child. "We want to fix things."

"I don't like being lied to."

"We understand. We wouldn't like that either."

"No, you wouldn't," snapped Jacobs. "I have new demands. To begin with, I'll need more money. After everything I've given them, I'm enti-tled to it. Or perhaps they would prefer if I went to their newspapers. Is that what they want?"

Malloy clasped his hands together and had no answer. His assign-ment didn't include knowing these things. He didn't even know who this mysterious *they* were. He looked down at the thick Oriental rug at his feet—authentic undoubtedly. Everything in the living room—the chan-delier, the grand piano, the fine antique furniture—screamed of opu-lence, of serious money. He studied old man Jacobs and realized he was genuinely curious as to who this arrogant little person really was.

"You don't have to do anything drastic, Mr. Jacobs," he finally ven-tured. "We're going to work this out tonight. Here and now."

"I'm tired of their lies," muttered Jacobs.

Malloy nodded and listened to the muffled sound of the faucets run-ning. The flowing water became clearly audible as Malloy watched his partner slowly step down the stairs into view. The man cut through the kitchen and suddenly appeared directly behind Jacobs. His name was Regnier, and he hadn't said a word to the old man, which wasn't unusu-al; he rarely said much to anyone. He was half a head shorter than his seated companion, but stocky. He held a heavy wooden cutting board in his thick, powerful hands.

"So," continued Malloy, quickly now, "I want to make sure we understand where you're coming from. You want more money and—"

"Enough of this. I want to meet with Taylor. He's the only one who can help me."

Regnier had silently stepped into position. His eyes flicked to Malloy's and got the silent affirmation. He raised the board slightly, held it for a moment, and then with a sweeping arc slammed it against Jacobs's head. The old man pitched forward with a groan and sprawled onto the coffee table in front of his seat.

Malloy was on his feet. The two of them converged upon the old man and carried him quickly across the rug to the stairway. Regnier led the way up, following the sound of the running water to the bathroom. The tub was sufficiently full. Malloy turned the knobs off and then began to unbutton the old man's shirt.

"Help me with this."

Regnier bent down with a grunt and removed the old man's shoes and socks. He undid the trousers and pulled them off along with the underwear. They tossed the clothes to the corner in a heap.

Malloy stooped down to the crumpled, naked body. He hoisted the upper torso over the edge of the tub until the forehead dipped into the water. Red drops fell in a steady trickle from an oozing scalp wound. When the head was completely submerged, the body abruptly revived. The old man began to flail his arms and splash both men as they leaned their weight into him and kept his head beneath the surface. It was not difficult. The arm movements lasted only a few seconds, but they continued to hold him under for an additional minute. A bubbly ribbon of pale yellow bile rose up to the surface of the water.

When they were satisfied, they eased their grip on him and lifted the rest of the body into the tub, leaving it facedown in the now pinkish water. Malloy tossed a bar of soap in with the corpse before they exited to the hallway.

They divided the house strategically, beginning with the garage. Their search took an hour and a half. It was nearly 11 P.M. when the two men finally returned to their car and drove off into the night.

CHAPTER 1

THE PIVOTAL MOMENT of the negotiation had arrived, the point in the dialogue when pen was poised over contract. Nick Merchant studied his latest clients and felt his pulse drum at his temples. They were simple people, probably possessing no learning beyond the ninth grade, if that. They sat across from him—Emma McClure in her faded floral dress and house slippers, and her son, a greasy, yellow-toothed biker named J.P. They huddled on their worn living room couch looking like two expectant parents. Nick expected their reaction to his forthcoming disclosure to be on a par with being told they held the winning lottery ticket.

"Do you have any further questions, Mrs. McClure?"

"I can't think of any."

Nick leaned over the table and pointed to the blank line that read *Client*. J.P. looked over his mother's shoulder.

"Sign it, Momma."

"Quiet, J.P."

"He wants you to sign it."

"I told you to hush, boy!" she hissed. "Don't you be hanging over me like a vulture when I'm tryin' to think."

Nick searched his mental data bank for the few properly placed words that would sway Emma McClure to give her autograph. Twelve thousand dollars hovered like the horseflies buzzing in the stagnant air of the McClure shack. He leaned forward and tried to speak soothingly. "You seem a bit unsure, Mrs. McClure. Is something unclear?"

"Well, it's just that ... well, things like this don't usually happen around here."

"I understand," said Nick, with a smile. "I know this all seems a little strange. Do you have a copy of the yellow pages by chance? I'd like to show you something which may reassure you."

J.P. rose from the couch at his mother's prompting and returned with the phone book. Nick took it and flipped through it till he came to the heading Private Investigators.

"Here we are—Merchant and Associates. Our firm is a completely legitimate, family-owned business. We've been licensed by the state of California as private investigators for the last twelve years now. Our reputation in the field is excellent. If you'd like to check into us, you can call the local Better Business Bureau. I'm sure they would be happy to tell you all about us. I encourage you to do that if it will ease your mind."

"He's bein' honest, Momma," begged J.P., his voice almost frantic.

"You pipe down!" she snapped. She turned to Nick. "I don't think I'll be needing to call 'em. I believe I can trust you, Mr. Merchant. You say your family owns this business?"

Nick shifted in his chair a bit. He didn't want to lie to the old woman, but he felt it was best to shield her from the complete truth. "My father started the company, ma'am. He retired four years ago."

Emma looked over at her son. "I suppose a family-owned business couldn't be all bad, huh, J.P.?"

"Sure," replied J.P., happy to agree.

Nick nodded earnestly. "Ma'am, I promise you—there's nothing to be worried about. I wouldn't come into your home and lie to you. I guarantee you'll be very happy once you sign." He directed her gaze to the line requiring her endorsement.

Mrs. McClure frowned. Her life had never been complicated by important matters such as this, but Nick Merchant had a boyish, honest face, and even though she hadn't been brave enough to admit to him that she didn't really understand half the things he had explained to her that past half hour, she did feel that she could trust him. She gave J.P. one last uncertain look and, seeing nothing but encouragement on his face, scrawled her signature across the line. She handed Nick the contract and his pen and sighed.

Nick glanced over the signature and felt his saliva glands finally start working again. "Thank you, Mrs. McClure, and congratulations. This is a happy day for the two of you." He placed the contract into the folds of his portfolio. "I'd like to give you the details on your inheritance now."

"I'd appreciate that."

"The money is coming from your uncle, Andrew Thomas Galloway." He paused, gauging her reaction.

"My goodness," she stammered. "I . . . I don't—"

"My research indicates that you probably never even met him."

"You know, I never did, but my mother mentioned him a few times when she was alive. They had some sort of a feud goin'. Hadn't spoken to each other since the sixties."

Nick frowned sympathetically. Company research indicated that Andrew Galloway had not spoken to Emma McClure's mother since 1958. His research had uncovered more than dates, though. Andrew Galloway was actually a borderline psychotic with an unnatural attraction to young boys. But there was no need to bring out the darker side of his findings.

"Your uncle had been living up north in Placerville. He died about six weeks ago."

"And he remembered me in his will?"

"Actually he died without a will. When an individual dies without a will in California, the laws of inheritance are based on genealogy. Bloodlines. You're his closest living relative, so you get the entire proceeds of his estate."

"How much?" asked J.P., his entire body tensed.

"Brace yourselves, okay?" said Nick, breaking into a smile now. "There was slightly more than sixty-three thousand dollars in his bank accounts. That's the entire value of the estate. Congratulations."

Mother and son remained motionless, and Nick could read no reaction until J.P.'s yellow grin spread across his face like a hairline fracture in glass.

"Sweet Jesus," said Emma, fanning herself with a magazine.

"It's all yours now, folks."

"Sixty-three thousand!" shouted J.P., rising to his feet.

Nick focused on Emma McClure. He was more concerned with the heir's reaction.

"I can't believe this," she muttered, her head in her hands.

"I'm happy to say it's true, ma'am. Let me tell you how it'll work: my attorney will arrange a court hearing where we'll ask the court to release your uncle's money. Once they okay our petition, it'll take about five or six weeks for my attorney to receive the checks from the county and send you your portion."

"And then you'll mail me the money?"

"I'll deliver it to you personally. The county will mail my attorney two checks—one for your portion, the other for my company fee. As soon as my attorney gets the checks, I intend to drive back down here and hand you your portion myself."

"I appreciate that."

Nick reached into his coat pocket. "I want you to have my card, also my attorney's card, and a copy of the contract you've signed. Be sure to keep that in a safe place." He closed and latched his briefcase. "If you have no more questions, I'll need to be on my way, but please feel free to call me anytime at my office if you feel the need. My number's right there on the card."

She smiled at him, misty-eyed. "This is a godsend—a *godsend*, Mr. Merchant. Do you know how long I've wanted to patch the roof here? I . . . I just can't . . ."

The words were lost. She stood and took a step toward him, her arms extended. Nick blushed a bit as she gave him a quick hug.

"I'm happy to bring you the news," he said, smiling. "I'm sure you'll put the money to good use."

"Oh, we will, won't we, J.P.?" she replied, dabbing at her eyes. J.P. beamed.

"Thank you again, ma'am. Remember—any questions, you call me."

She nodded and Nick said goodbye.


The San Francisco office of attorney-at-law Douglas Spinetti reflected the prosperity of a well-established young practice. The interior decorator had placed the earmarks of success—the polished hardwood floor partially covered by an ornate royal-blue Persian rug; textured white walls adorned with fine paintings from the city's hippest art galleries; and the oval-shaped-full-length swivel mirror with cherry and red oak borders, perfectly positioned for self-admiration. The law degree from Georgetown hung like a divine scripture on the wall behind the grand mahogany desk. With his newly purchased Jaguar and recent membership in the Olympic Country Club, Doug Spinetti now felt the equal of an older brother whose law practice had reaped similar trophies. At six foot four with artificially tanned movie star looks and a full head of wavy black hair, Doug was a formidable presence in probate court. With him at the helm, Merchant and Associates had never lost a court battle, a fact Doug did not let Nick forget.

Doug was chattering away on the phone when Nick entered the office. The private investigator flashed his attorney the thumbs-up sign and approached the mirror, straightening his tie. He was exhausted again, and it showed. Deep bags had found homes under his eyes, and the eyes themselves were streaked with seemingly permanent little threads of red. He took two steps back and looked himself over. He was six foot one with a youthful face and thick black hair sprinkled with slight beginnings of a gray that hardly complemented his thirty-five years. His jaw was long and thick, his mouth often tired but always ready to smile. He was a loner but didn't mind it because he enjoyed his life, and his work was the biggest reason why. Heirs always needed finding, and to him nothing was more exciting than that simple fact.

Doug hastened his conversation along and finally hung up.

"Goddamn, I'm glad you're here. I need some good news." He spread his arms. "Talk to me—done deal?"

"What do *you* think?"

"I think we bagged ourselves another one," said Doug, flashing the victory grin that seemed to reveal every polished tooth in his mouth. "Percent?"

"Twenty."

"*Twenty?* That's it?"

"That's it. Yeah, yeah, I know. You didn't see their house, Doug. These people were about an inch from the poverty line."

Doug's face had assumed an expression more suitable for the thought of lost income.

"I swear to God, Nick, you missed your true calling in life. You should be over in India passing out loaves of bread or something. Nick Merchant, missionary."

Nick smiled and took the expected lumps. "You need to come along with me one of these times. You might learn something."

"No, *you* might learn something—how to run a business and not a damn charity. Your pops knew how. I don't know about his bleeding-heart son."

Nick was chuckling now. "Answer me honestly, Doug. Would seventy-five percent be enough of a cut?"

"Eighty sounds better." He shook his head. "So did these lovely poor folks give you any problems?"

"None. Couldn't have been in there more than half an hour. Real nice lady. She was in tears after I told her."

Doug attacked his desk calculator with his hand. Nick watched in amusement as the fingers pecked like a hungry bird. Doug leaned back with his hands behind his head. "Twelve point six—not too shabby. Could've been sweeter, though."

"Not too bad for three days' work," said Nick, rubbing his eyes. He had gotten only ten hours sleep out of the last seventy-two and exhaustion was hitting him like a freight train.

"Any other companies contact her?"

"Nope."

Doug leaned forward, studying him closely. "You seem a little mopey for someone who just made twelve grand. Talk to me, pal. What's up with the frown?"

Nick shrugged. He gazed absentmindedly at the certificates and diplomas affixed to the wall directly behind Doug's desk—a wall of medals proven in the battlefields of court. "I'm fine. Little bit distracted—I keep thinking about New York. It's almost show time over there."

"Yeah, what's the deal with Alex?"

"You know what the deal is. Two o'clock, Columbia County. She'll have five grand in her pocket, ready to go. The deputy attorney's pretty jumpy about the whole thing, but it's all set up."

"How many files you think this guy will have for us?"

"I don't know. I'm guessing we'll get six or eight cases to work. With the early jump, I'll solve 'em all. The worthwhile ones anyway."

Doug drummed his fingers on his chin, his smile wide. "I could barely sleep last night thinking about this, Nick. Thank God we're finally wising up. We've been getting our ass kicked more than we should."

Nick nodded. Despite the occasional Emma McClure, Doug's assessment was correct. The victories were nice, but they were really nothing more than table scraps from the big heir-finding firms like General Inquiry and Hogue and McClain. Hopefully the New York State money would be a step toward reversing that imbalance. Nick hoped so. He and Alex had spent several long nights on the phone discussing whether or not they wished to enter the shady realm of bribery. Although neither of them was comfortable with it, they were in agreement that Merchant and Associates would not survive without lining an occasional pocket.

"I want you to call me the second you hear from Alex," said Doug. "I'm not gonna be home tonight till about nine, but I want to know how it went."

"Will do. Where're you off to tonight?"

Doug leaned forward on his elbows, his frown inconsolable. "Oh God—another ballet recital for Carey. Kimberly wants to enroll Nicole in ballet class next month when she turns six." He shook his head. "If it ain't ballet, it's piano; if it ain't piano, it's gymnastics. Man, what I'd do for a G.I. Joe doll and a baseball mitt. Next one's got to be a boy, Nick."

"Then you'd just be bitching about Little League and Boy Scouts."

"I can handle that stuff. You don't know how bad it can be, buddy— I'm surrounded by girly things every hour out of the office. Barbie dolls and ballet. Kimberly wants another next year, and I'm scared to death it'll be another girl."

Nick laughed. "It's called justice. For all the hearts you stepped on before you got married." He glanced at his watch and shot to his feet. "I gotta get outta here. I'll call you later."

"Don't forget. I got a really good feeling about this deal."

Doug followed him to the door, giving him a playful punch in the shoulder as he left.


Alex Moreno rapped her nails impatiently on the surface of the Columbia County deputy attorney's desk and waited. She had five thousand dollars cash in her pocket and another seven thousand in her purse. She was nervous, but it wasn't just because of the illegality of the bribe. It was an excited kind of nervous, like a child on Christmas Eve who was not sure just how many gifts were going to be under the tree in the morning. She could barely sit still.

She dug her fingers under the collar of her blouse and gave it a slight yank. The thing felt like a noose and allowed about as much circulation. She had spoken with Nick the night before and agreed to dress "professionally." What a joke. Alex—the professional briber! She frowned. Blue jeans and a T-shirt were about as formal as she liked to get on the job. The blouses and skirts she had worn as an attorney hadn't left the closet in four years, and that was just fine with her.

"Mr. Koenig will be right with you," said a clerk, poking her head into the office.

Alex nodded and glanced around the typically drab government office. She was in the Columbia County Clerk's Building, in the office of Deputy Attorney Lloyd Koenig. The walls were bare, a dull off-white, the carpet a worn gray. Koenig's desk was box shaped, an imitation-oak construction with a dull finish and chipped edges. One small window looked out to Union Street in downtown Hudson. She shuddered at the thought of working in such confinement as she slipped her hand into her pocket and felt the envelope again. She had gone through it twice that morning to verify that it was indeed five thousand dollars. All that was needed now was Koenig and the probate files.

Nick was the one who had arranged this very special meeting. It was a desperate move, really—a move for survival. With heir-finding monster General Inquiry strengthening its bribery-fed stranglehold on the larger California counties, it was time to either fight fire with fire or sink out of sight. Neither she nor Nick had any intention of packing it in. With considerable reservations, they had finally decided to cross an ethical boundary.

Nick had negotiated the terms of the payment with Koenig one day over lunch. For five thousand dollars, Merchant and Associates was to be given an exclusive ten-day sneak preview of the county's monthly probate files, a 240-hour head start on the official county release date, when the competition would get their first look. Ten days—an eternity for a capable heir finder to wrap up a case. In light of this fact, five thousand dollars was a small price to pay.

"Ms. Moreno?"

Alex stood and faced him. Lloyd Koenig was short with thinning gray hair, and he wore a charcoal pinstripe suit, suspenders, and what looked to be a Rolex on his wrist. A walking billboard of Italian-tailored success. He offered his hand as Alex caught his eyes roam down her healthy five-foot-seven-inch frame.

"Lloyd Koenig, deputy attorney, here. Sorry to keep you waiting."

He gestured to the chair and Alex sat down again. Koenig dropped to his swivel chair and smiled, his leer making Alex cringe inwardly. He was gawking at her as if he had just heard a nasty story in the men's locker room.

"So how're you doing today?" he asked, showing a row of smoke-stained teeth.

"Fine, thanks," she answered, removing the envelope from her pocket and dropping it to the desk in front of him. "We may as well get down to business, Lloyd. Five thousand. Go ahead and count it if you'd like."

Koenig looked blankly at the envelope and then back at Alex. He said nothing.

"Is something wrong?" Alex asked, suddenly confused.

Koenig maintained his stare unflinchingly. The air was very quiet. "We need to talk," he said.

"About what? Is there a problem?"

"It's about the arrangement." He scratched his nose. "I'm afraid we're going to have to . . . renegotiate the terms."

"I thought everything had been squared away with Nick Merchant, Lloyd."

"Well, it *was*, but that was before I knew what I had here."

"I'm a little confused," she said, feeling a warm flow of blood to her cheeks.

"I'll be blunt. I want more money. This is just too damn big."

Alex studied him. Too damn big? "So what are we looking at here?"

"After what I've seen in these files, I think ten thousand's damn cheap."

Strictly for appearances' sake, Alex assumed a stunned look. She had anticipated worse. Koenig continued.

"I should be asking for a lot more than that. I've only got four files for you, but one of them is worth it all by itself. Easily."

"I'd like a figure."

Koenig considered his response carefully. "More than six figures. That's the last I'll say until I see cash."

Silence gripped Alex by the throat as Koenig let it all sink in. She felt a trickle of sweat run down her neck. More than six figures? The implication was obvious. And barely believable. "Are you saying you have a million-dollar estate?"

Koenig frowned, noncommital. Alex could see that she would get no more information until payment was rendered.

"Usual terms, Lloyd?" she finally asked. "One week?"

"Return the file to me in exactly a week and there'll be no problems. Seven days or we never do business again."

"We know how it works," Alex replied. "We've never been late before."

"Just be sure to keep it that way." He leaned back in his chair. "A

Bank of New York is right across the street. You have the funds to cover it?"

"I've got it all right here, Lloyd. Anything else we need to discuss?"

He frowned and shook his head. Alex rose to her feet and removed the envelope. She dealt out five thousand, then reached into her purse and counted out the rest. Koenig gathered it up like a miser when she was done.

"Give me a minute," he said, rising to his feet. "One other thing: I don't want you looking at the files here. Take them back to your car and get out of here. Understand?"

"No problem."

He left the office, closing the door behind him. Alex felt positively giddy. A seven-figure estate! If what Koenig was saying was true, they were indeed making out. A deal? Hell, this was an outright steal. She leaned forward on the desk and waited.

CHAPTER 2

THE MEMORANDUM CAME in a routine and innocent enough manner—the ringing of the telephone followed by a solitary beep and the winding of a paper through the facsimile machine. Memos arrived every minute in the Washington, D.C., office of the director of the Federal Bureau of Investigation, and this single sheet, the latest in an incessant stream of information exchange, sat untouched in the plastic fax tray for nearly an hour before the occupant found the appropriate ten seconds to examine it.

Arthur K. Gordon, acting FBI director, was sixty-seven years old and top man in the Federal Bureau of Investigation for the last two years. A former federal prosecutor and judge, Gordon was a towering man with cotton white hair and closely aligned gray eyes who seldom saw a memo that he judged worthy of his immediate attention. This latest arrival was an exception. Upon reading it, he reached for his phone and instantly had Edmund Arminger, his deputy director in New York, on the line.

"Tell me what you found and when you found it."

"Per the directive," replied Arminger, "my field agent sought to establish weekly voice contact with Jacobs this previous Friday. When Jacobs could not be contacted after a dozen phone calls, I dispatched two agents to his home in Hudson. They gained entry that night when

Jacobs failed to respond to the doorbell. They found him facedown in a bathtub full of water. From their initial inspection, it appears Jacobs slipped entering the tub, hit his head, and drowned. County coroner's got him now."

"Hmm. Any signs of foul play or forced entry?"

"None. The house was locked tighter than a drum."

Gordon leaned forward on the massive desk and tapped his fingers on his temples in an effort to gather his thoughts. "Any noticeable wounds or injuries?"

"Pretty solid gash on the right side of the head," replied Arminger. "Looks like a slip to me."

"So other than the head wound, no other visible signs of trauma?"

"Not that they could see, Arthur. We'll have the full coroner's report in a little while. Do we have reason to suspect anything other than an accident?"

It took Gordon a moment to reply.

"We don't have reason to suspect anything," he finally said. "If the coroner finds anything suspicious, we may take another look at it, but I don't expect anything unusual to come of that autopsy. One thing I want to make clear, Edmund: under no circumstances are we involving the local police."

"Fine. We can close the book on Mr. Jacobs, then?"

"I don't anticipate anything out of the ordinary on our end. Do what you need to do to close it out."

"Jacobs was a strange one," said Arminger quickly. "Did you look the file over? It's very incomplete. I don't understand why this man wasn't screened better."

"We've got the same file. It is a bit . . . lacking in some regards."

"Why exactly were we hiding this man?"

"I don't have the specifics in front of me," replied Gordon. "I assume there's a reason we weren't provided with the particulars, and I don't have a reason to feel interested at this point."

"I'm *very* interested, Arthur. I need to know about all WP's in my jurisdiction."

"He's not your problem anymore," said Gordon. "A death in Witness Security means less work, not more. Bury your curiosity with the old man and move on."

"That's not easy with this one."

"But it's smart. Don't get preoccupied with this, Edmund. When you're in my seat, you'll learn more than you want to know. Close this out by the book and forget about it."

"That's what I intend to do, Arthur."

"Good. Call me if you have any other questions."

He hung up and ran his hand across his face. Of the hundreds in witness protection, something was distinctly different about this eighty-seven-year-old. Gordon frowned as he reached for the phone. He knew enough about the Jacobs file to suspect he wasn't about to be enlightened.

## CHAPTER 3

NICK AWOKE FROM dreamless sleep and squinted into the half-darkness of his bedroom. The clock indicated he had slept for nearly an hour, a solid nap but not nearly enough to make up for three nights of neglect. He let his head fall back to the pillow as a police car screamed by on the street. As it always did, the wail of the siren brought him back.

He turned his head to the framed picture on the nightstand, a three-by-five-inch portal to a previous life. He studied his expression in the photo, the smile of a twenty-three-year-old rookie cop in his department-issued black uniform, shaking hands with a proud father who had worn the badge himself for twenty years. Bill Merchant would have gladly worn that piece of metal another ten years if he hadn't discovered his true passion.

He had read about heir finding in a PI magazine article and proceeded to build Merchant and Associates from nothing, turning his company into a tiny yet persistent thorn in the behind of General Inquiry, Hogue and McClain, and all the other big players. With his only son moonlighting from SFPD as his part-time partner, forty-seven-year-old Bill Merchant had found himself a calling. And what a wonderful calling it had turned out to be. For eight years, father and son had the time of their lives finding people and telling them all about inheritances they never knew they had.

But it had all ended quickly one night. Despite what Nick had told Emma McClure, Bill Merchant hadn't retired at all. That wasn't even close to the truth.

Somehow Nick knew the drinking would have a hand in it. It didn't matter whether it was behind the wheel, on the street, or in bed; the bottle would have its final say. As chance would have it, it happened outside a bar, a dive Bill Merchant probably shouldn't have been in by himself. A knife was pulled, and William Merchant—cop turned PI, widower turned drunk—was dead in the gutter. A handful of witnesses to interview but ultimately no arrests. Four years had passed since that terrible moment—no arrests, no new leads. Just another unsolved homicide gathering dust in a file cabinet.

For Nick, quitting the force was really no decision at all. Merchant and Associates had been orphaned just as the son had been. He decided in his grief that if there was anything he could do to ease some of the hurt, it was preserving and maintaining this final piece of his father. Merchant and Associates would exist—would *thrive*—as an ongoing tribute to its founder. This was a promise he had dedicated himself to keeping.

Nick pulled himself from the bed and opened the living room blinds. He studied the joggers and dog walkers going about their business on the grassy Marina Greens. Alcatraz sat in the middle of the bay like some immense freighter at anchor. Another black-and-white cruised Marina Boulevard toward the wharves. Nick focused on a shapely brunette jogging along the gravel path by the bay. The water was gray, a tinge darker than the fog-choked sky.

He entered the bathroom and turned on the faucet. He had always considered heir finding a bizarre line of work, more suitable for Sherlock Holmes than Dirty Harry, but he had come to see that he was better suited for finding people than he was for handcuffing them. The track record seemed to prove that. A four-year tally revealed that he and Alex had solved over two hundred cases and signed over five hundred heirs in fourteen countries. And even now, even after four years of it, the entire business remained wonderfully strange to him, kind of like working for the Publishers Clearing House Sweepstakes, only instead of one winner a year he found several dozen. All that and he got paid for it too.

He leaned over the sink and splashed frigid water on his face. He needed to wake up. There was no telling what Alex would find in

Columbia County. He dabbed himself dry as he surveyed himself in the mirror. His face remained youthful despite the creases around the eyes, the lines in the forehead. He smiled at himself weakly. He was doing fine. Four years after the murder and he was finally doing okay.

The doorbell rang. He glanced at his watch. Noon. Alex's call was long overdue, but at least his secretary was on time.

"How can you live out here?" Rose asked as she stepped inside. "I had to park almost four blocks away."

"This is where all the successful young people like me live," answered Nick, with a wink.

Rose dropped a stack of files on the kitchen table. "You're not so young anymore, Nick. Look at Doug. He's barely older than you, and he's got two kids already. Time for you to stop acting young and start thinking about settling down."

"You have someone in mind for me? A young Raquel Welch who can cook? I'm all for that."

"I might be able to arrange something," she said as she took a seat at the kitchen table. "My niece Patricia is single, and she's very sweet. She's a big girl who'll keep you well fed and happy. I think it would be good for you to meet someone new."

"I meet someone new every day."

"I'm not talking about old dead people, Nick. I'm talking about someone young, someone with a *pulse*, for goodness sake."

Nick smiled and shook his head helplessly. Taking on Rose two years ago as full-time secretary had been one of his better moves. With nearly thirty years of executive secretarial experience behind her, she had quickly made Merchant and Associates a fortress of organization.

The phone rang. Rose grabbed it, drawing an amused look from Nick. She held it out to him after a moment. "Alex. She's hyperventilating."

"She's what?"

She shrugged. "She's excited about something."

This was nothing unusual. Nick took the phone. "Hey, girl."

"Nick! Nick, you aren't going to believe this!"

"That good?" he asked, taking a pen and paper from Rose. "How many estates?"

"Only four, but you are *not* going to believe the fourth."

"Lay it on me."

"The name's Gerald Jacobs. Gerald Raymond Jacobs. That's

J-a-c-o-b-s. Died five days ago upstate, and I'm not kidding you about this figure. Are you by your fax?"

"Yeah. Why?"

"Because I'm sending it now. I'm not even going to waste my breath telling you about this one. You need to see it for yourself."

"Well, quit yakking and start faxing."

"Call me the second you're done reading it. No—book a flight out here first. We've got to get moving on this, Nick."

"I'm hovering over the fax, sweetie. Talk to you in a few."

Nick placed the phone down and rubbed the side of his face. Alex's enthusiasm was a strong point. It was one of many reasons he enjoyed their partnership so much.

Rose was staring at him. "Well?"

"She's excited, all right. Must be a nice one."

Rose dismissed this with a wave of her hand. "She gets excited doing her nails," she commented dryly.

Nick smiled and grabbed an apple from the kitchen. The fax suddenly rang. He approached it as a sheet slowly began humming through. He snatched it before it could fall to the tray. One part only he needed to see—the Inventory and Appraisement section. He found it on the third sheet.

"Oh my God . . ."

He let himself fall backward onto the couch. His mouth was locked open. Rose watched him from the kitchen doorway.

"Nick?"

"Jesus Christ," he muttered, not looking up. "Is this right?"

"What is it?"

His eyes were seeing it, but even with the act of reading it, of holding it, he found belief to be lagging. But there it was, as undeniable and real as a punch to the jaw. Was it a typo? He narrowed his eyes into slits and read the number again.

Twenty-two million, three hundred forty-six thousand dollars. And change. He leaned over the documents and continued reading.

The decedent, Gerald Jacobs—a.k.a. Gerald Raymond Jacobs—had died at his residence, which was located at 198 Michael Drive in Hudson, New York. The death had occurred just five days ago, and the county public administrator had been authorized to handle distribution of the estate assets. It was a scenario Nick had seen in hundreds of cases. After a cursory search for blood relatives, the PA would in all likelihood find no related heirs. Being bogged down with dozens of other estates, he would then file away the Gerald Jacobs case until time would allow for further examination.

Nick found the order of administration, the document appointing the county public administrator as caretaker of the estate. Due to the absence of a will and the apparent nonexistence of blood relatives, the assets had been taken over by the county court. The money would remain with them until further information became available.

Nick handed the sheets to Rose and rubbed his forehead. He felt Alex's excitement seize him. Somewhere—*somewhere*—there had to be heirs, and he felt damn confident he could find them. But from that point on, every second was crucial. He reached for the phone.

"I need a one-way ticket to Albany out of San Francisco. As soon as possible." He bit his pen. A flight that evening was absolutely essential. "Today, three-thirty P.M.? That's perfect. One ticket, yes . . . yes, it'll be on my Visa card. . . ."

He hung up and looked at Rose, who was still scanning the probate filing.

"My God, Nick."

"Unbelievable. I'm gone. My flight's in three hours."

He entered his bedroom and found his garment bag. He took five shirts and half a dozen ties from his closet.

"Could it be a mistake?" asked Rose, watching him pack.

"No chance. It's all spelled out nice and clearly."

"You think you can solve it?"

"The real question," answered Nick, reaching for one of his suits, "is whether I can solve it before anyone else does. If the East Coast outfits know about Jacobs, this might already be over. I'll know soon."

"You're supposed to call Alex back, Nick."

"Thank you," he said, reaching for the cordless.

Alex answered on the first ring.

"Nick?"

"You're right. I never would've believed you."

"What do we do?"

"Same thing we always do, baby—we build ourselves a family tree. Listen to me—I've got a three-thirty flight this afternoon to Chicago with a connecting flight to Albany. I should be out at your place no later than two A.M."

"I'll be waiting," said Alex. "Is this a dream, Nick? Twenty-two million and no relatives making a claim?"

"Well, if there *are* relatives, you and I are going to find 'em, partner. But don't go out and buy your yacht just yet. Something tells me this ain't gonna be easy. Who knows who else Koenig talked to? I figure General Inquiry's a safe bet. He's probably getting paid off by a bunch of heir-finding companies."

"He could make a million off the information alone."

"He's a fool if he didn't. He has no loyalty to us, that's for sure. There's just no way that we could be the only ones who know about this." He checked his watch. "It's three-thirty over there. What can you do in the next hour and a half?"

"A bunch. I've got our runners picking up the death certificate and the obituary. A couple of couriers are checking marriage records too. I'm going to the archives as soon as we hang up."

"Good girl. We'll be off to a running start tomorrow morning. I'll be knocking on your door about two A.M., okay?"

"Coffee'll be waiting."

"Make it strong. See you in the morning."

They could do it, Nick thought as he hung up. No doubt about it. The tools were in place. The fiche readers, volume after volume of skip-tracing manuals, law books, phone directories, and genealogical texts. The collection of birth and death records data, adoption records, marriage and divorce records. The business was on-line with almost every state-of-the-art database currently in existence for finding people and the dirt on those people. The essential networks were ready, the phone numbers in place to a small army of private investigators and researchers. The company was equipped to go to war with anybody. Even General Inquiry.

Nick reentered the bedroom. Rose had his flight bag packed and ready to go.

"You're all set, Nick," she said, zipping the bag closed. "You've got three suits and plenty of shirts and ties—"

"And enough underwear and socks to last through a nuclear winter. You're a lifesaver, Rose. Hey, I know I said I'd give you the afternoon off, but do you think—"

"Don't worry about it," she replied. "Let's get to the office and get your things together."

Nick nodded and wondered how he had ever gotten along without her. He slung his garment bag over his shoulder and found his keys. He held the door open for her.

"I can't wait to see my bonus check after you get this one," she said with a smile.

"That'll be one monster bonus, Mrs. Penn."

He locked the door, and they headed for the elevator.


The McCarthys were a cautious old couple, one of the more wary he had seen that month, but the old man secretly loved the challenge of it. Lawrence Castleton, sixty-four years young, still felt a passion for his business. Founder of Los Angeles–based General Inquiry, he had been in charge of the heir-locating giant since its inception forty years ago. He was a large man, six foot four and close to three hundred pounds, with thinning white hair smoothed back along his head and a large woolly mustache that gave him a grandfatherly appearance. He insisted that all employees address him as Lawrence, and he disliked titles such as *president*, much preferring the term *chief adviser*. He was the living legend of the industry.

"Mr. Castleton," said Mr. McCarthy, "it's not that we don't appreciate your company contacting us about the inheritance. We're just looking for some assurance that we won't be stuck paying any surprise fees."

Castleton nodded. A not uncommon concern of prospective clients. "I assure the two of you that you will never incur any expenses whatsoever, and I want to—" He stopped as the conference room door suddenly swung open. His chief investigator, Richard Borg, craned his neck around the door.

"Pardon the interruption, folks. I need to speak with you, Lawrence. It's urgent."

Castleton gave a tight, irritated smile. "Be out shortly, Richard."

"Lawrence, you need to come see this now."

Castleton glared at his friend. He hated being interrupted midway through a presentation, especially when a three-hundred-thousand-dollar estate was the topic. He rose to his feet and excused himself, meeting Borg in the hallway outside.

"Hope it's good, Richard."

"It's better than good. Follow me . . ."

Castleton stepped quickly to keep up with his second-in-command as he led him down the first-floor hallway of the Sachmann Building, a three-story company-owned structure now perfectly adapted for the business of people-finding. The first floor, consisting of the lobby and twelve suites, was accessible to the public. Clients were entertained and courted in the centralized conference room. The second floor held eight additional offices and a company gym, which included weights, treadmills, and a spa. The third floor was a genealogical library and research center containing over four thousand genealogical texts and manuals and a dozen workstations with hundreds of databases at the ready. Mormon heaven, as Castleton called it.

They entered the president's suite at the end of the hall, and Borg quickly shut the door behind them. Borg, the genealogist instrumental in the solving of the million-dollar Luchetti case in 1989, reached for a small collection of papers on the desk and extended them to Castleton.

"Read, Lawrence."

Castleton didn't need to read every word, the Inventory and Appraisement section being the only part he was interested in. He quickly flipped through the pages until he spotted it. His forehead instantly furrowed.

"Well, holy . . . shit . . ."

"Just came through the fax."

The president of General Inquiry continued to read as his hand cradled the faxed sheets like a newborn. "Columbia County?" asked Castleton, giving a quick incredulous laugh. "This is a joke, right? We never get anything out of that godforsaken little burg."

"No joke," said Borg. "We've got our people moving on it right now. We'll have the obit and death certificate shortly."

"What's the name of our contact out there?"

"Lloyd Koenig."

"How much did he take us for?"

"I told him we'd give him a contingent thirty grand *after* we solved it. Based on a fee of thirty percent of the estate, that's about one half of one percent of the gross."

"Good job. Who can we send to New York?"

"I've already spoken to Risso and Lake."

"Excellent." He slammed his fist into his hand. "I want fifty-state searches for marriage, divorce, census, immigr—"

"Lawrence, before all that, we do have one little problem. Koenig sold it to another firm."

Castleton rubbed his chin, hardly surprised. He had been in the business too long to let news of the competition catch him off guard. "So who're we up against? Hogue and McClain? Vanguard?"

Borg shook his head. "Alex Moreno."

"Who?"

"She's with Merchant and Associates. Remember that San Francisco firm?"

"*Them?* What the hell are they doing all the way out in New York?"

"Moreno lives there, remember? She runs a route through the local counties."

"So what other companies?"

"Koenig swears they're the only ones. I think he's on the level."

Castleton grunted. He leaned against the edge of his desk and crossed his arms on his barrel chest. "This Koenig character's a real fucking genius, isn't he? I would've paid him a hundred grand free and clear if he had just had the common sense to deal with us exclusively." He waved his hand in the air. "What's done is done. I don't see a problem going against a rinky-dink operation like Merchant and Associates. Do we know when they got ahold of the file?"

"About an hour before we did."

Castleton instantly glanced at his watch. It was 7:10 P.M. in New York. The hour had gained Merchant and Associates almost nothing. If they were lucky, they might have gotten hold of the death certificate. But a head start of any kind was still disturbing.

"It doesn't matter," Castleton said. "Merchant won't be a problem. The father never gave us problems—why should the boy? I'm looking to have this wrapped up in twenty-four hours."

Borg was clearly not overwhelmed with the pep talk.

"I hope so, Lawrence. I keep thinking about Omar Morales."

"Well, *don't,*" growled the president, confirming a huge sore spot. "It was pure, dumb luck, Richard. We got sloppy and Merchant slipped in and stole one—big deal. That isn't going to happen here, I promise you that."

Borg nodded and said nothing. It *was* a big deal—a $21,000 big deal. They had called the Omar Morales case an aberration, a freak event, but it demonstrated a sobering fact—they weren't as invulnerable as they liked to think.

"When does the Lear land in New York?"

"Midnight."

"Crack of dawn I want Risso and Lake in Hudson at the neighbors' front doors."

"They will be."

"Good," replied Castleton, nodding importantly. "We'll solve it, Richard. Merchant can't touch us. I want to check something upstairs on our friend Mr. Jacobs. You have time?"

Borg nodded. At the door, Castleton grabbed his friend's shoulder.

"One last thing—let's keep this Jacobs business our little secret. Don't breathe a word of this to anyone else in the firm besides Risso and Lake. I don't want to get everyone else here all wound up. Nor do I want to slice this pie up into too many pieces. *Capice?*"

Borg nodded his approval.

"Let's go, then."

CHAPTER 4

Jimmy Demello was frightened. He was on his knees, opening drawers and shoving files indiscriminately into his suitcase. Now that he was inside his East Harlem office, he felt a heightened, almost panicked sense of urgency. Ten minutes—he needed to be out and on the road in ten minutes. He ran his sleeve across the wetness of his forehead and cursed. Even close to midnight it was sweltering, the dry air hanging like smoke over the carpet. He was tired of that heat. He would move somewhere cooler, somewhere by the ocean hopefully. It didn't matter where actually; he just needed to put some serious miles between himself and the Gerald Jacobs assignment. He intended to do that immediately.

He was reaching for another drawer to empty when he heard a creak, like a foot stepping on aged floorboards. He froze, too scared to move. He listened. He was about to remove the gun when two men slipped into the half-darkness of the office.

They were an odd-looking pair. One was tall and long-limbed, the other thick and muscular. They both looked dangerous as hell to Jimmy Demello. His stomach suddenly hurt. He hadn't noticed them staking out the parking lot, but apparently they had been there all along. Waiting for him.

Malloy and Regnier both held pistols affixed with silencers.

"Strange hours you keep, Demello."

The PI felt his bladder loosen at the mention of his name. He swallowed hard and tried not to show how scared he was. "Can I help you guys with something?"

"Oh yeah," replied Malloy, with a barely perceptible smile. "I think you know what it is we're looking for."

"Excuse me?"

"Cut the bullshit. You and your partner like taking pictures. Where are they?"

The smile was gone now. The thick man named Regnier had stepped to the left, spreading the distance between himself and his companion. Demello thought of reaching for the pistol in his belt but knew it would be suicide. He would try begging.

"The old man's got 'em all. I swear to God. He's got everything."

"The old man's dead, Demello. You didn't know? Bathing accident, from what I hear."

"Look," said Demello, his hands out and shaking now. "I got no reason to lie. If I had the pictures, I'd give 'em up. I'm tellin' you—we gave 'em all to Jacobs. He paid for 'em, we handed 'em over. It was just a regular job."

"If it was just a regular job, we wouldn't be here, would we? Where's your partner?"

"I don't know. I swear to God I don't."

Malloy slowly stepped toward him. "You don't know much, do you? That's too bad. And too bad for your partner when we find him."

"Oh God, please—"

Malloy's gun fired first, followed by Regnier's. Jimmy Demello fell backward, dead before his head hit the carpet.

The two visitors went to work, ignoring the body. Their work didn't take long—the office was small, a few desk drawers and two dented file cabinets holding nothing of interest. The killers checked Jimmy Demello's car before entering their own and driving away.

Edmund Arminger leaned back in his black leather executive's chair and pored over the Jacobs file yet again. For reasons even he wasn't entirely certain of, he felt drawn to it. He sensed a deeper story within its pages, a secret he was expected to safeguard but not to share in. He felt a mild resentment toward Director Gordon for trying to stifle his curiosity. He was Senior Deputy Director of the country's most power-ful crime-fighting organization; he would not be dissuaded so easily.

He placed the file aside. For the third time, he could see nothing. The report was routine but brief, revealing scant detail. Jacobs was, oddly enough, a foreigner, a Swiss whose real name was Martin Schmidt. There were dates, placement arrangements, a thin personal background report, and little else. Reason for placement was given in the vaguest possible terms: *protection of key witness.*

Arminger glanced at his watch. It was 1 A.M., Wednesday morning, a time of day when most other deputy directors were home with their wives. Since his rather acrimonious separation two years before, he saw little reason to spend time in an empty house. After all, it was dedica-tion and hard work that brought men to the top of their professions, and he would be living proof of that very shortly, just as soon as Arthur Gordon hobbled off into the sunset. In his opinion, it was high time his chief did just that.

Deputy Director Arminger was forty-nine years old, five foot ten with unstylish flat hair, pale skin, and an unremarkably thin voice. Physically unimpressive, he was a man who might easily be overlooked were he to enter a room of unsuspecting agents. Those who knew Edmund Arminger recognized him for what he truly was: a shrewd and, some would say, cold leader, brilliant enough to be considered the imminent successor to the director himself. Every agent in the Eastern Region knew this and deferred to him because of it.

Arminger raised his head to the sound of voices in the hallway. His guests had finally arrived.

Director Gordon came with his usual escorts but left them in front of Arminger's office, closing the door behind him. His eyes were red and heavy. The glare of the neon lights above made them look absolutely tortured. Arminger studied him and was startled at how old his chief looked that morning. Not much longer until the old man called it quits.

"I know this is unexpected, Edmund," said Gordon. "It's important. I just found out that Jacobs will require a bit more than we thought."

Arminger wasn't disappointed to hear this. He leaned forward on his desk and brought a hand to his chin as Gordon took a seat in front of him.

"We have new duties," said Gordon. "First thing we need to do is assign an agent to go down to the county courthouse and remove the Jacobs probate file. The plan eventually is to pull the death certificate, the property deed, and any other documents with his name. We're erasing Jacobs from the public record."

"Lot of attention to give a dead old man," commented Arminger thoughtfully. "I still don't understand why Dalton didn't brief us about this person if this was so important."

Gordon crossed his legs and frowned. His predecessor hadn't had time to do much. Director James Dalton had lasted barely three months after his diagnosis of stomach cancer.

"We can't possibly be versed on every last person in witness relocation," Gordon said. "Let's just get this over with, Edmund. This Jacobs business is becoming a nuisance." He removed a handkerchief and honked into it.

"What's to be done after we take the file?"

"We get a warrant to clear out the house. I'll need you to get a moving truck there within the next day or two and haul out everything that isn't nailed down. I want every table, chair, and napkin out of there."

"And once we're done with that?"

"Same as always. The file goes to archives and gets buried."

Arminger nodded and reached for a folder in front of him. "I want to show you something," he said, extending a piece of paper to Gordon. "Take a look at 'Cause of Death.'"

Gordon scanned down the death certificate. "'Drowning.' What about it?"

"Look at 'Other Significant Conditions.'"

Gordon read it aloud. "'Lower chest bruises.'" He looked at him, unimpressed. "What's so interesting?"

"I talked to the medical examiner who performed the autopsy and asked him his opinion. He thinks the locations of the bruises were a little bit odd. He said a paranoid person might make a case that Jacobs had his head held under water. That would explain the wide chest bruise. The side of the tub was pressing against him as he was held down."

"Old people bruise getting out of bed—I speak from experience. Does this coroner think he's a detective or something?"

"It's just odd," replied Arminger. "Lower chest bruises? Sounds as if someone had a score to settle with the old man."

"That goes without saying, doesn't it? He was placed in the program for a reason."

"And that reason was *protection*, Arthur. I don't like the idea of a placement being murdered in my jurisdiction. It's a reflection of my post. I need to know what's happening in my own backyard."

Gordon let out a breath as they stared at each other. Every week now it seemed his New York deputy was finding something new to get snappy about, pushing when he should be showing restraint. It was troubling to him, and increasingly irritating.

"Don't get worked up over this. A few chest bruises on an eighty-seven-year-old is not convincing evidence of murder. If that's what you're basing your case on, I'm not impressed." He turned away from Arminger. "Let's just get this under wraps. If there's anything rotten, we'll deal with it at the appropriate time, but for now let's treat it like any other witness protection closedown. As I told you, the local police are not to touch this. I don't want a cop near that house."

"No need to worry about that," replied Arminger. "I told the medical examiner that we would handle any investigations. He'll keep his mouth shut if he likes his job."

Gordon took a seat.

"I wouldn't expect to find much to investigate. Nothing surfaced while Jacobs was alive, so why should he all of a sudden become an issue now?"

Arminger nodded slowly. He had ideas but thought better of sharing them.

"Standard procedure, then," said Gordon. "Investigations, homicide or otherwise, are only going to keep the old man around. I want an agent by the Columbia County courthouse first thing in the morning to pick up that file."

"He'll be there."

"See that he is."

N ICK REACHED ALBANY at ten minutes before two in the morning. He stepped from the cab and double-checked the Morris Street address. This was it. The porch light was on, the only one on the block still shining. He glanced down the street in both directions. It was a quiet, pleasant neighborhood from what he could tell, and Alex's two-story, brown Victorian was like any other on the block. He stood for a moment and admired her newly purchased home. He was proud of her—damn proud. It had been a long, painful road from the roach-infested Spanish Harlem neighborhood of her childhood. She had fought and scratched every inch of the way out of there. He knew his childhood had been a cakewalk in comparison to that.

His finger was inches from the doorbell when the door swung open. Alex wore a huge smile as she stood and stared at him, her finger on her chin.

"Hmm," she said thoughtfully. "I think I recognize this face."

"I just couldn't take being away from you," replied Nick, smiling back.

"How sweet. And I suppose a twenty-two-million-dollar case has nothing to do with it, huh?"

They embraced tightly. Nick caught a trace of a perfume he remembered from years ago, and the memories of their days (and nights) together at Texas U. washed over him. He had forgotten the name of the fragrance, but whatever it was, it still smelled incredible. He took a step back and looked her over. With her perfect olive-toned skin and wide brown eyes, Alex could still easily pass for a newly enrolled coed. The product of Spanish and Cherokee parentage, she was every bit the head-turner she had been fifteen years before. The beautiful, big-boned frame always seemed to carry those extra five or ten pounds so perfectly.

Nick slung his bag over his shoulder and looked about the interior of her home. "The place looks great. I want the full tour before we get to work."

"Well, follow your tour guide."

The house was roomy but comfortable. Three bedrooms, two baths, and a spacious den. Alex was glowing as she showed him around. He could see it in her eyes; she was proud of herself, and she had every right to be. She had beaten some pretty nasty odds from day one, and Nick was happier than anyone for her. She was the only one in her family who had earned a college degree, who had made anything of herself. She had happily abandoned her career as a lawyer when Nick had introduced her to heir finding.

The coffee was ready in the kitchen. Alex filled two mugs and offered one to her partner.

"Let's take these upstairs, Nickie. I've got some good stuff to show you."

They climbed the stairs to the second-floor office. Nick looked about his East Coast base of operations approvingly. Alex had made positive renovations. She had purchased the high-backed leather chair he had recommended and a large executive's desk, and the fax, computer, and copier were smartly placed and unobstructed by the mess of papers he was accustomed to seeing. He also noticed the fire safe he had been nagging her to buy.

"Like what you see, Mr. Nitpicker?" asked Alex.

"Love it. Hey, and it only took you four years to get organized."

"Be nice, Nick. You remember how tiny my apartment was."

Nick removed his sport coat and settled down at the desk. "Let's talk Jacobs. We got documents?"

"And more," Alex said, pulling up a chair next to him. She reached for a small photograph and handed it to him. "Special bonus, courtesy of a friend in the coroner's office. Say hello to Mr. Jacobs."

The photo was a Polaroid, taken from the shoulders up. The head was nearly bald, the doughy face a sunken collection of wrinkles. The milky-white flesh of the corpse contrasted sharply with the cold gray of the medical examiner's gurney.

"Handsome devil," said Nick, placing it aside. "What else?"

"Lotsa documents but a whole lotta nothing," said Alex, handing him a sheet. "Here's the DC. We've got ourselves a real *unk* man."

Nick scanned the death certificate for the most important section. Both "Father's Name" and "Mother's Maiden Name" gave the same classification: *unk*—unknown. He followed his finger down the document as Alex spoke.

"Eighty-seven years old, died at home. Cause of death says drowning. Must have slipped in the tub or something."

Nick nodded. "'Marital Status: single.' Damn. Lifelong bachelor?"

"Looks that way. Our couriers checked the state marriage logs from the years 1925 to last year. He never got married in New York."

Nick rubbed the sweat from his forehead. The house was warm and stuffy.

"'Usual Occupation: glassworker.' What's that supposed to be?"

"No clue," replied Alex. "I couldn't find any unions or anything, so I think it's pretty worthless."

"Social Security number's got an 087 prefix. Isn't that . . . ?"

Alex nodded. "Issued in the state of New York."

"We've got a contact." He read from the death certificate. "Informant's name: Bonnie Schliegel, mailing address, including zip code: P.O. Box 16, Stony Point, New York."

"I think this lady is key," said Alex. "She's in the obit too."

She leafed through her collection of papers and found a photocopy. Nick took it and read. It had been copied from the previous day's edition of the *Albany Times Union*.

**Jacobs, Gerald Raymond**—at his home in the city of Hudson, September 7, age 87, had been a resident of the city for 3 years, retired skilled laborer. For information on memorial gathering, please call Bonnie Schliegel at 518-555-2893. Contributions to your favorite charity preferred.

"Resident for three years," Alex said. "The old guy's a transplant."

"So where was he residing his previous eighty-four years, my lady?"

"Twenty-two-million-dollar question." She twisted a lock of hair thoughtfully. "I called Bonnie about eight o'clock last night."

Nick looked at her quickly. "Tell me you didn't. Alex, we need a face-to-face with this woman. Phone calls are too risky—"

"Relax, Nickie. I just called to see what her voice sounded like. She sounds like a sweet little old lady on her machine. Your specialty. I've got a PI doing a real address search on her. He promised it by seven A.M."

Nick glanced at the wall clock. It was 2:45 A.M. "It's late. How you holding up?"

"Horribly. I need a couple more hours."

"Me too. Let's finish up by three." He wiped his forehead again. "You got the heat on in here?"

"You wimp. The windows are open."

"I'm cooking."

"You're whining."

Nick smiled and looked back to the desk. "What else we got?"

"You'll like this." She opened her portfolio and found another sheet of paper. Nick took it and gave her an incredulous stare.

"How'd you get this so quick?"

"Rayford has a crush on me. He says he loves my voice."

"He should see the rest of you."

Having a contact within the Internal Revenue Service was expensive, but it paid huge dividends. A divorced fifty-year-old with four kids, Murray Rayford apparently didn't mind committing a federal crime to make a few extra thousand a year.

Nick began reading the IRS profile from the top.

1.  First, Middle, Last Name: Gerald Raymond Jacobs
2.  Street and Number: 198 Michael
3.  Post Office, State: Hudson, New York
4.  SSN: 087-81-7691
5.  Employment status: Retired—receiving Social Security benefits
6.  Business Address of Present Employer: ——
7.  Date of Birth: 1/10/13
8.  Place of Birth: England
9.  Mother's Full Maiden Name, Living or Dead: Patrice Margaret McIntyre
10. Sex: Male

**11.** Color: White

**12.** Give Date You Became an Employee: ——

**13.** Filing Residency Status: Citizen

"Here we go," said Nick, snapping his fingers. "Place of birth and Momma's name."

"Take a closer look at that name before you start doing cartwheels."

Nick read the mother's name again and felt his enthusiasm fade. "McIntyre. Oh boy."

"In England too," said Alex, shaking her head. "Good luck. We'd have a better chance finding a Joseph Smith in the States."

"We don't even have a city to narrow it down. So much for the IRS."

Nick placed the paper down and slouched back in his chair. He felt overwhelmingly exhausted. Or was it deflated? They had reviewed several key documents—documents that would normally kick-start a case investigation—and found next to nothing.

Alex rose and walked behind him. She began to massage his shoulders hard.

"I got a chance to go by the County Recorder's office this afternoon and check the property record at 198 Michael. I was hoping a family member might have signed the note."

"Good thinking. Anything?"

"Nope. The realtor signed it. Jacobs was a real loner, Nick."

Nick closed his eyes as she really ground into him. "Not a rousing start," he said. "That's okay. The neighbors and Bonnie should have something to say tomorrow morning."

"They'd better," said Alex, squeezing his muscles mercilessly. "The guy's a complete blank so far."

"Man oh man. You like hurting me, don't you?"

"You used to be able to take it." She slapped the side of his head lightly. "I'm turning in. The bed's all made up for you in the guest room."

Nick pulled himself up and found the bathroom. He brushed his teeth and washed his face before entering the guest room. The small room had a bed, a dresser, and some neatly placed pictures on the wall. Alex was still a ways from furnishing the place.

He stripped to his shorts and got under the sheets. Fifteen years ago, they would have been in her dorm room, or his apartment, slipping

under the blankets together. They had been strictly friends their first
year at college, then clouded the relationship by taking it to the bedroom. Their fling had lasted one semester, collapsing upon itself after
four months of friction. Nick felt primarily to blame. He knew he could
be hard to take, intense almost to the point of being obsessive. Alex's
patience had run its course after sixteen weeks. It had been a mutual
decision to cool it.

Nick was thankful that they had remained friends after college.
Alex had become one of the few constants in his life, a supportive
force through his hiring as a police officer, the death of his father, his
struggle to establish himself as an heir finder. When he had made the
decision to expand the business, she had been the obvious choice as
partner, and the arrangement had worked out well. Although they had
experienced some shaky moments back in college, Nick felt the relationship had grown into a friendship they never could have realized
while in school. Just maybe they were coming to understand each
other after all.

Alex entered the room and pulled a chair next to his bed. She had
changed into an oversized T-shirt and shorts. The shirt hung on her a bit
lopsidedly, revealing a shiny bronze shoulder.

"So I suppose Doug's just a little excited about all this," she commented.

"Who, Doug? Excited about twenty-two million? C'mon—no big
deal to him."

"Yeah, right. He must be running around the office like a chicken
with its head cut off."

"Sounds like me you're describing."

She smiled. "My mother says hello, Nick."

"How is she?"

"Fine. Still in the same dump. Soon as we solve this one, I'm getting
her out of there."

"She kind of likes it there, I thought."

"That's a load of crap. She *thinks* she does. I tried to get her to
move in here with me, but she's stubborn. Doesn't want to impose."
She shook her head. "I guarantee you I'm getting her out of there
soon. I don't care if I've got to tie her up and carry her out myself, I'll
do it."

Nick nodded and said nothing. He remembered how things were.
Alex's mother still lived in Spanish Harlem and worked long hours in a

garment house in downtown Manhattan. He knew Alex still sent her a portion of every check she made.

"I really want this case, Nick."

"You and me both. But we're up against the big boys here, Alex. I bet we're not the only ones who bribed that attorney. We've got a shot, but don't go booking any cruises."

"Hell with the cruises. I'd love to buy my mom a house, get her out of that hellhole."

"You can buy her a castle if we solve it."

"She already lives in a dungeon." She leaned forward toward him. "You know what's strange? Why's a guy who's worth twenty-two million living in Hudson? There's no way I'd live there if I had that kind of money."

"I was thinking the same thing," said Nick, sitting up in bed. "Hudson isn't some well-to-do community, is it?"

"Not really. It's kind of changing. All these ritzy antique shops have cropped up on the main strip, so you have all these yuppy types coming in to shop on the weekends. But overall it's still an old town with a lot of crime and unemployment."

"It doesn't add up. Take it a step further, though. Where'd he get all this money? As a glassworker? I don't think so. Unless we're talking about fourteen-karat glass. Maybe he was a jewelry broker."

"Maybe he won the lottery."

"Can we check?"

She shrugged. "There must be some sort of a state lottery headquarters. I don't know if they'll release any information, though."

"Worth a shot," said Nick, lying back down. "About the only thing we can conclude about the old man so far is that he was a big-time loner. If he's got family, none of them seem to care about him very much. Either that or they've just lost contact with him."

Alex failed to stifle a yawn. "So what's the plan in the morning?"

"I'll be up at six. I want to see Jacobs's neighborhood, take a look at his house. How about I go talk to his neighbors and you go visit that woman Bonnie?"

"Sure. I hope my PI's reliable. He said he would have that address by seven."

"Call him by seven-fifteen if we don't hear from him."

"Yes, master. Anything else?"

"Sure. How about finishing that massage?"

"Your masseuse is worn out." She mussed his hair with her hand and got up. "Close your eyes and pray for some heirs."

Nick watched her legs appreciatively as she walked from the room. He clicked the nightstand light off and turned back to the ceiling. An eighty-seven-year-old dead man stared down at him in the dark.

*Gerald Raymond Jacobs—who were you?*

There was an incongruity here, this pairing of a seemingly humble immigrant worker and an eight-figure fortune. Something odd was buried in his grave.

Castleton awoke at 5 A.M. In recent years, he had allowed himself to sleep in until six-thirty, but the appearance of the Jacobs case mandated a return to the old ways. In the office at 6 A.M. to review the current probates. And today there was only one.

Richard Borg could read it in Castleton's face. Borg was a former Detroit police officer whose yearnings for private investigation had driven him to General Inquiry some twenty-one years earlier. As Castleton's chief researcher and senior associate, he was the one Castleton sought out when his brilliant mind was stymied. And today Borg could see the tension. Even during the million-dollar Luchetti case in Italy several years ago, Castleton had remained at his usual ease. The old man had his game face on now.

"What do we have, Richard?" Castleton asked sharply.

Borg hoped his news would loosen him up. "It's looking like the old guy was never married in the States. We've checked the marriage indexes in forty-eight states, as well as Puerto Rico and Guam. Nothing. I'm still waiting for responses from my Delaware and Wyoming people. What I'm really anxious for is a callback from our man in the Federal Immigration Archives."

"Jacobs was an immigrant?"

"Looks that way. Immigrants from the twenties and thirties who came to America alone and unmarried statistically had very low marriage rates once they were here. This matches with Jacobs. Once we get our hands on the immigration record, we'll have an English port of departure. Then our people in the UK will do the genealogy."

Castleton twirled the hairs of his mustache thoughtfully. "When are Lake and Risso due to arrive in New York?"

"They're already there. This morning they're approaching the neighbors." He reached over his desk and found a paper. "Here's the obituary."

Castleton took it and read. "Not much here."

"That's good. Merchant must be pretty lost right about now."

Castleton walked silently to the third-floor windows, his arms folded behind his back. "So are we certain no other companies are on this?"

"I know that Hogue and McClain aren't. If they don't know about it, I doubt anybody else would. I checked up on Merchant's office. His secretary says he's out of town."

"He's in New York already."

"He's in way over his head, Lawrence. Jacobs is looking like one tough nut. No wife, no children, no family stepping forward. I guarantee Merchant isn't finding much."

Castleton had his chin buried in his hand as he paced in front of Borg. "Sounds like we're dealing with an alias."

"I wouldn't be surprised. We'll know soon."

"Omar Morales was an alias. Somehow Merchant found that out before we did." He stopped and looked at Borg for a response.

"I don't see any parallels besides that. Lawrence, Merchant doesn't have some special knack for uncovering fake identities. You said yourself he got damn lucky with Morales. I can think of at least a dozen other cases involving aliases which we landed. Where was he for those?"

"He can't get that lucky again."

"He doesn't have people in England. That's where this is going."

Castleton rubbed his chin and looked thoroughly sour. "Once Lake and Risso talk to the neighbors, I want one of them to follow Merchant. We need to know what he's up to."

"*Follow* him? Jesus, Lawrence—"

"Don't fight me, Richard. I'm not taking any chances here. We know where his partner Moreno lives in Albany, right? I want a tail on that son of a bitch today."

Borg nodded and reached for the phone.


Blue sky had suddenly torn a hole in the gray morning clouds of Albany. A thick-bearded, middle-aged man sat in Washington Park with his hands deep in his coat pockets. He smoked a cigarette and watched disapprovingly as an old woman tossed handfuls of seeds to an army of pigeons. He couldn't stand the flying rats, and he hated people who treated them like pets. He was angry that he had to sit and watch this disgusting display, but he had agreed upon the arrangement.

His name was Kragen, and he had driven all the way from his home in Brooklyn Heights for this special early morning meeting. His contact had told him to be at the park at 6 A.M. and to wait on the bench nearest the lake. He thought the cloak-and-dagger stuff was unnecessary, but it amused him in an irritating kind of way, and as long as money factored into the equation he would of course play along.

At ten minutes past the hour, a figure holding a briefcase walked casually toward him along the paved walkway by the lake. Kragen straightened up a bit on the bench and purposely looked away from the approaching stranger. Just an innocent early morning stroller, he thought—to anyone else's eyes. He flicked his burning cigarette butt away and waited. He wasn't particularly nervous, but something about this group always made him feel strangely tense. His gun was in his coat. You never knew.

The visitor reached him and sat on the opposite side of the wooden bench. Several seconds passed before the new arrival spoke.

"We have something else for you."

Kragen nodded and looked at his shoes. The two of them watched the pigeon woman dump the remains of her paper bag at her feet as a hundred gray wings flapped about her. She stood muttering in the center of the mess, watching her babies eat.

"What is it?" asked Kragen. He knew the man was getting to that, but he was tiring of the dramatic pauses.

"Within the next day or so, the house in Hudson will be emptied. Everything will be loaded up and taken away. We want you to simply watch the house for a day or two until it's cleared out. Send the same two men as before. Can you have them there by noon?"

"No problem. All you want them to do is watch the place?"

"That's all."

"Are you expecting anything unusual to happen?"

"No. It's just a precaution. Just make sure it stays secure at all times."

"No problem."

The man reached for the briefcase and opened it on his lap. He found a thick manila envelope and handed it to Kragen without looking. "As agreed upon. That's for Hudson and the city job."

Kragen didn't bother to count it. As weird as these characters were, they had always been reliable when it came to payday.

The man stood. Kragen looked up at him and studied the spectacled, bland face. He wasn't intimidated, but something about these people was just plain spooky.

"Have them there by noon."

"You got it, buddy."

The man nodded stiffly and walked away down the concrete. When he disappeared from sight, Kragen got up and walked back through the silent trees to his car.

CHAPTER 6

NICK HAD NEVER been through Hudson before. He consulted his map and took Mill Street on the northern edge of town to Harry Howard Avenue, and after two errant passes found the street sign he was seeking.

Michael Drive was off Michael Court in the northeastern corner of Hudson, about as far from the river as one could be without leaving the city limits. Nick wasn't surprised about the locale. One of the more isolated parts of town, Jacobs's neighborhood was far from the commercial strip of downtown, a dead-end street rarely frequented by anyone but residents. Knowing what he did of Jacobs, it seemed appropriate.

Making a sharp right onto Michael Court, Nick realized just how excited he was. But nervous. Neighbors could be a pivotal source of information—or a huge waste of time. Getting them to talk usually didn't pose a problem. The trick lay in finding someone who actually had information worth hearing.

He drove to the end of the street, reaching the ninety-degree turn to Michael Drive. He parked on the corner of Michael Court and dragged a sleeve across his brow. It was 8:30 A.M. and a muggy seventy-five degrees. He was glad to be getting his visit over with before the mercury could climb any higher.

He stepped from the car and walked casually around the corner to Michael Drive. Overall the neighborhood was more impressive than he had expected. The homes were actually a curious mix of shabby Victorians and larger, more elegant Greek Revivals. The lawns were neat and spacious, the streets wide and tree-lined. It appeared to be a quiet neighborhood devoid of much traffic, a place where a barking dog might pose the most serious threat to the pleasant stillness of the air. Pleasant enough, thought Nick, but still odd. A perfect neighborhood perhaps for someone who didn't want anyone to *know* he was a millionaire.

He headed north on Michael Drive, scanning each home. It was hard to feel inconspicuous walking on a dead-end street, but he was doing his best. He stuck his hands in his pockets. Outside of a couple of joggers running the opposite way, the sidewalks were barren. Just another Friday morning.

Gerald Jacobs's house was the fourth from the corner, a two-story white and gray colonial with large windows and a prominent brick chimney. It was one of the nicest on the block, albeit a bit neglected looking. The paint was cracked and peeling in large sections, and the front yard was unkempt, weeds encroaching over a stone walkway that led to the front porch. The shrubs and bushes adjoining the front stairs were overgrown and untrimmed. Gardening didn't appear to have been the old man's favorite pastime.

He walked slowly along the sidewalk, his eyes on the house. What he saw wasn't a home—it was nothing more than a giant, double-floored treasure chest, not full of gold or precious stones, but secrets—the glimmering, private gems of a wealthy recluse's life. He frowned. Everything he needed was probably in that house.

He approached the building to the right of Jacobs's house. All neighborhoods shared one characteristic—residents normally loved to talk about each other, especially the strange ones. From all indications, Jacobs may have been the oddball on the block. He needed to play off any possible animosities.

Nick sidestepped a small boy playing on the front steps and pressed the front doorbell. A woman of about forty quickly opened the door.

"I hope you're not selling anything," she said, pointing a stubby finger at a brass No SOLICITORS sign affixed to the door frame.

"No, I'm not, ma'am. My name's Nick, I'm a skip-tracer with the credit bureau of New York. I've been trying unsuccessfully to contact your next-door neighbor, Mr. Jacobs. I was hoping you might have some idea where he is."

"I've got an idea all right. They pulled him out of there about a week ago."

"Pulled him out? Is he . . . ?"

She nodded. "As a doornail. What's this all about?"

"Mr. Jacobs owes a number of creditors a little bit of money."

"You don't say," she said, suddenly interested. "Well, what is it you need to know?"

Nick smiled slightly. A busybody—the investigator's best friend. "How long did you know Mr. Jacobs and what did you know about him?"

"Well, I tell you, George and I have been here for nineteen years now, and Mr. Jacobs moved in about three years ago. I don't know that we even exchanged three *words* with the old grouch. He was a strange one. Liked to keep to himself, real unsociable. The kind of grumpy old man who wouldn't wave back if you waved at him. You know, the type who'd turn off all his lights on Halloween just so the kids would leave him alone. He just wanted nothing to do with his neighbors."

*Small wonder*, thought Nick. "So you really didn't know much about him . . ."

"I didn't know a damn thing about him," she said. "And that was just fine with me. I don't know what his problem was. Never waved, never said hello. Just crazy if you ask me. Makes you wonder who showed at his funeral."

"Did you ever see anyone visit him? Any friends or next of kin?"

"Oh, who'd want to? I never ever saw anyone visit that man. As far as I could see, he was all alone. That's the way he wanted it, I guess. Stranger than strange."

Nick was convinced she knew nothing. He turned to leave. "Thanks for your time."

"So Jacobs owed some money, huh?" she asked after him. "How much?"

"Nothing to get excited about," he replied, not looking back.


Five remarkably similar interviews later, Nick opened his car door and collapsed onto the seat. He hadn't expected it to be easy, but he was getting nowhere fast. No one had any clues, any leads. The man was a complete question mark, as mysterious an individual as he had ever investigated. He leaned his head back against the headrest and thought of Alex. Her meeting with Bonnie was suddenly looking absolutely pivotal.

He stared over the steering wheel and frowned. All the answers were in that house. Short of breaking and entering, he didn't see much hope in getting a peek.

He stepped from the car and walked back around to Jacobs's home. He paused, then strode up the cracked stone walkway leading to the deserted house. Miss Busybody was probably watching from behind her curtains, but that couldn't be helped. He stepped up to the porch. Wiping what he assumed to be the living room window with his hand, he narrowed his eyes and peered inside. A thin white curtain obscured his view, and he couldn't see anything but vague, dark shapes. The furnishings seemed to be in place. He approached the front door and tried the knob, gave it a little shake. Flimsy, weak wood. Not even a dead bolt. God, this was tempting.

He stepped over the side rail of the porch and walked down a cobblestone pathway to the back fence. He stopped at a side door and placed his face up against the glass. Another curtain blocked his view from what probably was the kitchen. He walked to the sturdy-looking six-foot fence, placed his hands on the top, and hoisted himself up for a look. The yard was rectangular with several concrete paths traveling the length of a poorly maintained garden. Overgrowths of plants and shrubs bordered the yard, and cheap plastic furniture dotted a wooden patio by the back door. Nick lowered himself to the ground and noticed the curtains in the house next door rustle. Probably a good cue to take off.

He was walking back down the pathway toward the street when something caught his eye directly to the right. Jacobs's mailbox was stuffed to capacity with mail. Envelopes and colorful junk mail jutted out of the garage mailbox slot like a growth of weeds. He walked over and grabbed the bulging stack. Miss Busybody would probably have a conniption when she saw that, but she would get over it. He returned to the car and placed the pile of mail under the passenger seat. At least he had something to show for the morning's work. He slid the key into the ignition.

"Neighbors don't know much, do they?"

The voice startled him. The man noticed and seemed to enjoy the fact. He wore a suit and tie and an arrogant grin on his face.

"Sorry," said the stranger. "Didn't mean to scare you. Nick Merchant, right?"

Nick nodded and said nothing. He knew immediately who the man was, or at least who he worked for. It was only a matter of time before he or Alex crossed paths with one of them.

"Tough case, eh?" commented the man. His eyes flicked to the mail by Nick's side. "Danny Risso—General Inquiry." He extended his hand with a smile. Nick looked at him and the hand momentarily before offering his own.

"Any luck so far?"

Nick smiled weakly. As if he would tell him. "We're doing okay."

Risso laughed a bit, a chuckle that grated on Nick. "Hell of a case, huh? I mean, who would've thought something like this would ever come out of Columbia County. Or anywhere, for that matter . . ."

"Who would've thought it."

Risso stuck his hands in his pockets and glanced around the street. "Kinda strange the old coot lived here, huh?"

Nick shrugged, noncommittal. He had heard enough of the idle chatter. He had already broken his own rule of not speaking with the competition. He wasn't about to sit there and have public enemy number one pick his brain for clues. He started the ignition. Risso backed away. The oafish smile was back.

"Gotta run, huh? Hey, good luck there, Nick. By the way, in case you haven't figured it out already, you don't have a prayer of solving it."

Nick snapped his head to him. Their eyes locked. Risso's grin had shrunk to a smirk. A variety of choicely worded responses filled Nick's head, but instead he gave a smirk of his own and pulled the car into the street.

It took half an hour and two map references of the town of Cedar Hill for Alex to finally find Acacia Street. She slowed the car to a steady cruise as she strained her eyes for 978 Acacia. A dull brown ranch-style home provided the number. She made a quick U-turn and eased into a spot directly in front of the home. According to the address provided by her PI, this was the current residence of one Bonnie Schliegel.

Alex took a moment to calm herself. Nervousness was standard before meeting a key client, but this time the feeling was amplified. Bonnie was potentially the key piece to a puzzle worth twenty-two million dollars. All questions had to be asked with the utmost tact and delicacy. Alex tilted the rearview mirror and dabbed at her hair. Being well-groomed and presentable never hurt with the little old ladies.

With a determined frown, she stepped to the curb. An older-model Oldsmobile in mint condition was parked in the driveway of the home, and a well-kept bed of flowers along the front perimeter of the house shimmied in the breeze. Alex half expected to see a woman in a bonnet in the middle of it, snipping roses. She looked around. This was the kind of neighborhood she wanted for her mother—a quiet community with a police force that had trouble keeping busy.

She glanced at her watch. It was 8:30 A.M.; she could see her mother on the subway en route to work—eight hours of drudgery to earn a check that would have put her on the street years ago were it not for her daughter's support. She closed her eyes. Ten years ago, her mother had regularly sent a portion of her minuscule weekly paycheck to help pay her daughter's college tuition. She had wanted that degree even more than her daughter did.

She stared at Bonnie's house and gave a determined frown. They needed to find these heirs.

She approached the front door and gathered her thoughts momentarily before pressing the bell. Instantly she could hear a hysterical little dog yapping and scratching behind the door. Several seconds passed, but there were no other signs of life. She pressed the bell again, further inciting the dog. Suddenly there was a rattling of chains and dead bolts from inside. The door opened several inches, and an old woman—her thin white hair a scraggly mess—peered out. Alex could see several chain lengths still attached to the inside of the door. They stood staring at each other momentarily before the woman spoke.

"Yes?"

"I'm sorry to disturb you this morning, ma'am. Are you Bonnie Schliegel?"

"Yes, that's me."

The door was open barely five inches. Alex reached for her business card and extended it toward the gap.

"Miss Schliegel, my name is Alex Moreno. I'm a private investigator from Albany. I was hoping—"

"One moment," the woman said, turning abruptly to the howling little beast at her feet. Alex heard her scolding the frenzied animal as she led it away. The woman had not taken her card, so Alex put it back in her pocket.

"Now, what were you saying?" the woman asked, her face framed in the five-inch gap once again.

"Yes, ma'am, I was saying that I'm a private investigator from Albany. I'm here researching Gerald Jacobs's family. The reason I'm visiting you is because your name was mentioned in Mr. Jacobs's obituary and I was hoping that you might know something about him."

Bonnie squinted. "Are you with the IRS?"

"Uh . . . no, ma'am. I'm not with anyone. I work alone."

The woman eyed her as Alex pondered the significance of her question. Something in the eyes told Alex that there were at least a few screws rattling around upstairs.

"What do you want to know about him?" Bonnie asked, a bit harshly.

"Did you know Mr. Jacobs?"

"As well as anyone did."

"Would you mind sitting down with me for a few minutes to answer a few questions about him?"

Alex held her breath. Bonnie looked her over warily and abruptly closed the door. Alex's heart sank momentarily until she heard the chains being unlatched. The door swung open.

"I suppose it's okay, but if it turns out you're with the IRS, I'll have nothing to say to you."

Alex thanked her and stepped inside. Bonnie led her into a musty living room and motioned her to a chair. Several cats lounged about a worn couch, unimpressed with Alex's appearance. Bonnie guided the annoying little dog away to another room and returned, sitting across from Alex on the sunken, hair-coated couch.

"I don't normally let strangers in my house, but you say you're here about Gerald. That makes you . . . interesting to me."

*Gerald,* thought Alex, folding her hands in her lap. The fact that she was on a first-name basis with him was a very promising sign.

"I appreciate this."

Bonnie lit a cigarette and held it back over her shoulder. A striped tabby leapt into her lap and curled into a ball. "What did you say your name was?"

"Alex Moreno. I know that—"

"Are you Mexican?"

"Uh, no. Spanish and American Indian."

"American Indian, eh? The IRS has been terrible to you people. They think they can make it all better by giving you those casinos to run. Well, thanks for nothing. They're making more money off those places than you are. I learned all about it on *60 Minutes*. . . ."

Alex nodded and folded her hands on her lap. It was clear the IRS was the enemy. Bonnie had provided her with a way to bond. "The IRS hasn't been fair to my people at all."

"They're never fair," commented Bonnie through her smoke. "Gerald had a hell of a time with them."

"What can you tell me about Gerald, Bonnie?"

The old woman took a deep breath on her cigarette and eyed her. Her free hand scratched the lazy feline's chin. "I have a question for you first. You said you were doing research into Gerald's family. For who and why?"

Alex was surprised by her bluntness. She had underestimated her. Apparently Bonnie wasn't going to give any information until she screened her guest. She was ready with her response. "I'm here on behalf of a life insurance company. It seems Mr. Jacobs had a sizable policy that's payable to his family. The authorities and I are having difficulty locating them."

"That's no surprise," replied Bonnie, with a laugh. "I think someone else in your company already called."

Alex felt her heart pound. She knew who that someone was, and it was the last person in the world she wanted Bonnie speaking with. "Did they?"

Bonnie nodded. She got to her feet and pressed a button on an answering machine in the hallway. Alex heard the voice clearly. *"Barry Lake, General Inquiry . . . Important matter to discuss . . . give me a call . . ."*

"I was at the supermarket this morning," said Bonnie. "Someone you know?"

Alex smiled to herself. You needed a little luck in the game sometimes. She was doing pretty well all of a sudden. "Yes, I know who Barry is. He's calling about the same business I'm here for. You don't need to bother with him."

"Is that right?" the old woman replied sharply. "You're sure about that?"

Alex tried to appear disinterested as she turned back to the living room. "Barry just wants to talk to you about what we're already discussing. You can call him, but I don't think you'll enjoy repeating yourself."

Bonnie's eyes narrowed in suspicion. Alex held her breath momentarily, then relaxed as she heard the old woman press the reset button. Frowning, Bonnie returned to join her at the couch.

"As I was saying, Miss Schliegel, we'd like to see the money from this policy go to Gerald's family, not the State of New York. His heirs need to know about this so they can collect."

"I don't think I know anything that can help you."

"Were you friends with Gerald?"

"Friends—that's a good word."

"How long did you know him?"

"For about two years. I met him at the Sunday concerts in the park. We both loved classical composers. Gerald loved to play Mozart on his piano. He was an excellent pianist before he got his tic."

"I'm sorry—his tic?"

"Yes, his hands shook and he couldn't play like he once did. It bothered him."

Alex nodded respectfully. The tape recorder continued to run silently in her jacket pocket. "Did he ever mention his family?"

"Not really. About a year ago, I took Gerald out for a meal, and afterward we spent some time at his home. I was playing the piano for him and we were listening to the phonograph—just having a grand time. Now, Gerald must have had a good amount of wine, because he started speaking of a sister he had, but when I asked him about her, he put an end to it. This was the only time I remember him speaking of family. He was a very private person."

"So he never told you this sister's name?"

"No."

"He never told you any names or cities where the sister lived?"

"Never."

"Is there anything else you can tell me that might be helpful?"

"Let me think for a moment."

Alex felt her frustration growing. Hopes were riding on the old woman, but she seemed to know very little. Where was this sister?

"I think Gerald had an eye for me, actually," continued Bonnie. "He was a sweet old man and a good friend for two years. I enjoyed his company. He was so sweet, yet strange."

"What was strange about him?"

"He was very secretive about his life. But I think he was lonely too. I felt so awful when he died that I made the funeral arrangements. It's a terrible thing to die alone, you know."

Alex thought of her mother for some reason but quickly dismissed the thought. She nodded at Bonnie to continue.

"Something else odd: he said he was from England, and he did have a thick accent, but it wasn't British. It was German. Now, how can a person be raised in England and have a thick German accent?"

"That is strange," Alex agreed. "Did you ask him about that?"

"Yes. He said his father had lived in Austria."

"You've been in his house, Bonnie. Did you ever see any family pictures or anything?"

"I never took much notice of his house, although I can tell you that it was decorated beautifully. You would be amazed at the inside of that little house. Such beautiful paintings, a grand piano, exotic rugs. He must have had money to burn."

"Did he ever mention other friends or past employment? What did he do for a living?"

"He didn't talk about it. He was an old man when I met him, well into his eighties and long retired. And I never saw him with anyone or heard him mention any other friends."

Alex rubbed the back of her neck as the cold realization set in. Bonnie knew nothing. Jacobs loved classical music, had no friends, and spoke with a German accent. But it didn't add up to a thing. She sat and thought as the little mutt barked himself hoarse from the other room.

"Were you ever in any room of his house other than his living room?"

Bonnie looked aghast. "Certainly not."

"I didn't mean it that way. I'm sorry if I offended you."

Bonnie nodded grudgingly as she stroked the cat. Alex reached down and touched one of the purring animals. The old woman had been harping on the IRS earlier. It was worth a shot.

"Did Gerald work with the government, Bonnie?"

"Why do you ask?"

"You mentioned the IRS earlier. I was just wondering."

"No, he didn't," she snapped, her expression suddenly guarded again. "Why are you so concerned with this insurance policy, anyway?"

"I've been hired to take care of it."

"Well, I don't know that there's anything more for us to discuss," she said, grouchy now. "I've told you what I know. Gerald didn't have family or friends. Enemies maybe, but no friends. Maybe you should look for *them*. They might be easier to find."

Alex stared at her hard. Bonnie frowned and shifted uncomfortably in her chair. The words had slipped.

"Can you tell me about Gerald's enemies, Bonnie?"

"He was going to take care of them. He had a plan and he was going to get them good. He . . ." She stopped herself and made an exasperated sound. "I know what you're up to, and it's not going to work. I promised I wouldn't tell and I won't go back on my word."

"Don't you think Gerald would want you to tell me if he knew it would help his family?"

"No, I don't think that at all. His family never bothered to visit with him. What kind of family is that?"

"Did Gerald—"

"Stop picking at it," she snapped. "Just because he's dead doesn't mean I can go blabbing things around." She tossed the cat from her lap and stood. "I don't have anything else to say to you. I want you to go now."

"Bonnie—"

"Do I have to call the police?"

Alex felt a spark of anger, almost lost it. She took a deep breath. Bonnie looked shaken, even a bit frightened. Getting her more worked up might not be the wisest decision. She got to her feet and reluctantly made for the front door. She waited for Bonnie to open it for her before stepping into the morning sunlight outside. The door closed quickly behind her, and chains were rattling again. She stood momentarily before turning down the path and back to the car.


On the road, Alex tried to form some sort of picture. An immigrant glassworker from England who talked like a German. Twenty-two million dollars. A hatred for the IRS—nothing rare there. It was colorful stuff lacking significance, murkier than sludgy water. Alex would have been more concerned about her lack of headway if she hadn't noticed the car in her rearview mirror.

She first spotted it in Albany, just a few miles from her home. She confirmed her suspicions with a series of turns. Four lefts, three rights— the gray car maintained its position two blocks behind, no closer, no farther. It looked like a single occupant.

She considered her options. She could try and lose him or she could force an encounter. She knew the smarter choice was probably the former, but after sitting through the Bonnie interview she felt more than ready for a face-off. Especially with some General Inquiry jerks.

She slowed her speed for several blocks and reduced the distance between herself and her pursuer by half a block. She continued a slow deceleration as she drove randomly through residential Albany. After several blocks of a twenty-five-mile-per-hour pace, the car abruptly took a left and disappeared down a side street.

Alex pulled over on Colonial and sat for several minutes, watching her rearview mirror. She felt mildly disappointed—a confrontation with the competitors would have been a welcome release of tensions. She put the car into gear again and continued home without incident.

Edmund Arminger leaned forward on his desk and studied his field agent carefully. Derek Hanson was an experienced agent, the recipient of several internal commendations over the past five years. Out of a pool of nearly one hundred agents operating out of Manhattan, he had been selected to retrieve the Jacobs file. It was a simple task that had suddenly gotten complicated.

Arthur Gordon wasn't surprised. He sat to Arminger's side and remained silent during the discussion, deferring to his deputy. The conversation he was quietly witnessing was only adding to an already splitting headache.

"What did you say this attorney's name was?" asked Arminger.

"Lloyd Koenig."

"Start from the beginning. You approached Koenig and . . ."

"When I showed him the warrant and asked for the file, Koenig was clearly uncomfortable. After stalling for a minute or so, he broke down and admitted he didn't have it. By then he was practically shaking."

"Where did he say the file was?"

Agent Hanson looked to a small notepad. "He said he loaned the file to a private investigator from Albany named Alex Moreno, who was there on behalf of a San Francisco company called Merchant and Associates. He said he also passed on a copy to a PI firm in Los Angeles called General Inquiry. He claims these were the only two firms he had spoken with."

"Did you get a contact at General Inquiry?"

Hanson handed over the notepad. "The name's circled, sir."

Arminger read it as Gordon finally spoke.

"Agent Hanson, did Koenig say why he was giving this file to these investigators?"

"He said they were interested in looking into the estate for the purpose of finding heirs."

Gordon nodded.

Arminger thought for a moment, then rose to his feet. "That'll do for now."

Agent Hanson nodded and left.

Gordon waited for the door to shut before he leaned back in his chair and exhaled loudly. Now his head was hurting too. "Why are private investigators interested in Jacobs?"

"What do they know that we don't?" asked Arminger, not hiding his frustration. He looked to the pad again. "Alex Moreno, Lawrence Castleton. Merchant and Associates and General Inquiry."

"Have you ever heard of these outfits?" asked Gordon.

"I don't care who they are—I want to know why they're getting involved." He hit his intercom. "Carol, I need background checks on two individuals. Alex Moreno, out of Albany, New York, and Lawrence Castleton out of Los Angeles. The names are spelled just like they sound. I want full bios on their companies as well."

"Yes, sir."

"The names are General Inquiry and Merchant and Associates. They're in Los Angeles and San Francisco, respectively."

"Yes, sir."

He clicked the intercom and nodded at his chief. "This Jacobs business is getting interesting."

"Not for me," replied Gordon, looking steadily at him. "You're getting too wrapped up in this. I don't want you going beyond these background checks until we get more answers."

Arminger frowned defiantly. "I don't like being kept in the dark."

"Nor do I. I agree that it's time we were briefed. I'm going to arrange a meeting back in Washington."

"I think it's time, Arthur. We need to know. Ten or fifteen minutes, we'll know exactly who these PI's are."

"I'm delighted. But both of us need to be careful until I know more."

CHAPTER 7

A LEX HATED THE look. She used to draw it from him in college.
It grated on her, that look of thinly veiled skepticism. After all
those years, it still made her mad.

"Don't give me that little smirk, Nick."

"What are you talking about?" replied Nick, no longer smirking. He
was leaning back on her kitchen countertop. "Why would I be smirking?"

"You do it when you don't believe me."

"Why would anyone follow you, Alex? Other than trying to get your
phone number, I can't think of any reason."

"It's GI. They know we're on this and they're trying to see what
we're up to. You were probably being followed yourself—you just
didn't notice."

"As if that's something I'd miss. Hey, I don't necessarily see it as a
bad thing if they were following you. Indicates to me that they're as
clueless on Jacobs as we are."

"I don't like being followed."

"Take it as a compliment. If it's them, they're showing us respect.
Too much, I'd say."

"What if it wasn't them?"

"Who would it possibly be if it wasn't them?"

Alex turned away, angry that she had no answer. She noticed the kitchen table behind Nick was covered with several small stacks of paper.

"What's all that?" she asked, pointing.

"Jacobs's mail. I grabbed it from his mailbox when I was looking around his house."

"Anything good?" she asked, taking a handful of letters.

"Zero. About as boring as *my* mail."

She began to look through the little piles. "Did the neighbors know anything?"

"Nope. Jacobs was the neighborhood outcast. Never talked to any-body." He picked up a piece of mail. "I ran into the GI investigator out there."

"With the car, I hope."

"No such luck. Impression he gave me was that they weren't ex-actly setting the world on fire either. Jackass made some smart quip: 'You'll never solve it.' Like he was trying to bait me or something. I laughed in his face and drove off." He dropped the envelope back on the table. "How'd it go with Bonnie?"

"Not too well. She knew things, but she wouldn't come out with them. I pushed her a little too hard and she threw me out."

"What do you mean 'she knew things'? What was her relationship to him anyway?"

Alex pulled a bottle of mineral water from the refrigerator.

"A friend. She knew him for two years. She kept talking about the IRS, how much she hated it. She got all bent out of shape when I asked her if Jacobs was connected to them somehow. Said she'd promised him she would keep her mouth shut. Then she started talking about his *ene-mies*. Next thing I knew she wanted me out. I'm talking massive mood swings here."

"Sounds like she definitely knows something."

"I've got it taped. She said that he mentioned a sister once."

"That's *great*. What about this sister?"

"She said they were sitting around drinking one night and he just came out with it. She didn't press him for more because he didn't like to talk about his family. She didn't know anything about her."

"Well at least we know he does have family. Nothing else?"

Alex took a swig of her bottled water.

"She said he had a German accent. He told her his father was

Austrian. That's the bulk of it, Nick. She wouldn't tell me the good stuff."

Nick did a slow, thoughtful pace about the kitchen. "So we have an extremely wealthy old man with a German accent. An Austrian, supposedly."

"Maybe he was a Nazi," said Alex. "That might explain his money."

Nick gave a bemused smile. "I was thinking the same thing. What the hell would an old Nazi be doing in Hudson, New York?"

"Same thing they're *all* doing—hiding out, I guess."

"It's a pretty crazy theory. Being a wealthy old man with a German accent doesn't make you a damn Nazi." He thought for a moment, then looked up at her quickly. "I want to hear this Bonnie conversation."

Alex found the recorder and placed it on the kitchen counter. Nick rubbed his chin and listened silently as she continued going through the mail. He didn't speak until the tape ended.

"She knows things, all right. Think it would do any good to have me go talk to her?"

"I doubt it," replied Alex, studying a Jacobs bank statement. "You heard how stubborn she was."

"Don't bother with the mail," said Nick, reaching for his notepad. "We've got thirty-four pieces. Twenty-five pieces of junk mail, seven bills, one bank statement, and a statement from a mutual fund company. No family information at all."

Alex frowned and took a seat. She was still feeling irritable about being followed.

"One strange thing I did find in the mail," said Nick, handing over a stapled set of papers. "Look at this and tell me what you think."

Alex recognized it immediately. A phone bill. She glanced over all six pages. The charge was over two hundred and fifty dollars for the month. "He liked to blab on the phone."

Nick pointed to the list of long-distance calls. "Look at those calls. What do you see?"

"Lotsa 202 area codes."

Nick nodded. "Washington, DC. Look at all these different numbers, Alex. I called some of them. I got the Justice Department, FBI headquarters, the Pentagon message center, for Christ's sake."

Alex placed her fingernail on the phone bill. "Look at this. On August 25, he called this one number at 8:10 P.M., then again at 8:12, 8:14, 8:16, 8:19, 8:21 . . ."

"I noticed that too. There's a bunch of patterns just like that."

She shrugged. "So he was probably one of those wackos who thinks the government planted a computer chip in his head or something."

"I agree—he's probably nuts. But maybe not. We've been wondering where this guy got twenty-two million. Could be he was involved in something big, possibly with some sort of government agency."

"Probably so," said Alex. "I wouldn't be surprised if he had something to do with the JFK assassination."

He gave her an irritated look. "Ha-ha. I'm trying to be serious here."

"Who cares what he was involved in," she said, spreading her hands in the air. "We need to find some family."

"Well, we're doing a pretty crappy job at the moment." He slowly shook his head. "I can't remember a case where we had so many key documents and so few clues. I wonder if—"

The phone rang. Alex got to her feet and answered it. "Hi, Rose . . . really . . . hold on a second. . . ." She covered the receiver. "Rose, Nick. She says she just got a strange call. Go pick up the line upstairs."

Nick jogged upstairs and found the phone. "Hi, Rose."

"You guys, I got a really weird call a minute ago."

"What was it?" asked Nick. His secretary's voice sounded excited and shaky.

"I'm not sure. I just got off the phone with some screaming attorney in New York by the name of Lloyd Koenig. Said he needed you to return the Jacobs file to him immediately. He claimed it was absolutely urgent that you get that back to him today. He said some pretty nasty things—"

"What was he so upset about?"

"He said an FBI agent had just been in his office asking about that file—"

"*What?*" said Nick, nearly crushing a pen in his hand.

"He said that this agent wanted the Gerald Jacobs file and names of all the people Koenig shared it with. He gave him your name, Nick. Yours too, Alex."

"What else did he say?" asked Alex.

"He said the agent told him that he would be back for the file and that if he was lying about anything, he'd regret it. He was very rude—"

"Did you tape it?"

"Just the tail end. Hold on a second . . ."

A winding noise could be heard, then a sound of humming static. Rose's voice suddenly rang clear.

"—do for you, sir?"

"Just get hold of your goddamn boss, lady. Tell him to call me immediately! I need that file back today! I got goddamn FBI breathing down my neck. Tell him I need that file back now or I will have his ass! I'll drag his ass down with me—!"

"I'll pass along the message, Mr. Koenig."

"I better hear from him soon!"

"I'm sure you will. He'll be checking his messages."

"I'll be waiting!"

Nick could feel the fear in Koenig's voice. He felt a bit shook up himself all of a sudden. "Okay, Rose, thanks for the call. If anyone else besides Doug calls for me, just say I'm out of town and there's no number to reach me at."

"Okay. Be careful, you two."

He placed the receiver down and rubbed his chin. When Koenig had handed over the file, he knew he had been taking a minor risk, a one-in-a-thousand chance, but for ten thousand tax-free dollars, he had opted to take that chance. The roulette wheel had landed on his number now, though. In all likelihood, he could kiss his cushy little career with the government goodbye.

"Why is the FBI getting involved in this, Nick?"

Alex stood in the doorway. She was rubbing her arms up and down, a nervous habit from college that Nick remembered well. He shrugged and tried not to show his own concern.

"Wish I knew. Maybe my ideas aren't so crazy anymore, huh?"

"This isn't good."

"No, it isn't. It matches with what we were just talking about. Jacobs must have been somebody special, maybe in the witness protection program or something. That might explain the money."

"Koenig's in big trouble."

"He knew the risks, Alex. We'll send the file back, but I don't think it's going to help him too much now."

She nodded slowly. "Do you think the FBI will come after us?"

"For what?"

"We bribed him, Nick."

"They won't bother us," he said with more confidence than he was feeling. He twirled a pen in his fingers. "Koenig's in enough trouble as it is. If he tells the feds we offered a bribe, he'll be admitting that he took it, right? He's looking to save his skin. He's not going to add to whatever charges he's already facing by admitting his role in a bribery."

"So what will he say—he just *gave* us the file?"

"As lame as that sounds, it would be the smartest thing he could do."

Alex's face was skeptical. "They're going to call us. Watch. I guarantee they'll call."

"Hey, they might. I don't know what they'll do."

"I don't like this, Nick."

"You think I do? I don't want to mess with the feds. But until I'm given a valid reason to stop what I'm doing, I intend to keep working on Jacobs. The entire investigation may soon be a moot point anyway at the rate we're moving." He rose and walked by her. "I need some lunch. What do we have to eat around here?"

She followed him downstairs into the kitchen.

"Maybe that person following me today wasn't with GI, Nick."

"I don't know who it was. I really don't think it's anything to worry about." He peered inside the refrigerator and made a face. "What's with all this fat-free stuff?"

"Forget your stomach for a second, okay? I'm concerned about this."

He pushed the refrigerator door closed and leaned back against it.

"I understand that, Alex. I just don't think this is cause for panic."

"I'm not panicking—I just don't like being followed." She turned away from him. "This case is weird, Nick. There's something else going on here."

Nick stuck his hands in his pockets. The FBI's involvement undoubtedly confirmed his partner's statement. "We need some fresh air," he said. "Feel like going for a drive?"

"A drive? We need to sit down and talk about Jacobs."

"That's exactly what we're going to do, gorgeous. I've got an idea."

Edmund Arminger paced the carpet of his Manhattan office and considered the latest information. He didn't know exactly what it all meant yet, but at least he knew part of the story.

The bio sheet on General Inquiry was enlightening. The company was a licensed private investigation firm established in 1956 by Lawrence Milton Castleton. The company specialized in "asset recovery and estate research." Their main source of revenue was heir finding—the locating of persons entitled to unknown assets for a fee consisting of a percentage of those assets. The company employed thirty-eight researchers and was enormously profitable.

"Heir finders," he said, in Gordon's direction. "They find heirs to estates. They sign them to legal contracts which stipulate a percentage of the inheritances to their companies."

"Now I've heard of everything," said Gordon as he read the sheet.

"Sounds like a shady racket," commented Arminger. "Jacobs must have died with some bank accounts."

"So what do we have on the other company? What was the name again?"

"Merchant and Associates. We've got nothing yet on the girl—too damn many Alex Morenos in the database. The company's main office is in San Francisco. Nothing much is coming up on the system, although it does show them as having a PI license. Seems to be kind of a fly-by-night operation. Much smaller than General Inquiry, but they're in the same business."

"So these companies bribed the attorney to get this file before their competitors did."

"I assume there was bribery, yes. Apparently the official release date of that file isn't for another week or so. So they bought themselves a weeklong head start on their competition."

Gordon rubbed his chin slowly. "More complications . . ."

"I wonder if there are any heirs to be found," said Arminger. "I guess we're going to find out."

"Guess again," said Gordon. "We're calling both of these companies right now and ordering them off Jacobs. Last thing we need are some meddling PI's sniffing around where they shouldn't be."

Arminger nodded and took his seat. He liked looking down at Gordon from the higher perch behind his desk. Not too much longer . . .

"So how do we want to do this?"

"Secure a line and make the damn call. Just be firm."

Arminger took the bio sheet of General Inquiry and reached for the phone. The president of General Inquiry was on the line almost immediately after the deputy director identified himself.

"This is Lawrence Castleton."

"Mr. Castleton, this is Deputy Director Edmund Arminger with the

New York City office of the Federal Bureau of Investigation. How are you?"

"Just fine," answered Castleton, after finding his voice. "What can I do for you?"

"An important matter crossing my desk this morning has made this call necessary. Do you know a Lloyd Koenig out here in Columbia County?"

"I believe I know that name, yes," replied Castleton, innocent as could be.

"I believe you do as well. We're aware, Mr. Castleton, of the . . . relationship you've enjoyed with Mr. Koenig. I can tell you I'm not very pleased with this special arrangement. As chance has it, I'm not calling you to discuss any illegal activity you may have been a part of—I'm calling about the latest file you've received from Koenig. The Gerald Jacobs probate file. Is *this* name familiar to you?"

"Yes. Yes, it is."

"You're currently trying to find beneficiaries to Mr. Jacobs's estate, correct?"

"Yes, we are," said Castleton, his voice growing softer by the moment now.

"Gerald Jacobs had a very close relationship with the Bureau while he was alive. It's not in anyone's best interest—certainly not yours—for the details of this relationship to suddenly become public."

"That's definitely not my company's intention."

"I'm sure it isn't, but I'll still insist on your cooperation. We need your company to drop any investigation into Jacobs immediately. I fully expect this as of this conversation, Mr. Castleton. Do you agree?"

"Drop it?" asked Castleton, his voice catching.

"Drop it and dispose of all memos related to it. Completely erase its existence from your files."

"And may I ask why?"

"You may, and I'll tell you only this: bringing Mr. Jacobs's name and past into probate court will only raise issues better left untouched. You understand, of course, why I can't give you more information."

"I see."

"We can count on your full cooperation, then?"

Castleton's reply came after an uncomfortable pause. "I've always had respect for the FBI, Director Arminger. I'm slightly confused, though. My company's been in operation for over forty years now, and something like this has never happened before."

"I understand the request is unusual, but I wouldn't be making it unless this was a matter of FBI security."

"Well," said Castleton, after another pause, "I'll bring this up to my associates for immediate discussion—"

Gordon held the headset and shook his head slowly at Arminger.

"Perhaps I'm not being clear enough with you," said Arminger. "I'm telling you to drop this matter. If you comply, I personally guarantee that the FBI will not pursue an investigation into any alleged bribery of county employees in New York State. Nor will the IRS be on your back for the next twenty years. Am I making myself clear now?"

"Quite," responded Castleton, his voice like ice.

"Very good. If that's all, then, I'll—"

"Before we end our friendly discussion, Director Arminger, I feel obligated to let you know that we aren't the only ones aware of Mr. Jacobs. There's a certain party working out of San Francisco who is also trying to find Mr. Jacobs's beneficiaries."

"We're aware of Merchant and Associates—"

"That's good," interrupted Castleton. "If we're expected to leave the Jacobs investigation alone, I'd expect that Nicholas Merchant would be told the same thing."

"He'll be given the same instructions. You don't need to be concerned about him."

"It just so happens I'm very concerned. I have some of Merchant's particulars in front of me right now if you're interested in conducting your background checks."

"What kind of particulars?"

"The basics. Nicholas William Merchant: born in San Francisco, Social Security number 569—"

"I won't be needing any of that. But thank you for your cooperation. Have a pleasant day."

Arminger hung up the phone and looked over at Gordon. "Firm enough?"

"I'm impressed. The part about the IRS was a good touch. Let's give Merchant and Associates a call and lay this to rest."

Arminger found the San Francisco number and reached for the phone again.

Lawrence Castleton buried his face in his hands and groaned. He felt as if he had just been shaken awake midway through the most wonderful dream of his life. He suddenly had the overwhelming urge to take the rest of the day off. The week, for that matter. He pressed the intercom to Richard Borg's office. Borg was in front of him twenty seconds later.

"Did the market just crash?"

"Imagine the worst news we could possibly get," said Castleton, ignoring the joke. He stared at Borg with glassy, defeated eyes.

"Merchant found heirs!" said Borg, going white.

"Almost as bad. We've just been ordered off the Jacobs case."

"Ordered off? By who?"

"I just received a call from Deputy Director Arminger with the FBI."

Borg studied his face to confirm that his boss was completely serious. "The *FBI*?"

"It seems that our man Mr. Jacobs was, somehow or another, affiliated with the Bureau. They don't want us touching it, Richard."

"*What?* Why the hell not?"

"He wouldn't give me a reason. Just told me point-blank to forget about Jacobs." He shook his head in disgust.

"What was his tone like?" asked Borg. "Did he threaten you?"

"He said we shouldn't expect any problems with bribery charges or the IRS if we comply. If we don't play along, well—I'm sure you get the picture."

"Are you certain this was legitimate? Could it be a—"

"I traced the call to FBI headquarters in Manhattan. It's legitimate."

Borg clenched his fists. "This is bullshit! They can't tell us not to do our work!"

"Unfortunately they just did."

"What about Merchant? Did you tell them about him?"

"He said they know about him and would be contacting him to pass on the same message. I threw out his name just to reinforce it in his head. If for some odd reason Merchant is allowed to solve Jacobs, we'll of course sue the hell out of the Bureau."

"I can't believe this!" blurted Borg. "Twenty-two million sitting there and we can't work it? Why the hell—"

Borg held his tongue at the expression of his friend. General Inquiry's founder had folded his burly arms over his chest, and the edges of his mouth curled upward into a half scowl, half smile. "I never said we were dropping it, Richard."

Borg looked at him. "Are you thinking of—"

"You're damn right I am. Hell with the FBI and their bully tactics. The feds aren't going to stand in our way on this one. This is our livelihood, dammit. This is America! Who are they to *order* us not to make our living? We're not doing anything illegal. We're supposed to just forget about this because it inconveniences them? Well, it inconveniences me to be cut off from legally pursuing my business."

"So you're saying . . . ?"

"I'm saying the hell with the FBI—we're working it. I'm not passing up the case of the goddamn century."

Borg nodded. "What kind of problems can they cause for us?"

"We'll be fine. We'll have someone anonymously represent us in probate court. They'll never know we're behind it. After we win the court battle, we'll stick the money overseas." He nodded in smug satisfaction. "I'm not afraid of the feds, and as for the IRS, I'm not paying those accountants top dollar for their goddamn penmanship. We've been expecting them to target us for years anyway. They want to audit us, let them. Even if we lose two or three million in penalties, we'll still rake in close to ten from Jacobs. That's a trade-off I'll take any day of the week."

"Another thing to consider," said Borg. "Merchant probably won't drop it."

"Why would he?" asked Castleton. "The Bureau's got no leverage on him. Hell, they probably won't even be able to find him."

"Keep going then?"

The president leaned back, nodding his head savagely. "Let's find these goddamn heirs."

Richard Borg smiled widely. General Inquiry's president wasn't the type to bow to intimidation. They had waited their entire professional lives for something this enormous. Even the Federal Bureau of Investigation wasn't about to stand in their way.

## CHAPTER 8

I T WAS A casual Wednesday afternoon drive through Hudson. Alex was watching the restaurants and antique shops of Warren Street stream by as Nick kept his attention on the road. He was looking for a place where they could talk, a locale more conducive to planning. At the end of Warren, he made a left on North Front, then a right over the bridge spanning the railroad tracks. He parked in the boat launch facility, then slipped through a hole in the gate, jogging down the embankment to the edge of the Hudson River.

Alex followed him through the fence, first taking a look around to see if anyone was watching them. Frowning, she walked halfway down the incline, then took a seat on a log, her arms crossed on her chest.

Only a few feet from the water, Nick stooped and picked up a rock. It was smooth and flat, perfectly suited for its purpose. He took two quick steps toward the water and sent it skimming. He counted five skips before it collapsed into a series of compact splashes and sank. He was convinced that rock skipping, like heir finding, was in the genes. His father had been a master of both.

Alex sat on the embankment above and waited impatiently. The rock-throwing exhibition wasn't impressing her, and she focused her sight on the shoreline homes a half mile across the river in Greene County. Why Nick had dragged her down here was a mystery to her.

She certainly didn't see any answers to Gerald Jacobs floating by in the cold waters of the Hudson.

"May I ask what we're doing here?"

Nick threw another stone across the gray-green water. This one curved crazily at the end of its journey after hopping at least six times. He reached for another. "Thinking. Fresh air's good when you're stuck on a case. Know what I did a couple of Saturdays ago? Caught the ferry out to Alcatraz and just walked around. Thought a lot. A day later I found the last Johnston heir."

"You went to Alcatraz by yourself? Time to get a girlfriend, Nick. Oh, I forgot—you're no good at the relationship thing."

The joke drew a look from Nick. Alex's arms were folded, her lips a tight smirk.

"I wasn't that bad, was I?" he asked.

She gave him a noncommittal shrug. Nick frowned and approached her.

"It just so happens, my little smart-ass, I do some of my best thinking when I'm alone. I'm thinking right now about our friend Mr. Jacobs. The plan's coming together." He extended his hand to her. "Get down here. I want to see you throw one."

"No thanks."

"Just do it. I'll tell you my plan if you do."

She gave a disgusted sigh and took his hand. At the shore, he found a suitable rock and placed it in her palm.

"This one's perfect," he said. "I want to see at least five skips."

She threw it in an arc that ended with one clumsy splash.

"You need to get lower than that," said Nick, putting his hand on her waist. "Bounce on your knees a little bit. Take a couple steps, kind of sideways. Come on, you should be a natural. Remember back in Texas how you used to launch bottle caps with that little wrist snap of yours?" He raised his hand to his shoulder and snapped his fingers.

"That was a long time ago."

"Fifteen years ago, not fifty." He threw a rock violently over the surface of the water. "Hey, this reminds me—remember that weekend we went down to the Rio Grande?"

"Yeah. It rained all weekend and I nearly caught pneumonia. Fond memories."

She walked back up the embankment and retook her place on the log. He joined her.

"Lighten up, grumpy," he said, brushing off his hands. "We're not giving up yet."

Alex cupped her chin in her hands. "This case is going nowhere."

"You haven't heard my idea yet. Ready?"

"No, I want to watch you throw rocks for another half hour."

"It's a simple enough plan. A little risky, though."

"Would you please spit it out?"

"We get inside his house."

Alex looked at the gravel at her feet and laughed slightly. "Just like that, huh? I didn't know you had the key."

"I don't."

She turned and studied his profile. The thought had crossed her mind as well, but not as a viable option. "And here I thought you were an ex-*cop*, not an ex-*con*."

"Just listen for a second, Alex. When I was visiting the neighbors this morning, I took a look around Jacobs's house, gave the front door a little shake. Felt pretty flimsy to me. I've been through my share of doors. The only problem would be noise. It's a quiet little neighborhood. But that's where you'd come in."

"Who says I want to come in?"

"You'd be the lookout," continued Nick, ignoring her now. "We'd have you parked somewhere nearby to keep an eye out for windows lighting up or cops driving by. You wouldn't be at risk of getting caught."

"Thank you for worrying about little me," said Alex. "I'm not afraid to go in, Nick."

"I know you're not, but we need to have someone outside. All those years of being a cop taught me a little about getting through doors. You still have those little two-way radios we used to play around with?"

"Somewhere in the garage, I think. I don't know if they even work anymore."

"We'll buy new ones if they don't. Any sign of trouble, we'll need instant communication. I think one in the morning might be a good time to arrive. I'd need a good chunk of time in there to be thorough. Friday night isn't the best night to do it, but it's risky to wait."

"Isn't there any other way in besides the front door?" asked Alex, feeling reluctantly swept up in his enthusiasm. "Seems a little conspicuous."

"We can't break windows, and I'm not about to shuffle down the chimney. The front door's actually fairly concealed. There are these overgrown bushes surrounding the front steps. Once I get to the porch, I'm pretty well covered." He studied her. "What do you think? Are we crazy?"

"*You* are," she said. "Bribing somebody's one thing, but breaking and entering?"

"You talk like we're burglarizing the place. We're not stealing anything. We aren't hurting anyone. We're just . . . taking a little look around."

"Just like walking through a museum, huh, Nick? No different at all."

"Alex, please. Is this really so bad?"

"Bad enough to land you behind bars."

"Only if I get caught. We'd probably get off on a trespassing charge. I'm not sticking around to get caught, though. If I run into problems at the door, I'll just bail out of there." He fell to a knee in front of her. "I say we do it, Alex. Something like Jacobs will never come around again. We have to give it a shot."

Alex wouldn't look up. He brought a finger to her face and used it to gently raise her chin. They stared at each other for a moment, and she fought back a smile. Nick burst into a grin and knew the battle was won.

"That's my partner," he said.

"The sensible one of the two," she replied.

He rose and turned to the water. He was talking about it so matter-of-factly, as if it were no more difficult than going to the supermarket. But if something went wrong, there would be consequences. Laws varied from state to state, county to county. It could get a lot uglier than six months in the county jail. He rubbed his face. He felt confident now but wondered how his knees would feel walking up those porch steps.

"I can't believe it's coming to this," Alex finally said.

"It's the only way."

Both sat in silence momentarily, Nick biting at a hangnail, Alex staring across the river. Nick reached down and sent a final rock into the silent waters.

"Let's take another look at Michael Drive," he said, heading back to the car. "We've got to plan this right."

CHAPTER 9

A T 1 A.M., the rented midnight blue van pulled quietly from the driveway and down the street. They drove silently to their destination. Everything had been discussed, every scenario played out, and they were as comfortable with the plan as they could possibly be.

Nick sat in the passenger seat and felt perspiration bead up on the back of his neck. In eight years with SFPD, he had never seen much to make him sweat. He had seen mangled bodies, dead children, and shotgun suicides, and he had never shrunk from any of it. *You become immune after the first year,* Bill Merchant had told him. *You get an iron stomach.* His father had been right. He wondered how long it took criminals to develop iron stomachs. His was in knots.

The early hours of the morning were coal black, no moon in the sky to throw a spotlight on them. Upon arrival they made a pass down Michael Drive, scanning the street for any signs of life. Nick was encouraged to see that the streetlamp directly in front of Jacobs's home was burned out. The first break had gone their way.

Alex pulled the van to the curb around the corner and cut the engine. Nick glanced over his shoulder down the block and strained his eyes toward Jacobs's house, the fourth one from the corner.

"Conditions are about as good as they could be," he said, sounding more confident than he felt. "I doubt we'd have a better night to try this."

Alex nodded. "Houses are dark except for that one across the street."

Nick looked himself over yet again. He was wearing a heavy army jacket over a pullover. Inside the jacket was a crowbar; over his shoulder, a backpack. His hands were fitted with black leather gloves, and his radio was secured in his front jacket pocket. They had tested the clarity in Alex's backyard and been satisfied. Nick had remembered to remove the van's license plates before they had set off for Hudson.

"You look like Rambo," said Alex with a nervous little laugh.

"Let's hope I pull this off like Rambo," replied Nick. He grasped the door handle, hesitated, and looked back at her. "You all right?"

"I'm all right."

"You sure?"

"Ask again and I may say no. Get your butt moving before I start thinking too much."

"Okay. If all goes well, you'll hear from me in less than ten minutes on the radio. If anything goes way wrong, I could be back here real quick, so just be ready to gun it."

"I'll be ready," replied Alex. "Be careful."

Nick stepped to the curb, closed the door gently, and disappeared around the corner.

John Malloy slouched behind the wheel of the car and listened to his partner gurgle. The breathing was rhythmic, almost hypnotic. With every wheeze and snort, he felt himself grow drowsier. He pinched himself and glanced at his watch. Twenty minutes after one. Another forty minutes and it would be his turn to be annoying. His partner would hear some real snoring then.

They had parked at the end of Michael Drive, beneath the long shadow of a tree. Their vantage point was completely perfect. It was boring, simple work, but at least the money was right.

Malloy was almost glad to see the pedestrian. Watching him would kill a few minutes. He reached for the binoculars and raised them. The solitary figure was moving quickly down the dark sidewalk of Michael Drive. He immediately felt suspicious. The stranger wasn't jogging, didn't have a dog by his side. Malloy studied him and wondered what the hell he was up to.

Nick walked briskly along the sidewalk toward the Jacobs home, feeling every thump of his heartbeat. Despite his reconciliation with the plan, he couldn't purge a distinct uneasiness in his gut. The Jacobs case was about to become unique in more ways than just money. He had always respected the law, and despite his and Alex's rationalizing, he knew this was wrong, wrong, wrong. He thought of his father and wondered if he could see him right then, see his only son drifting to the other side of the law. Under the circumstances, he wasn't too certain old Bill Merchant wouldn't be doing the same damn thing.

The surrounding houses were silent and dark as Nick approached the front walkway of the Jacobs home. Before second thoughts could surface, he cut to his left and quickly moved up the walkway leading to the front porch. Boards creaked loudly as he gingerly stepped to the door. He crouched down like a soldier in a foxhole, temporarily sheltered from enemy eyes. The bushes adorning the front garden were effective allies; their shadows were covering him like a shroud. He was thankful the old man hadn't made use of the hedge clippers.

He grabbed the cold hard steel of the crowbar, feeling the solid weight of it in his hands. Before he could think too much, he turned to the door. He felt the doorknob, and with the full force of his weight, wedged the crowbar firmly between the door frame and the knob. He bent the door outward, knowing he could snap it from its hinge quickly, but noise was the concern. He would need to lean against the crowbar and slowly increase the pressure.

"Dammit—"

The wood was creaking in protest, flexing to its limits. With an ear-splitting crack, wood fragments exploded outward. The door creaked open. Nick cursed and ducked in quickly, pushing the door shut. With no bolt to hold it, the door swung slightly inward. He reached into the darkness and grabbed what felt like a coffee table, propping it up against the door. He placed the crowbar to the floor gently and peered through the peephole. Another light in the house directly across the street had flickered on. He reached for the radio.

"Alex . . ."

The response came instantly.

*"Are you in?"*

"Yes. We're home free. Watch for cops. I'll be out as soon as possible."

*"The house across the street lit up—"*

"I know. Just watch for cops. Toughest part's over."

*"Just hurry up, Nick . . ."*

Nick stared into the inky blackness. For better or worse, he was in. He had gained his entrance relatively easily, but that didn't mean some nosy neighbor wasn't reaching for a phone. He strained his eyes and glanced around the living room.

*Where to start, dammit, where to start?*

The house was almost completely black. He reached for his pen-light and shot a laser beam of light around the room. The beam was weak, but he could still see the lavishness with which the old man had surrounded himself. A dust-coated crystal chandelier hung from the ceiling, and a thick Oriental rug covered the floor. To the left, elegant nineteenth-century gilt chairs with burgundy upholstery surrounded a stately antique dining table. A heavy gold-framed mirror hung direct-ly behind the table, and the walls were covered with imposing works of art with elaborate gilded frames. He ran a gloved hand down the surface of one, feeling the rough texture on his fingers. It felt authen-tic.

Uncertain where to begin, he turned and promptly slammed his shin on a table. Stifling a curse, he grabbed two books that lay on the table and examined them. One was a biography of Chopin, the other an illus-trated translation of Dante's *Inferno*. Finding nothing between the pages, he placed them aside and scanned the living room with the pen-light. A grand piano stood in the corner like a casket.

Moving through the living room and into the hallway, Nick gazed up a long flight of stairs leading upward. People usually kept their personal mementos hidden away in their bedrooms; it would be a good place to start. He was about to head up when his eye caught a tiny flashing from the hallway. He approached the rapidly flashing light and quickly saw what it was. The answering machine's message light was flashing like a pinball machine. Odd, he thought—a recluse getting that many calls. He pointed the light on the machine and popped it open, taking the tiny message tape. It would make for interesting listening later.

He quickly stepped up the hardwood stairs. Two large portraits adorned the wall to his right. One depicted a somber elderly man with a flowing white mustache staring out over a cliff; the other a young woman in an elegant white dress holding a parasol. He firmly grasped the portraits and lifted them from the wall, noting the surprising weight. Placing them gently at the bottom of the staircase, he returned to the wall and began pressing and feeling the uncovered wall space. He tapped on it lightly and heard no echo.

*Seen too many detective movies, Nick. Quit wasting time . . .*

Thinking of the initial racket of the entry, he thumbed his radio. "Alex . . ."

*"What's happening?"*

"Nothing much. I'm heading upstairs. How's it look out there?"

*"We're okay. That light went off across the street."*

"You should see this place. Nothing at all like the outside. The old man had a hell of an interior decorator."

*"Quit sightseeing and get to work."*

"I'll try not to take more than an hour."

*"An hour!"*

"At least. Talk to you soon."

The hallway upstairs was darker than the rooms below, and the penlight seemed dimmer. Four doors beckoned: one directly ahead, one to the left, and two to the right. Nick grabbed and gently twisted the first knob on the right. A windowless closet with six shelves. A lightbulb cord hung from the ceiling and Nick pulled on it, flooding the tiny room with light. He grabbed towels from the top shelf and quickly shook each piece, discarding them in a pile as he went. In two minutes' time, the entire contents of the closet lay in a heap in the hallway. Nothing was found.

The next door on the right was the bathroom. Nick foraged through all drawers and the medicine cabinet, finding nothing except prescription medicine bottles and lotions. He quickly examined the labels of the medication bottles, making a note of the prescriptions. If necessary, he would find time to call a pharmacist to see what the medications might reveal about Jacobs's health. He pulled aside the shower curtain, looked in the tub, and saw nothing. He remembered the death certificate and ran the light around the inside. A faint pinkish ring was visible.

A bedroom was the first room on the left side. From the sparseness of the decor, Nick assumed he had entered a guest room. A single twin-size bed, neatly made, sat primly against the right wall. The curtains were open, and faint indirect light from the window facing the street streamed in weakly across the floor. He considered drawing the curtains but quickly thought otherwise. Feeling hot suddenly, he removed his jacket and placed it on the bed. He approached the closet. One by one, he tossed sport coats, sweaters, and overcoats aside as he checked every lining, every pocket. Boxes on the top shelf of the closet held some old turntable records and a wide variety of hats, gloves, and dusty books. Many were printed in German. Nick looked through one of them. Bonnie had been right about that—Jacobs was German. Or Austrian. The books seem to substantiate it.

He leafed through each of the books, looking for the postcard, the scrap of weathered paper, the birthday card—anything that would give that crucial family contact. After spending five minutes looking in drawers, under the bed—even under the throw rug—he crept toward the door at the end of the hall. If there was nothing of value in the old man's bedroom, there was still the garage, the dining room, the living room, and any other closets. Something had to turn up.

Malloy laughed to himself incredulously. Despite the overgrowth of bushes blocking his view, he felt fairly certain now that the prowler was inside. Breaking and entering—this bastard had balls. But that didn't mean they were going to let him get away with it. He nudged his companion awake with his elbow.

"Wake up. Something's going on here."

Regnier grunted and sat up straight. Malloy nodded in the direction of the house.

"Some guy just walked up and busted in. I heard him with the listener. He's been inside for a while now."

Regnier grabbed the binoculars and quickly brought them down.

"All I see is bushes."

"He's not sitting on the porch swing. Trust me, he's in there."

"So what do we do?"

Malloy considered it. Nobody was supposed to show up and pull a stunt like this.

"Instructions are to keep the place secure. Shit! I didn't agree to this." He reached to the back and found his gun. "I'll have to go introduce myself."

"Why not get him on the way out? We'll take him out on the sidewalk and drag him off quick."

Malloy shook his head as he shoved the clip in with a loud click.

"We can't let him roam around in there all night. I'll give him five minutes. If he ain't out then, I'm going in."

*          *          *

Holding his breath, Nick twisted the doorknob of the second floor's final room and stepped inside. The smell was musty and stale, the air heavier than the inside of a crypt. The curtains were drawn, and the room was almost completely lightless. The penlight cut through the dark and traced the edges of furniture. Jacobs had a gigantic bed, almost regal with its elaborate upper frame and curtain attachments. Nick shuddered at the medieval appearance as he approached the large dresser directly across from it. Methodically he emptied each drawer, his anticipation and disappointment growing stronger by the moment. He turned to the closet. It held shirts, jackets, boots, books—even rifles—but Nick could find nothing pertinent to Jacobs's personal life. Flustered, he stood in motionless confusion among the piles of clothes and bedding. He glanced at his watch and saw that he had been in the house for twenty-five minutes. He thought of the garage and moved toward the door but then remembered to check under the bed. No stone unturned.

Nick dropped to his stomach and scanned under the bed. He saw a dark, square-shaped object and reached for it. An empty tissue box. He cast it aside and turned back to the door, catching his foot in a small throw rug and nearly tripping. He kicked it aside gently and then paused. He had caught a glimpse of something odd as the light ran over the floor, an irregularity in the floorboards. He shone the light and confirmed it. Stooping, he ran his fingers over the floor. He could see a barely visible ridge. Some kind of small door was carefully cut into the floor where the throw rug had been. He tried to pry it open with his fingers but couldn't get a decent hold. He hurried back down to the kitchen and found a sturdy knife. *If what I'm looking for isn't in there,* he thought as he jogged back up the stairs, *it won't be anywhere.*

He jammed the knife into the crevice and propped it open enough to allow his fingers to reach down and get a hold. He pulled the hatch open. His light beam immediately caught the dull glimmer of steel. He reached to it and felt cold metal, and his mouth went dry.

Placing the container on the bed, Nick saw under the light that it was a metal security box. His pulse was moving fast now. He tried to open it but saw that it was locked. He tried to pry the knife into the edges but found that it was too thick. Walking briskly back downstairs with the box under his arm, he entered the kitchen. He found a thinner blade and took it and the metal container into the living room. Placing it on a coffee table, he jammed the blade into the hinges with all his might. After prying and twisting for several moments, the mechanism suddenly gave.

Inside the box was a jumble of letter-size envelopes, one larger manila envelope, and three aged black-and-white photographs. He examined the three small photos first.

One was a photo of a young boy, perhaps nine years old, holding an infant in his arms. On the back of the photo, in faint pencil, was written *1922*. The other two photos were of two young women. The women's expressions were somber and reminded Nick of passport photos. On the back of one was written *Monica 1935*. The other was blank.

"Hello, Monica," he whispered as he took the envelopes.

He spread the papers on Jacobs's living room floor and found that he had about a dozen brief handwritten letters, two blank New York City postcards, and a greeting card. The greeting card was a Hallmark, a cartoon cover with colorful ribbons and streamers. The printed message inside was generically simple—*Many Thanks!* The sender had scripted his own note beneath the generic one. The writing was labored and crooked, the handwriting of an elderly person.

Thank you for the chocolates, my friend! Congratulations to you for your new life!

Otto Kranzhoffer
September 25, 1997

Here were key words, thought Nick. Important words. *My friend. Your new life.* The card was in its envelope. The return address was Rue de Malatrex 23, Geneva.

He turned to the handwritten letters. The print was similar in each one. His suspicions were correct, then; they were from the same person. Someone named Claudia. The letters came from an address in Germany.

Nick placed the photos and letters into his backpack. They could be examined more thoroughly later. He opened the manila envelope and found two dozen large color photographs. Odd—the pictures were of men in suits, men talking, men getting out of cars. He shoved them back into the envelope and into his backpack as well. Now wasn't the time. The garage still needed attention. He walked quickly through the living room, the figures in the portraits staring at him as he hurried by.

He reached the door on the left side of the hall and found the garage. He crept inside. The penlight stabbed into the black, revealing a tidy garage and the glimmering reflection of a well-preserved Mercedes. Nick traced the far wall with the light. Seven identical cardboard boxes were placed neatly against the wall. He slid one of the boxes from the top of the stack, placed it on the floor, and opened it.

Inside the box were hundreds of single sheet documents. Each document was emblazoned with what appeared to be the letterhead of some kind of a financial institution. Nick examined a dozen of the documents. Despite minor variations, they all shared a similar look. He flipped the lids off several of the other boxes. Similar documents filled each.

The crackle of the radio made him jump.

*"Nick!"* Alex's voice was a panicked whisper. *"Someone's outside on the sidewalk! He's right outside the house!"*

Nick brought the radio to his mouth. "Cop?"

*"No way. He's . . . oh my God, Nick, he's coming up the walkway! Nick!"*

Nick didn't have time to analyze things. He quickly crammed a thick stack of the documents into his backpack and shot to his feet.

"Get ready to step on it."

*"What—"*

Alex's transmission died abruptly as Nick turned the volume down. He dashed back into the living room as quickly and quietly as he could. Already he was too late. A shadow had fallen across the curtains and then the front door was slowly being forced open against the coffee table. Nick dove for the grand piano and scooted under it.

From his stomach, he watched the intruder ease into the house. He felt a chill. The man was holding a large handgun.

The newcomer darted from doorway to doorway, his arms extended and locked. Nick tried not to blink as the stranger swept the weapon through the room.

The gunman seemed to be satisfied with his examination of the first floor, and he quickly approached the stairway. He began climbing the stairs, glancing back as he ascended every few steps. Nick tightened the straps of his backpack and readied himself to move. When the man was out of view, he slid out of his hiding place and quietly hurried to the front door. A flashing of lights froze him, reds and blues flickering in the darkness. The cops were on the scene.

*Would've been happy to see you guys a few years ago,* he thought grimly.

Nick hurried to the rear door and eased out the back. He ran over the back deck, inadvertently kicking a patio chair and sending it skittering loudly over the deck. Bolting to the eastern fence, he catapulted himself to the top. He took a quick glance at the gauntlet awaiting him. There were three homes between himself and Alex, each with a fenced backyard. He would need to make like an Olympic hurdler to get to her.

He swung his legs over the first fence and toppled into the neighbor's yard. Dashing fifteen yards through a garden, he pulled himself up the next fence as the wood near him suddenly splintered with the impact of bullets. He fell into the next yard and stumbled forward. He could see the streetlight on Michael Court where Alex was waiting. He tossed himself over a third fence as more bullets dotted the wood behind him, and he felt his ankle give as he rolled into the yard just adjacent to the street. Lights were flicking on in houses. Nick felt the full weight of his 190 pounds as he pulled himself over the final barrier. Alex was at the curb with the engine running. He plunged to the sidewalk, the crowbar flying from his jacket with a clatter as he stumbled up to the van. He threw himself in and held on as Alex spun out noisily and accelerated down the street.


Malloy leaned out the bedroom window and listened to the screech of spinning tires. He slammed his hand down on the windowsill and swore. He couldn't believe he had missed. Bad angle or not, he normally made shots like those in his sleep.

He hurried from the bedroom and approached the flight of stairs. He was one step down when the sound of the police radio halted him in his tracks. Cop lights were shining through the curtains. He heard a car door slam.

He drew back into the shadows as the front door opened. A single cop entered, his service revolver ready. Malloy cursed. He hadn't planned on this. But he wouldn't be the one left holding the bag. He raised his weapon, fixed the sight on the officer's chest, and squeezed the trigger.


In fifteen minutes' time, they pulled safely into Alex's garage. From all appearances, the getaway had been clean. Nick collapsed onto the living room couch. He shook his head, still unable to calm himself completely. Alex was too nervous to sit.

"What happened, Nick?"

She wanted a comforting response, something to slow her throbbing pulse. Nick could only shake his head.

"I'm not sure. Whoever that guy was, you can be damn sure he was no cop. He was opening up on me when I was hopping fences."

"He was *shooting* at you?" asked Alex, the horror thick in her throat. "But I didn't hear any—"

"Silencer," replied Nick. "A good one too. All I heard was the fence popping all around me." He looked at her. "They were watching that house, Alex."

"*Who* was?"

"Somebody."

Alex looked overwhelmed as she paced the carpet. "Everyone on that street must have seen us tearing out of there, Nick."

"No plates, remember? Stop sweating it. This was about as clean as it gets."

"Who would stake out that house, Nick?"

"Wish I knew. Why do it at all?"

"My God," said Alex. "If that guy wasn't a cop, what happened when the real cops found him in there?"

"Hopefully they nailed *him* for the break-in. We're scot-free, Alex. Forget about it."

"Sure, Nick. You nearly get killed, we nearly get arrested. Forgotten—just like that." She stopped pacing and leaned up against the wall, raising her face to the ceiling. She took a moment to gather herself. "Did you find anything in there?"

He stood and grabbed the backpack. "Christmas came early this year." He removed a mess of papers from the backpack, waving them emphatically. "I think we may have hit the jackpot."

"What have you got?"

"For starters, we got letters from someone named Claudia in Germany. Looks like our man Jacobs was German. I don't suppose you know any *Deutsch,* do you?"

"Any what?"

"Never mind. I've got some photographs and some other documents out of his garage. I don't know what they are or if they can help us, but they're interesting. C'mon, get away from the curtains and get over here."

He pulled the manila envelope from his backpack and put it aside. Alex joined him, and the two of them focused on the letters.

"Looks like we've got two solid contacts," Nick said. "Otto and Claudia. Claudia intrigues me the most. She addresses Jacobs as *Mein Liebling. Mein* I know is 'my'—what's *Liebling*?"

"No idea. What kind of dates do we have here?"

They both shuffled through their small piles. Nick waved one triumphantly.

"This one's June 5th of last year. Fifteen months ago! We've got a return address in Germany. Schönes Luft, Bernauerstrasse 445, D-8340 Berchtesgaden." He looked at her. "Who do we have for a translator around here?"

"I've got somebody downtown," said Alex.

"We'll call them at dawn." Nick began to pace about the room and continued to speak, as much to himself as to his partner. "We fax these letters to the translator at daybreak. We have them completely translated and dissected. If it looks good, I'm on a plane to Germany to meet Claudia."

"Not a cheap flight," commented Alex. "How are we doing on money?"

"We're set. I just had Rose transfer twenty thousand from the line of credit to our business account. We've got another thirty grand on top of that if we need it." He cast his eyes about the room. "Where's your atlas?"

"Up in my office. I'll get it."

Alex bounded up the stairs and came back down again almost immediately, carrying the large book. Nick took it from her and thumbed through the pages to the map of Germany. He ran his finger down it.

"Berchtesgaden is in the state of Bavaria in southern Germany. Salzburg, Austria, looks like the nearest airport." He reached for the phone. "Yes, I'd like to know if you have any flights available to Salzburg, Austria. The sooner the better. I'll hold. . . ."

Alex was looking at the photographs. Nick placed the phone down and clenched his fist.

"There's a flight to Frankfurt, Germany, out of JFK tomorrow. From Frankfurt I'll catch another flight to Salzburg. I'm all set."

"I'm going too, right?"

"What do you mean? I need you here, Alex. If Claudia gives me names of relatives, I'll be passing on the information to you. You may be making the approach."

She put her hands to her hips. "You're doing all the good stuff and I'm stuck here being your little errand girl."

"Alex, are you listening to me? I said you may be approaching the heirs. What more do you want? Don't give me a bad time here."

She slowly turned back to the photos. "Where did you find these pictures?"

"Under the floorboards in his bedroom."

"What? Under the floorboards?"

"Believe it or not. There was this . . . compartment hidden under his bedroom floor. Found it by luck. I'm telling you, this old guy was a lot craftier than we've been giving him credit for." He took several of the pictures and glanced them over. "These photos are strange."

"They look like surveillance photos," said Alex.

Nick studied them and saw that that was exactly what they looked like. They were high-quality color snapshots of half a dozen men in suits. They were congregating by two large cars and talking in small groups. The setting was parklike, with trees and shrubbery in the background.

"Some of these people look familiar," commented Alex.

"Not to me they don't," replied Nick. "Which ones are you looking at?"

Alex pointed at one of the faces. It was a youthful, skinny face, serious eyes behind black-rimmed glasses. He seemed to be glaring directly into the lens.

"Doesn't he look familiar? Kind of?"

Nick stared hard but didn't recognize him. He put the pictures down on the table and shrugged.

"Nobody I've ever seen."

Alex's eyes suddenly widened. "Oh my God, Nick—look at this one."

She gave him another picture. It was the same group of people, but this time a withered old man stood in the middle of them. He was stooped and the only man not wearing a suit.

"Where's our file photo?" asked Nick quickly.

Alex handed it to him. Nick compared the coroner's photo with the new photos. There was no doubt in his mind.

"It's Jacobs, all right. He must have hired someone to snap these photos. Why, though? These men don't seem to be doing much."

"It's not *what* they're doing that's important," said Alex. "It's who they are. These people are obviously important to Jacobs in some way. Hmm . . ." She studied the back of one of the pictures and offered it to him. "This is sweet. Look."

The photo was an enlarged face shot of the skinny man Alex had just pointed out. Jacobs was standing next to him. On the back, in smeared black ink, someone had printed *Cut Taylor's throat!*

"Lovely sentiments," commented Nick.

"What's that all about?" Alex asked, looking a bit chilled.

Nick shook his head helplessly and then began sliding the photos back into the envelope.

"Let's not waste time on these right now. We know Jacobs was nuts, probably paranoid as hell. Let's just concentrate on this lady in Germany. I think she's our family link."

Alex was looking over the greeting card from Geneva.

"This Otto character is a friend of Jacobs."

"We'll be checking him out too."

"I can't believe you found all this."

"That ain't all either." He handed Alex the three small passport photos. "Something else I came across . . ."

*"Monica 1935,"* she read. "Sister maybe?"

"I'm optimistic."

"Anything else?"

He shook his head, then stiffened. "Damn! I just remembered." He reached for the tiny tape in his pocket.

"Is that—"

"Yes, it is. Where's your little tape player?"

Nick followed her upstairs into the office. She found the recorder and inserted the tape. Nick took a seat as she pressed play.

*Beep . . . click . . . bzzzzzz . . . beep . . . click . . . bzzzzzz . . . beep . . . click . . . bzzzzzz . . .*

A dozen times, the pattern.

"Somebody didn't want his voice taped," commented Alex.

"Makes you wonder if—"

The sound of a voice silenced Nick. It was a male voice, a bland monotone.

*"Mr. Jacobs, we have a message from Taylor . . . we're coming to see you. . . ." Click . . . bzzzzzz . . .*

Nick was about to comment when another male voice came through.

*"Yeah, Jacobs—it's Demello . . . I need you to gimme a call today . . . it's important . . . call me . . ." Click . . . bzzzzzz . . .*

"What do you think?" asked Nick.

"I think they're up to no good," replied Alex. "The way they talk. Short, unrevealing sentences. They're being careful what they say because they know they're being taped."

"I think so too. It's—"

Another message interrupted him. This time the voice was quick and agitated. A rough tone—a voice from the streets.

*"Yeah, Jacobs—it's Demello . . . pick up the phone . . . don't play around, old man . . . call me back or I'll be at your goddamn doorstep. . . ." Click.*

"Same guy," said Nick. "And he's pissed this time."

The tape ran out after half a dozen more hang-ups and clicked itself off.

"Two dozen hang-ups, three messages," said Alex thoughtfully. "Jacobs had some people upset with him. That Demello guy especially."

"And once again we have Taylor. Jacobs took pictures of him for some reason, and now we have him calling the old man."

"These messages are scary," Alex said. "I wonder about this bathtub accident, Nick."

Nick slowly nodded. He rubbed his chin and thought for a few seconds. "Let's say that Taylor or Demello bumped off Jacobs. Would they be dumb enough to leave their names on his home answering machine?"

"Demello doesn't sound like an Ivy Leaguer to me."

"True, but Taylor's caller sounds smarter to me, kind of refined. I wonder if . . ." He bit a fingernail for a moment, then waved his hand in the air. "This is all very interesting, but all I'm concerned with right now is Claudia." He glanced at his watch. "It's late. I've got a long flight ahead of me. I need to close my eyes for a little while before morning."

"It *is* morning."

Nick took the tape player and headed for his room. His eyes stung, and his ankle ached from hopping the fences. He reached the bed and spread out on his back. Alex appeared in the doorway.

"I really need some sleep, Alex."

"We didn't talk about these yet."

She was waving the bank documents he had found in the garage. His head fell back to the pillow.

"I pulled those from his garage. I think they're bank statements."

"They're more than that," she said, sitting on the edge of the bed. "You know what these are? Authorization letters. Swiss bank accounts, Nick. Ownership certificates." She looked at him quickly. "Jacobs might have another twenty-two million over in Switzerland."

"And it doesn't mean a damn thing unless we find heirs."

Alex was paging through them rapidly. "Every one of these has the name *Ludwig Holtzmann* on them. Maybe Jacobs is Ludwig Holtzmann."

Nick sat up. He took a small stack from her and scanned through it. "There's a bunch of other names listed too, though."

Alex kept turning pages. "But *Holtzmann* is the only name I see on all of them. Jacobs has to be Holtzmann, Nick."

Nick lay back down on the bed. "Could be, but we'll need more than that to go on. There must be hundreds of Holtzmanns in the database. No—we need to check this woman out in Germany. That's the next step."

He draped a rolled-up T-shirt over his eyes. Alex crossed her arms on her chest.

"You're crazy if you think you'll actually be able to sleep."

"Not with you blabbing in my ear."

"When are you going to call Doug?"

"In the morning. Now beat it."

"Nighty-night, grouchy."

She closed the door behind her. Nick opened his eyes and stared at the ceiling. In his mind he could hear the voices from the tape

*"Call me back or I'll be at your goddamn doorstep. . . ."*

He thought of the drowning accident in the tub. Was it just an innocent slip of the foot? With the events of that morning, he greatly doubted that now.

He raised the recorder in his hand and pressed Rewind. He listened to the gadget's whirling and again thought of the gunman in Jacobs's home. Adding him to Taylor and Jacobs meant he had *three* mystery men to ponder now, and he didn't have the foggiest idea who any of them might be.

He pressed Play. The battery was weakening, the voice draining away like a dying man.

*"Mr. Jacobs, we have a message from Taylor . . . we're coming to see you. . . ."*

## CHAPTER 10

O N   T H E   C O R N E R of Pine and Broadway in Albany, the man named Kragen held a cup of coffee and watched the early morning pedestrians go about their business. He was operating on maybe four hours' sleep, and they had been a lousy four hours. He was in a nasty mood over the events of that morning.

When the limousine eased to the curb in front of him, he ditched the coffee and climbed inside. His contact this time was a familiar face, a pale, skinny man who liked expensive ties and white dress shirts. Something about this tidy little man rubbed Kragen the wrong way. He disliked even sitting next to him, but there were few people whose company he enjoyed.

"What the hell happened, Kragen?"

"Take a deep breath, chief. I get nervous when people raise their voices at me."

The limo moved into traffic again as they both glared at each other. The smaller man blinked nervously, then lowered his voice.

"Tell me what your people saw."

"They were watching the house," Kragen explained. "Just like you wanted. About one-fifteen, this guy walks up out of nowhere and goes up to the place. He disappears up the steps and then they hear this noise. Like a crash."

"A crash? What do you mean?"

"Just what I said—a crash. You know, like someone kicking a door in or something."

"Somebody broke in?"

"That's right."

"So what did they do?"

"They were set to go in after him, but a minute later a cop shows up."

"Oh Christ," said the man, sitting back and rubbing his forehead. "Then what?"

"The cop walks up to the front door, and then they hear the shot. Took a few seconds to figure out what happened. Turns out this burglar had a gun. Apparently he was waiting for the cop inside. Second the cop reached the front door, he went down."

The man rolled his eyes in dismay and looked straight ahead. The car moved by Kiernan Plaza, drawing a honk and a shouted curse. The driver, blocked from sight by a darkened divider, didn't respond.

"Are you sure about this? How do you know the cop was the one who got shot?"

"They said they drove by and saw him lying there in the front doorway."

"Dead?"

"Couldn't tell you."

"Did they see the prowler take off?"

Kragen shook his head. "Must have run out the back. He never came out the front."

"Why didn't they chase him?" demanded the man. "He shoots a cop and they let him just walk away?"

"My boys weren't there to play hero, chief. Besides, it's not like they had a lot of time to think things over. Five minutes after the cop went down, there were squad cars everywhere."

The stranger looked distressed by what he was hearing.

"No one told us this was going to happen," said Kragen, angry but restrained. "Your friend at the park yesterday morning said there wasn't going to be any trouble. My men didn't expect anything but a little surveillance. What's the deal here?"

No response came.

The car was heading south on North Pearl now. Kragen was tired of sitting next to the little man. His head hurt from lack of sleep. Money or not, this guy was hard to take.

"What time did the break-in occur?" asked the man suddenly.

"Must have been about one-fifteen."

"And the cops showed up right after this burglar broke in?"

"Couldn't have been more than five minutes."

"So he couldn't have been inside any more than five minutes—is that what you're saying?"

"That's what I'm saying."

The man nodded. He reached forward and rapped on the divider with his pen. The limo eased to a stop at the curb. Kragen could tell his host was upset. He could see little balls of froth at the corners of his mouth.

"You've been paid for your time. We may need you again at very short notice. Can your people be ready quickly?"

"Quick as the money's out."

"It will be. Wait for my call."

Kragen stepped to the curb and wondered if he would ever hear from him again. He wasn't sure he even wanted to.

Moving day was going smoothly. Two large men in white jumpsuits maneuvered a sofa carefully through the doorway of 198 Michael. A half dozen federal agents were pitching in as well, entering and exiting the home like pillaging rodents, their arms full of whatever they could scoop up. They were opting for the smaller or lighter furnishings—the towels, the clothing, the chairs, the kitchen appliances. The refrigerator, dressers, and other heavy furniture were being left for the professionals. Every one of them was wondering how the movers would get the piano through the doorway.

Deputy Director Arminger stood on the sidewalk, his arms folded on his chest. Despite the absurdity of the assignment, he was actually enjoying his role of moving supervisor. He was breathing fresh air, and that by itself was a pleasant change. He was convinced that the Bureau office in Manhattan with its endlessly recycled ventilation had almost certainly planted the seed of some terrible cancer in his lungs. He was resigned to an early end, and he fully accepted that. He inhaled the crisp Saturday morning air and watched his men working. He could only hope the annoying presence at his side would eventually give up and go away.

"We still need to dust the place," said the police captain. "What's so urgent that your men can't wait an hour?"

Arminger exhaled. "I told you already, Captain, this is now a federal matter. There's nothing further for you here."

The captain frowned beneath a flared salt-and-pepper mustache. "One of my men was almost killed here last night. My detectives have a right to get in there and look around. You're hauling out evidence, goddamnit."

"Evidence which will get proper attention from the FBI crime lab. I regret that the officer was hurt, but—"

"Waiting an hour or so wouldn't make a difference and you know it," the captain snapped. "Why don't you quit being so damn stubborn and show a little flexibility?"

"We have nothing more to discuss, Captain."

"I want your boss's name."

Arminger turned and faced him.

"I *am* the boss. Go bother someone else now."

Arminger made his way past the cop and up the walkway. He examined the entrance. The door frame was cracked, the bolt hanging like a broken limb. Brazen, he thought. The gunman had seemingly walked right up and kicked the front door in.

He stepped inside and looked around the living room. Things were thrown about. Books were on the floor, a coffee table was on its side. A security box on the couch gaped open at him like a metal oyster. He walked over to it, his hands in his pockets. If there had been a pearl inside, it was long gone now.

He took the stairs to the second floor. The movers were fighting with a mattress now, and he sidestepped them as he made his way up. The hallway above was filled with towels and bed linens.

"Rogers," he said, stopping a passing agent. "What's this mess?"

The agent shrugged. "It was like this when we got in, sir. Place has been all torn up."

Arminger proceeded down the hall, reaching the master bedroom. He stopped in the entrance and paused. Now, this was interesting. A kind of trapdoor was propped open out of the floor. He approached it and looked inside. A small space, now empty. Recently emptied. The thief had made off with a serious haul.

He made his way back outside to the front yard. A police officer was leaning against his patrol car watching the movers. Arminger approached him.

"Morning, Officer. Were you here last night?"

The cop nodded, his eyes to the house. "The cop who got shot's a good friend of mine."

"How's he doing?"

"He'll make it. He'll be on his back for a while, but he's going to pull through."

"Good news. Were you here when the shots were fired?"

"En route. I think I might have seen the guy disappear off Joslen. A van maybe—black or dark blue. We lost 'em in the side streets."

"Is this your neighborhood normally?"

"Yeah."

"Ever have any kind of trouble at this address before?"

"Never. What's going on in there? My captain's pissing fire."

Arminger was thinking of the backyard. He turned and walked back toward the house. "I'm glad the officer is going to recover," he said over his shoulder. The deputy director reentered the house and walked through the living room again. The movers were looking at the piano and scratching their heads. The agents were busy avoiding eye contact with them.

Arminger stood and surveyed the backyard from the patio. There was no mystery regarding the old man's gardening habits. The yard was a dry brown mess of weeds and dead rose bushes. The concrete paths were barely traceable through the tangle of roots. An agent was walking along the eastern perimeter, his eyes trained to the ground.

"Lose something, Davis?"

"Just looking around, sir," replied the agent. "Look at the table there."

Arminger followed the agent's finger to the patio table. A small black device lay flat on its surface. He took it and gave it a cursory look.

"So what's this?"

"It's a two-way radio, sir."

"Thanks for clearing that up. My turn to show and tell now?"

"I found it by the fence," replied the agent, approaching him. "The power was on."

Arminger looked at the radio with new interest. It was a cheap, mostly plastic model—a toy really. But a functional toy. He popped open the battery compartment. A nine-volt, brown acid oozing.

"The power was on, eh?"

"Yes, sir."

Arminger nodded and considered his suspects. It was a short list. He lowered the antenna and placed the radio in his coat pocket.

"Let me know if you find anything else."

CHAPTER 11

THE SUN WAS falling to the west as another day faded to black. It was 5 P.M., Thursday evening.

Nick shielded his eyes from the glare of the runway and yanked the window shade closed. As soon as Flight 438 out of JFK taxied to the runway and lifted from the ground, he would start planning strategy. He would have plenty of time to do so. The flight to Frankfurt would be nearly eight hours. From there, he would switch planes and fly to Salzburg, Austria—another hour. He anticipated being well rested by the time he finally drove back over the German border to Berchtesgaden. He would need to be. Germany would be uncharted territory, but that had also been the case in Japan, Australia, Denmark, and the other foreign countries he had visited to find heirs. He would find his way around just as he always did. He had already made arrangements for a translator to accompany him to Berchtesgaden. Things would proceed smoothly from there.

The plane had positioned itself for takeoff when his phone suddenly rang from his pocket like a muffled bird. Rose's voice had a frightened edge to it.

"Nick, what's going on here? I just got in from running my errands and these two men were here waiting for me. They said they were with the FBI. They were asking all sorts of questions about you."

"They showed up there at the *office*?"

"Two of them. And they weren't very friendly."

Nick tried to swallow a knot in his throat but failed. He hadn't expected anything beyond a simple phone call from the feds.

"What exactly did they say, Rose?"

"They told me to get hold of you. They wouldn't leave, Nick. I didn't know what to do. I finally told them I'd been paging you all day and you hadn't called me back."

"So they left?"

"Yes, but they left a phone number in Manhattan. You're supposed to ask for Deputy Director Edmund Arminger."

*"Deputy Director?"* Nick blurted, far louder than he had intended.

"Yes. This Deputy Arminger has left several messages on the answering service. Sounds like he's very concerned about something." She took a moment to catch her breath. "What's going on, Nick? I don't want to get in trouble."

A stewardess walked by and gave Nick a scolding look. The plane was set to move.

"You won't get in trouble, Rose," he said, lowering his voice. "I don't know what these people want, but it definitely has nothing to do with you."

"Well, I'm worried just the same. I think you better call them right now."

Nick bit a fingernail as his eyes darted about the floor. "Give me their phone number. . . ."

The jet engines howled to speed, and the sickening sensation of liftoff fluttered through his stomach. It never got better. Flying was something he still couldn't bring himself to enjoy. He laid his head back and closed his eyes.

The FBI couldn't be ignored, as much as he would have liked to do just that. Safe to say, all this special attention wasn't good news. They certainly hadn't come by the office to offer him a job. He had heard stories of the federal agents—the dirty intimidation tactics they used—and he probably didn't know the half of it. He would have to call them, but if he did it now, it would in all likelihood mean the end of the Jacobs investigation. The thought of that brought a sharp frown to his lips. He made his decision, a compromise of sorts. He would call them, but only *after* he acquainted himself with Claudia. Until then he was going do a wonderful job of playing dumb.

He reached over and pulled down the shade, doubting if he would be able to sleep.

He woke some time later, feeling disoriented and stiff. His watch revealed that only slightly more than an hour had passed. He raised the shade and looked out at the last purple rays of the sunset. Below, the dark gray of the North Atlantic lay in wait like an enormous dormant monster.

He cracked his neck and thought of the hours he had to kill. He dismissed a few lingering thoughts of the FBI and decided to look over his notes. They were more interesting than last month's *Time* anyway.

They had delivered Claudia's letters into the hands of Alex's Albany translator at daybreak. The conclusions to be drawn were hardly definite. The text of the letters was incoherent and rambling, but in each of them, the writer referred to Jacobs as *Liebling*—"darling." Claudia would ramble on about Germany and the weather, and then reverse direction and talk about war, the 1930s, and other scattered topics. Alex was certain that Claudia was Jacobs's lover. Nick felt less convinced. He felt more certain that she was crazy, or at the very least suffering from senility. The translator had agreed with that summation. It was irrelevant. Claudia knew Jacobs—that was enough. She needed to be checked out.

Time moved like a stubborn tortoise. Nick divided the hours between his notebooks, broken sleep, and a movie. Scattered dreams merged. He saw the gunman at the Jacobs home. He saw Emma McClure and her son sitting on their shabby living room couch. He saw his father lying in the morgue, his face drained white and sunken, his naked, desecrated body like some alien mass of bone and tissue. He woke abruptly and ordered a cocktail. It didn't seem to help.

From Frankfurt the connection was met smoothly, and the flight to Salzburg lasted almost exactly an hour. Nick watched the ground rush by as they descended to Austrian soil. It was misting, dreary—he saw the tiny headlights of cars traveling along winding country roads. Unknown territory, an unknown land. He had never flown back from a foreign country without clients. This was not the case he wanted his luck to run out on.

The plane jolted to the runway through a light rain. Nick rose to his feet and reached overhead for his bag. He felt exhilarated. He passed through customs and wove his way through the terminal of the Salzburg airport. The loudspeaker overhead blared announcements in a pleasant fräulein's voice. The terminal was filled with travelers, most of them blond-haired and blue-eyed—an odd spectacle for him after countless trips through San Francisco International. He found a cab outside and was taken to auto rentals. Within fifteen minutes, he was speeding through the rolling Austrian countryside along southbound Autobahn 312 and passing through customs at the German border. His map showed it to be a simple route—a half-hour trip on the autobahn would lead directly into the heart of Bavaria. And Berchtesgaden.

Nick marveled at the view surrounding him on the rapidly ascending roadway. The drizzle of the German border had vanished into a brilliant blue sky which shimmered off the pavement of the autobahn. To the right, massive limestone and granite mountains rose and fell magnificently into the greenery of the surrounding valleys. Alpine meadows sprinkled with color and bordered by thriving forestland blanketed the countryside. The views opened up further as the valleys seemed to sprawl deeper within the shadows of the Bavarian Alps. He lowered his window slightly and enjoyed the cool, pine-scented air.

The natural beauty of the drive was soothing, so much so that he nearly missed his turnoff, a winding cobblestone road that shook the wheel in his hands. According to his map, he was about to enter a small mountain village just outside of Berchtesgaden, a town with a name he wouldn't even dare attempt to pronounce. He glanced at the map. Bischofswiesen.

The road evened out as Nick found himself in the center of the tiny town. He slowed the car. He was in the town plaza now, alone on the road. An open marketplace, teeming with older ladies bustling about in search of choice produce, lay to his left. To his right was a cream-colored hotel with dark wooden balconies and colorful flower boxes. Locals lounged under table umbrellas in front of a cafe.

He found the address he was looking for and pulled to the curb. With arrangements already made, it took only a minute to hire a stout, middle-aged fellow by the name of Rolf as translator. A generous wage equivalent to twenty-two dollars an hour was negotiated.

Back on the road, Rolf asked if he could smoke. They lowered the windows. Nick feared the German's hairpiece would be lost in the torrent of wind. He could feel his ears popping as they continued to ascend.

"Yes, Berchtesgaden is less than five minutes from us, Herr Merchant. Just stay on the road. Your exit is coming shortly."

Nick nodded and looked at his speedometer. He was flying along at a speed that would earn him a serious ticket back home. He was enjoying himself, savoring the thrill of traveling the autobahn at seventy-plus. Rolf reclined in contentment with his hands folded on his ample belly, seemingly unconcerned with their speed.

"Where exactly are we going in Berchtesgaden, if you don't mind me asking, Herr Merchant?"

"A retirement home by the name of Schönes Luft. Heard of it?"

Rolf nodded his head and yawned. "Oh yes. Very exclusive home. Have you relations there?"

"No," replied Nick, reading a mountain road sign as it flew by. "Just doing some work on behalf of a client in the United States."

Rolf pointed forward. "Your exit is coming here. Slow down or you'll pass it."

Nick eased off the accelerator. Claudia was so close he could feel her presence. He ground his nails into the steering wheel as he pulled from the autobahn. As he slowed, the car proceeded along a winding road that skirted a massive outcrop of boulders. To the left, he saw rustic chalets, some built into the rocks of the mountain towering above. A gray double-steepled stone church appeared ahead, its twin spires pointing to the sky like daggers. Carved figures in various states of rapture stared out blindly from its niches.

He passed the church and veered to the left as instructed. The road climbed upward. After about a twenty-second ascent, the road leveled and opened up into a circular parking area. A stately, white-pillared structure loomed before them like a mausoleum at the far end of the lot. Nick pulled the car to the front of the building and parked. He placed his recorder in his jacket pocket, double-checking that the tape had been rewound to the start. He looked to Rolf.

"I've no idea if the woman I want to see speaks English. If she does, you may not be needed. You'll of course be paid for your time." Rolf nodded, unaffected either way.

Nick stepped from the car and eyed the Schönes Luft. Stark white with four twenty-foot granite pillars flanking the entrance, the structure looked sturdy enough to withstand a World War II air raid. He wondered if that had been the designer's intention. It looked secure, if not warm and friendly.

At the entrance, they passed through an elaborate display of flower beds and hanging plants and entered the building through a pair of massive oak doors. From the foyer of the building, he looked for someone to approach. An older woman dressed in white wrote at a front desk, and as his shadow fell on her paper, her stern gray eyes met his.

"*Ja?*"

"Hello," Nick said with a smile. "Do you speak English?"

"How can I help you?" she asked, her look guarded.

"I'd like to speak with one of your residents if possible."

"You are a relative of one of our boarders?"

"No. My name is Nick Merchant—I'm a private investigator from the United States. I have important news for one of your boarders regarding a family matter."

"Have you an appointment?" she asked, reaching for a large leather-bound book. "We usually require appointments for visitors who are not family."

"No, it's an urgent matter and I didn't have time to call."

"What is the person's name?"

"Her first name is Claudia. I'm unsure of her last name. She sends letters to relations in the United States."

The woman's mouth had shrunken into a tight pucker of displeasure. "I'll need to speak to the authority on duty," she said, rising to her feet.

"I appreciate that."

Nick nodded uncomfortably at Rolf. Authority on duty? He thought this was a rest home, not a prison. The staff certainly had a warm touch. He hoped he would never end up in a place like this.

He looked beyond the reception area and into a large sitting room. The walls were adorned with rich tapestries and pictures, the carpet was thick and new, but somehow it was like colorful camouflage. The place had a cold feeling to him. It seemed more a hospital ward for the terminally ill than a retirement home. He wondered if Claudia was completely infirm.

The woman returned in a moment's time with an even sterner looking companion. The newcomer was a formidable presence, a pinkish-skinned woman with wide shoulders and a thick neck. She eyed Nick disapprovingly.

"You're the one who wishes to see Claudia Dorsch?" she demanded.

"Yes, I believe she's the one."

The woman walked slowly from behind the counter, examining Nick and his translator.

"I'm the Directing Custodian here. This retirement community is a private home. We don't let just anyone wander in to see our guests. Many of our boarders are not in the best of health. Unexpected visitors can be upsetting, Herr . . . ?"

"Merchant. Nick Merchant." Nick extended his card and let her read it.

"You've traveled far, Herr Merchant."

"Yes, I have, Frau . . . ?"

"Brausch."

Nick motioned to his translator. "Why don't you step outside for a moment and let Frau Brausch and myself have a word in private?" Rolf exited. "Is there somewhere where we can perhaps sit down and talk, Frau Brausch?"

"What is this concerning?"

"A family matter pertaining to one of your residents. Please—just a few moments and I promise I'll be on my way." He took extra care to speak softly. The woman seemed too ready for confrontation.

"This can't take long. I have too much to do. Follow me."

Nick focused on the back of her thick neck and gathered up his resolve. A cranky old nursemaid wasn't going to stop him so close to the summit. Persuasion combined with the proper amount of half-truths would do the trick.

They entered a small, brightly lit office. Frau Brausch did not sit down and did not invite her guest to do so. Nick clasped his hands in front of himself and began.

"Frau Brausch, I have a small business in the United States, a business which does genealogy on families. Through my research I've learned a great deal about Claudia's family, some of whom live in the United States. Claudia may be entitled to a sum of assets in the United States which have been left to her by a recently deceased relative. I simply wish to speak with her briefly, to establish for legal purposes whether or not she is the person I believe her to be, and then inform her of her inheritance."

"She has never mentioned relations in the United States. I think you may have the wrong person."

"Well, it shouldn't take me more than ten or fifteen minutes to find out. All I need to do is ask her a few very specific questions."

Frau Brausch was holding firm. "We've had problems in the past with unexpected visitors. Why didn't you telephone ahead first? Frau Dorsch is in no condition to even understand any of your . . . legal phrases."

"I'm requesting just ten minutes and then I'll leave. I promise I will be very gentle with her. Please—I've come a long way. . . ."

Brausch was biting her lower lip in frustration. He was wearing her down.

"As her guardian," continued Nick, "you're watching out for her best interests, aren't you?"

"Of course I am," she snapped.

"Well, let me find out if she's who I believe she is so that I can provide her with what's legally hers." He spoke firmly but softly.

Brausch exhaled in defeat. "Ten minutes. That's all you get. If she's sleeping, you'll just have to come back. If you upset her in any way or—"

"I promise I won't. I'm glad I haven't come all this way for nothing."

"Yes, yes, yes—follow me and I'll check on her. If she's asleep you'll just have to wait."

"Does she speak much English? I've brought my translator along with me."

"You won't need him. Now come along."

Nick found Rolf by the front garden and sent him off to do as he wished until he was done with Claudia. He then followed the acerbic custodian as she led him up a stairwell.

Nick was barely even aware of his surroundings. His hands felt a bit shaky. This was potentially the most important moment of his professional life, and the fact was flashing in his head like a thousand-watt strobe light. He wasn't used to this. This wasn't the happy-go-lucky heir finder strolling into the McClure house with a smile and a contract. This was Game Seven of the World Series, bottom of the ninth, bat in his hands, and a hundred-mile-per-hour fastball heading his way. He had to make good.

They reached the second floor and proceeded down a tiled hallway. Small white marble busts peered at Nick from cubbyholes in the walls as they walked by. They would serve as his silent witnesses.

At the hallway's end, Frau Brausch stopped at a door and faced him. "If she's sleeping, you'll have to wait," she repeated.

Nick watched from the doorway as she entered. An elderly woman was sitting upright in bed, with another woman in a wheelchair facing her. The woman in the bed was speaking and looked gaunt and frail. Brausch placed her hand on her shoulder, and the old woman turned her squinty eyes up to her. They exchanged words in German and Nick saw her nod absently. There was a blankness in her eyes he had seen before. It wouldn't be the first confused, elderly person he had to extract information from. It had never been easy.

Brausch walked quickly back to the doorway.

"She's very disoriented, but she wishes to hear you out." Brausch peered over her shoulder at the women. "Her friend Magda won't disturb you. I'll be right outside this door if there are any problems."

"Thank you very much."

Brausch nodded and closed the door partially behind her. Nick looked at the old women and walked toward the bed. A large open window revealed the Alps, a sight probably unappreciated by the room's boarders. The bedridden woman happily babbled to her friend in the wheelchair. She turned to Nick as he drew closer, and he saw her eyes, vacant pale-blue pearls. Nick smiled, glanced at her equally confused friend, and reached for a chair. He took a moment to rethink his strategy before speaking.

"Hello, Claudia," he said softly. "My name—"

"Yes, hello, hello. You wish to speak in English, eh? Yes, Magda and I still remember it from the old days. We still like to practice it when old friends come to see us. Isn't that right, Magda?"

Her companion spoke in a smoker's rasp. "He looks just like my brother Karl."

The eyes were completely blank, the smiles blissfully serene. Nick now fully saw what he was faced with. Forget trying to explain who he was or what he had come for. He needed to get her talking about Jacobs.

"You're feeling better, Claudia?" asked Nick sweetly, as if he were talking to a child.

"Yes, I am, and I wish you would come visit more often. You are Uncle Willie's young nephew, eh?" Her fingers fidgeted incessantly as she leaned against the headboard of her bed.

"Yes, I am," replied Nick without hesitation. "Uncle Willie says hello. . . ."

"Tell him I'm not happy about that girl he chose. Not at all." She pursed her lips and looked agitated. Magda frowned in agreement.

"She wasn't a very good choice, was she?" asked Nick.

"She's a Pole! I don't approve of her."

"A Pole—how terrible," added Magda, making a little clicking sound of disapproval. Nick nodded, his face duly concerned.

"I don't care for Poles," continued Claudia. "For Willie to mix his blood with her is wrong. Do you know where her family is from?"

"Where?"

"Danzig!" She spat the word from her mouth as if it were a poison.

"Danzig?" repeated Nick in mock astonishment.

Both Claudia and Magda shook their heads dejectedly.

"It's terrible," said Claudia.

Nick nodded, his face a mask of empathy, while he processed what he was hearing. Was Uncle Willie actually Gerald Jacobs? If not, he needed to change the subject, and fast. He scooted his chair forward. It was time to be more direct.

"I haven't seen Uncle Willie in some time, Claudia. He hasn't moved, has he?"

"No. He was born in Düsseldorf, he will die in Düsseldorf. The family is still there."

"And how is Gerald? Gerald Jacobs?"

Claudia's face immediately brightened. Something had clicked.

"Monica's letter came the other day." She reached to the nightstand by her bed and grabbed an envelope. "You can read it if you like."

"Thank you," he replied, remembering the name on the back of the passport photo taken from Jacobs's home. He opened the decrepit envelope carefully. It was in German and was dated August 2, 1972. Nick looked up and saw both women staring at him.

"So . . . how is she?" he asked awkwardly, drawing a confused look from Claudia. "Monica. How's her health?"

"Much better. After the war, I think she and I will go to Dresden for a long vacation." She tilted her head to Magda. "Maybe you will come, Magda?"

Nick frowned. After the war? The woman was completely gone, living in some long-dead past. Anything out of her mouth was dubious. He needed to get to the heart of the matter.

"What about Gerald Jacobs, Claudia?"

She paused, her hazy mind struggling to gather fractured pieces of decades-old memories. "Ludwig," she sighed, "poor little Ludwig, my darling."

Nick froze. Ludwig? He thought Jacobs was her darling. Alex was right, then—Jacobs was Ludwig Holtzmann.

"How is Ludwig?" he asked, prodding her along. "I've not seen him in a long time."

She smiled. "Ludwig used to have the most golden hair that I've ever seen. Everyone thought he was the dearest man."

"I'm sure they did," replied Nick. "How is Ludwig, Claudia?"

"Ludwig is fine. He now lives in the *verdammt* United States."

"What city, Claudia?"

"Eh?"

"What city in the United States does Ludwig live in?"

Her face went blank, almost as if a synapse in her brain had misfired at that moment. "I don't . . . remember."

"You don't remember?" Nick asked. She did not respond.

"Near New York City," Magda interjected.

"How do you know?" he asked, turning to Magda.

"Because she told me." Claudia glared at Magda and she looked down.

Nick abandoned his previous tact and shot right to the point. "Magda, is Claudia Ludwig's sister?"

"No," she whispered, a hand shielding her mouth. "His sweetheart."

"Not brother and sister?"

"No." She looked at Claudia cautiously before continuing. "Lovers."

Nick turned back to Claudia. "Has Ludwig ever married? Does he have any children?"

Claudia shook her head adamantly. "No, Ludwig was too dedicated to his work."

Nick nodded. He was close—so very close. He reached into his jacket and produced the picture of the girl he had found in Jacobs's room.

"Who was Monica, Claudia? Who was she?"

Claudia stared at the picture for five long seconds and then smiled widely. She pointed her crooked finger at the photo. "That is Ludwig's sister, Monica."

Nick looked at the picture, his heart pounding his rib cage.

"So many questions," Claudia said. "Tell me when Willie will come visit."

"I'm not sure," replied Nick, feeling his patience begin to slip. "How are Monica's babies, Claudia? How are her children?"

"Ah yes—Monica's little boys. And one little girl too. Monica shouldn't have disgraced them."

"What do you mean—"

"She fled the country. Went to America."

"And she had three children?"

"At least the little ones didn't suffer through the war."

"What were her children's names, Claudia?" he asked, almost pleading now. He touched her hand gently. "Do you remember their names?"

"I don't know," replied the old woman absently.

"Think, Claudia. You can remember—I know you can. Where did Monica live? What city in America?"

"Monica just wrote to you, didn't she, Claudia?" asked Magda.

"Yes. I told her to come to Germany, but she never comes."

"Where is Monica now?" asked Nick.

Claudia pointed. "Magda, give me my jewelry box."

Magda nodded, lifting herself slowly from the wheelchair. She slowly shuffled over to her dresser, opened a drawer, and removed a small wooden case.

Nick scrutinized the box approvingly as she returned. Good things often came in small packages. Magda handed it to Claudia and she pried it open with her withered, skeletal fingers. She removed what appeared to be a small stack of envelopes. Nick leaned forward and wet his lower lip. Claudia held the letters to her heart and smiled sadly.

"These letters are precious. My dear family—someday we will be reunited."

"Claudia, may I see them please?" Nick asked.

He reached for them and, meeting no resistance, slid them gently from her grasp. To his relief, Magda began chattering away to Claudia, and their focus shifted away from him.

He thumbed through the stack of envelopes. Some were in English; most were in German. He scanned several that were written in German, looking for names or addresses that might be useful, and found nothing.

One letter caught his eye. It was in English and dated just over six years ago. From what Nick read, it contained the kind of everyday trivialities that elderly people normally love to hear. It had been sent from

Des Moines, Iowa. The letter began "Dear Claudia." The envelope, which Claudia had so meticulously saved, gave a return address of 11 Pinecreek Road, Des Moines, Iowa, 50312. The letter had been sent from a Monica Von Rohr.

Before he could decipher the significance of the find, he noticed a letter unlike the others. The typewritten ink was faded and a bit smeared, but it was in English and completely readable:

Dearest Claudia,

I pray this letter finds you in improved health. I am well and bring you news, both good and bad. I have agreed to the Americans' conditions. For my full cooperation they in turn have agreed to arrange my release and provide me with compensation. Unfortunately they require that I make my new home in America. Proximity is the only way they believe they can insure my silence. I have little choice in my current position but to accept their terms.

I would have hoped to see you a final time, but my obligations begin the moment I am free. My situation has presented me with two damnable options. Having endured nearly fifty years of one, I hope you understand my decision to live my final years under the rules of the other. Please destroy this letter and the accompanying document after you read and commit them to memory.

Love always, Ludwig
July 30, 1997

Affixed to the letter was a yellowed, poor-quality photocopy. Nick glanced at the women and then back down to read. The paper was faded, the words almost illegible. The seal of the Federal Bureau of Investigation was stamped at the top.

Burdoc 863348
CroRef 8741,-2,-3
24 July 1997
Re: Ludwig Wilhelm Holtzmann

Pertaining to the matter of the now existent Gerald Raymond Jacobs, relocation shall occur in the city of Hudson in the state of

New York. Manufacture/creation of all vital documents and testi-monials shall reflect the adoption of the Jacobs identity. FBI Director Dalton given complete autonomy in selection of agents to initiate placement. The number of agents shall in no circum-stance exceed two. Full implementation to begin on 14 August 1997.

Nick let a breath out slowly. The picture had come into focus a bit more. The FBI had placed Gerald Jacobs, who was actually Ludwig Holtzmann, in Hudson, New York, back in 1997. But evidently the cur-rent FBI administration had been asleep at the wheel when he died. They hadn't expected heir finders to descend on the body quicker than flies. A careless mistake.

The women were too absorbed in their conversation to notice Nick slip the Von Rohr and Holtzmann letters into his inner coat pocket. He took the Bureau document as well. He then placed the slightly thinner stack on Claudia's nightstand. They would never notice the difference, and he would definitely return them just as soon as the investigation was over. He rose to his feet.

"Claudia, Magda, it's been nice talking with the two of you. I really must be leaving, though. Thanks so much."

Claudia's eyes momentarily twinkled. "Won't you stay for dinner?"

"I'm afraid I can't." He gently took her hand. "It was nice seeing you."

He turned from them, feeling a bit guilty. He had deceived them, but if anything he had brightened their day by paying them a visit.

Frau Brausch waited for him outside the door, her arms folded across her chest.

"Find what you were looking for?"

"I just may have," he replied, hurrying by her. "I appreciate your help."

Nick hastily descended the staircase to the main floor, his mind reel-ing the entire walk. The names reverberated in his head. FBI Director. Ludwig Holtzmann. And the trail was now pointing to Iowa. Somehow he sensed that Des Moines wouldn't be the last stop on this wild ride.

He exited out into the sunlight of the front court and entered the rental car, beginning a slow cruise back down the road they had come on. He spotted his translator sitting along the way and five minutes later returned him to Bischofswiesen.

Before returning to the autobahn, he pulled the car into the lot of a small inn by the side of the road. He began punching in Alex's home phone number, then paused. The FBI was on to them. He hung up and tried her cell phone instead. It would be a harder line for them to trace

"It's me."

"What happened?" Alex's voice was drowsy with sleep.

"Something big, I think. I got this woman to pull out some old letters. Jacobs *was* Holtzmann, Alex. I think we have the old man's sister in Iowa."

"Oh my God—Nick! What—"

"Write down this name. Monica—that's M-o-n-i-c-a—Von—V-o-n—Rohr—R-o-h-r. Last name is two words. Address: 11 Pinecreek Road, that's P-i-n-e-c-r-e-e-k Road, Des Moines, Iowa, 50312. Read it back." She did. "Okay. Get on the computer and do an occupant check. Call the operator out there and confirm that she's still at that address. Get up and get on it right now."

"I'm up."

"After you confirm the address, do a complete background check. I'm en route back to the Salzburg airport right now. Hopefully when I get there you'll have a confirmation on the address and I'll be hopping on a plane to Iowa. What time is it there now?"

"Little after four in the morning."

"One other thing—see what you can find out about this Ludwig Holtzmann person. After you're done researching Monica, go to a library or something and see what you can find. Find out whatever information you can on those bank letters too. We need to know exactly what those are."

"There might be another few million there," said Alex.

"You got it, baby. If so, we'll tack 'em on to the estate and claim those too. Listen, we've both got our hands full. I've got to run now—"

"Wait a second, Nick. Have you spoken with Rose? The FBI—"

"The FBI's looking for me—I know all about it. I'm not doing anything about that until I check out Iowa. I'll hear them out once we find our heirs. I found some document over here that links them to Jacobs. Look, I'll tell you all about it when I get back. Just check out Monica for me and I'll get back to you in a while."

Nick replaced the phone and pulled off onto the road.


Friday morning in Albany had been spent on the links. Philip Cimko had been in a fairly decent mood—that is, until he spotted the cart. It rolled into view down the side of the fairway as he was set to tee off on the eleventh hole, and the sight of it told him his peaceful day was done.

The cart eased to a stop and off tottered O'Connor, chief aide and unofficial bearer of bad news. Cimko grabbed a small hand towel from his cart. He didn't bother looking at his sudden visitor. Looking would only irritate him further.

"I've got the full story on that situation upstate, Philip."

Cimko dabbed the sweat from his forehead and smiled humorlessly.

"I'm sure it's a wonderful story at that." He sighed in resignation. "What do we have?"

"Two private investigation firms—one's in Los Angeles, the other's in San Francisco. What they're trying to do is find heirs to Jacobs so they can sign them to some sort of inheritance contracts. These are legal agreements which entitle—"

"I prefer the shorter version."

O'Connor blinked nervously as he tried to think of a shorter version. Cimko traded the towel for his rapidly warming mineral water as his subordinate cleared his throat and walked around to him.

"In order to find these heirs, both of these companies are digging up everything they can on Jacobs's past—"

"Heirs—what are these mythical heirs you keep mentioning? The old man shouldn't have any family."

O'Connor swallowed and tried not to blink too much. "*Shouldn't* have any family, no. But these PI's were probably behind the break-in. Supposedly the place had been ransacked."

"We already know there's nothing in there, O'Connor. Our people checked the place out already, remember?"

"So why did one of these PI's fly to Germany last night?"

Cimko looked at him sharply. "How do we know this?"

"Credit report. Same person just made another reservation to Des Moines."

"Des Moines?"

"Iowa."

Cimko's shoulders seemed to sag. He pushed his sunglasses to his forehead and wiped his eyes. The unseasonable heat wasn't helping matters.

"So what, O'Connor. What exactly can he fucking do?"

"Big damage maybe. From what I understand, these PI's need to show the court the old man's family tree to prove the heirs are related.

They're going to need to dig up everything from his past to find out exactly who he really was. It's the only way to link the heirs to him. All the findings would come out in open court and be filed at the court-house. Public record, Philip."

"How? How could they dig all this up? What the hell's there to find? I'm telling you, the old man *had* no family."

"Probably true, but do we want them even looking? They already know something's going on, what with the FBI's involvement. Do we take the chance of underestimating these people? Philip, for a piece of twenty-two million they're not just going to go away."

Cimko studied him, then cursed and climbed back into the cart. He was a youthful thirty-eight years old and very slender. "We'll need to take action then," he said. "Thomas expects us to handle our end of this. I want you on the phone with our Brooklyn contact."

"Brooklyn? Jesus Christ, that business in the Bronx was supposed to be the last of it."

Cimko tossed the bottle aside and glared at him.

"Yes, it was, O'Connor. The Bronx was going to be the last of it, and before that Hudson was to be the last of it, and before that it was Switzerland. Unfortunately it seems the Band-Aids are no longer work-ing. It seems we now have massive fucking hemorrhaging, and the only thing that will stop it now is a tourniquet. Tightened, O'Connor—tight enough to stop the bleeding." He took a breath and refound his com-posure. "We were all caught off guard by this. Even Thomas didn't anticipate it. Christ, who had ever even *heard* of heir hunters?"

"What is Thomas going to do?"

"Everything he possibly can. He arrives in Washington today."

"My God. What's his plan?"

"He has to fill in Gordon. There's no avoiding it now."

"Fill him in? Just how is he going to do that, Philip?"

"By being very careful," replied Cimko, leaning over the wheel of the cart. "He knows the President has been very supportive of the committee. Marshall will back him up, if for no other reason than to make himself look good. I don't think we'll have a problem there." Cimko grabbed a folded section of newspaper and began fanning him-self.

O'Connor stared at him grimly. "I hope you're right, Philip."

"I usually am."

"Thomas better know what he's doing," said O'Connor.

Cimko laughed scornfully. "I really wish you would think, O'Connor. For once in your life, think before you open your mouth. Of course Thomas knows what he's doing. He isn't a fool. Do you think he would have ever gotten involved with Jacobs in the first place without having a safety net in place?"

O'Connor was shaking his head. His face looked pained. "This could get completely out of hand."

"Have faith, O'Connor. The plan will work. Once Gordon is taken care of, we'll be in the clear."

"And what if the plan doesn't work?"

"It *must* work. Thomas will see that it does." Cimko climbed back into his cart and removed his sunglasses, wiping them with the towel. He felt calmer now. His rare Sunday away from his desk had been ruined, but he was over it. "Thomas expects me to quell this any way I can," he said. "I want you on the phone. How soon can Kragen have people in L.A. and San Francisco?"

"Immediately. But—"

"No buts. It has to be done."

Nick was seated outside Gate 26 of Salzburg International Airport when he got Alex's call.

"I found Monica, Nick."

"Great. What do we have?"

"I'll give you the bad news first. I found her in the Iowa death index. She's been dead for about two years—"

*"Damn,"* said Nick, clutching the phone. "What about the good news?"

"Her maiden name was Holtzmann. She's got three children— Jessica, Matthew, and Timothy. Jessica's still in Des Moines. Matthew's in Sacramento. I've got a flight reserved to California."

Nick watched a line of travelers entering a boarding tunnel. "What about the other brother?"

"He's not coming up on any of the searches I ran. Let's just wrap up two-thirds and worry about him later."

Nick hesitated but quickly realized there was nothing to think about. "Do it. You run background on Jessica?"

"Sure did. She's an attorney, Nick."

"Oh man. So much for a quick and easy presentation."

"Probably pick over every little word and phrase of the contract," said Alex.

"I can handle her. Listen, there's a fax service available here at the airport. I want to get these reports in my hands now. I've got a lot of flight time to kill. How many pages are we looking at?"

"Ten."

"Great." He gave her the fax number. "Get that to me, and I'll call you right after I see Jessica."

"It's on the way. We're so close, Nick!"

He hung up and hurried through the terminal.

CHAPTER 12

A STRANGE CALMNESS SETTLED over Nick during the Iowa
flight. He watched the descent into Des Moines and told himself
that things were now out of his hands. He and Alex had done their best,
pushed themselves to the limit. They couldn't possibly have moved
quicker on the Jacobs investigation than they had those last three days.
If they had been beaten to them by their competitors, so be it. At least
then they wouldn't have to concern themselves with the FBI anymore.

From State Highway 5, Nick pulled the rental car onto the Fifth
Street exit and made a left on McKinley. A long, tree-lined street led
him to Pinecreek, his next left. He slowed to a cruise until he read the
address he was looking for.

The house at 11 Pinecreek Road was a ranch-style dwelling with
beige paint and brown borders. It was a modest, simple home, and Nick
hoped this was indicative of the owner. He felt encouraged by what he
had read of her background during the flight.

Alex had done her usual thorough work. She had first traced one of
Jessica Von Rohr's billing addresses to a law office. An Internet search
through the Martindale-Hubbell legal directory confirmed that Jessica
was an attorney specializing in real estate, with an emphasis on farming
law. She had completed her undergrad studies at the University of Iowa
and received her law degree from NYU.

Their IRS contact provided more information. Miss Von Rohr's W2 tax forms showed her to be earning in the range of sixty thousand dollars each of the previous five years. She was doing well income-wise, but not well enough for Nick to be concerned. For some reason, the most difficult clients had always been the wealthier ones, a fact that had always mystified the partners.

A credit report showed Miss Von Rohr to be carrying minimal credit card debt, a student loan of twenty thousand dollars, and a forty-five-thousand-dollar debt with the Bank of Des Moines—a mortgage loan, Nick assumed. Her home was owned under her name, and an occupancy check revealed no other boarders. She was single.

The Iowa State Department of Transportation gave further key data. Thirty-one-year-old Jessica Anne Von Rohr was born in Ames, Iowa. She was five foot four, one hundred and fifteen pounds, with blond hair and blue eyes. She drove a 1994 Saab—apparently rather quickly. She had received two speeding tickets in the last fourteen months.

A general Internet search on her name had provided two final hits. Jessica had a current State of Iowa fishing license and was also part of a local jogging club.

Nick put the papers aside. He felt optimistic. Jessica was a rural attorney with country roots and a decent income. Any woman who liked to fish couldn't be *too* uptight.

He glanced back over at the house. The Saab was parked in the driveway. He checked his tie in the rearview mirror and smoothed his hair.

From his coat pocket, the phone rang.

"Hey, Alex."

"Do I sound like Alex?" asked Doug. "I've been waiting for your damn call. What's the latest?"

"I'm in Des Moines getting ready to approach a possible heir. I think I—"

"Jesus, you got an *heir*? Why the hell haven't you called me?"

"I can't call you every fifteen minutes, okay? Gimme a break. I'm about to make an approach here. Heir or not, I'm going to be on my way home this evening, which reminds me—can you pick me up at SFO?"

"What time?"

"I don't know yet. I'll let you know as soon as I book the flight. With a little luck I'll be walking out of that boarding tunnel with the biggest smile you've ever seen."

Doug liked the sound of this.

"Man oh man, I wish your pops was around to see this, Nick. Who would've thought we'd pull something like this off?"

"Haven't pulled anything off yet, buddy."

"You will, man. Hey, I called to let you know I got our petition together. All I need to do is fill in the blanks."

"Well, I hope to give you a name in a little while here. Listen, I'm right outside her place. I'll call you when I know what the story is."

"Soon as you're out, Nick."

"Soon as I'm out."

He put the phone away and paused. Doug was right—his father would have enjoyed being a part of this one. Nick would have loved for him to be there too. But present or not, his father was a part of the Jacobs case—a part of *every* case and nothing was ever going to change that. He stepped to the curb.

An unfamiliar nervousness hit him when he was on the walkway. The presentation he was about to make would be Merchant and Associates' greatest triumph, dramatically changing several lucky people's lives for the better. He would be one of those lucky individuals, but only if it went right.

He reached the door and paused, staring at a motionless set of wind chimes. The very first thing he had to do was determine unequivocally that Jessica was indeed an heir. That would be done with his very first question. He pressed the doorbell and immediately saw movement inside.

The young woman who answered the door wasn't what he had been expecting. This was not the slipper-clad, bathrobed client so typical of rural cases. She was dressed in purple running shorts and tank top, an elastic white headband holding golden hair back over her forehead. She seemed shorter than five foot four to him, but she was very pretty. The eyes, bright and intelligent, met and held his.

Nick straightened up a bit and tried to remember his script.

"Good afternoon," he said. "I'm looking for Jessica Von Rohr, daughter of Monica Holtzmann."

She leaned against the doorway, a confused look on her face. She looked him over carefully before speaking.

"I'm Jessica Von Rohr," she said. "What can I do for you?"

*Bingo,* he thought. "Looks like I caught you on the way out."

"You may have," she said. "Depends on what you're selling. Salesman, right?"

"I'm happy to say I'm not," replied Nick, showing his private investigator's ID. "My name's Nick Merchant, I'm a private investigator from San Francisco. I've come here with news of an important family matter."

She took his card and looked it over. "Okay," she said, handing it back. "What kind of family matter?"

His smile came from sheer nervousness. "I'm pleased to say that I have good news for you, Miss Von Rohr. I think you may be an heir to an estate."

"Really," she replied, her expression skeptical. "And what estate would this be?"

"I'd love to tell you all about it. I do have some documents I'd like to show you, though, first. Can we perhaps sit down for a few minutes and talk?"

She raised her chin slightly as she leaned against the doorway. It was a small, delicate chin, held confidently. Her face was classically attractive—full lips, oval cheekbones, clear, smooth complexion. She stared at him, bright green eyes under dark blond eyebrows.

"Did somebody at the office put you up to this?"

"Absolutely not. Scout's honor."

She rubbed her chin thoughtfully for a moment before stepping aside and motioning him in. "I can give you a few minutes. You better not try to sell me life insurance."

Nick tipped his head graciously and entered. He could kick himself. Her good looks had rattled him, turned him into a babbling amateur. Scout's honor? Good God! But at least he was in, and one thing was resoundingly clear: if another heir finder had gotten to her first, she would have known exactly why he had come. He was first!

Nick took a seat on a large sectional couch and looked around. The living room was tastefully furnished but not lavish. A picture facing him from an end table caught his eye. A gray-haired woman and a young lady he assumed was his host smiled at him from the frame. They were standing in front of a river and were wearing frayed hats and long rubber pants. The older woman held what looked to be a sizable trout on the end of her line. Apparently that fishing license came in handy.

Jessica sat in a recliner next to him, leaning forward with her elbows on her bare, toned legs.

"I notice you creek-fish," Nick said, nodding to the photograph.

"Not too much since my father passed away," she said with a slight smile. She glanced at her watch. "I need to be somewhere pretty quick here. Why don't you go ahead and tell me what this is all about."

Nick nodded and reached for his portfolio. He didn't want to rush this presentation, but his prospective client appeared to be all business, maybe even a little uptight. He removed a folder that held an inheritance contract stipulating a 30 percent fee. Jessica Von Rohr brushed her hair back behind her ear and waited.

"Thanks again for sitting down with me. I'll make this as quick as I can." He cleared his throat. "Let me first start by explaining my business. I've a company located in San Francisco called Merchant and Associates which specializes in doing private research for families. Specifically my firm locates missing family members who are entitled to assets of relatives. We've connected dozens of people with assets which were previously unknown to them."

"So I'm a missing family member," she said, nodding intently. "And I didn't even know it."

"Technically I suppose *estranged* is a better word. My latest research leads me to believe that you can become our client. Based on the findings of an investigation we've conducted, I think you may be entitled to a sum of assets from an estate."

"Sounds good to me." She crossed her arms. "So you actually do this for a living?"

"Yes, I do," he replied with a smile. He had heard that question so many times.

"I'm jealous," she said with feeling. "You mean you can actually *make* a living doing this?"

"If you're willing to work hard. I admit my business is different, but it's completely legitimate. We're a licensed private investigation firm which has been working with estates for twelve years now. I've brought a list of professional references as well as examples of work my company's done for other clients."

"Good. I'll need to see all that." She swept a stray hair from her face and leaned forward. "So what about my inheritance? Come on— enough buildup. You're on the clock here."

"Sure. Miss Von Rohr, there's just one aspect of my business I do need to explain before I tell you about the inheritance. My company earns its money when a person agrees to become our client. All this means is that they sign an agreement which assigns to my company a fee—called a finder's fee—which is a percentage of the assets we've told you about. By being a client, you pay no out-of-pocket fees whatsoever. Merchant and Associates pays all legal fees related to obtaining the assets. Our compensation is received directly from the estate. You never have to come up with a penny. Due to the fact that my company does need to guarantee its fee, the sources of the assets are not revealed until *after* the client signs our contract."

"So you don't tell me until I sign, huh? I don't know. I mean, I understand contingency fees, but I'm not too wild about signing anything blindly. I'll need to look over all your materials before I commit to anything."

"I understand," said Nick, hiding his disappointment. "How would you feel about signing a contract like this if you determined it was legitimate?"

"I probably would," she said, with a less than convincing shrug. "If I'm entitled, I'm entitled, right? What percent are you asking for?"

Nick considered it momentarily. He had been hoping for a quick close, but his client hadn't been as easygoing as he would have hoped. Alex had been right with her attorney comment.

"My partner and I think twenty-five percent is fair," he said.

She nodded, her reaction to the number unreadable. "I'd like to see the contract, if I may."

Nick handed it over to her and held his breath. Jessica brought her legs up off the floor, curling them into her seat as she read the contract. He watched her as she read. This was very appropriate. The most attractive heir he had ever met signs the most beautiful contract he had ever written. He felt as if every nerve in his body were tingling. He licked his lower lip quickly. The boys at General Inquiry would die when they heard. They would have to carry old man Castleton out on a stretcher. Hell, they would need a *forklift* for that job.

"Pretty basic," she said, handing him back the paper. "So what kind of assets are you talking about here?"

"Mostly bank accounts, but we're also looking at some real estate and other personal property."

"Really." She was silent for a moment. "What if I told you that I may already know whose estate this is?"

"Do you?" asked Nick, trying to remain poker-faced.

"I think I've got a hunch. You kind of tipped me off when you asked if I was the daughter of Monica Holtzman. This has to be coming from my mother's side of the family. Am I right so far?"

Nick winced inside. She was right, and getting warmer by the second.

"I bet you this is coming from my mother's brother, Ludwig," she said, staring at him. "Is it?"

Nick hesitated. Clients had correctly guessed the source of inheritances before, and he had usually handled it one way: full disclosure. With the proverbial cat now out of the bag, he could only be hurt trying to hold on to nonexistent leverage. But his hidden ace was still intact. With Ludwig Holtzmann's hidden identity, the advantage was still his. Unless she already knew, she would never guess Holtzmann and Gerald Jacobs were one and the same.

"I'll be honest," he said. "Yes, it is. It's coming from your Uncle Ludwig."

She nodded, satisfied with her deduction. Nick remained silent as he focused on her. She was very attractive, but beyond that he was having a difficult time getting a good read on her. She was obviously very sharp, a client who would not be led by the nose to the dotted line. Something about her almost seemed a bit arrogant, but maybe she had just had a rough day at the office.

"I've found that your uncle was a pretty mysterious person," he said, hoping the comment would open her up.

"That could be," she replied. She paused, then suddenly rose to her feet. "I really need to get going. Tell you what—leave all your documents and testimonies and I'll give it all a good look. I do need to be somewhere, so if you'll excuse me . . ."

Nick was feeling very uneasy now. He scratched the back of his neck and tried to recover. He had dealt with plenty of heirs who didn't immediately sign, but this one was acting strangely. The conversation had ended too abruptly.

"I think I should let you know that it's a substantial amount of money we're talking about here."

"All the more reason for me to think about this."

"Miss Von Rohr, I apologize, but I'm a bit confused. I've done some research into your uncle and found—"

"Look," she said, rather abruptly. "You seem like an honest guy. I know this is your job, and I respect that, but there's nothing I can do for you right now. Let me call you in a few days, okay? I promise I will." She reached for a ring of keys. "I really have to get going now."

Nick began gathering his papers together. He had a dozen questions, and a dozen more after that, but he saw that he wasn't going to get his chance to ask them. He closed his portfolio and stood. She was by the door, waiting for him.

At the bottom of her porch stairs, he waited for her to lock the front door. He had to try one last time.

"Jessica, I respect your feelings on this, but I have to ask out of curiosity: What did you know about your uncle? Is there anything at all you can tell me about him?"

She walked down the steps and made her way quickly over the front lawn toward her driveway. Her hand was up, palm out, as if she was fending him off.

"Maybe later. I've got your card, okay?"

She entered the Saab. Nick stood for a moment, his mind flooded with questions, before slowly walking back to his car. He watched her reverse into the street and drive off before he started the ignition.


With the disclosure came silence. The client's face went blank. He sat in a motionless stupor, unable to react. Finally a laugh came, a quick, nervous snort that built on itself and became a rhythmic chuckle. He looked down at the scuffed Formica surface of the kitchen table and shook his head.

"Yeah, right. Whatever you say."

Matthew Von Rohr's skepticism wasn't surprising. Alex smiled at him and dabbed sweat from her forehead. The combination of her euphoria and the one-hundred-degree Sacramento heat was making it hard to think straight.

"I've got the documentation to prove it, Matt."

She reached for the copy of the probate file and found the appropriate section. Matt Von Rohr inched his chair closer to hers. Their knees touched. Alex put the papers down in front of him and placed her fingertip on the number.

His jaw fell open. He gripped the papers roughly and shot to his feet. "Jesus Christ," he said. "Jesus *Christ*. You *aren't* kidding. . . ." His expression now was utter shock. He seemed to sway a bit before settling back down in his seat. He stared at her, his face as dazed as a happy drunk. "This can't be right. There's no *way* this can be right."

"It's hard for me to believe too, Matt. It's all true, though. Congratulations."

Von Rohr placed his hands on the side of his head and gave a bewildered smile. Then he turned his head to the ceiling and let out a whoop that echoed throughout the tiny apartment. Alex broke into a smile and used every ounce of strength to prevent herself from doing the exact same thing.

"You've got to be kidding me!" he yelled happily.

"About four weeks and it's all yours."

She was being attacked now. He launched himself to her and grabbed her in a joyous embrace.

"Oh my God!" he shouted in her ear. "Oh my God!" He pulled back, still holding her shoulders. "An hour ago I was arguing with the caterer over sixty bucks. Sixty bucks!"

"I'm happy for you," said Alex, smiling. "Your fiancée's going to faint."

"Faint? She's gonna die! Twenty-two *million*!"

"One-third, Matt—remember. Your sister and brother are entitled to their portions too. Your share comes to roughly seven point four million, minus our fee, of course."

"Sure, sure—plenty to go around." He turned and pulled the refrigerator door open. "We need a beer. We're gonna have ourselves a cold one right now, Alex. Jesus Christ!"

Alex didn't argue. If this didn't call for a drink, nothing did.

Von Rohr flipped the top off and placed a Heineken in front of her. He extended his bottle to her, his face radiant.

"To Alex . . . Alex Marina . . . Is that right?"

"Moreno."

"To Alex Moreno. The first woman to ever change my life—for the better!" He brought the bottle to his lips but stopped himself. "No, wait! To Gerald Jacobs!" He thrust his bottle to the ceiling. "Rest in peace, Uncle Gerald, you old buzzard! Whoever the hell you were!"

They clinked bottles. Alex filled her mouth with cold beer and smiled. Thirty percent of Matt Von Rohr's one-third cut was about 2.2 million. Two point two million! And Nick had undoubtedly doubled that figure with the sister. They had done it!

"Jamie's gonna die, Alex. She's going to absolutely die when I tell her."

"When's the wedding?"

"End of next month."

"Well, it's going to be a wonderful honeymoon."

"You're telling me. We'd planned on going to Hawaii but that almost seems kinda cheesy now."

"Hey, might as well make it Paris or Rome."

Von Rohr took a gulp of beer and shook his head, still in a daze. He sat next to her, placing his hand on her leg and rubbing it a bit.

"I'm in shock. Thank you. Thank you so much."

Alex smiled as she removed his hand. She took another swallow of beer as her mind traveled back to New York, to a dark room with torn furniture and a small, blurry-screened television. One month, two months max, she was going to buy her mother a new home, a home far from the dirt and grime of the barrio. Once they tended to the loose ends of the Jacobs case, it was as good as done.

"So you guys haven't contacted Jess yet?"

"My partner's in Des Moines right now," she replied. "You think your sister will go along with this?"

"Oh man, why wouldn't she? Jess is all right—kind of an intense person sometimes—but I don't think your partner will have any major problems with her. She's an attorney, so she'll probably have a few more questions than I did."

Alex nodded. She wanted to bypass the next topic but knew it was unavoidable. "Matt, there is of course a chance that she won't sign our contract. There might even be a chance that she could try to go around us and claim the money on her own—"

"I don't think she'd cheat you guys, Alex. How could she if she doesn't know where the money is?"

"Well," said Alex, hesitating slightly, "she might call you."

Matt Von Rohr laughed. "I see what you're getting at. Don't worry about that. First, I don't think she would call me. We're really not that close to begin with. Second, even if she did, I think it would be wrong to cheat you guys after your hard work. I wouldn't tell her anything, Alex."

"Will that cause a problem between you two?"

"I can handle Jess," he replied with a wink.

Alex smiled and relaxed. "How much did you know about your uncle, Matt?"

"Nothing," he replied. "I knew my mother had a brother in Germany, but she never talked about him, and I never cared enough to ask. I always thought he died years ago. What have you found out about him?"

"Almost nothing. We have no idea how he made his money or why he changed his identity. His death certificate says he was a glassworker, but there's obviously more to it than that. Luckily for the sake of the inheritance, all we need for the court is to prove the genealogy, and that's all taken care of."

"Who cares who he was?" replied Von Rohr, grinning. "Whatever he did to make that cash, God bless him." He guzzled his beer and headed for the refrigerator.

"What about your brother? Is there anything you know that could help us track him down?"

The topic of his brother seemed to subdue him a bit. Von Rohr returned to the table with a full green bottle and sat.

"I wish I did, Alex. It's been about seventeen years since I spoke with Tim. We've thought about hiring a PI to look for him, but somehow—I don't know—we just never got around to it. It just seemed so hopeless."

"Well, I see no reason why we shouldn't be able to find him. If he's . . ."

"Alive," finished Von Rohr. He picked at the label on his beer bottle. "I've wondered that myself. Tim was the crazy one in the family. Wild friends, drugs, drinking—you name it. You'd think you'd be safe from that crap out in Iowa. Not quite. Tim tried to straighten up when he was eighteen by running off and joining the Navy. That was seventeen years ago. I haven't heard a thing since."

"Were you close growing up?"

"Yeah, I always thought so. Hell, we were brothers, you know? It's not like we ever had any serious fights or anything, at least nothing beyond the normal kid stuff." He looked down. "You see, this is why I wonder if he's alive. I just can't believe he would disappear like that. Not even a phone call."

"Do you know where he was based in the Navy?"

"San Diego, I think."

"How about his ship assignment?"

"That I don't know."

The tape machine on the table clicked off. Alex found a new tape, placed it in the machine, and pressed Record.

"We have access to some good military databases that could turn up something. You said Tim was born in Ames, Iowa, right?"

"Right. We all were."

"We'll need to order his birth certificate as well as your own to present to the court. We have your approval to do that?"

"Oh yeah. Jess's too, I'm sure."

"Great. Matt"—she extended her hand—"thank you, it's been fun. I'll let you make that phone call to your fiancée in private now. I'll be meeting with my partner and planning our strategy on finding your brother. I want you to call me if any questions come up."

"I appreciate it, Alex." He took her hand once more. "Thanks again. Do me a favor—let me know what you find on Tim. Even if it's bad. I want to know."

"I sure will."

They said goodbye. When Alex reached the sidewalk, she jogged to her car.

In the terminal of Des Moines International, travelers met and parted like ants in the frantic ritual of air travel. Nick ignored the crowd as he made his way through to Gate 42. The seats were half full, a few dozen loners sitting by themselves. Nick found an isolated row, dropped his garment bag, and sat. He was an hour early for the flight, and he had bought the latest *U.S. News* to kill time. He knew the latest problems in Iraq and the most recent sex scandal on the Hill wouldn't be enough to divert his attention. His mind was on Gerald Jacobs. That was the only story he was interested in knowing.

He kept thinking of Jessica Von Rohr. She had said nothing about her uncle, but her entire manner suggested that she knew something. He wanted to sit down with her and try to get some answers, but if the day's meeting was indicative of her normal attitude, he saw little chance in that. He wondered if she would even sign the contract. At least they wouldn't have to bother with the FBI if she didn't, but at this point that was small consolation.

He glanced at his watch and groaned. An hour until he was out of there. He needed desperately to get out of Des Moines and get back home. He preferred to forget about these last several days, if it was actually possible to forget. Maybe he needed to take that long-overdue vacation. Head down to Mexico and drown himself in tequila and sun. He would make his plane reservation as soon as he got home.

His cell phone rang, and he seriously considered not answering. But he had to talk to Alex about it eventually.

"He signed, Nick! We've got a client!"

"He . . . did?" asked Nick, dropping the magazine between his feet.

"Thirty percent. He loved me! Thanked me a hundred times. He was a great guy."

"He signed," muttered Nick.

"What about you? You sign Jessica yet?"

He paused and took a deep breath. "There was a problem, Alex. She wouldn't play ball. Things went okay but she decided she needed to think it over."

"Oh God," she said, her voice thick with disgust. "I can't believe it. What was her problem?"

"I don't know. It was tough to get a feel for her, Alex. I really have no clue which way she'll go."

"Probably try to cheat us. Attorneys! What did I tell you? I knew she'd analyze it to death."

"You were right. She basically guessed that it was coming from her uncle. She'll never be able to trace it to Gerald Jacobs, though. Unless she goes to Matt Von Rohr."

"We're safe there. Matt said he wouldn't tell her, and I believe him. Did you tell her how much the estate is worth?"

"I tried to, but she was in a rush and pretty much shuffled me out the door."

"Oh my God," she said. "Everything we've put ourselves through and she doesn't want to sign? This is *unbelievable.*"

"Not much we can do about it now. I'll have to come up with another approach later." He scratched the back of his neck. "Hell with it—tell me about the brother. I thought for sure you'd have the same problem."

"Not at all, Nick—he was great. Just a regular working stiff, engaged to be married. He was overjoyed. He seemed fairly certain that his sister would sign. He also said his brother Tim was in the Navy in San Diego seventeen years ago."

"What kind of reaction did he have when you told him it was coming from his uncle?"

"Reaction? He was *toasting* the old geezer. Laughing about it. He said he never knew anything about him and never wanted to either."

"You've got the contract with you?"

"No, I left it by the side of the road—of course I've got the contract, silly man."

"Where are you right now?"

"Highway 80, approaching SF."

"Drop that contract off at Doug's office before you go to the airport.

I want to wrap Matt Von Rohr's third up quickly. The deeper we get into this, the harder it'll be for the FBI to pull us out."

"Are you going to call them?"

"I think I better. I can't blow 'em off anymore. By the way, I'm flying straight back to San Francisco. I have some military contacts in SF I can contact to get the search going on Tim."

"Should I wait here for you or . . . ?"

"There's no need to, Alex. Get back home and I'll call you in a day."

"You better. Hey, I think this calls for a name change."

"Huh?"

"A name change. *Merchant and Associates* sounds so stiff and boring. How about *Merchant and Moreno*?"

"Whatever you say, girl."

CHAPTER 13

A T THE MAIN office of heir-finding giant General Inquiry, the 8 P.M.
chime of the clock barely caused a ripple among the busily working investigators. Two secretaries were dispatched to the deli for take-
out dinners and sodas, but most scurried about their desks while trying
to make themselves useful and inconspicuous. The talk of the day had
been the Henry Orville Roque estate. Jerry Acosta was lead investigator, and he had already utilized the skills of half a dozen colleagues in
his search for heirs. Progress was slow and tempers short, as little had
been gathered on the decedent, a friendless World War II veteran who
had died in tiny Amador County. The classic loner, a completely unremarkable man with nothing to his name but a single bank account holding $380,000. Death had made Mr. Roque suddenly quite popular.
Everyone in the building knew his name now.

The two employees in the firm not concerned with Henry Roque
were behind closed doors. President Lawrence Castleton knew his
second-in-command well enough to know by his expression that something had gone horribly wrong.

"Merchant filed papers."

In a single swift movement, Castleton took the glass paperweight
from his desk and hurled it against the wall. Borg didn't flinch. Violence
wasn't unexpected. Depression would surely follow.

"*Sonofabitch!* How? How did he do it?"

"He's only got one, Lawrence. We can get the other two."

A light knocking came from outside.

"Go away!" shouted Castleton, on his feet now. He rubbed his great bowling-ball head and looked disconsolate. "How could we get beaten, Richard? Have we slipped this much? Why wasn't Merchant called off? The FBI said they were going to contact him—why didn't they!"

"They probably did. We never thought he would drop it, remember?"

Castleton fell to his couch and fanned himself. His head was beaming red and looked like a giant swollen beet. "Who are the heirs?"

"Two nephews and a niece. Merchant's only got one of them. The sister refused to sign and the other brother's missing—"

"So why are we sitting here talking about it?"

"I've got people working on it right now."

"Why am I the last to know?" Castleton demanded.

"Because if I came to you first, you would've screamed at me for not getting our people moving quickly enough."

Castleton looked stricken as he mopped his forehead with a handkerchief. Borg hoped his heart could take it. The thought of having to perform mouth-to-mouth wasn't pleasant.

"Why wouldn't the woman sign?"

Borg shrugged. "Don't know. All their filing says was that she was contacted."

"We have an address?"

"Des Moines. Lake's on the way."

"I want him to talk to me before he makes the approach." The president's composure was slowly returning. "What about this other brother?"

"The file says he's missing. Neither sibling has seen him in years. We've got nothing so far, but the wheels are turning. We know he's got a criminal record. A real loser. We may be looking at a street person or a possible incarceration. I've got our Prison Bureau people moving, but it'll take a while."

Castleton grasped his head again. "How could this happen? Head-to-head and we lose? To *Merchant*? I used to wipe up the floor with his father."

"It's not over yet."

"How much did he get?"

"Thirty."

The old man slid down the leather upholstery until he was on his back. Borg was certain another outburst would trigger a coronary.

"We'll get forty," said Borg. "From both of them."

"Merchant's still out there. What if he finds the brother too?"

"I doubt that, Lawrence. He wouldn't have filed papers and given us the names if he thought he had a chance."

"The other companies will be in on it now."

Borg shook his head. "They won't have any reason to jump on it. There were no cash amounts given in the filing. By the time somebody else bothers to investigate, we'll have it wrapped up."

Castleton bolted to his feet quickly. Borg marveled at this sight. This was easily three hundred pounds in motion.

"You said Lake's en route to Des Moines?"

"Right."

"Where's Risso?"

"Here. I was about to reassign him."

"Well, don't. I've got something for him. He's going to San Francisco."

"San Francisco? For what?"

"Something I should have done a long time ago. We're done playing around."

Doug insisted on a celebration, and Nick didn't have the energy to fight him. His attorney took Highway 101 from the airport straight to the city. He passed through South of Market and crossed Market, then up Van Ness to Sutter. The table was reserved at Burris' Steakhouse, a swanky, dimly lit landmark that catered to the important few who felt the need to order beef at thirty-two dollars a slab.

Nick pulled his tie a bit looser and squinted around the restaurant. A dignified looking older man in a tux was tapping out a forties tune on a piano in the corner. The large round table next to theirs was filled with a mix of drunk Japanese and Americans in suits. Nick wondered what kind of deal was being finalized over the steaks and creamed spinach.

Doug finished the remainder of his second rum and Coke and hung an arm over the leather backing of the booth. His smile had been a fixture.

"Get used to places like this, buddy. Your life's just taken a sweet turn."

"Nice. Very romantic. But if you pull out a ring, I'm gone."

"You notice some of the women walking around this place? Man, if I were still single . . ."

"Never stopped you before," said Nick, looking around. A stunning young blonde had just settled into a booth fifteen feet away. In the half-light, she looked familiar.

"Take a look over your left shoulder when you get a chance, Doug. Don't make it obvious."

Doug nodded and rubbed the back of his neck. He turned after a few seconds and did his best leer. The blonde caught it and gave a little head toss.

"Jesus. Can we switch seats?"

"No chance," said Nick, motioning the waiter over. "Another Beck's for me and a rum and Coke for him." The waiter bowed and left.

"Oh, before I forget," said Doug. "I need that Dawson contract from you."

"Fiftieth time you've told me."

"Usually takes that many times to get your attention."

"It'll be at your office tomorrow morning. Rose is going by my place to pick it up."

"She's got your apartment key now?"

"She checks my fax and mail when I'm away. Even does my laundry occasionally."

"You serious?"

"Not about the laundry part." Nick gave the girl another look. "I know who that blonde reminds me of. She looks just like Jessica Von Rohr."

"That good?"

"Real close. Christie Brinkley in running shorts. Kind of short, though."

Doug snorted. "Too bad she was such a little bitch."

"She *was* kind of uptight. But real sharp. I barely had to explain anything to her."

"Well, there's the problem," grumbled Doug. "Stupid fool thinks she knows everything. She's probably planning on backdooring us."

Nick shrugged and stared at the candle between them. "Who knows. Something else is bugging me, Doug. She knew something about Jacobs. I could tell. Man, I'd pay a thousand bucks just to know what was going through her head."

"You just paid a couple million. How hard did you push the contract?"

"As hard as always. I thought it was in the bag, but she was being a real hardass."

"She get mad at you?"

"No, it wasn't like that. She was calm but very adamant. She just was *not* going to sign."

"She's cheating us, Nick. Just you watch."

"She may try. We've got no control over that, though. I just wish I knew what the story was with her uncle."

Doug shook his head and reached for his drink. "All you need to know is we're out about two million bucks if she doesn't sign. Who cares who her uncle was?"

Nick leaned back and watched the pianist go to work on the keys. "There may be some family skeletons there. Could be something pretty ugly, like an abusive past or something. Remember the Harrison case? That woman told my father to get lost for a quarter million dollars. Later on we found out the dead guy had molested her when she was a kid."

"Quarter million's a quarter million," said Doug. "This is twenty-two mil, buddy. Why'd we have to get a flaky heir for *this* case?"

Nick shrugged. "What I plan to do is give her a little time, let it cool off a bit, and then maybe visit her again. Hell, we'll lower our fee to maybe fifteen or twenty percent. If she doesn't go for that, we'll just have to write it off. As long as we've got her brother, I won't really care. It's still a dream case. Think about how lucky we are, man. A multi-million-dollar estate with no heirs hovering around? It's *unheard* of."

The waiter returned with the drinks and asked if they were ready to order. Doug chose the lobster; Nick, the pepper steak.

"I think it was a mistake filing the papers so quick," said Doug. "Everybody and their mother will be out looking for this brother now."

"He'll be a tough find. I've already run his name through a dozen databases and gotten nothing. I mean zero. The guy may be dead."

"I still think we should have waited a day or two."

"I want to see this done, Doug. We still have the FBI to contend with. Which reminds me, I need to call them first thing in the morning. They can't tell us to back off if we've got our client already going through probate court."

"Yeah, you hope not."

*       *       *

The front bar was a bustle of happy businessmen and businesswomen. Coats were off and ties were loosened. One man sat by himself and ignored the revelry. He would not be eating, and he was not waiting for a dinner guest.

Regnier lifted his glass of wine. Red, always. He let the wine stand in his mouth before swallowing. He gave the booth a careful, casual look. The investigator and his attorney were getting drunk and foolish, and this was perfect. They had just ordered and would be in the restaurant for at least another hour. This would be plenty of time. His cohorts wouldn't need that long to finish their work. He, meanwhile, would indulge himself in another glass. The bartender responded to his nod and brought a full glass over.


Rose parked in a spot stenciled *guest* and stepped to the concrete. She was always happy to run an errand in exchange for an early day at the office. Nick was good about things like that. And with the signing of the Jacobs heir, she knew she would now become one of the higher-paid secretaries in all of San Francisco. She was lucky. Her boss was a good guy.

She thought of her niece Patricia as she waited for the elevator. Patricia was thirty-two now and anxious for a husband and babies. Nick was thirty-five and available. And lonely, she had always sensed. She was confident the two of them would get along nicely. If Patricia lost a little weight, it was a certainty.

She exited on the third floor and walked down the corridor. Yes, she would set up a lunch date down by the wharf, something casual and low pressure. They would get to know each other slowly over calamari and crab cakes.

She reached apartment 302 and found her key ring. Nick's apartment key was the one with the gray electrical tape on the end. She held the keys and paused. Listened. A noise, nothing more than a light tinkle, sounded just behind the door.

"Nick?"

She found the key and slid it into the knob. A split second before the flash, Rose heard a shout from within, then the eruption came, tearing through the front wall. It impacted her squarely, lifting her from her feet. The fireball billowed from the apartment in a wave of blinding heat and tore straight through the hallway and into the unit across. The windows exploded outward to the street, spewing fire and showering the sidewalk with burning debris. Everything was silently illuminated on the street momentarily, then the hypnotic effect of the flames wore off and people began to shout—frightened calls against the backdrop of a distant fire engine's wail.

As expected, neither man was in any kind of condition to drive. Nick and Doug slouched in the backseat of a taxi and laughed at stupid things they hadn't joked about since the last time they had gotten tanked together. Doug was gagging with loud laughter and undoubtedly annoying the hell out of the cabbie.

"Hey," he said loudly in Nick's ear. "That reminds me—remember that time we snuck into that boarded-up house on Anza Street?"

"And that old derelict came out and chased us?"

"We were like ten years old," laughed Doug. "Hey, we didn't know what we were on to then. Turns out that was just a warm-up for old man Jacobs's place."

"That crazy bum was scarier than any gunman."

"You're a cat burglar at heart, Nick. You're one gutsy bastard." Doug turned to the front. "Hey, buddy! Brown corner house on the left."

The driver nodded and pulled to the curb at the end of Franklin Street. Doug threw a twenty in Nick's lap and fumbled for the door handle.

"I need a ride down to my car tomorrow morning. Can you swing by and pick me up?"

"Seven-thirty?"

"See ya!"

"Enjoy the couch."

Nick watched him zigzag to the front door. He laughed. Kimberly was really going to let him have it. *Move over, Fido—you got company tonight.*

He leaned back as the taxi took off again. His vision was really starting to swirl now. He let his head fall back as he watched the wavering glitter of Lombard Street pass by in one nauseating river of white and red neon. He hadn't planned on getting stewed, but hell, they had a valid enough reason. Gerald Jacobs had been the toast of the night. Tomorrow would be an ordeal, but who gave a damn? He could close shop for good now if he wanted to, and the way he felt at that moment, he might do just that. He could just fly off somewhere and never come back.

The road was gently buffeting him. As he sat his mind drifted, a kaleidoscope of faces and pieces of the last week. For some reason, he could see Alex's mother, sitting in her bedroom of crucifixes and candles, clutching a rosary to her breast. The picture show shimmered and changed, settling in the Columbia County Clerk's office, with Lloyd Koenig, the attorney with the slick suits and ten thousand dollars in his pocket. There was a bathtub behind him—a red water bath with an old man's corpse floating facedown in the mess. Jessica Von Rohr now, standing in her living room and shaking her head slowly back and forth . . .

The cabbie's words registered, cut through the fog of a half dream. Nick pulled his head up with great effort and blinked groggily. The driver whistled and repeated the words, his first of the ride.

"Big fire, mon . . ."

The sight of it seemed to sober Nick up just a bit. He straightened up out of his slouch and put his face to the window. They were on Marina, all right. Two large fire trucks were shooting jets of water at a building. His building?

A cop appeared in the middle of the road and motioned them down a side street.

"Stop, driver. Let me out."

The driver parked around the corner. Nick paid him and broke into a run, making his way quickly back around to Marina. As he approached his building, he saw people standing behind the police lines, pointing and watching the firemen applying the finishing touches. A fine mist from the hoses hung in the air and dampened his clothes. He looked up and in a sickening flash recognized whose unit it was. He approached a cop.

"Officer, I need to get through," he said. "That's my apartment."

He walked unsteadily past the barricade and scanned the street. Could it be that . . . ? No. Rose was home. Had been for hours.

A powerful hand squeezed his arm.

"You deaf, buddy? Nobody goes near that place until we get the okay."

"That's my apartment," he protested loudly.

"Back behind the line or I'm taking you in."

Nick muttered something and stepped behind the line. Two girls who looked no older than eighteen stared up the building, eyes wide as they snapped gum.

"You two see what happened?"

One of them looked at him suspiciously. "Yeah, a gas line blew."

"A gas line? How do you know?"

She looked irritated. "What else? The whole building shook."

Nick turned back to the firemen and watched, even more confused. He felt foolish for having had so much to drink. He could barely think straight.

The crowd was slowly dispersing back into the night. A woman in pajamas stood miserably by a cop and cried. Nick spotted a police officer standing alone and walked up to him.

"Officer," he said, trying to focus on the cop's face. "That's my place." He gestured weakly toward the building.

The cop looked him over warily. "What's that?"

"That's my place," Nick repeated emphatically. "I live up there. That's my apartment."

"Your unit?" the cop said, giving him more attention now. "Can you come with me please?"

"What was it?" asked Nick as he followed him through the crowd. "What happened?"

The cop led him to a man in an overcoat with a thick gray mustache and a hard scowl. Nick knew without asking that he was a detective. The man held a cigarette and was talking with a fireman by one of the trucks. The detective turned to the approaching cop and gave him a little head nod.

"This man says it's his apartment."

The detective squinted at Nick and gave him the once-over. "Number 302?"

Nick nodded. The detective gave the cop a get-lost look and then they were alone.

"What's your name?" the detective asked.

"Nick Merchant. When did—"

"Just getting home, Mr. Merchant?"

"Yeah. I want to know what happened."

"You aren't the only one," the man said. He took his time removing and lighting another cigarette. "A very powerful explosion of some kind tore through your apartment about half an hour ago."

"An explosion? What do you mean?"

"An explosion. You know . . ." He spread his fingers in front of his face. "*Ka-boom!* You keep anything combustible or explosive in your place?"

"Like what?"

"Like dynamite," he snapped. "Help me out, will you?"

"Ask a sensible question and I might," Nick answered angrily.

"Where have you been this evening?"

"At a restaurant," replied Nick. "I got in on a flight from Des Moines about eight o'clock and went directly out to dinner."

"Uh-huh. What do you do for a living?"

"I'm a private investigator."

The detective gave a knowing little frown. "Work out of your home?"

"No, I don't."

"Ever had any problems with your work? Threats maybe, sour business deals?"

"I can't say I have, no."

The detective nodded condescendingly. Nick was irritated but trying to keep cool. The man was asking the proper questions. He had asked the very same ones while he wore the badge.

Something in Nick's peripheral vision suddenly grabbed his attention. He noticed his neighbor from 305 sitting on the curb with a rag to his chin. The young man looked up at Nick slowly as he approached. He was shirtless.

"Did you see what happened, Jay?"

The man was staring at him reproachfully. The rag in his hand was spotted red. He and Nick had gotten to know each other fairly well those past few months, sharing laughs as they periodically ran into each other in the hallway. Now his eyes were suspicious, his face hardened and accusative.

"Yeah, I saw it," his neighbor said. "I was just getting home from work. That lady you know came and tried to get into your place. The second she went in, it blew."

Nick collapsed to a knee as his mouth went dry. "The lady I know?"

"Yeah. I've seen her here before."

"About fifty or so? Five foot five, hefty?"

"Yeah, the one I've seen going in there before. What kinda alarm system you got in your place anyway?"

Nick sat next to him and felt the wet grass seep through the seat of his pants. He buried his face in his hands and shuddered. He had instructed her to go and pick up those papers. He had sent her there! A nausea swept over him.

The detective approached him and spoke in a softer tone. "Can you talk to us?"

"Just give me a minute," he replied numbly.

A mist hung in the air, soaking through Nick's clothes and making him shiver. He looked down at his shoes. The puddles of water looked reddish. The blood was running from his neighbor's chin, forming little red rivers between the pebbles and dirt.


A new detective now—younger, his face clean-shaven and softer. "Are you Nick Merchant?"

"Yes, I am," said Nick.

"You're in apartment 302?"

"You got it," he replied from his soggy seat in the grass. He was still drunk, but he didn't really care now. "Look, I just got back in town. The cab dropped me off and I saw the fire. I have no clue about any of this."

"Do you keep anything combustible in your apartment?" asked the detective.

"No, I don't."

"You say you know who the dead woman might be?"

Nick closed his eyes tightly. "I might. My neighbor says he saw a woman who fits the description of my . . . secretary entering my apartment a second before the blast."

"Does your secretary have the key?"

"Yes, she does. She was picking up some documents."

The detective stooped down closer to him. "Do you have any roommates?"

"No, I don't."

"You don't?"

"That's what I said. No roommates."

"Okay then," the detective said. "Anybody else have the key besides your secretary?"

"Yeah, the landlord."

"Besides him. We're trying to figure this out, friend."

"Nobody—nobody else has the key. Why do you ask?"

"We're trying to figure out who the other body inside the place is."

Nick looked up at him. "Inside?"

The detective nodded. "Male, as far as we could tell. Any idea who that might be?"

Nick looked up at the smoky shell that was once his apartment and shook his head. He had no idea. None whatsoever.


He sat a while longer until the cold forced him to move. The trucks were still there, but the hosing had stopped. His apartment was a black cavity in the building, like the burnt husk of a candle.

The younger detective approached him.

"Where can we get ahold of you, Mr. Merchant?"

Nick didn't respond. He didn't know the answer. He looked at his watch. Eleven o'clock.

The detective noticed that Nick didn't look entirely steady.

"Are you all right?"

"I'm great," he mumbled. "Just . . . great."

"Keep this," the detective said, offering his card. "We'll need to talk soon."

Nick nodded remotely and took the card. The cop turned and left.

The scattered few who still needed to stand and gawk were finally getting bored now that the spectacle was over. Nick loped across Marina Boulevard to the parking lot in the back of the complex. He saw his car under the wooden canopy of what used to be his apartment. It looked untouched. The lot was poorly lit and empty. He scanned it. If they knew his apartment, they could find his parking spot. Despite the artificial courage of the booze, he turned back. He was in no condition to drive anyway.

He walked south on Bay Street toward Chestnut. Considering the hour, the streets were fairly crowded. He was drawing looks—his suit was wet, the seat of his pants dirty. He looked like a mugging victim and felt much worse. He reached Lombard and ducked into a taxi.

"The avenues."

"Which one?"

"Take Doyle Drive to Park Presidio."

They moved through the nighttime traffic of the Marina. He wanted to purge himself of the alcohol and think clearly, but he knew it would now have to run its course through him. He rubbed his face and thought of Rose again. His instructions had sent her there. His instructions! His eyes shut tightly, then flew open again. There was someone else he needed to speak with immediately.

He pulled his phone from his jacket and called her cell phone first, then her home phone. He heard her fumble for the receiver, dropping it once. Her sleepy voice made it sound as if she were heavily sedated.

"It's me, Alex. Where's your cellular?"

"It's two-thirty in the morning, Nick—"

"Something's happened here. Get up and turn on your cellular. I'm calling you back in ten seconds."

"What's going on—"

"Alex, *do it.* Something bad's happened over here."

"All right, all right . . ."

He waited ten seconds and called her again on the secure line.

"Nick?" Alex said as the connection went through.

"Rose is dead."

"What?" She went silent momentarily. "What are you talking about?"

"Rose has been killed. Someone planted a bomb in my apartment last night and Rose walked into it. She's dead."

"Oh my God, Nick!" said Alex, fully awake now. "Where . . . where are you right now?"

"In a taxi. Just listen for a second. We're into something bad with this Jacobs thing. You need to pack up and get out of there. You're my partner and they'll know that. They're going to come after you too—"

"Who's they?"

"I don't know, but you have to get up and leave."

"Leave? Where am I supposed to go?"

Nick ran a hand through his hair. He noticed the driver watching him in the rearview mirror, obviously hanging on every word.

"Keep your eyes on the damn road," he snapped, glaring at him. He turned back to the phone after a moment and lowered his voice a bit. "Alex, listen to me, okay? Rose is dead. She's been murdered. It was in my apartment, so there's no question it was meant for me. If you stay in your house, they're going to find you. If they find you, they'll try and kill you. What more do I have to say?"

"But why don't—"

"No buts, Alex! You were being followed the other day, remember? I really hope it was GI, because if it wasn't it may have been someone a helluva lot nastier. *Get out of there.*"

"Okay, okay, I'm leaving."

"Bring all of the Jacobs stuff. Everything. The mail, the pictures, the tape—all of it. Grab a few changes of clothes and just get someplace safe. You still got your .22, right?"

"Yes—"

"Load it and bring it with you. Get moving now, okay?"

"I'll call you as soon as I get there. Wherever *there* is."

"Be careful, Alex. I mean it."

"Have you been drinking, Nick?"

"Yes. Call me as soon as you can."

Nick clicked the phone off and felt a measure of relief. The only people in the world he needed to be concerned with now were Alex and the Spinettis. He doubted Doug would be a target, and his family would be fairly useless to anyone looking for him. All he needed to do, then, was watch his own back. Being alone in the world had its advantages. His emotional baggage could fit in his back pocket. This fact would only make it harder for them to kill him.

The taxi went through Golden Gate Park, emerging on Lincoln Way and making a right. Nick had the cabbie stop in the Outer Sunset, and he walked two blocks east on Lincoln to the Travelers Lodge. The old woman behind the counter looked him over warily as he filled out the papers. She asked him if he was okay. He nodded and asked how much for of her cheapest room. "Forty-five dollars," she croaked through a cloud of cigarette smoke. "You're lucky—you got the last one." He checked his pockets and found thirty-six dollars. He paid with plastic and took the outer staircase to his second-floor unit. It was a dim room with two saggy queen-size beds. He threw off his jacket and sat down with the lights off.

The Battery Street office complex was dark and vacant at 1 A.M. A sixty-one-year-old security guard dozed at his desk in the east wing. At the furthest reaches of the west wing, two men in dark pants and black pullovers cut the lock on the chain-link fence bordering the complex and entered the parking lot. Each man had lengthy criminal records for burglary, assault, and extortion. They had been approached and paid handsomely by a man who had identified himself as Henry Fields, although his real name was Danny Risso. The assignment he had given them was simple.

Both men lugged two six-gallon buckets through the gate. One of them stooped at the side door of the building and placed a thin metal spike into the door lock. The mechanism was stubborn but they were inside after half a minute. They walked in silence, the contents of their covered pails sloshing. A tiny flashlight skimmed the door of each unit. They stopped at unit number eight and placed the buckets on the floor. This lock took a full two minutes of tinkering before they were inside. They quickly inspected the two rooms comprising the unit before beginning the night's assignment.

The file cabinets received first attention. Each drawer was emptied in the center of the room. All books were then gathered and added to the pile. The phones were ripped from their connections. The three computer video monitors were smashed, their insides soaked with fluid. In fifteen minutes' time, all but the furniture lay in a center mound, a grotesque pyramid of Merchant and Associates' vital innards.

A fire safe presented the most formidable obstacle. The key mechanism was an unfamiliar German design with little free space to maneuver in. They were set to abandon it when it suddenly gave. They opened the two drawers and quickly added the fiche and papers to the pile. They stood back and surveyed their work, an ugly mound of papers and office equipment. Then they ripped the covers from the buckets. In seconds the pile was dripping with fluid. The excess was used on the remaining furniture, carpets, and walls. The man who knew locks placed his bucket aside and nodded at his companion.

The two of them stepped to the hallway as a book of matches was removed. The lock picker struck a match, ignited the book, and tossed it through the doorway. Lines of fire streaked across the fluid trails, climbed the walls, enveloped the pile. The flames first sought out and devoured the lifeblood of the company—its vital documents, its signed contracts, its licenses, its court affidavits. Then they set upon the tools and hardware. When the fire engines arrived fifteen minutes later, the entire unit was an inferno.

\*     \*     \*

Nick leaned against the headboard of the sagging bed as his mind slowly came back under his control. He had been out on his back for at least an hour, but now the alcohol had started to dissipate as the early stages of a hangover set in. He sat in the dark and stared down at the quilt beneath him. The cold reality of the evening's events was sinking in with a sick finality.

Rose was dead. Rose had been murdered. It was horrible, horrible to the point of being unreal. She had a huge family, several dozen relatives in the Bay Area alone. He imagined standing there at the funeral, catching the occasional glance, hearing the hushed whispers in between the crying. *There he is,* they would say. *It happened at his apartment.* He felt sick.

He found the bathroom and bent by the sink, turning on the faucet. The cold water provided a needed jolt as he splashed some on his face. He reentered the darkness of the bedroom and lay back down on the bed. All he could do now was think.

Whoever these maniacs were, they clearly were traceable to Jacobs. If it was another heir finder, the motivation to remove him was obvious. He could think of twenty-two million reasons right off the bat. But a murder attempt with a bomb? He wasn't sure he could buy that. Still, given the enormity of the Jacobs estate, he couldn't rule it out. He had crossed ethical boundaries himself on this one.

He considered the FBI. He'd heard of them pulling some pretty dirty maneuvers, but bombings and murders were not their domain. Then again, they probably had all the right connections to people who specialized in just those kinds of activities.

Nick stared into the dark and felt the beginnings of a headache. He would call the FBI at daybreak. He could only imagine the icy reception *they* were going to give him. After dealing with them, he would call a contact at SFPD and find out if the body at the apartment had been identified. The detective said they had found a man's body *inside* his unit. It seemed clear now. Rose must have walked in on them setting the trap, a trap meant for him.

He hugged his knees and felt alone, more isolated than he could ever remember feeling. He kicked off his shoes and picked his jacket up off the floor, placing it over a chair. The streets outside were silent in the dead of the early morning. He couldn't even hear a car in the distance. He lay back on the bed with his arms at his sides and tried to will himself back to sobriety.

*     *     *

He woke sometime later, disoriented and still woozy. A noise had cut through the haze in his head—a car door shutting. He jerked his head up as he heard another sound, softer but very distinct. A voice. Two voices?

He crept to the blinds and nudged one aside with his finger. He was just in time to see two figures in long coats disappearing from sight under the walkway. He glanced at his watch. Four in the morning—an odd time to be checking in. He thought of the woman downstairs, speaking through her screen of cigarette smoke. *You're lucky—you got the last one. . . .*

He stood still for a moment, a vague uneasiness sweeping through him, then hurried into the bathroom. The window was five feet from the floor and maybe a foot and a half by two. He moved a small potted plant from the ledge and slid the window all the way open, revealing a bug screen. He thrust his palms at it hard. It popped free on the second attempt and landed silently in the bushes below. He stuck his head out and looked around. It was maybe fourteen or fifteen feet to the ground. A thick drainage pipe snaked down the wall an arm's length away.

He stole back to the front window and cursed his stupidity. One way or another, this would be the last time he used a credit card issued in the name of Nick Merchant. He pressed himself against the wall; his finger holding the single blind. He could just barely see the end of the walkway where the stairs rose from street level. The two strangers would either come up the stairs or return to their car and drive off to another motel. In the reflection of a car's windshield, he could see the neon sign, bright and impossible to miss—No VACANCIES.

It was then that they rose into sight. This was almost surreal now. They were coming up the stairs, their hands deep inside their jackets.

Instantly his mind seemed to clear. He ran to the bathroom, locking the door behind him. He approached the window and extended his arms through first, then leapfrogged into the frame on his stomach. He reached for the drainage pipe and used it to pull his legs out behind him, but his weight proved too much. His hands lost their grasp on the slippery metal and he fell feet first, into a thick patch of shrubbery directly below.

From above, he heard the sound of the bathroom door shattering. Someone swore from the window as he sprinted across Lincoln Way and into the park.

Nick ran blindly, ducking his way around the trees and dense foliage. He assumed they wouldn't be following him out the window, in which case he would have a good ten seconds before they could run around the building and chase him. Ten seconds to put as much distance as possible between himself and them. A world-class sprinter he wasn't, and tearing through bushes was noisy. He could take his chances hiding. The park was covered by a canopy of trees and almost completely black. Thick patches of bushes were everywhere. He looked back and felt chilled to see the glare of flashlights. They were a good distance behind but running hard.

He made a sharp left, ran thirty yards, and dove into a thicket, pushing himself down deep into the brush. Something squeaked in the darkness behind him and scurried away. He stifled his violent breathing and froze. The light beams were bobbing and shaking and getting closer by the second, but they were veering from his path slowly. They stopped fifty yards to his left. He held his breath and watched through the tiny branches and leaves. Two men dressed in dark clothes, both of them thick and formidable. One of them skimmed the other with the flashlight. Nick shuddered as he caught a quick glimpse of him. The man was tall and ponytailed, and he cradled a large automatic weapon in his arm. The man was slowly scanning the park with a pair of goggles. Nick swallowed hard. If those glasses had thermal capability, they would spot him in seconds.

Both strangers were sweeping their flashlights in wide arcs through the park. Nick closed his eyes to avoid any retinal reflections and shrunk back as they slowly took a few steps in his direction. The beams skimmed by him once, then again as his heart was slamming his chest. He could hear them talking, hushed comments he couldn't make out. They lingered for another minute before suddenly splitting up. One of them began quickly heading south, skimming the bushes with his flashlight. Nick's eyes widened. The other thug was in a crouch, heading north and coming directly toward him.

Nick felt the hair on his neck stand. He reached back blindly for something, anything, to wield as a weapon. His hand grabbed frantically but found only dirt and twigs. He held his breath. The man was barely twenty yards away and on course to step right on top of him. Nick found a small rock, held it for a second, and then tossed it into a clump of bushes behind the gunman. The second the thug's head turned, he launched himself from his hiding place and charged him.

The man heard him move and wheeled at the sudden sound, but Nick had a crucial split second, and he used every ounce of his weight to drive his shoulder into the man's ribs, separating man from gun and driving him into the dirt. A quick elbow to the face took the remaining fight out of him.

"Who are you?" Nick demanded, pinning the man down. "Who the *fuck* are you?"

The man was gape-mouthed, wheezing desperately for breath knocked clean out of him. Nick looked up as he heard a voice in the distance. The other flashlight was heading back in their direction now, and quickly.

Nick groped wildly in the dark for the gun but found nothing. He grabbed the flashlight, clicked it off, and sprinted away with it. He stumbled down a mossy incline, half expecting bullets to tear through him at any moment. He ran west through the park for five minutes straight, paused for thirty seconds, then ran for another five minutes.

Exhaustion finally forced him to stop. He hunched in the darkness, shivering and listening to himself wheeze. The giant eucalyptus trees of the park swayed and creaked in the wind around him.

Things were happening too quickly. Whoever these people were, they were not wasting a second of time. They hadn't even let the smoke clear from his apartment before coming at him again. But he had left them a convenient trail. From here on, he would make himself invisible. Untraceable. He only prayed Alex had gotten out of her place in time. God forbid, if they had found her . . .

Painfully he began jogging north toward the lights of the Richmond District, looking back every few seconds. At the edge of the park, he scanned both directions, then darted across Fulton Street. He would disappear into the avenues, find a safe place to plan. When morning came, he would finally make a long-overdue phone call.

## CHAPTER 14

THE TEMPERATURE GAUGE was at 122. Lawrence Castleton sat hunched on the wooden bench, his giant folds of skin glistening with droplets of sweat. The Saturday morning ritual was never missed. Stationary bikes for three miles. In the sauna by 8:30 A.M. At the desks finding heirs by 9:30 A.M. A decade-old formula for success for the chief executive of General Inquiry. He had weighed himself that morning—a svelte 303. He had actually dropped a couple of pounds.

The door opened and Borg quickly slipped in. Castleton didn't open his eyes.

"Nine o'clock, Richard? Can't keep up with the old man anymore?"

Borg plopped down on the bench across from him.

"One of the Sandoval heirs called me at home. Crying about the usual crap."

Castleton threw a spray of sweat from his forehead. In the half-light, the president looked like an enormous poached egg.

"I'll never let an heir ruin my favorite morning of the week," he said, his eyes still closed. "You'll carry me out of here someday, Richard."

"I don't doubt it," Borg replied, wondering which four investigators would help him.

"What's the news up north?"

"Sounds like it went well. Risso said it took three trucks half an hour to douse it."

Castleton's eyes snapped open.

"Three trucks? Goddamn it, this was supposed to be a *controlled* fire. I didn't want to torch the entire fucking building."

"Relax, no one got hurt. It went perfectly."

"Is Risso in yet? I want to talk to him."

"Wait a minute, Lawrence—there's something else you need to know. Get a load of this—someone blew up Merchant's apartment last night."

Castleton swung his head to Borg quickly, whipping spray from his forehead. *"What?"*

"Someone planted a bomb in his place. From what I'm told, two people were killed."

"What people?"

"Bystanders, I guess. I know it wasn't Merchant. He showed up at the scene while they were cleaning up the place. Anybody's guess where he is now."

"Risso didn't have anything to do with this, did he?"

"God, no, Lawrence. Are you crazy? It's a bizarre coincidence."

"I don't like bizarre coincidences. If his office gets traced back to us, we'll be the prime suspects in this bomb thing."

"It can't be traced. The people we used never even saw Risso's face."

Castleton leaned back and closed his eyes again. "Who'd blow up his place?"

"I don't know. Other heir finders?"

"No other heir finders even know about this. None of them are crazy enough to try it anyway. No, it's all related to this Jacobs business. The FBI knows exactly what's going on."

The ceiling intercom crackled. *"Lawrence?"*

It was Danny Risso. Castleton quickly pressed a button.

"Go ahead."

*"We've got a break on Jacobs."*

"I'm listening, Danny. What is it?"

*"We found an heir."*

They stared at each other.

"Meet me in my office in ten minutes."

They grabbed their towels and hurried to the showers.

*          *          *

Danny Risso was waiting in the president's office. He was grinning like a proud new father.

"What do we got?" asked Castleton.

"We got ourselves a jailbird," replied Risso, smiling.

"I knew it!" said Borg, punching his hand. "I *knew* he was a con."

"Where is he?" Castleton asked Risso.

"San Quentin. My flight's at noon."

"You're going with him," said Castleton to Borg. "I want forty-five percent from this son of a bitch." He turned back to Risso, who looked a bit deflated to hear he would have a partner. "What's he in for?"

"Drugs. Nine-year sentence. Out in five months."

"Make it fifty percent," said Castleton. "This guy has no bargaining power. I want you to get whatever you can."

"The more we get, the fatter the bonus checks," said Borg, with a grin.

The optimism had returned to the president's face again, the familiar glow he hadn't shown in days. Lawrence Castleton's sense of euphoria had distracted him just enough to prevent him from noticing the midnight blue van parked forty yards down the street, or its occupants, who had just listened to every word of the conversation he had enjoyed with his associates.


The limousine drove through Manhattan in silence. Director Gordon watched Times Square stream by as his deputy director sat and simmered. Arminger was tired and irritable. He enjoyed long hours of work, but the time put into the current project was producing no tangible results. Jacobs was four days old, and he still didn't know what was going on. His lack of knowledge and his chief's seeming indifference were making him all the more irritated.

"Why do you think it was him?"

"Seems obvious," replied Arminger, with thinly veiled condescension. "The day after the break-in, Merchant was off on a flight to Germany. The day after that, he signs up the heir. He found something in that house. Must have been damn good for him to shoot a cop on the way out."

"What evidence?"

"Evidence won't be a problem. He's the only suspect."

Gordon frowned and watched Broadway through tinted glass. Anger, impulsiveness, stubbornness—traits he was seeing all too often in the DDNY. He sat next to the future of the Bureau, and the future frightened him.

"It's time to go after him, Arthur."

"He hasn't returned our calls. I admit he's acting every bit the guilty man."

The car circled around Federal Plaza and found the entrance down into the parking lot. They took the elevator to the second floor and entered the office of the deputy director. Arminger found the coffee machine and poured himself a cup.

"Anything interesting in the house?" asked Gordon.

Arminger blew steam from the surface of the coffee.

"Nothing I saw. Merchant had gone through it pretty thoroughly the night before. If—"

The intercom interrupted him.

"I'm with Director Gordon, Carol."

*"I'm sorry, sir. You have a Mr. Nick Merchant on line one . . ."*

They stared at each other for three seconds before Arminger responded.

"I'll take that, thank you."

Arminger found his seat behind the desk. Gordon placed the headphones on and nodded. A finger pressed the flashing light.

"This is Deputy Director Edmund Arminger."

"Nick Merchant . . ."

They raised eyebrows at each other. Arminger moistened his lower lip.

"Does it normally take a dozen phone calls to get your attention, Merchant? I feel sorry for your clients if that's the case."

"What do you want with me?"

"Nothing terribly complicated. We're insisting that you drop your investigation into Gerald Raymond Jacobs. Don't dig around him, don't look into him at all. This is a federal matter and I strongly advise staying clear of it."

The line was silent. They could hear what sounded like traffic in the background. The tape would be analyzed later.

"Why do you want me to drop it?"

"Mr. Jacobs had a very close association with the FBI. I'm afraid that's all I can say and about all you need to know."

"What if I don't back off?"

"Then your problems will only be starting. I should tell you that the FBI is now handling the investigation of the attempted murder of a Hudson police officer, as well as the break-in of the Jacobs home. I understand the list of suspects is very short."

"Wait a second. Attempted murder? What attempted murder?"

"You know exactly what I'm talking—"

"I don't know a damn *thing* about any attempted murder!"

"Yes you do, Merchant. Yes you do. Once we get this investigation under way, I'm sure we'll find all the evidence we need to build a very strong case against our single suspect."

A long pause settled over the line before Nick again spoke.

"Sir, I don't know what happened with this police officer, but I'm telling you right now I didn't shoot anyone. I'll make you a deal— I'm willing to help you if you're willing to help me. I'd like to know who this Jacobs person really was. I'd also like to know why people are trying to kill me. I assume it's all part of the same story."

"What are you talking about?"

"I'm talking about a bomb that was placed at my front door last night. I was fortunate enough to walk away from it, but my fifty-five-year-old secretary wasn't so lucky. Oh, and before I forget, there was this other little incident: two lunatics tried to fill me full of bullets this morning. Do me a favor, sir—go pick up a morning edition of the *San Francisco Chronicle* and read the front page. Tell me if it sounds to you like someone's trying to kill me."

Arminger shook his head at Gordon and received a puzzled look in return.

"I don't know anything about that, Merchant. I assure you we will not be giving out any information pertaining to Mr. Jacobs, though. The only thing we're interested in is that you end your investigation. It's a simple solution."

"Yeah, real simple. So simple I can't believe I didn't think of it. Just go back home—if I had a home—lie down, and forget all about this. I guess I'll just tape a note on the door telling whoever tried to kill me that they don't need to bother with me anymore because hey, I've wiped my mind clean of old Gerald Jacobs. Then you guys can come over and arrest me for some murder charge I had nothing to do with. Yessir, that's a great solution you thought up. Can I tell you something?"

"Go ahead."

"I have no assurance whatsoever that whoever tried to murder me last night will stop trying if I drop this. Hell, in their eyes I probably already know way more than I should. As much as I'd like to back out of this, I just don't think I *can* anymore. If I try to go back to my life, I'm either going to wind up dead or in jail."

"So you won't cooperate."

"Cooperating on your terms will get me killed. If you want to help me figure out what's really going on here, then let me know. Otherwise I need to do two things, sir. I need to find out who killed my secretary, and I need to do whatever it takes to keep myself alive. If that includes finding out *everything* I possibly can about Mr. Jacobs, then that's what I'll do. I don't care about your little secret, but I do care about my life."

"Merchant, you're only bringing more trouble down on your head by—"

"This conversation's going nowhere. Go talk to SFPD. Maybe you'll understand my position better."

The line went dead. Arminger held the receiver for a second before replacing it. Gordon removed the headsets and placed them on the desk. Then they looked at each other.

"Sounds as if he's made up his mind, doesn't it?" Gordon said.

Arminger's response came swiftly. "We'll go after him hard. He can't be allowed to roam free on this."

"I'd like to speak with SFPD before we make any decisions. I want to hear about this so-called bombing." Director Gordon rose to his feet and rubbed the small of his back. "I'm tired of this, Edmund. I'm about to fly back to Washington, and I assure you, I'm not leaving until I get some answers. It's time I went directly to the source."


The Lexus slowly moved among the warehouses until Kragen saw Pier 11. He turned right and parked along the waterfront, facing the gray waves of the East River. Across the expanse, the outline of Brooklyn Heights. His favorite home had been purchased there with cash two years ago. The others were in Florida and Aspen, but he was partial to New York and always considered it his home base. It was where most of his work was, and work had never been better these last few months.

Kragen checked his watch and waited. His role in the Jacobs situation had been permanently expanded, and he was pleased with the particulars. The compensation was right, and the resources were available to earn it without too much difficulty. For the kind of money being offered, he would have actually considered coming out of retirement himself were it a physical option. But he was forty-nine years of age, with a disfigured hand and half a dozen metal fragments inches from his heart, courtesy of a VC booby trap. He was keenly aware of his limitations. But that was the beauty of having others do the work for him.

After ten minutes, the limo appeared from behind a warehouse and pulled alongside him. The back door opened before the tires came to rest. Philip Cimko was in his suit pants, white button-down, and burgundy wingtips. No tie. Kragen hated the thought of taking orders from the arrogant little punk. He lowered his window and lit a cigarette as Cimko approached.

"Your boys really fucked up, Kragen. What happened?"

Kragen felt the blood rise to his cheeks. Money or not, he didn't need this loafer-wearing pansy chewing him out. He smiled and blew a cloud of smoke out of the side of his mouth.

"Good morning to you too."

"You killed an innocent woman."

"Accidents happen, junior. I lost someone too."

"You can't be involving innocent people, Kragen. It's unacceptable."

"It was his damn secretary. How innocent could she have been?"

"It can't happen again. You're getting paid too much not to be perfect."

Kragen looked across the river and smiled slightly. All mistakes were forgivable. "I get the picture, okay? I assume you didn't drive down here to lecture me."

Cimko looked around. The wind was picking up and his GQ hairstyle was now a flailing mop. "Can I sit in there?"

Kragen gave an ambiguous head toss and reached for another smoke. He would have the punk gagging. Cimko entered and immediately coughed.

"Change of plans, effective today. I have two more to add to your list."

"Same money?"

"Same money. These should be very simple for you."

"More PI's?"

"Don't worry about who they are. We'll have you all the information you need by tonight. It needs to be done quickly. How soon can you mobilize your people?"

"How quick can you pay for 'em?"

"Instantly upon completion. You have any experience tracking down missing people?"

Kragen frowned. "Can't say I do. Doesn't mean I can't learn fast. Is Merchant still the one you want to focus on?"

"He's one of them. After last night he's probably gone underground, but he'll slip up eventually. You have to find him when he does."

"Do my best."

"Don't do your best, Kragen—do your job. You have to find him."

"Listen, junior, this guy's a PI, and now he's wise to the fact somebody's after him. Probably knows all the tricks about hiding. I guarantee he's not sitting around waiting for a bullet like those stupid bankers were."

Cimko was enraged. "Don't ever bring them up again. *Not ever.*" He took a long second to calm himself. "You've got to find Merchant by Wednesday. If you're as good as you claim, it shouldn't be a problem."

Kragen crushed his cigarette in the ashtray and licked the residue from his teeth. "So what about those two bigwigs in L.A.?"

"Nothing's changed there. You should have plenty of motivation with what we're paying, Kragen. Do you still have people in San Francisco?"

"Yep."

"Keep them there until we reach you later today. We're going to have them travel up north in a few hours."

"Where up north?"

"You'll know in a while. Just make sure they're ready to move."

CHAPTER 15

A FLOWING TIDE OF fog engulfed the upper segments of both towers
of the Golden Gate Bridge. Penetrating winds billowed in from
the outer reaches of the Pacific. Under the southern end of the bridge,
a blue Buick rented by Michael Dean Collier rolled past Fort Point and
to the edge of the bay.

Nick stared at the foam-tipped waters, his mind still numb from his
discussion with the FBI. He had wondered what had happened when
the cops had walked in on the gunman in Jacobs's house. Now he had
his answer. Their simple little break-in had become a nightmare.

He looked up at the fort, the century-old sentinel at the mouth of the
ocean. It had been twenty-two years since he had ventured down there,
a thirteen-year-old on the seventh-grade field trip, the only boy in class
without a paper bag lunch or a mother to pack it. Bleak, lonely days,
mornings when he would wake up in the empty little house in the
avenues to find a few dollar bills on the kitchen table and a scribbled
note from a father who would already be off on his beat. His dad had
done the best he could.

A quick toot of a horn shook him from his thoughts. A car rolled
slowly into the spot next to him. Doug's cheeks were pale and
unshaven. Nick stepped from his car and joined him in the Jaguar.

"Your property manager called me this morning," his attorney said softly. "The entire office is gutted. Ashes. Even Matt Von Rohr's contract."

"I thought you had that."

"After I filed the papers, I brought it over and put it in the fire safe. Seemed like a good idea."

Nick rubbed his eyes and exhaled. The amount of pending business in the office was staggering. Every contract and crucial court filing they had was now gone. The Wallace case alone had thirty-nine signed contracts.

"How did you rent the car?" asked Doug.

"Michael Collier did," replied Nick. "Thank God I got that ID a couple years ago."

"Keep using it. Don't even think of putting your real name on anything."

"As if you need to tell me that."

They both sat and listened to the breakers slam against the shore. The wind carried a fine mist to the car windshield, and the blare of the foghorns rose and died in the wet air.

"What I don't get," said Nick, "is why they burned down the office if they expected me to be dead. Why bother?"

"It's GI, Nick. This is all about Jacobs. They're trying to wipe us out completely so we can't make a claim."

"Why do all this *after* I've found heirs? If they really wanted to screw us, they would have done it before we found them. Besides, do you really think they would resort to murder?"

"It's a lot of money, Nick. I wouldn't put it past them."

Nick studied his friend. In the gloomy shadow of the bridge, Doug looked old and tired. They sat in silence and watched a barge ease out into the open sea.

"I'm not sure what to do," Nick finally said. "Home's gone, work's gone. Where do I start with this?"

"First thing you need to do is get a gun, Nick. You know where you can get one?"

"That won't be a problem."

"What about the FBI? You called them yet?"

Nick told him about the conversation he had shared with Arminger. Doug looked worse now.

"Jesus Christ. You think they actually have something on you for shooting that cop?"

"Whether they do or don't, they're perfectly capable of coming up with something. If they want to keep this Jacobs thing quiet badly enough, they'll dig up whatever they can to build a case against me."

"Why didn't you just tell them you were gonna leave it alone?"

"Because I have the feeling that they're coming after me regardless."

"Dammit," said Doug, rubbing his forehead. "Fuck! What are you gonna do?"

"Do I have a choice? I've got to investigate this Jacobs guy. I need to know what I'm up against. After what's happened to Rose, I can't just go slinking off. There's nowhere for me to go anyway."

"But what—"

"Look, buddy," said Nick, swiveling to him, "I'm going to need you. I have to know if you're in or out. No hard feelings if you're not. What's it going to be?"

Doug stared at him momentarily, then gave him a disgusted look. "What am I, some scumbag attorney? I've known you forever, Nick. I was right there when your dad started the business. You *know* I'm in."

"Just checking."

"I'm just not sure what 'being in' means now."

"It means being there if I need your help. That's all. If I call you at three in the morning, you'll be there for me."

"Hell, yeah, I'll be there," Doug said.

Nick gave a weak smile. "Look, I'm sorry for being so punchy."

"Understandable after the night you've had."

Nick reached into his pocket and removed a scrap of paper.

"I've got something I need you to do. The cops said they found a body in my place. A man's body. I called a contact of mine at SFPD this morning and got the dead guy's name."

He handed it to Doug, who read out loud.

" 'William David Brecker.' You think he—"

"Damn right I do. Son of a bitch was planting the bomb when Rose walked in. You want to know something? I bet you and I were being watched at the restaurant last night. They knew where I was and thought they had plenty of time—"

"But Rose shows up and takes it instead," said Doug, looking pale. "Jesus Christ, Nick . . ."

A carload of tourists drove by them slowly. Nick watched them until they were out of sight.

"I want you to run every possible background check you can on this guy. I want to know exactly who this piece of garbage was."

"I'm on it," said Doug, putting the paper in his wallet. "What are you gonna do in the meantime?"

Nick frowned and drew a deep breath. "Let me tell you my plan. . . ."

It had been six years of unabashed glory. By most measures, the promises of a revitalized America, a reenergized economy, and a return to the sacred tradition of solid family values had been fulfilled. President Robert Marshall now enjoyed record approval ratings, the press likening his administration to a kind of modern-day Camelot. The youthful fifty-seven-year-old sparkplug who had taken the country's reins six years before was a PR man's dream, a squeaky-clean leader adored by both young and old.

This day, the great leader was in his usual upbeat mood. Arthur Gordon was always impressed by the constant optimism of his commander in chief.

Gordon took a seat in front of the President and crossed his legs. He personally didn't buy into the popular perceptions of Marshall's divinity, but his duty was to serve whomever the American people chose as their leader. Only four more years with this one—if he was reelected.

"I understand this witness protection thing has become a real pain in the ass for you, Arthur."

"It's been a frustrating few days," agreed Gordon.

The President sat behind the great desk of the Oval Office and joined his hands thoughtfully in front of his chin. A cigarette smoldered in an ashtray in front of him—a habit very few people knew about.

"We need to reach a resolution here," said Marshall. "It's very troubling how things have gotten to this point."

"I agree," replied Gordon patiently. "It would be helpful if I knew exactly what I was dealing with here, Mr. President."

"And you will, Arthur. I didn't realize you were in the dark on this. I've invited someone to join us who can explain Jacobs a bit better than I can."

A knocking came from behind as the President rose to his feet.

"Perfect timing," he said with a smile.

The double doors opened, and in stepped a Secret Service agent along with a guest Gordon knew immediately. The unexpected visitor was an imposing six foot three, with salt-and-pepper hair, intense gray eyes, and a solid chin. Unmistakable.

The President made the obligatory introduction. "Arthur, of course you know Senator Newland."

New York State senator Thomas Newland—war hero, friend to business, and probable presidential successor—flashed his toothiest smile. He purposefully approached the old man in charge of the FBI and extended his hand. "How are you, Mr. Gordon?"

The director clenched the powerful hand and nodded, confused. The three of them sat. Gordon decided to adjust his preplanned strategy until the senator's appearance explained itself.

"You don't mind if the senator joins us, do you, Arthur?" Marshall asked.

Gordon gave a slight gesture, more of a shrug than anything. He wasn't sure if he minded or not, but he would see where this all went.

The President turned to Senator Newland. "I'm hoping to get this resolved here and now, Tom. I'm stepping in because I know it's important to you and that committee of yours. Get me up to speed here. What was the old fellow's name again?"

"Jacobs," replied Newland. "Gerald Jacobs."

"Right," said Marshall. "Director Gordon is naturally concerned being that the Bureau has been Mr. Jacobs's caretaker these last few years. He would appreciate if you could fill him in on some of the background of the situation."

Newland frowned sympathetically and turned to Gordon. "I'm happy to do that," he said. "I regret not getting the opportunity to brief you on this earlier, Mr. Gordon. Hopefully I can clear up the confusion you must be feeling."

*Be my guest,* thought Gordon, nodding at the senator to continue.

"For the last four years," said Newland, "I've been chairman of a very special committee, a group of which I'm very, very proud to be a part. It's a special investigative body set up to work in conjunction with a large number of Swiss banks, the purpose of which is to determine the location and rightful ownership of lost assets. I'm sure you've read about some of the settlements achieved in recent months with a number of Swiss banks. Much of this is due to the efforts of my committee. And those of Mr. Schmidt . . ."

Gordon waited. He had been aware of the senator's committee, but he needed to hear more before he said anything.

"As you're aware of, Gerald Jacobs was actually a person by the name of Martin Schmidt. Mr. Schmidt was quite a valuable find for us, a Swiss citizen with banking experience dating back to World War II. He provided us with an amazing amount of information—account owners, numbers, dormancy periods, contents of security boxes. Schmidt basically laid out the complete holdings of a major Swiss bank for us and also versed us in exactly how things are done over there. We're nearing significant settlements with a number of Swiss banks because of his insider's knowledge."

"So why exactly was he brought to us?" asked Gordon, cutting to the chase.

"I'm surprised that isn't in your file," replied Newland. "Mr. Gordon, if I had known Director Dalton had neglected to share this information with you, I would have made a point to seek you out and personally explain things. I'm glad to do that now, however tardy I may be." He leaned forward, his eyes narrowing slightly. "The information Schmidt was passing us is extremely sensitive. We believed there was a reasonable possibility that he was in serious jeopardy because of it. Swiss bankers are a tightly knit community. Their clientele is very wealthy and powerful. They do not appreciate their trade secrets being passed about or their names being sullied. As a stipulation for his help, Schmidt actually *insisted* on protection. For what he provided us, we were happy to oblige."

The director nodded, still off balance. The senator and his information were so unexpected he was having difficulty digesting what he was hearing. He had been out of the loop on Jacobs, and to be briefed in front of the President was both frustrating and embarrassing. He was angry he hadn't known much sooner.

Newland continued. "Negotiations with a number of Swiss banks are going to drag on for quite some time, Mr. Gordon. The groundwork we've laid the past few years will be seriously compromised if Mr. Jacobs's true identity is revealed."

"And I don't want to see that," said President Marshall, with emphasis. "Tom is doing remarkably well with a very difficult situation, and I don't want his project to fail. His committee is doing the right thing to help correct a terrible wrong, and this is something that will also reflect very favorably on the Party next election. I'll be damned if some greedy private investigators will undermine four years of honorable work. Speaking of which, have you established contact with these PI's yet, Arthur?"

"I just spoke with the last of them this morning."

"And has he given his word not to investigate?"

"Actually, no. He says that he can't promise us anything in regard to that."

"Now, which one is this?"

"Nicholas Merchant."

"Right. The small outfit."

"That's correct."

The President nodded and looked to Newland. The senator spoke.

"Mr. Gordon, as I understand it, the reason these investigators are so interested in Jacobs is because of his estate. Isn't there some way we can get into the appropriate county and drain these accounts? I'd think this would remove any incentive for these PI's to even continue with this."

Director Gordon was having difficulty paying attention to the question. He was still processing what he had just heard of the Jacobs background.

"I'm sure there is a way, Senator. The problem is that we have no true jurisdiction in a state county probate proceeding. With some maneuvering, we could do it, but I think we'd only draw the attention of God knows how many state employees to the situation. The press surely wouldn't be far behind, and that's exactly what we're trying to avoid. If we allow this probate hearing to proceed but simply close it off to the public, we'll alert fewer people of the estate's existence. We've been immediately confiscating the court records as they're being filed."

"I think that's wise," commented the President. "Now then, what about this police officer who was shot the other night? I believe you told me he was a City of Hudson policeman?"

"That's correct."

"Who are your suspects in that?"

"Nicholas Merchant is the primary suspect."

"Do you have your evidence?"

"Not at the moment."

"It's clear he had every reason to enter the home."

"The motivation is obvious, yes."

"And this does involve the witness protection program. Quite obviously your jurisdiction."

"That's correct," replied Gordon.

"Then run with that, Arthur. I'd like you to take over any investiga-

tion into this attempted murder as well as the burglary. Clearly the burglar and the shooter are one and the same, wouldn't you say?"

"Quite possibly."

"Quite *likely,* I would think. I'd like you to gather your evidence and
file your charges against this Merchant person. Didn't you tell me that
he used to be a police officer?"

"In San Francisco, yes."

"San Francisco? Is he a homosexual, by chance?"

"I have no idea," answered Gordon.

"Well, find out. Have your agents check that house up and down. We
need evidence, Arthur. It's very important that we nail this man if he's
insisting on pressing this investigation forward. We do not need undue
attention brought to this Jacobs fellow, not after all the fine work the
senator's committee has done."

"Mr. President, the house has been cleared out and handed over to
the New York Department of Justice. Those were your instructions."

"Yes, and that was a favor to Senator Newland. Knowing his involvement, I'm giving him a certain leeway on this situation." He crossed his
arms on his chest. "Arthur, I'm not looking for anything complicated
here. Just get in there, find the evidence—a few fingerprints perhaps—
and file the charges. This needs to happen quickly. I wouldn't be so
insistent if it weren't very important to Senator Newland and his committee."

"Is Merchant's firm very large, Mr. Gordon?" asked the senator.

Gordon kept his eyes on the President when he spoke. He didn't like
being questioned by Newland, nor did he feel comfortable with the senator's involvement in this part of the discussion.

"A two-man show, basically."

"So you take care of Merchant and his operation pretty much shuts
down."

"That's probably true."

"Sounds like a clear solution," Marshall said, a bit too quickly for
Gordon's liking. In the silence that followed, the director saw his opening.

"What will be required of the FBI if Merchant by chance brings any
of this out?"

"I'm counting on you to make sure he doesn't," Marshall said, clearly
irritated now. "Goddamnit, the longer we sit here and chat, the more
likely it is we'll see problems. I want you two to work together here. If

you have any more questions, pick up the phone and call each other. Frankly, I feel I've spent more than enough time on this, and I'd like to get on with running the country. Did you have any more questions for Tom, Arthur?"

Gordon slowly shook his head. He wanted to pick at it more, but he resisted the urge.

"Good," said Marshall. "Now that Senator Newland has been good enough to brief you, you can move on with this. It sounds as if it's no big deal if it's just taken care of in a firm manner." He turned to Newland. "Tom, I trust I won't need to intervene any further."

"I agree, Mr. President."

The three of them rose to their feet and exchanged handshakes. The President ushered them to the door and said goodbye.

Gordon followed the senator into the lobby just outside the Oval Office. Newland turned to him and said, "It was good to clear the air today, Arthur. I appreciate your help on this. I want you to feel free to contact me if you have any more concerns."

Gordon nodded and said nothing. He felt certain he would have further questions, but he doubted if he would be approaching Newland for answers. He let the senator walk off, then he took several steps through the lobby before stopping and looking back. The President's door was shut.

He finally turned away, a vague uneasiness nagging at him. This would not be the end of it. There were complete answers somewhere, and he planned to find them. Soon.


The fishermen were returning to their berths at the Marina Greens. They were largely older men, grizzled, hardened types with foreign accents who rose before daybreak to ensure they found favorable spots on the water for their small, barnacle-encrusted boats. For ten years now, they had waged a losing war, for the bay was in slow decline. Health officials spoke of toxicity levels and mercury content, of fish too poisonous to eat, but still the fishermen set out in the misty mornings with their ten-foot poles and assortment of multicolored lures. They had nowhere else to go.

Nick lowered his window completely and felt little relief. The morning fog had lifted, removing the city's only defense from the sun. Indian summer was in the air—two weeks or so of intolerable heat that native

San Franciscans endured rather than enjoyed. The smell of sea salt and bird guano blended sickeningly in the faint, almost nonexistent breeze. Nick fanned himself slowly with a newspaper. Ever since college, he had hated heat, hated those dusty hundred-degree afternoons in East Texas where the nearest relief was some godforsaken water hole miles down a simmering hot concrete turnpike. Indian summer was coming at a bad time this year.

It was one in the afternoon. He had hours to kill before his flight would leave, and until then all he could do was sit. A newly purchased garment bag lay on the backseat, and two large shopping bags sat on opposite sides of it. He had purchased new pants, shoes, shirts, and underwear. It had been charged to the tune $970 on a credit card issued to a Michael Dean Collier, a fake ID he had kept for years but until now never used. The billing address on the card was a post office box—worthless to anyone looking to find the cardholder. He felt reasonably safe using it. He had a driver's license and passport to match. From that moment until some undetermined point in the future, he would be Mr. Collier.

Nick slouched in his seat and watched the fishermen come and go. One horrible image would not dislodge itself from his mind: the thought of a fifty-five-year-old grandmother on a metal slab. He had rubbed his temples raw thinking about Rose.

His pager began to vibrate. A New York area code—thank God. He reached for his phone.

"Where are you?"

"Schenectady," Alex replied. "I got a one-month lease on a studio. If I have to hide out, I at least want to be comfortable. Where are you?"

"Near Fisherman's Wharf. Anybody follow you?"

"I don't think so."

"You don't *think* so? Did you look?"

"Yes, I looked. I can handle myself, Nick."

"Just watching out for you. Listen, something I didn't tell you earlier—another person was killed in that blast last night. The cops found a man's body *inside* my apartment. I got his name from a cop friend of mine. I'm gonna have Doug run it and see what turns up."

"Let me know as soon as you have something."

"I will. What did you manage to bring out of your place?"

"The laptop. Some clothes. That's about it. You yelled at me to get out of there quick, remember?"

"What about the Jacobs stuff? You didn't forget that, did you?"

"I got it, I got it."

He rubbed his eyes with his fingers. "Good. Have you found any-thing yet on Ludwig Holtzmann?"

"I haven't gotten a chance yet, Nick. I'm not even sure what exactly you want me to do."

"Whatever you can. Go to a library or research center or something and see what you can dig up. Find *anything*, Alex. This guy was German or Austrian, right? Take that and go with it."

"Fine. What are you going to do?"

"I think Jessica Von Rohr knows some of Jacobs's story. I have to get it out of her somehow. I'm catching a flight back to Des Moines later today."

"And what makes you think she's going to give you the time of day?"

"Because I'm gonna be very damn insistent. Listen, I need to get hold of a gun once I touch down there. Remember those heirs we found in that little town south of Des Moines about two years ago? Their name was like Reichart or Reinfeld or something like that. . . ."

"Reinbeck," said Alex. "I remember them. The town was called Indiana or—"

"Indianola," said Nick, snapping his fingers. "Two brothers, if I'm correct. Couple of hunting-and-fishing country boys. I'll have Doug dig up their addresses. If anybody out there can get me a gun, it would be those two characters."

"What—you're just going to show up at their door and ask for a gun?"

"If you have a better idea, I'm all ears."

"You don't have to snap at me, Nick. We're both in the same mess here."

"I'm sorry. I'm afraid I've got another lovely bit of news to share with you."

"Oh God, what now?"

"Someone torched the office early this morning. Every contract we had there went up in smoke, including Matt Von Rohr's. Doug brought it over from his office and it got destroyed too."

He could hear her slowly let a breath out.

"Any other good news, Nick?"

"Now that you mention it, yes. Two men tried to kill me last night and I'm alive to tell you about it."

Alex was silent. "You're not joking, are you?"

"Not much of a joke, is it? You have to watch your back, and do *not* use any credit cards issued in your name. Use your fake ID at all times. How did you lease that apartment?"

"Cash. Debra Ramos."

"Good job. We know what we have to do then: I go to Iowa, you do the Holtzmann research. One of us will have to get back to Matt Von Rohr and have him sign another contract. Just another thing to add to our list."

"Who'd do all this to us, Nick? Do you think the other heir finders are behind it?"

"I don't know. The only other people who know about Jacobs are the FBI, which reminds me: I spoke with one of their deputy directors this morning."

"What did he say?" she asked, her voice hushed.

"Just what we thought—he demanded that we back off Jacobs. I told them I can't guarantee them anything. But he did tell me one thing, and you better brace yourself for this one . . ."

"What is it?"

"They told me the cop who showed up at Jacobs's house the other night was almost murdered. That gunman must have shot him, Alex. They want to put that on me."

"Jesus," she said. "What proof do they have that we were even there?"

"I don't know," he replied. "Maybe they're getting their evidence together right now."

Both of them held the phones and were silent. Nick spoke before she could think too much.

"Listen," he said. "Sitting around worrying isn't going to help us. I want you to get moving on the Holtzmann research. Let's just keep in close contact and check in with each other before we do anything. Okay?"

"I'm scared, Nick."

"So am I. Just please be careful."

"You too."

Nick exited the lot and headed back toward the avenues.

## CHAPTER 16

ALEX DROVE THROUGH the side streets of residential Albany
with a nagging pain in her gut. She had realized her mistake
twenty minutes after the conversation with her partner. She tried to lay
blame on Nick, and he *was* partially at fault, the way he had frantically
ordered her out of the house. She had been so busy grabbing clothes
and underwear, she had overlooked the one thing they could not afford
to be without. She had forgotten the Jacobs pictures.

She made a pass down Morris Street. Nothing odd. Nobody suspicious. Absolutely normal. Mr. Tomiki was across the street, watering
his lawn for the tenth time in the last three days. The streets were
empty, as usual. She drove several blocks both directions from her
house. Clear. A few cars—all unoccupied. She frowned. The whole
hiding thing seemed slightly absurd. She would just slip into her home
and slip out with the pictures. Nick wouldn't even have to know
about it.

She calmly drove back to her home and parked in the next-door
neighbor's driveway. The couple who lived there would be at work until
six and wouldn't mind in the least. She placed the .22 in her jacket and
stepped from the car.

The house was fine. Slightly lonely looking maybe, but untouched.
She cut down the adjoining pathway and walked to the back fence. The

hinges of the wooden gate creaked as she pushed it open and hurried through to the backyard.

She entered from the kitchen side door. The gun was out now. She did her best Angie Dickinson around the corner into the living room and scanned it. Home sweet home. Any psychopaths in the closet? She smiled and quickly jogged upstairs in a crouch, gun extended. She stopped at the top of the stairs. Her throat went dry as dead leaves. The office door was closed.

There was a simple reason she always left that door open. Air flow. Kept the house from getting musty. She never, ever closed that door. But there it was in front of her—shut tighter than a vault.

Her arm shook a bit. The house was still, a deafening dead quiet. She stepped toward the door slowly. The gun felt warm and slippery in her palm. The floorboards were creaking under her feet like little firecrackers. One thing she was certain of—she had left the Jacobs photographs on the edge of the file cabinet. She reached for the knob, turned it, then threw the door open hard against the wall. Three or four loose papers fluttered to the ground from the sudden breeze. She braced herself outside the doorway, gun extended, her finger lightly tickling the trigger. She could see the pictures, just as she had left them. She exhaled. If someone had been in there, they couldn't have missed them. She approached the file cabinet and grabbed the envelope.

She was halfway down the stairs when the doorbell rang. She froze, then crept to the curtains. It was only her mailman, an older guy with roaming eyes. He was holding a package. She reached for the knob but quickly drew her hand back. A gasp passed over her lips as she slowly lowered herself to one knee.

Somehow it had registered in her peripheral vision, just a black blob, a dark incongruity against the varnished brown door. She stared at it, eyes wide and unblinking. It was at the base of the door, a metallic looking black box, no larger than a brick. A pair of thin wires—one white, one green—ran from the top of it and reconnected at the base. On the very top was a red crystal, flashing twice every three seconds or so.

The doorbell rang again, but she barely heard it. She backed away from the door slowly, vaguely aware of her heart thumping in her temples. She gripped the gun and looked about wildly. This was no longer her home. Someone had entered and turned it into a house of horrors, a place she could no longer fathom sleeping in.

She made it to the hallway. Her eyes, keen now, spotted the second black brick instantly. It sat at the foot of the door leading to the garage—her normal point of entry into the house. Any other day, she would have pulled her car into the garage and come in from there. Either that or parked in the driveway and entered from the front. The same horrible fate awaited either choice.

In the kitchen, she could almost see the intruders now. The window hung open barely an inch, the latch bent slightly askew. They had broken in and seen the three doors leading in from outside. Having only two devices to plant, they had opted to play the percentages and arm the two most likely entryways. Only blind luck had saved her. But she wasn't even supposed to have gone back there. Nick wouldn't need to know about this.

She walked quickly to the side door, double-checking the doorway thoroughly before exiting. She crept down the side walkway between her house and the neighbor's. The streets were clear. She entered the car quickly and thrust her key into the ignition. She felt heartsick as she watched her home disappear in the rearview mirror. She would not be returning in the near future. Whether she would be returning at all remained to be seen.


A small crowd had gathered at both sides of the glass. Even the warden had found time in his schedule to be present for this special meeting. It was he who personally took the contract behind the glass to inmate number 235150.

Timothy Von Rohr didn't bother scrutinizing the piece of paper. He turned back to the crowd hovering behind him and raised his hands helplessly. "Can't sign it with my finger, Warden."

The warden nodded at one of his men. The guard slapped at his pockets helplessly in search of a pen. Finally the warden rolled his eyes and produced his own pen, a glimmering Mont Blanc.

Von Rohr took it and scratched his name across the line. It was a messy attempt, like a fourth grader's, but this was understandable. It was his first signature in nearly nine years.

The warden took the paper back around to Richard Borg and Danny Risso, reading as he walked. He handed the paper to Borg and gave him a serious nod. "Ten minutes, gentlemen."

Borg nodded and verified the signature before turning back to the prisoner. "I'll keep it simple, Timothy. You've just signed a claim legally entitling you to one-third of an inheritance. Your fifty percent share of that comes to approximately three point seven million dollars."

Von Rohr leaned back and crossed his thick, tattooed arms on his chest. He gave a snort and glanced up at one of the guards hanging over his shoulder. "Who's gonna leave me that kind of money, buddy?"

"Your uncle," replied Danny Risso.

"Yeah. My uncle Donald Trump."

Risso smiled dryly. "Your uncle's name was Ludwig Holtzmann. Remember him?"

"Nope. Sure you got the right guy?"

"We're positive we got the right guy," said Borg. "We wouldn't waste our time coming here if we didn't. When do you get out, Timothy?"

"Five months."

"What we'll do—if you'd like—is set up a trust account with a local bank here in the Bay Area. The money will be perfectly safe there for five months until you're free to claim it. Does that sound reasonable?"

Von Rohr gave another chuckle. Everything the two visitors said seemed to be eliciting a laugh.

"You two walk in here, give me three point whatever million, and ask me if it sounds reasonable? Yeah, sure, it's sounds reasonable, all right."

"Good. When the trust account is set up, we'll send you a letter with all the details." The investigators rose to their feet. "Thanks again, Timothy. Any last questions?"

"Yeah," he replied, throwing a glance to the warden. "Would you guys mind sending a dozen long-stemmed roses to Uncle Louie's funeral? That would mean *so* much to me."

"Time's up," said a guard. "Let's go, Von Rohr."

"What a joke," mumbled the convict as he was led out of view.

Borg looked at Risso and smiled slyly. He couldn't agree more. Three point seven million in twenty minutes. What a joke.


Matt Von Rohr reached for his jacket and broke into his thousandth smile of the week. He slipped his card into the machine and felt the chomp of the time stamp. He waved good night to a few of the warehouse grunts and pushed through the exit to the lot. T minus seven days to freedom. Seven days until his life started all over again.

He had gotten the call two hours ago. She sounded nervous, probably more than a little embarrassed, but that was understandable. It was slightly unbelievable to him how it could happen. While it was true there was no protection against a fire or other acts of God, you would at least think anyone with a piece of paper that valuable would put it in a bank vault or something. No big deal. Alex was cool. Besides, he had checked everything she told him by calling the Columbia County offices and verifying his uncle's estate. Merchant and Associates was sending a new contract express airmail and he would be returning it to Alex's P.O. box the same way.

He drove through his Sacramento neighborhood and felt absolutely gleeful. They had planned on raising their children there. They had scraped up enough for the house and made sure it wasn't too far from the best schools in the city. But they could scrap that plan now. His fiancée was thinking big, talking about a four-bedroom in San Francisco or Hawaii and a cabin in Tahoe for the winter. Yessir, tough choices they were facing nowadays.

He pulled into his driveway and checked his watch. They were going out to celebrate over dinner. He was getting used to this. He slammed the door of his Corolla and envisioned a black 944 with a sunroof. He shook his head and laughed. This was no dream.

He grabbed the mail and found the front door key. He found a beer in the fridge and headed upstairs. He needed a shower badly. Eight hours of warehouse dust and grime was penetrating his pores. Another week and a half of it. And that's only because he was nice enough to give them two weeks' notice. He took his shirt off, threw it in the corner, and undid his belt.

The blow hit Matt Von Rohr from behind, a stiff shot to the neck that put him on his stomach. From the floor the room was spinning. He turned his head up painfully. Two men looked down at him. Both held guns. One of them circled around him, his head tilted thoughtfully.

"Your brother Timothy—you know where he is?"

Von Rohr looked at the gun and shook his head. He was teetering on the edge of unconsciousness. He shifted to his side, his pants wrapped around his ankles.

"When did you last see him?"

"What do you want with me?"

"When did you last see your brother?"

"Christ, not for years. What—"

They each fired a shot, one of them applying a final bullet to the head. The two gunmen walked downstairs and entered their car, taking Brooke Street to the freeway.

CHAPTER 17

THE PLANE BEGAN its descent at 6:30 P.M. The ground below was
coal black as the sun's final rays broke the horizon.

Nick turned from the window. He was rested and felt a bit calmer.
He had managed to doze off somewhere over Nevada, and it had
been deep, dreamless sleep. His fear and confusion over Rose's
murder had been replaced by an angry determination to find
answers.

He took the Fifth Street exit off State Highway 5 and parked the car
on the corner of Euclid and Second. As promised, the white pickup
truck was parked and waiting. Nick made a U-turn and caught a
glimpse of the face behind the wheel.

Dave Reinbeck was just as Nick remembered. The cheeks were
still red, the whiskers still unshaven, the hair still a wavy blond mess.
Little had changed from the day two years ago when Nick had
appeared at his front door with the news of Stanley Reinbeck's death.
It had been the first bit of news Dave Reinbeck had gotten about his
father since the old man had walked out on the family nearly thirty
years ago.

They shook hands on the sidewalk.

"Glad I could help, Nick," said Reinbeck, handing over the small
wooden box. "Just get it back to me as soon as you can."

"You bet, Dave," replied Nick, placing the box under his arm. "I appreciate you coming out here."

"No problem. I work only about five minutes away from here." He stuck his hands in his pockets. "So what's going on anyway? You're not in trouble, are you?"

Nick opened his car door and placed the box on the passengers seat.

"Everything's fine. I had to catch a quick flight out here and didn't have time to clear a gun with airport security." He shut the door. "So how's your brother doing?"

"Real good. Still working in construction. He's says hello, by the way. He wanted to know if you had any more money for us."

Nick smiled. "I wish I did."

"Oh well. Guess I only got one deadbeat dad, huh?" He shook his head and pulled out his truck keys. "I'm runnin' late to dinner. Good seein' you again, pal. Lemme know if you need anything else."

"Thanks again, Dave."

Nick gave him a wave as the truck pulled off onto the road. He entered his car and removed the lid of the box. The pistol was a six-shot, snub-nosed revolver, hardly heavy duty but better than nothing. Dave was nice enough to include a box of ammunition as well. Nick slipped six bullets into the cylinder and placed the gun in his coat pocket. The weight against his chest was reassuring.

His phone rang. Doug's voice had an unrestrained urgency.

"I got the full background on that Brecker guy. It's pretty ugly, Nick."

"Give it to me," said Nick, reaching for his notepad.

"For starters, we got a 1980 assault with a deadly weapon charge. Charges eventually dropped. Another assault charge, 1983. Charges dropped again. Here's the kicker: a 1984 arrest for murder. Went to trial and found not guilty. You getting all this?"

"Every word," replied Nick, writing away. "Anything else?"

"That's the best of it. Or the worst, I guess I should say. The only other thing is a 1992 misdemeanor conviction in Nevada—possession of a loaded firearm in his car. Six months' probation."

"That's it?"

"That's it. Jesus Christ, you want more?"

Nick bit his pen and considered everything he had just heard. "Anything else there about this firearm charge?"

"What? Two assaults and a murder charge and you're asking—"

"Will you just answer the question please?"

"It says the guy was caught with—quote here—an unlicensed custom-suppressed McMillan M86SR rifle with tritium night sights and a laser-aiming device. That's all it says."

Nick closed his eyes for a moment and felt chilled. "What about employment?"

"You'll love this. Phoenix police officer, 1974 to '78. Just the kind of guy you want on the force, huh?"

"What else from employment?"

"Nothing."

"What do you mean, nothing?"

"Nothing, Nick. No work, no taxes paid, no permanent addresses since '78. Big zero."

"What about voter's and property? Postal atlas? How about credit and utilities?"

"I ran 'em all. He doesn't show up anywhere. That's absolutely everything, man."

Nick continued chewing his pen. Absolutely everything wasn't much. Outside of the arrests, William Brecker had ceased to exist in 1978. He found that very, very frightening.

"You talk to Von Rohr yet?" asked Doug.

"I'm a few miles from her place. It's barely seven P.M., so I'll give it another hour before I approach her."

"I slept like shit last night. This whole thing's making me a nervous wreck."

"Imagine how I feel."

"Try and sign her, Nick. If you have to go through all this misery, you might as well get rich doing it."

"I'll call you later."

Nick put the phone away and started the engine. He had no desire to walk away from this case rich; all he wanted to do was just walk away alive. He checked the rearview mirror. Whoever had tried to kill him at the apartment was not about to stop trying now. If anything, they were going to double—*triple*—their efforts.

He reached for the steering wheel and noticed his hand wasn't quite steady.

\*     \*     \*

He parked across from her house at 7:30. The front blinds were drawn, and he couldn't see any lights on. The evening was clear and still. He decided he would wait a few minutes before ringing her front door.

He turned his attention back to William Brecker. The background report he had just gotten was more disturbing than he had anticipated. Assault and murder charges weren't even that shocking. After the events of the prior day, he had almost expected them. It was the weapons charge that was really sticking in his head. He had heard of the M86SR rifle. It was a pro's tool—accurate from long distances, powerful, deadly. It had not been made for duck hunting.

The employment information only made him more uneasy. From 1978 on, Brecker had dropped out of "normal" society—no work, no taxes, no address. The conclusion seemed obvious—Mr. Brecker made his living pulling discreet, cash-only jobs. Dirty jobs. How many others had he murdered?

Nick leaned his head back. The fact that a killer-for-hire had been sent for him was not nearly as frightening as the cold knowledge that his breed was always disposable. William Brecker would be replaced, and probably very quickly.

He looked over at Jessica's home. A dim light was suddenly turned on in the living room. He stepped from the car.

The cold reality of the situation swept over him when he was halfway up the walkway. He could barely believe the circumstances bringing him to her doorstep this time. He felt a touch of anger toward himself. The FBI had tried to tell him, had tried to warn him off, but no—Nick Merchant wouldn't hear of it. Nick Merchant had to find heirs, Nick Merchant had to be so curious. That curiosity had come back to haunt him now, and it had killed a hell of a lot more than a damn cat. He had to do what he could to prevent another tragedy.

He pressed the doorbell. In five seconds' time, the door swung open. Nick opened his mouth to speak but had to pause at what he saw. The face at the door was white, the eyes wide and frightened. Nick's rehearsed introduction was instantly forgotten.

"My God," he said. "Are you okay?"

Jessica Von Rohr looked beyond him wildly, scanning the front yard. "What are *you* doing here?" she asked, her voice charged.

"I . . . I need to talk to you," Nick stammered. "Is something—?"

"I just got a call from a detective in Sacramento," she said. "He said my brother's been murdered."

Nick blinked several times, then reached for a post to steady himself. For a brief moment, he forgot where he was.

"My brother's dead," Jessica said numbly, almost as if she were convincing herself of it. "He's been murdered."

Hearing her voice brought Nick back. He glanced furtively down both sides of the street, then stepped into her doorway. "We need to talk."

"No," she said, blocking his path. "What's going on here?"

"Can I please step inside for a moment? I've got some information you need to hear."

Her eyes were defiant. Nick spoke softly but firmly. "I'm not here to talk about inheritances, okay? We need to talk about what I've learned about your uncle." His hand caught the door. "Dammit, Jessica—your brother isn't the only one who's been killed."

He could see in her eyes that this statement registered. Slowly she stepped aside. Nick let a breath out and followed her in. They entered the living room but did not sit this time.

"What happened to Matt?" Nick asked.

"Someone broke into his home and shot him. I got the call half an hour ago. Can you possibly tell me what this is all about?"

Nick shook his head helplessly. "I'm not sure where to start," he said, walking to the front window and sneaking a quick look out. "Last night, someone booby-trapped my home with an explosive. A friend of mine was killed."

"Who? Who would do this?"

"I don't know enough to give you an answer." He walked up to her. "I need to know as much as I can about your uncle. These murders have something to do with him."

"How do you know?"

"I'm guessing, but I know I'm right. I need to find out more so I can prove it."

She rubbed her forehead and abruptly sat down. She looked up at him, her face tired. Her skin was clean, her perfectly clear complexion exposed. She was dressed in a business skirt and white blouse. The call must have caught her just getting home from a Saturday workday.

"I don't know *anything* about him," she said. "My mother hadn't spoken to him for years. He was kind of a . . . family outcast."

"Your mother must have told you something."

"We always knew that my mother had a brother, much older than she. She told us he was dead, killed back in Germany. She never went into much detail."

Nick shook his head back and forth. He took a seat next to her. "There has to be more to it than that. Jessica, your brother and my friend are dead, and for all I know we could be next. *Think*. What else did she tell you? There's got to be more."

"There is no more!" she blurted out. "My mother's family was from Germany. They were there at the start of the war. My uncle . . . I don't know—he was in Germany the entire war. He might have been a Nazi or something, but I don't see how that's important."

"Why do you think this?"

"My mother said he was in the military. I don't know any more than that."

"A Nazi," said Nick emphatically, remembering Alex's earlier theory. "But this was no run-of-the-mill Nazi."

"I don't know what he was. My mother told us he had a desk job. That's all she ever said."

"And this is absolutely everything you know?"

She frowned. "There's one other thing . . ."

She got to her feet and stepped from the room. Nick felt deflated. He had somehow assumed she knew more. Much more. What this Nazi business added he couldn't see.

Nick crept to the windows and peered carefully through the shades. Paranoia was working overtime. He did not want to be in that house for more than another ten or fifteen minutes.

Jessica returned momentarily, holding an envelope. She opened it and removed a paper. "Your visit the other day got me curious. I did some digging around through some of my mother's papers and I came across something strange. I didn't even know I had it."

"What is it?" he asked, approaching her.

"A certificate of ownership to a box at Hahn and Konauer." She saw his confusion. "A private bank in Geneva, Switzerland."

Nick took the paper and noticed the date. The certificate had been issued two years ago. "You didn't know your mother kept this account?"

"No, I didn't."

"Was your mother mixed up with her brother somehow?"

"What do you mean, *mixed up* with him? She never saw him. Whatever business he was involved in, she had nothing to do with it."

"So what business did she have in Geneva?"

"I don't know, okay?" She glared at him. "Who do you think you are anyway—interrogating me in my own home. I'm the one who should be asking *you* questions. You're the one who showed up at my door the other day talking about inheritances."

Nick felt dangerously close to losing it. He instead kept quiet and forced himself to cool down. He needed her help, and she deserved his. He *had* been the one to first approach her.

"I'm sorry," he said softly. "I'm just trying to put things together here, that's all." He looked back down to the banking certificate and quickly said, "So you have no idea what might be in this box?"

"No idea," she replied, a measure of calm returning in her voice. "I'd like to find out."

Nick nodded but wondered if he was getting the full story. He looked back down at the bank document. It was no different than the ones he had found in the old man's garage. Whatever dwelled in that box had been untouched for four years now.

He looked back up at her. "Does the name Otto Kranzhoffer sound familiar?"

She shook her head. "Not at all. Why?"

The name on the greeting card he had found in her uncle's home. He hoped she wouldn't ask how he had gotten the name. "I think he may have known your uncle. I've found a greeting card sent by him to Holtzmann. It sounds as if they may have been friends."

"I've never known anyone by that name."

He nodded and tried to organize his thoughts as he sat back down on the couch. "I was hoping when I came here that you might be able to shed some light on why the FBI would be so interested in this man."

"The FBI? What? What are you talking about?"

He told her of his discussion with the FBI and their vaguely explained relationship with Jacobs. She leaned forward on the couch, her fingers wrestling with themselves.

"What business would the FBI have with my uncle?" she asked.

"That's what I'm trying to find out. Why would they set him up so comfortably?"

"I don't follow you."

"Holtzmann was worth twenty-two and half million dollars. We're not talking about any ordinary estate here. He obviously had some sort of . . . influence."

"This estate is worth twenty-two million? My God, why didn't you tell me?"

"You threw me out too quick." He stared at her. "Why? Would it have mattered?"

"It might have, yes. I thought this was all a hoax."

"No hoax, Jessica. Not after my friend gets blown to bits in the middle of my apartment."

"When did this happen?"

"Last night. They tried to get me a few hours after that, but I got lucky."

She seemed to bristle in her seat.

"Well, I've told you what I know. I don't want anything to do with this anymore."

"I'm afraid it may be a little late for that."

She gave him a sharp look.

Nick tried to speak softly. This was getting tricky. "Someone doesn't want your uncle being investigated. First they tried to kill me, but now they know I'm hiding. It looks like they may be changing strategies."

Her eyes were steady, but her cheeks once again seemed to be losing color. "Keep going."

"These people don't want private investigators digging around this estate, but they have no way of knowing how many PI's are involved. So they have an easier solution. If they can insure that there are no heirs, then they think that the heir finders will have no incentive to investigate the estate anymore. They think we'll drop it—"

"But I didn't sign any contract," she said. "They must know I haven't made a claim on the estate."

"But they still feel threatened by the possibility of you suddenly deciding to *become* an heir. If you do, all this goes to court and everything I've learned about your uncle becomes public information. As long as you're alive to sign another contract—"

"This is crazy," she said sharply. She stood. "Look, I have to go. I don't think we need to talk anymore."

"Your life's in danger," said Nick, not budging. "They came after Matt, and they'll come after you. Don't try to ignore this, Jessica. You'll end up dead."

She sat back down out of necessity now. Her eyes were glassy and ready to tear up. Nick regretted being so blunt but saw little choice. He entered the kitchen and found fresh tissue. She pushed his hand away when he offered it.

"Why did you have to show up here in the first place?" she asked, not looking at him. "Why didn't you just leave it alone? None of this would have happened if you hadn't dug this up."

Nick stood there and felt a twinge in his stomach. She was partially right. It could have been some other heir-finding firm that solved the case, but the fact was, it had been Merchant and Associates who had found her brother and filed those papers. As much as he wanted to tell her it wasn't his fault, the words just would not come.

"Fine," he said. "I'm not blameless here. But it has to work both ways. If I have to take a measure of responsibility for your brother, then I also have to take responsibility for our lives too."

She dabbed at her eyes a bit but didn't respond. Nick walked to the front window and stood for two minutes, staring out at nothing. Alex had said Matt Von Rohr had been so excited when she'd told him of the inheritance. Young, engaged to be married, and now incapable of anything.

Jessica was looking down, refusing to look at him. Considering what she had been through in the last hour, he thought she was holding up remarkably well.

"Listen," he said softly, "do you honestly think I would've touched this if I had known what was going to happen? You can't possibly think that."

"Someone has to take the blame."

"You're right. I think whoever killed your brother should." He sat next to her. "Look, I *will* find out what's going on here, one way or another. You can help me or you can run, but please *don't* ignore this."

"I really wish you would—"

Nick hushed her. He had heard it over her voice. It was an insignificant sound, but it resounded clearly in the still of the house, a hollow sound, a dull thud that vanished as quickly as it came. Under normal circumstances, he wouldn't have given it a second thought, but this situation was nowhere near normal.

He crept to the front blinds, his hand on the gun in his jacket. Two men were on opposite sides of her front porch. He looked at her quickly.

"Expecting someone?" he whispered.

Her eyes were wide and confused. She shook her head.

Nick reached for the bank certificate and shoved it down a pocket as the doorbell rang. He quickly approached her. "Come on."

He led her to the back door. The doorbell chimed again, and he pulled the gun free.

"What the hell are you doing?" she whispered, stepping away from him.

He didn't reply as he quietly opened the back door. Behind the property, perhaps thirty yards away, fenced farmland. Cornstalks, eight feet tall and thick.

Nick was about to speak when something suddenly slammed against the front door. Wood cracked loudly as another solid impact quickly followed.

Nick lunged for Jessica's hand and pulled her out the back door. They reached the field in seconds, ducking under the fence just as the back door of the Von Rohr home flew open behind them. The two of them ran fifteen yards blindly through the field, then veered abruptly to the right. An explosion of automatic weapon fire suddenly tore the air, ripping through the field behind them. Nick instantly pulled her flat to the ground. Several long seconds passed before silence settled around them.

Jessica was breathing so quickly that Nick had to hold a finger to her lips. She was squeezing his hand tightly, but he hardly noticed. A sound came into focus. A rustling, coming closer. The men had entered the field, pushing through the stalks after them.

Nick pulled her up and to the left. They hurried forward for half a minute, then stopped, collapsed to their knees, and listened. Nothing. The air again exploded with gunfire. They threw themselves flat as shattered husks rained down on them. Two seconds later it stopped.

Nick gripped the pistol tightly. There was no way he could get close enough to get off an accurate shot. He looked down at the ground, his eyes darting about the dirt, and listened. The air had gone still again. Silent. Jessica opened her mouth to speak, but Nick again motioned for her to remain quiet. Somewhere behind them, the gunmen were still as statues, listening, searching out their location. Absolute silence settled over the field, only a light breeze rustling the stalks. For what seemed like several minutes, nothing stirred.

The cell phone in Nick's pocket suddenly rang. He grabbed for it wildly, flipping it free to the dirt. Two full rings sounded, shattering the silence, before he could grab it. They looked at each other in horror.

Nick heard a distant movement, and then they were in the middle of a third barrage, their faces down against the dirt as the stalks whipped and spit around them. Nick raised his head when it stopped. Somewhere behind them—or was it in front of them?—maybe thirty or forty yards away—the stalks were snapping and rustling. He pulled her up to a crouch, and again they ran, staying as low as possible.

This time they kept moving—for how long Nick had no idea. All frame of reference was gone. They ran blindly, Nick pulling her along.

They finally stopped and ducked low again. He looked at her. Her face, her hair—her entire body—was coated with dust. Her eyes were wide with fear, but her panting was no worse than his own. He felt thankful she was a runner. He wished he could say the same for himself. His heart was slamming his chest, his lungs were in flames. He tried to swallow but couldn't. He studied the dirt, straining to hear. Nothing stirred except cornstalks, swaying gently in the warm autumn breeze. At first all he could hear was the thump of his own heartbeat. But then a distant, high-pitched noise intruded over the silence. He wasn't imagining it. Police sirens—slowly coming closer by the sound of it.

They heard a stirring from somewhere in the field not too far from them. Their attackers were on the move again and making no effort to be subtle about it. Nick gripped the pistol and waited, his finger on the trigger. They were running—he was certain of it—but in the opposite direction. They had heard the sirens too.

The two of them stood still for another minute, letting the sound draw nearer. Then Nick took her arm as they started toward the back of the field.

CHAPTER 18

IN THE MANHATTAN office of the Federal Bureau of Investigation, Edmund Arminger reached for the phone and got his boss in Washington.

"Anything new?" asked Gordon.

"We've got a confession from the attorney in Columbia County," replied Arminger. "Merchant and Associates paid him ten thousand for the Jacobs file, just as we suspected."

"Have teletypes on Merchant been sent?"

"Every department in fifty states. We're talking with San Francisco, Des Moines, and New York City and sending our profiles and photographs. I'm glad we're finally—"

"And you've spoken with the newspapers?"

"We're all set," replied Arminger. "I've spoken with Directors Hampton and Rivera and gotten commitments for half a dozen agents from each of their jurisdictions. We'll get him."

Gordon felt a bit irritated. "I'd like you to confer with me before implementing any future tactical maneuvers, Edmund. This has gotten too big to be making rash movements. I don't give a damn what the situation is—you let me know next time. My neck may be on the line here and if that's the case, so is yours. Are we clear on that?"

"Very clear," replied Arminger, after a brief but noticeable pause.

"Good," said Gordon. "I've spoken with the San Francisco Police Department. Seems there was something to that story Merchant gave us. Someone did blow up his apartment. His secretary—woman by the name of Rosemary Penn—was killed."

"He was telling the truth, then," said Arminger. "What the hell is going on with all this?"

"Let me tell you about my meeting with the President," replied Gordon. "*And* a surprise guest." The director told Arminger of his discussion in the White House.

"What do you make of it?" asked Arminger.

"Well, Newland's always had the President's ear," said Gordon. "On the surface, it's simple. The senator's committee is being jeopardized by the possibility of Jacobs's true identity being revealed. Neither the President nor Newland wants that to happen. From what I heard, I don't either. In which case we need to find Merchant and put him away."

"And is there something *beneath* the surface?"

Gordon paused for a long four or five seconds. "I don't know," he finally said. "The whole damn thing's an embarrassment. Closing a protected witness file shouldn't have been so damn difficult, but somehow we managed to screw it up, and now we have Newland to deal with. Committee or not, I don't like him being privy to our operations."

Arminger leaned back in his chair, frowning thoughtfully. "You think there's something else here, Arthur?"

"I didn't say that. But something doesn't feel right to me. Nothing I can put my finger on at the moment."

"So what do we do?"

"We'll do what we've been instructed to do—find Merchant as quick as we can. But that doesn't mean we can't do some digging of our own. If there *is* something more here, we want to make damn sure it doesn't sneak up and bite us."

"I agree," said Arminger. "I have another interesting bit of news out of Sacramento. The signed heir to the Jacobs fortune was murdered earlier today in his home. Merchant's out of the money. These heir finders are turning on each other."

"That's the obvious conclusion. Too obvious, I'd say. No, this may travel beyond a small group of PI's." Gordon paused and left the line quiet for a moment. "This murder may turn out to be a positive development. Now that Merchant has no client, we may not have to concern ourselves with a court hearing. I suspect he may be over the border by now anyway."

"I plan to find him if he's not."

"Someone will."


Night was falling quickly in Schenectady. Congested skies had smothered the city throughout the day, but dusk had at last brought a break in the clouds. The dry air hung heavy in the warm autumn evening.

Alex didn't care enough to notice. She drove south on State Street toward Albany. Her plan was basic—to find out whatever she could on Ludwig Holtzmann. She wouldn't be returning to the apartment until she did just that.

Her afternoon had been spent on the phone. Her calls had confirmed one fact, albeit one she already knew: the bankers of Switzerland were obsessively protective of their clients. She had contacted seven banks holding Holtzmann accounts—three in Geneva, four in Zurich—and received seven remarkably similar reactions. It had been a common refrain: without an original letter of authorization in her possession, she could be given no information pertaining to account holders or their accounts. Her trusty assortment of clever phone ruses, which normally worked so well with American banks, had gotten her nowhere. One banker had even hung up on her during her dead-relative sob story.

She made a right on Dove Street. If nothing else, she could now scratch the bankers of Switzerland from her list of contacts. She hadn't expected a treasure trove of information from them anyway. Her main hope that morning lay in her next stop.


The Balom Holocaust Museum was located behind a synagogue that had stood in midtown Albany for over fifty years. The synagogue had recently been renovated with nearly a quarter million dollars of worshipers' funds, its dry-rotted wood being replaced with new lumber. The congregation was largely elderly, a handful having faithfully attended since the onset of World War II. The current rabbi had survived one year in Auschwitz.

In the parking lot, Alex cut the engine and thought. Nick had pulled 270 of the bank documents from Jacobs's garage. She had counted them. On exactly 52 of these, "secondary holders" were listed. Ludwig

Holtzmann's name on top, the secondary holders' names beneath. She reached into her portfolio for the hastily scribbled list she had compiled earlier of the 52 names. With luck those names were about to confirm one of her nagging suspicions.

A wind was coming up from the east, scattering dead leaves about the parking lot. They crunched beneath her shoes, but the sounds didn't register. She combed her way down the list mentally as she walked to the entrance of the museum. *Saul Weinstein . . . Elsia Berman . . . Meir Ibrahim . . . Rebecca Wershowitz . . .* She felt strangely uncomfortable. They had speculated that Jacobs had been a Nazi. The names on the list sounded Jewish. A murky picture was developing, and she wasn't entirely sure she wanted to see it.

She pushed through the entrance of the Balom Museum and looked around. Old people lounged about on saggy cloth couches. Meticulously detailed murals filled the walls. The place looked more like a community center than a museum. She approached the counter, which was manned by a fortyish man in a lightweight sweater.

"Hi, my name's Debra Ramos," Alex said. "I spoke with Benjamin Roth this afternoon about some research."

"I'm Ben Roth." They shook hands. "Good to meet you. Shall we go to my office?"

They walked through the heart of the center, Roth greeting several people as they passed through. Alex followed him into a small office on the opposite side of the main lobby.

"Would I be prying to ask what this research is for?" asked Roth, sitting at his desk.

"Not at all," replied Alex. "I'm doing some genealogy on some prominent Jewish families. I suspect that some of the ancestors of the families I'm researching may have died in the Holocaust. We're trying to help them recover some assets."

Roth placed his elbows on his desk and nodded intently. "I'm happy to help with that. Wonderful that after fifty-odd years *someone* is making an effort regarding asset recovery. If you're trying to get these assets out of Switzerland, all I can say is good luck."

Alex removed the list from her pocket and laid it out flat on the desk. "I've a list of about fifty names of people who may have died during the war. I guess it's pretty much a long shot to find anything on them."

Roth took the list and scanned it quickly. "Not necessarily. What may help us is the fact that after fifty years of efforts by Jewish and Allied organizations, we now have a fairly complete picture of just who did perish in the Holocaust." He turned on a computer. "We may come up with some questionable name matches, but let's give it a shot."

"You've got some sort of a list on-line?"

"Oh yes. It's recorded in books, too, of course, but we have quite a few names to look up here. Shall we just start at the top?"

Alex nodded, pulling her chair around to get a better view.

"Hildi . . . Eva . . . Strauch," said Roth, reading from the list and tapping the letters in.

Alex looked about the office as Roth manned the keyboard. It was the first time she could recall ever having conducted research in a Jewish institution. The museum felt foreign to her, a glimpse into a world she knew little about.

"Here's a match," said Roth.

Alex's surprise made her pause. "Really?"

"Yes," said Roth. He read from the screen. "Hildi Eva Strauch, born 1897, Dresden, Germany. Daughter of Jaco and Maria Strauch. Died 1943. Treblinka concentration camp."

Alex took the sheet and placed a check next to the woman's name. "Let's try another."

Roth examined the list and typed in the name. "Here we are. Albert Saul Mamin, born June 1885, Krakow, Poland." He ran his finger down the screen. "Died in 1942. Auschwitz concentration camp."

Alex marked the sheet again, then looked for the next name. "How about Frances Gerta Rosen?"

Roth typed the name and waited. "This may not be a match. No— there she is. Frances G. Rosen, born 1926, Mannheim, Germany. Died 1945 in Auschwitz." Roth looked at Alex. "All these long shots of yours seem to be coming in."

Alex scooted her chair forward. "Do you have fifteen or twenty minutes to make a run down this entire list?"

"I can give you twenty minutes or so."

"Mira Ana Birowicz . . ."


Back in the car, Alex counted the checkmarks. Of the fifty-two names, forty-seven had been marked and traced to the death camps. That afternoon she had hoped to find information on two or three. She folded the paper up and stuffed it in her pocket. Nick had told her that Jacobs had seven full boxes of the letters in his garage. The two hundred or so taken that night, then, were barely a fraction of the total. The partners had speculated about Jacobs's past, and now they knew massive numbers of Swiss bank accounts were involved. It seemed likely that their Nazi theory was not theory but fact.

She frowned as she stopped at a red light. As heir finders, they had trained themselves not to care about the sources of assets. The fact that assets existed was the only point that was supposed to matter. But this was simply too chilling to ignore. If the FBI was so panicked to keep Jacobs a secret, then his past must be something truly awful. She saw no other conclusion to be drawn.

She drove back to the apartment, purchasing a newspaper from a street rack and glancing at the headlines casually. The President's latest whipping boy was tobacco, and Yeltsin had just checked back into the hospital. Liver problems, undoubtedly.

She entered her unit and put the paper aside. World events could wait until much later. She clicked the laptop on. She needed to put her findings down in some sort of orderly fashion. She took the mouse and created a file, naming it Jacobs 1.

Her phone suddenly rang. Nick checking in, most likely.

"Hello?"

"Hello, I would like to speak with Debra Holtzmann."

Alex paused. The female voice had a thick French accent and sounded very distant.

"This is Debra Holtzmann," she replied.

"My name is Simone Giron. I am with the Alban-Witz bank in Geneva."

Alex blanked for a moment, then remembered that she had left her phone number with one of the banks she had called that morning. She grabbed a pen and paper and took a seat.

"Oh, yes—yes, Miss Giron. Thank you for calling me back."

"Our director wishes to speak with you regarding your inquiries."

"Uh, sure . . ."

Alex waited anxiously, half expecting to be berated. To her surprise, the voice that came on the line was exceedingly pleasant.

"Hello, Miss Holtzmann. My name is Victor Chagnon. I am managing director with Alban-Witz."

"Yes, Mr. Chagnon."

"Ms. Giron passed your name along to me. I understand you were inquiring into certain bank accounts?"

"Yes, I was." She decided to go with the old standby story again. "Let me explain. My uncle recently passed away here in the United States, and my brother and I have found some letters of authorization to several accounts in your bank. We're hoping to make a claim on these accounts very soon. I was hoping to obtain some basic information regarding them before we proceed."

"Certainly. I'm happy to help with that. Give me the number of the account your uncle held so I can pull the account information."

"There are several, actually." She read from one of the letters. "The first is ZA283-676752. I'd first simply like to know if this account is even open anymore."

"One moment, please."

Alex smiled at her luck as she waited. She had at least found *one* banker who wasn't a nut about confidentiality.

"Here it is," said Chagnon. "Your uncle was Ludwig Holtzmann, correct?"

"That's him. The account is open?"

"Yes, it is. And showing a rather sizable balance."

"Really. What does it show?"

"It shows your uncle has approximately three million Swiss francs. Or roughly one and a half million American dollars."

Alex's jaw dropped. She had chosen this account randomly. A lucky pick or were all the accounts just as large?

"Miss Holtzmann?"

"Yes," she said, snapping back. "I'm sorry. I wasn't expecting this."

"Of course," Chagnon replied, as friendly as could be. "Congratulations. You say you hold the original authorization letter to this account?"

"Yes, I do."

"Perhaps you and your brother are planning to visit Geneva and make your claim then?"

"Yes, we are," Alex said, still a bit dumbfounded by that balance.

"I would be happy to meet with you and settle this matter. And might I ask, Miss Holtzmann, your brother's first name?"

She paused, considering the relevance. "Nicholas," she finally replied.

"Ah yes," said Chagnon. "And I wonder what would you say to me if I called you a filthy liar?"

Alex paused, temporarily thrown by the question. "I beg your pardon?"

"You heard me quite clearly. You're lying to me. You have no brother, and your name isn't Holtzmann, is it?" The voice had taken on a decidedly vicious tone.

"I'm afraid you're mistaken," said Alex.

"I am not mistaken," replied Chagnon. "Nor am I a fool. Who are you? Who do you work for?"

"Mr. Chagnon, I really don't know what you're—"

"Don't play games with me!" he shouted. "I want to know who you are! Are you a friend of the pig Holtzmann?"

"I really don't—"

"No," snarled the voice. "*You* listen. I want to know who you are and who you work for. Talk! Give me the truth."

"Mr. Chagnon, I'm afraid you've mistaken me for someone else."

She heard Chagnon exhale into the phone.

"An accomplished liar," he said. "Very well. Tell Taylor his plan will fail. I've taken precautions. The end is coming soon for him."

The line clicked. He was gone.


Alex leaned back in front of the window, her eyes closed. The shades were drawn open, revealing dark city streets. She stayed that way for ten minutes and thought.

Finally she sat in front of the laptop and cradled her chin in her hand. She brought her hands to the keyboard and began to type. . . .

*Tell Taylor his plan will fail. I've taken precautions. The end is coming soon for him.*

She leaned back and stared at the words. So important, yet so utterly meaningless. Taylor. He had become ubiquitous. They had caught him now on an answering machine tape, in PI photos, and in an unexpected call from an irate Swiss banker. The name was springing up everywhere.

Alex reached for the bank letter from which she had given Chagnon the account number. Scrawled neatly at the bottom was a signature— Charles Chagnon, Managing Director. She did a double take. Victor had said *he* was managing director.

Alex cleared the surface of the kitchen table and brought her head down. Her temples were starting to throb. She felt as if she had reached mental saturation. She reached for the newspaper again.

This time she immediately saw the headline.

She bolted to her feet and gasped. The article was at the bottom of the front page, off to the right and highlighted in modest type. It's title was smaller and almost matter-of-fact—a local-interest story. She read it again. The *Albany Times Union* declared it like a death sentence: PRIVATE INVESTIGATOR SOUGHT IN SHOOTING OF POLICE OFFICER.

The cab maneuvered its way through the crush of evening traffic and reached its destination at Twenty-second and Tenth. The man named Malloy paid his fare and immediately entered the corner restaurant. His boss was seated facing the doorway. A pickle and a splotch of ketchup were all that remained of dinner. Malloy slid into a booth and nodded at him, receiving a frigid stare in return. Thick black eyebrows, black beard and mustache, dark eyes. Add an eye patch and a Jolly Roger hat and Malloy realized he would be looking at the perfect Halloween mask.

Kragen eyed his guest steadily as he drained the remainder of an iced tea. "Regnier just told me what happened. This whole thing's a bad joke."

Malloy wanted to look away but couldn't. The stare was withering him. He had hoped the anger had passed, but apparently a full stomach wasn't helping matters. "It's a joke," he agreed.

"Only I'm not laughing, Malloy. These numbskulls are costing me a lot of money."

The diner was still full with the Saturday evening dinner crowd, the noise level rising proportionately. Kragen slapped down fifteen dollars and slid from the booth.

"Outside."

They took seats at one of the tiny round tables on the street. Kragen found his tinted glasses.

"Next time something like this happens, I wish these idiots would have sense enough to lie to me. Tell me they went there and nobody was home. That way I don't have to think about all the money I should have in my pocket right now. What's the matter with those guys?"

Malloy remained silent. What was he supposed to say? There was no answer that was going to make it all better. *He* wasn't the one who had hired them.

"You're not gonna make excuses. Smart man." Kragen looked to the pedestrians. "I knew I should have sent you and Regnier down there."

"Where is Regnier anyway?"

"Los Angeles. At least we won't have to worry about that business."

The waitress came by. Kragen shook his head sourly. Malloy was dying for a cocktail but chose a mineral water instead.

"So tell me about these plates," said Kragen.

Malloy leaned forward on his elbows, relieved to be moving on to a new subject. "Seven cars on the street, not counting the ones in neighbors' driveways. Six owner owned, one with rental stickers. They checked the six with a contact at the state Office of Vehicle Registration in Iowa—all six were registered to people living there on that street. That leaves the rental. They went to the rental office at the airport but some girl at the counter was giving them lip about confidential information and all this other crap. They couldn't get her talking because the place was crawling with people."

Kragen's eyes widened behind the dark lenses. "Back up. Why didn't they just break into the car, for Christ's sake? The damn rental papers were probably sitting right there on the dash."

"Said they didn't have time. The cops showed."

"You're telling me they had time to copy down seven plates, but they couldn't find time to smash into one of 'em and check the glove box?"

Malloy raised his hands a bit and shrugged. "I don't know, okay? They said people were coming out of houses."

"Oh boy. Chased off by a bunch of hick housewives. That's great."

"Not to worry, though. They'll be flashing badges at the car rental place first thing in the morning. It had to have been his car. He's using a fake ID and credit card."

Kragen shook his head. "Yeah, and he's probably got ten of 'em. What if he paid cash and signed the papers John Smith. Then what, Malloy?"

"He's still got to show some sort of ID. We're gonna know first thing in the morning."

"We better. If we don't pull this off in four days, the deal's off."

"*Four* days? Why so soon?"

"Something big is supposed to happen by the end of the week. They're not telling me what it is or what it's all about, but this all comes to a head on Friday. We got ninety hours to do our thing or they're yanking their offer."

"We'll do it. I got a good feeling about it."

"Better be right. From here on, anybody who fucks up is out of the action for good. Pass that on to those idiots in Iowa." Kragen got up and brushed at his jacket. "Call me the second you hear on this plate. We'll need to move quick."

Malloy nodded, then watched his boss disappear into the crowd.

## CHAPTER 19

THE TAXI TRAVELED east over the Des Moines River, just north of the U.S. district courthouse and the police station. The driver stopped in the middle of a strip of faded motels and thrift shops and waited for his two passengers to exit the vehicle.

They rented a room in a plainly furnished, nondescript motel. Nick sat on one of the double beds and stared at the television screen. Jessica Von Rohr was on the other bed, sitting curled up, her head down. Her nylons were shredded, her skirt spotted with dirt. She hadn't spoken for nearly half an hour, and out of desperation Nick had turned to the television. He wasn't watching or hearing it, though; he was just sitting numbly, trying to think.

"We have to go to the police."

Nick looked up at her. She was standing at the foot of his bed.

"The police can't do much," he replied evenly. "They'll write us up a neat little report and send us on our way. You need to stop and think about this for a second."

She had the phone in her hand. "Yes, I need a taxi at . . ." She covered the receiver. "What was the address of this place?"

Nick reached over to the phone base and disconnected her. "Will you just wait a second?"

"Let go of that."

"No. Listen to me for a minute."

She glared at him before tossing the phone down and walking away. He spoke to her back.

"The police are not going to be able to help us, Jessica. Believe me— this is far, far beyond anything they've ever dealt with. If anyone should be involved here, it's the FBI, and frankly, I don't think they're very inclined to help us on this."

"*Us,*" she said, crossing her arms on her chest. "You keep saying us. I think these people are much more interested in *you* than me. They blew up your apartment and now they followed you here."

"They didn't come out to your doorstep looking for me."

"They followed you—"

"They didn't follow me," said Nick, his anger building. "They don't even know where I am. That's why they decided to come for you instead. That's why they came for your brother, Jessica. Look, I explained this to you already. No living heirs, no investigations. If they can't find the PI's, they'll try to find the heirs. That's the deal."

She ran her hands through her hair. "I can't believe this is happening. I can't *believe* this! I never wanted to be involved in this."

Nick's patience snapped like a pencil lead. He was almost shouting now. "And you think I do? I didn't ask to be a part of this, okay? It's *your* family's past that everyone's so pissed off about. Yeah, I may have stepped on this land mine, but it's *your* family who buried it. Go ahead and blame it all on me if that helps you hide, but this all goes back to your uncle. That's right—*your uncle.*"

She stared at him, a stunned look on her face. He pressed forward.

"Two people are dead," he said, stepping toward her. "When are you going to realize that, yes, you're involved now?"

Her eyes flared. She stood trembling slightly before sinking to the bed. Despite her best efforts, the tears came in powerful sobs. Nick walked past her to the bathroom and turned the faucets on. His face was hot. He filled his hands with cool water and doused himself. His cheeks were red with scratches from the cornfield, his hair matted together. He was dying for a drink, something with a nasty bite.

He sat on the other bed as he dabbed his face dry with a towel. She had gathered herself quickly, defiantly brushing away the tears. Neither of them said anything for ten minutes. She rose to her feet and went into the bathroom. Nick didn't watch her but he could hear the faucets start up again.

"Fine," she said, leaning over the sink. "You made your point. We don't go to the police. So what *should* we do?"

"I didn't say I had a lot of other ideas," said Nick, with a helpless shrug. "This isn't exactly your garden-variety situation."

They both went quiet. Jessica finally broke the silence as she was looking into the mirror.

"My uncle's past is something I haven't wanted to deal with. It's not easy to face up to the fact that you're related to a war criminal. . . ."

"War criminal?" said Nick, placing the towel aside. He approached her and stood in the doorway. "You never said anything about a war criminal."

She walked past him and sat on the edge of the bed. He followed her closely.

"Care to elaborate on that?"

She exhaled and glanced up at him. "Look, we have to come to an understanding here. We tell each other everything we know. No secrets. You agree to that?"

"I've told you everything *I* know. Sounds like you're the one withholding things."

She gave him a frustrated look. "Put yourself in my shoes, okay? One second I'm relaxing on the couch after a hard day's work and the next thing I know my brother is dead. And then there was our little jog through the cornfield. This may be another day at the office for you, but it's not for me."

Despite himself, Nick gave a helpless little laugh. "Believe me, running for my life from armed thugs is nothing I'm used to. I work in an office, just like you do. Spend most of my time doing research at courthouses, talking to little old ladies on the phone."

Her lips slowly curled upward. "You're shattering my images of the modern-day PI."

"It's not that glamorous."

"Maybe I should be holding the gun then."

"I used to be a cop. I can handle myself. But that doesn't mean you shouldn't be carrying a weapon too."

"I've been around guns," she said, curling up a leg and sitting on it. "You'll need to talk to your connections and get me one too."

Nick nodded. He was all for that. All he needed to do was find these mythical connections. He sat down next to her at the foot of the bed. "So what's this about a war criminal?"

She looked down at her lap. "My mother said her brother was a war criminal who'd been imprisoned."

"Why didn't you just tell me this earlier?"

"Because it was none of your damn business, that's why."

"What crimes was your uncle imprisoned for?"

"I don't know. My mother never said."

"Imprisoned where? Germany?"

She nodded.

"This sheds a different light on it," he said, unsure what that light was. "What else?"

"Nothing else. That's everything I know."

He kept his eyes locked on hers. "You fed me that line earlier. Why do I get the feeling you're just tossing me little tidbits here and there? Why don't you come clean with me?"

"I *am* coming clean," she replied firmly. "I swear to you. What reason do I have to hide things? I'm in as much danger as you are, right? Probably more."

Nick purposely held his stare an extra second before standing and approaching the nightstand. He pulled out a phone book.

"Ever been to New York?" he asked, knowing the answer already from her background check.

"Why do you ask?"

"Because you're going back there tonight with me."

"For what?"

"We're going to meet up with my partner and figure out what to do. You got yourself a free flight back East, courtesy of Merchant and Associates."

This time it was her fingers that disconnected the phone.

"There's no way I'm going like this." She stood and ran her hands down herself. "I look like a bum."

Nick checked her over. She was five foot four, all right—in heels. Somehow, in her dirty blouse and torn nylons, she didn't look half bad to him. Not bad at all.

"Is there a city nearby with a decent department store?" he asked.

"Ames. About ten minutes down the highway. They're open until ten on Saturdays."

"We'll take a cab there then. After we get clothes and a couple of travel bags, we'll go straight to the airport. Till then we sit tight."

"I have to call my office and let them know I'll be out for a while."

"A long while, I'd say. If they press you for details, I wouldn't get into it with them."

A car door slammed out in the street. Nick checked through the curtains. Jessica grabbed the remote and clicked the television off.

"I told you what I know—it's your turn now. I want to hear about everything you've found."

"That ain't much."

"Then it won't take you too long. I'm all ears, Mr. PI."

Nick sat across from her on the bed and started talking.

The Institute for Historical Review was an unremarkable little building situated between a Russian bakery and a twenty-year-old furniture store in downtown Albany. Three blocks east of City Hall, the institute was rarely frequented by pedestrians, but that would change today.

Alex had never taken much notice of the building the dozens of times she had been downtown, but now the modest two-story Victorian on Columbia Street stood out like a beacon. She found parking down the street and pulled to the curb.

She sat for a moment in silence as a fly buzzed about the inside of the car. She was thinking of her mother again, and the pit of her stomach had contracted accordingly. She knew her mother didn't read the newspapers. Her television time was almost exclusively dedicated to the Spanish channel. She probably wouldn't know of the charges against Nick, but with her blabbermouth friends, that could change quickly. And if one partner of Merchant and Associates was now a wanted fugitive, could the other be far behind? The thought of putting her mother through something like that was enough to make her shudder.

She stepped from the car, feeling slightly nauseous. She had called Nick immediately with the news but hadn't been able to reach him. Her partner didn't go anywhere without his phone. She couldn't think of a single comforting reason why he wouldn't be answering it.

A bell chimed against the back of the door as she entered the building. She looked around, a bit confused. Despite the distinguished title, the place had the look of a used bookstore. The room was dusty and poorly lit, with rows of dented book stands forming narrow passageways for several browsing patrons. The musty scent of aged manuscripts filled the air.

A lanky man of about forty emerged from a row. He approached Alex with a friendly smile, his arms holding several worn volumes.

"You must be Ms. Ramos."

"Yes—Debra Ramos," she replied, offering her hand. "Are you John?"

"Yes, I am—John Franklin. We spoke this morning."

"I appreciate you sticking around so late, John."

"Oh not a problem. Our senior researcher, Mr. Gruber, is here now, as usual." He brought a hand to the side of his mouth. "Old guy practically lives here. He'd probably stay all night if we'd let him."

"Well I'm definitely grateful," Alex said, scanning the interior. "What kind of business is this exactly?"

"We're a state-funded, nonprofit group which does historical research, mostly for universities and local government agencies." He noticed her expression. "Our funding hasn't exactly been abundant lately. Can you follow me please?"

Alex followed him back through the tight rows of books and into a small, poorly lit office. In the center of the room was a large, neatly organized desk behind which sat a bearded elderly gentleman. The man looked up from his papers and nodded at Alex with a cordial smile.

"This is Paul Gruber, Ms. Ramos," said Franklin. He turned to the seated gentleman. "She's the one who wanted the research done on Ludwig Holtzmann."

"Good to meet you," said the old man, smiling again. "You'll be pleased with what I've found."

"I'm very interested in seeing it," Alex replied.

The old man rose to his feet slowly and with great effort. "Come with me."

Alex followed him up a narrow wooden staircase and into a low-ceilinged attic. Here, neatly organized in domino-like book stands, were thousands of manuscripts and volumes. The old man walked purposefully to a desk and took a seat, motioning Alex to a chair on his left.

"An interesting figure you're researching," said Mr. Gruber, leafing through a folder. "I confess that I normally consider myself quite the expert when the subject is World War II personalities, but I admit I was a bit thrown by our dear Herr Holtzmann. It took me some time to find anything at all on him."

Alex watched him pull a single sheet of paper. He put on a pair of thick-lensed glasses and cleared his throat.

"Here we are—Ludwig Wilhelm Holtzmann. Born in Germany in 1913, died there in 1997."

"Died in Germany in 1997," repeated Alex thoughtfully. "How do you know this for sure?"

"The records verify it."

"Records can be falsified," she said softly. She saw his confused look. "I'm sorry. Please go on."

Gruber turned back to his notes. "Holtzmann joined the National Socialist party in 1934."

"National Socialist," said Alex. "A Nazi, you're saying."

"That's correct. A banker actually. Basically a bureaucrat of the worst kind. Received a war deferment in 1939—bad eyes supposedly. Humph. Whether this was a genuine infirmity or simply another case of a privileged party member having the right connections, we can't know. The latter I would guess." He found another sheet and extended it to her. "A photograph . . ."

She was anxious to see this. A studio shot—the young Gerald Jacobs. The face was as bland and generic as the biography she had just been given. A serious expression, a youthful face without a trace of humor. Tight, thin lips and bony jowls. The beady little eyes had a kind of subdued arrogance.

She handed the photo back and felt disappointed. She saw nothing remotely interesting about Ludwig Holtzmann. Certainly nothing notable enough to make him the center of all this attention.

"I'm confused about something," she said. "If he was just a banker, just a common bureaucrat, how is it you found anything on him at all?"

The old man removed his glasses and rubbed his eyes slowly. "I'm sorry. I'm afraid I'm not being very clear." He stood and walked toward a bare wall. "Perhaps a bit of footage can clear things up better than a forgetful old man can." He reached the wall and pulled down a hanging screen.

Alex swiveled in her chair, confused. "What's this?"

"You'll see," he said.

She let out a breath, impatient but trying to be courteous. She wanted information, not home movies. She opened her mouth to speak, but the old man had doused the lights. A film projector clicked into motion as a ray of light was projected to the screen.

"Mr. Gruber, I really don't—"

A blaring of trumpets silenced her. She looked to the screen. A grainy and dark image formed. The deep baritone of thousands of male voices suddenly boomed from the speaker. The picture focused on the dagger-beaked head of a bird as the camera slowly panned out. The bird became enormous, its fifty-foot wings pinned outward onto poles like a giant specimen in a butterfly collection.

Alex looked backward at the old man helplessly.

"Almost there," he said.

The camera now focused on two figures in military garb walking down the pathway through tens of thousands of perfectly aligned flag-bearers. The volume of the singing reached a resounding crescendo as the two figures in military garb ascended a great stairway upward. In several seconds, they had reached the summit. They parted, one saluting the other. One of them now faced the thousands of onlookers on his private pulpit. The singing in the stadium stopped. With a sudden thrust to the sky, he saluted the masses. As one, they responded, rhythmically, fervently praising their leader. The camera switched to an elevated box holding perhaps thirty dignitaries.

Alex watched in silent fascination. She was no history buff, but she recognized several faces. The rotund Göring, grinning widely in his gaudy white military uniform, his hands clasped together in unconcealed delight. The weasel-faced Goebbels, smaller but equally radiant in his joy in the moment. The picture suddenly froze.

"The Nuremberg party rally of 1938," said the old man in satisfaction. He approached the screen. "The hierarchy of the Third Reich. The most sinister lot of criminals the world has ever seen."

"Mr. Gruber, I appreciate this, but I really don't see what—"

"There he is, my dear," he said, walking to the screen. He raised his arm and patted a face. "Ludwig Wilhelm Holtzmann, vice president of the German Reichsbank."

"Vice president of . . . ?"

Her voice caught. She leaned forward in her chair and focused on the face of the man whose death had begun the incredible chain of events of the past week. He stood frozen in time, his mouth open, caught in the middle of a shouted salute to history's most notorious leader. She felt a shiver. This was no simple bureaucrat.

Gruber continued his narration almost triumphantly.

"I apologize for oversimplifying things. Saying that Ludwig Holtzmann was a banker is rather like saying that Lincoln was a politician. Ludwig Wilhelm Holtzmann was a little-known but instrumental figure in Nazi Germany's economic administration."

Alex said nothing. Her eyes remained locked on Holtzmann's face. He was young, bespectacled, with a short, little boy's haircut. He was dressed in full Nazi regalia.

The old man produced a paper and read from it.

"As I said, Holtzmann was born in Hamburg and educated at the University of Berlin. Joined the Nazi party in 1934. Held the position of Reichsintendant with the Ministry of Economics from 1934 to 1938. Vice president of the Reichsbank from 1938 to 1945 . . ."

Alex leaned her head back and looked at the ceiling. She needed to focus on something else. Anywhere but that projection screen. She raised her hand to her face and rubbed her eyes.

"In his position," continued Gruber, relentless now, "he held enormous power. Second only to Walther Funk in the Reichsbank, Holtzmann had ready access to nearly all assets of the German Reich. He could transfer huge sums with a simple signature, and he often did. He periodically authorized checks for millions of marks to Hermann Göring. When Funk learned of the transfers and sought to expel Holtzmann, only Göring's intervention saved his position."

Alex finally found her voice. "What happened to him?"

"With the end of the war, Holtzmann went on the run. He was tried in absentia in Nuremberg and—like Rudolf Hess and the others—given life in Spandau prison. He was captured in Italy in 1946 and returned to Germany to serve his sentence. He hanged himself in his cell just three years ago."

Alex nodded slowly. Three years ago—the same year a Mr. Gerald Raymond Jacobs arrived in Hudson, New York.

"Can I have that paper?" she asked.

"Certainly," said the old man, handing it to her. "I hope it's been helpful."

She rose to her feet slowly. "Do I owe you anything?"

"No," the man replied, waving his hand. "I don't mind sharing what I've learned."

Alex bowed her head graciously, then turned to leave. Her brain felt like it was just beginning to work again. She stopped.

"Why exactly did Holtzmann get sentenced to life in prison?"

Gruber looked at her as if the answer were obvious. "My dear, the Reichsbank held the entire assets of the Third Reich, all the plundered treasure, the stolen money, the gold plucked from dead men's mouths in Auschwitz. After Funk fell out of favor with Goebbels in 1943,

Holtzmann was thereafter almost completely in charge of the ill-gotten treasures. In that sense, he was a knowing accomplice to mass genocide."

Alex asked her next question very slowly and deliberately. "You said Rudolf Hess was sentenced to life in Spandau?"

"Yes."

"Did he die there?"

"Yes, he did. Somewhere around 1987, I believe."

She nodded. That information would come in handy later. She stole a final glance at the fanatical face on the screen, then thanked Gruber and exited down the stairway.

Timothy Von Rohr rose from his prison cell cot and threw a handful of cold water on his face. He grabbed his towel and stared at himself in the tiny mirror over his sink. It was true then. Incredibly, it was true. He smiled at himself and shook his head.

Warden Henshaw had done him a favor. After the investigators had left, the good warden had placed a very enlightening phone call to the State of New York, specifically the county housing in the city of Hudson. The county clerk had given him a quick confirmation of the enormous estate they were currently holding under the name of Gerald Raymond Jacobs.

Tim Von Rohr was ecstatic. He did a rough mental calculation. One-third was 7.4, and 50 percent of that was 3.7. Three point seven million! Not only would he be free in five months, he would be set for life.

The prison bars slid open. Von Rohr stepped into line as the crew of cons began moving through east wing lockdown. He frowned. The key now was to make sure none of the prison heavies found out about this. The blacks or the Mexicans might make a move on him if they knew about this bit of good fortune. He certainly wouldn't be telling anybody about Uncle Gerald. If the guards kept their big traps shut, he would probably be okay.

The line filed into the cafeteria. Von Rohr's head was reeling. He laughed to himself as he grabbed a tray. From San Quentin to Park Avenue. He had it made.

Tim Von Rohr didn't see the inmate rise to his feet at the table nearest him. The convict was already a lifer, and he had been paid with a year's worth of crystal meth and cigarettes. He had smuggled the small wood block out of the workshop and honed it into a blade against the rough concrete of his cell wall. His target's head was turned as he made his charge. A guard saw him moving, but his shout came far too late to matter. The shank was thrust into Von Rohr's jugular and twisted down, tearing it. The guards brought the killer down, but by then Timothy Von Rohr was on the ground, his life fluids draining red on the marble floor.

## CHAPTER 20

Nick and Jessica Von Rohr walked quickly through the terminal of the Albany airport. Alex's instructions had been firmly stated. Hurry out of the terminal and get to the departures ramp—she would be waiting in a rented van near the United Airlines sign. She would have the newspaper with her.

They exited to the street and Nick saw the van near the end of the terminal. It was dark blue and windowless. The engine was running. He grabbed the side door and slid it open. Alex was at the wheel, her face a greenish hue against the dashboard lights. Nick motioned Jessica into the back, then took the front passenger seat. Nick saw something resembling surprise in Jessica's face at the sight of Alex. Not the partner she'd envisioned, he thought. Alex glanced at Nick and waited for an introduction.

"Jessica, this is my partner—Alex Moreno. Alex—Jessica Von Rohr . . ."

Alex swiveled around and offered her hand. "I'm the one who met your brother Matt," she said. "I'm very sorry to hear the news."

Her hand hung in the air. Nick held his breath. Three unbearably long seconds passed before Jessica took it. They shook hands wordlessly, but their eyes were locked together. Nick spoke quickly.

"Let's get rolling, Alex."

Alex turned and took the wheel. Within minutes the scenery was a seventy-mile-per-hour blur. A silence that seemed almost frigid to Nick settled over the inside of the van. He remained quiet and watched the traffic. It was going to be a long drive back to Schenectady.

"Take a look down at your feet, Nick," said Alex, reaching for the radio.

Nick reached down and found the newspaper, bringing it low to his lap so Jessica couldn't see it. The FBI had been good on their word. Attempted murder committed in the commission of a burglary. Arminger had gotten one out of two right anyway. But it was the attempted-murder charge that had teeth. Alex had said she had even seen a local newscast about him. He was on television! People were sitting in their living rooms hearing all about Nicholas Merchant, the brutal cop-killer, the burglar of dead men's homes. And frighteningly enough, this was just the beginning. By now he knew a teletype would have been sent over the national police computer network. If that was the case, there wouldn't be a city where his name wasn't known. And if Arminger really meant business, he could make use of his fingerprints at the FBI crime lab in Virginia. Once he had the prints, he could do damn near anything he wanted.

Alex clicked on the radio, filling the van with a soft, generic jazz. The three of them sat and said nothing until they reached Schenectady.

Alex had rented a unit in Towne Villa, a small, tree-dotted apartment complex on Keyes Avenue in the south part of Schenectady. She found parking in the rear in spot number 204.

"We'll be right up, Alex," said Nick.

Alex caught the hint and stepped out of the van, leaving the two of them alone. Nick turned back to Jessica. Her head was back on the headrest. She looked drained.

"Pretty quiet back there. You all right?"

She lifted her head and nodded weakly. "Listen," she said, "what happened with Matt—I realize you couldn't have known. That's fair. I'm . . . glad you came out to my place. You probably saved my life. I want you to know I am grateful for that."

Nick nodded awkwardly and said nothing. Although absolved of blame, he certainly didn't feel worthy of any gratitude.

"You said you were going to come up with a plan during the flight," she said. "Any luck with that?"

"I have some ideas," he said, pushing the door open. "Let's head upstairs first. My partner needs to be a part of this."

The apartment was nearly empty. No couch, no tables besides the one in the kitchen. A television sat on the floor, looking small and pitiful all by itself on the living room carpet.

"Can I talk to you in here for a second, Nick?" Alex immediately asked, stepping past them.

Nick excused himself awkwardly and followed his partner into the bedroom. Alex closed the door partially and faced him, her arms folded in front of her.

"Think you know what I'm mad about?"

"Probably," answered Nick. "I'm not sure I want to hear it right now, though."

"Tough. Why is she here, Nick?"

"You already know the answer to that. Someone's trying to kill her and she wants to know what the hell's going on."

"She can go to the police."

"They can't do a damn thing for her and you know it. You know I'm right, Alex. They're not going to take her in and protect her."

"Oh, and you will? We're having enough problems watching ourselves without having to worry about someone who isn't even a *client*, for god's sake."

"What do you want me to do—dump her off on the side of the road? She's in this as much as her brother was."

"Her brother was our client, Nick; she isn't. That's an important distinction, I'd say."

Nick raised a finger to his lips. The discussion was one or two choice words from disintegrating into a shouting match. If not for the guest in the other room, he would almost have welcomed it.

"We need all the allies we can get at this point. She has a certificate to a bank box in Switzerland that may hold something important."

Alex approached him, her lips tight with frustration. "Fine, but she should do us a favor first. She should sign that contract, Nick. If you're making an effort to protect her, I think it's the least she can do."

"She isn't here for protection. She's here to help us find out what's going on. Alex, I'm slightly more concerned right now with clearing myself than I am about that contract. You should be concerned with the same thing. It's probably only a matter of time before your face is posted right next to mine."

"And just how are we going to clear ourselves?" she asked. "What are we going to find that's going to make these charges just go away? This isn't the Hardy Boys, Nick—it's *real*. It's time to move forward with plan B."

"Is there a plan A?"

"It's the same plan. We get her to sign, take our passports, and go on a permanent vacation. I intend to get out. Forget getting rich—I'm going to need that money to make it abroad, and when you finally figure out that these charges aren't going away, you'll suddenly realize you need it too."

Nick frowned and turned away. Taking flight as a fugitive was a last-ditch option. It was an alternative with a frightening permanence, and yes, it would require money to be feasible. His personal savings might last him six months, and that was only if the FBI didn't get to them first.

"Do you think I want to go through this crap and *not* earn a fee?" he asked. "You need to understand the immediate problem here: she's lost her brother. He's been murdered, remember? This is not the time to be shoving contracts in her face. We need to give her more time. She's too angry and full of distrust right now."

"We don't *have* a lot of time. We can't sneak around in the shadows forever."

"I know we can't. Doug's scheduled a hearing for her brother on Friday. We'll sign her before then and present her to the court as the heir in Matthew's place. For the next couple of days, though, we need to leave it alone."

Alex walked over to a sleeping bag in the corner and sat down. "She's mad at us, isn't she?"

Nick shrugged and looked at the carpet. "She was at first."

"Do you feel guilty about this? About Matt and Rose?"

"How am I supposed to feel? I certainly don't feel good about it. About any of it. I'm very confused right now, to tell the truth."

"We can't take full blame for what happened to Matt, Nick. I can understand her anger, but she can't possibly believe that we could've known any of this would happen."

"She knows that. Look, we'll just give her time, okay? It's the smartest thing for now."

"What about the charges? We can't tell her about them, can we?"

Nick frowned. He had already pledged his total honesty, but telling Jessica that he was wanted for attempted murder would shatter any last hope for a trusting relationship. And yet he couldn't risk her finding it out on her own.

"I'll have to eventually," he said. "I need to win her over a bit more first."

"She'll find out one way or another."

He rubbed his forehead in frustration. There were too many variables, too many things to keep account of. "I'll deal with it. When the opportunity arises, I'll tell her."

"How are you going to do that?"

"I don't know how, okay?" he pleaded. "Please, let's deal with this one crisis at a time."

They remained silent for ten seconds before Alex spoke again.

"So what's this about a Swiss account?"

Nick told her about the bank certificate Jessica had found. Alex slowly paced around him, her chin in her hand.

"There's some sort of a Geneva connection here, Nick. Listen to this . . ." She told him about the day's research and the strange phone call she had gotten from the Swiss banker.

" 'Tell Taylor his plan will fail,' " Nick repeated thoughtfully. "What was the rest of it again?"

" 'I've taken precautions. The end is coming soon for him.' "

"This banker knows who Taylor is," he said, quick with his conclusion.

"Take his words on face value, Nick. We can't be sure what he knows."

"Well, he obviously knows *something*. We can safely conclude one thing: from what you told me of his tone, there's little doubt of his feelings toward Taylor. He doesn't like him. That's good—I don't either. We're on the same page in that regard." He thought for a moment before looking up at her. "I want to have a chat with this Mr. Chagnon."

"Easier said than done," she replied. "I must have called him back four or five times. They told me he was permanently unavailable and then hung up on me."

Nick glanced at his watch. "In another hour I'll be able to call Geneva. If we can think of the proper approach, we may be able to talk to this guy. If I can just get him on the damn line, I think I can convince him that I want Taylor too."

"What if we *can't* get him on the line?"

"Then I may be hopping on another plane. Jesus Christ, this is crazy." He let out a long breath. "Let's get out there and talk things over with the heir. She's part of this."

He stepped to the door but paused in midstride when he caught Alex's look. He could see something in her deep brown eyes he had never seen before.

"What is it?"

She sat down on the sleeping bag in the corner. He lowered himself down next to her, so close their shoulders rubbed.

"What's going to happen to us, Nick?"

Nick put his arm around her. He had been so busy running around, he hadn't even had time to dwell on their long-term prospects. His partner clearly had found the time. It was startling to see. Alex had always been the gutsiest woman he had ever known, but he could now see real fear in those wide eyes. She needed something other than hopeful words. He pulled her to him. She hugged him back and put her face on his shoulder.

"We'll make it, girl. If we just rely on each other and plan this right, I think we can find our way out. But we've got to do it quick."

Like an electric jolt, the call came suddenly in the dark. Arthur Gordon rolled away from his wife of thirty-five years and reached blindly for the phone. Either his youngest daughter was having more marital problems or a break had come in the Merchant investigation. His deputy's voice indicated it was the latter.

"Merchant was in Iowa with one of the heirs."

"How do we know?" Gordon asked, propping himself up on a creaky elbow.

"Des Moines called us. There was an incident at Jessica Von Rohr's home yesterday. Two gunmen showed up and shot the place up."

"Gunmen? Wait—how do we know Merchant was there?"

"Neighbor says she saw a man matching Merchant's description show at Von Rohr's door maybe an hour or so before the shooting started."

"Any bodies?"

"Nothing. We've assigned two agents to watch the house, but the odds of her coming back are slim."

"Do we have full airport coverage in New York and San Francisco?"

"Full coverage. And partial coverage in half a dozen others."

Gordon nodded as his wife rolled over and muttered something next to him. He lowered his voice. "You think Von Rohr's with Merchant now?"

"I think so, yes. He lost the first heir so he's trying to make his payday with the sister. Probably wants to put a few million in his pocket before he leaves the country."

Gordon nodded as he stared into the darkness of his bedroom. "Send new teletypes. If they're traveling together, it's only going to make it easier for us. Did you find out when that court hearing is scheduled?"

"Wednesday afternoon. Are you sure we can't just drain these accounts?"

"Not without involving people in New York State. There's a better way to stop this hearing. Did you get that information I wanted on the attorney? What was his name again?"

"It's in my file. Apparently they've been together since Merchant and Associates started up. Known each other since childhood."

"That's good. We'll give him special attention starting tomorrow. By the time we're through with him, he won't be caught within ten miles of that courthouse."

"Merchant will just hire another one," said Arminger, disgusted. "There are a million other attorneys who'll jump on this opportunity."

"The point is, it could take him time to hire a new one. He'll have to reschedule the hearing while he makes new arrangements. It's another errand he'll have to run, another person he'll have to call, and that's exactly what we want. The longer he's in the States, the more likely it is he'll leave a trail. I want you to call San Francisco immediately and get started on that."

"I'll call them right now."

"Make sure they lean on this attorney hard," Gordon insisted. "He may be our key."


Alex and Jessica were at the kitchen table under a dim plastic hanging lamp. It was nearly three o'clock in the morning. Nick poured himself a cup of coffee and sat down with them.

"Everything's pointing to Geneva," he said. "We have Jessica's bank account to look into and Ludwig Holtzmann's friend Otto to visit. We also have a banker to talk to who may know quite a lot."

"This banker," said Jessica, her eyes narrowed in thought. "How did you get his name?"

Nick would have preferred it if she hadn't asked. Their source had been the bank documents taken from Jacobs's home.

"We discovered in our earlier research that Jacobs had bank accounts in Geneva. Alex made some phone calls and eventually got hold of this man."

Jessica leaned forward on her elbows, thinking too hard for Nick's liking. He turned to his partner before she could ask any more questions.

"What do you think, Alex? Feedback?"

Alex considered it for a moment. "I think we have to go. We have three solid leads to pursue in Geneva and very little to go on in the States, although I do have several things I need to see through here. I say you two go to Switzerland, and I stick around to finish my research in the States."

This made sense to Nick. It was safer if he and Alex didn't travel together anyway.

"What do you think?" he asked Jessica.

She exhaled and clasped her hands together on the table. "I don't know if I'm as concerned with uncovering mysteries as you two are. I just don't want to end up like my brother. Geneva sounds . . . safe, I guess." She brought her hands to her forehead and studied the surface of the table. "I'm sorry, but this is all new ground for me. You two are the professionals here."

"We aren't professionals when it comes to something like this," said Alex evenly.

"Well, I'm sorry to hear that, because all the amateurs seem to be getting killed," Jessica replied with a tight smile.

"It's decided then," Nick said quickly, nodding at Alex. "We take this to Switzerland; you continue whatever investigation you can here."

Alex got to her feet and left the kitchen. Nick gave Jessica an uneasy look and cracked a couple of knuckles. An icy silence was better than the opposite. He had zero desire to step between the two of them. Sounded dangerous.

Jessica suddenly stood and reached for her jacket. "I'm going for a walk."

"You what?" said Nick. "A walk? Wait a second—"

"Maybe I'll jog. I haven't decided yet. I noticed an all-night drugstore down the street. If I'm holing up in here all night, I'll need some things."

"Fine. I can give you a ride."

"She wants to walk, Nick," said Alex from the living room. "Let her walk."

Jessica was already at the door. She gave Nick a smart-ass wink and closed the door before he could say anything more. He approached the blinds and watched her until she was out of sight.

" 'I can give you a ride,' " mimicked Alex from the living room.

Nick turned to look at her. "What's your problem?"

"What's yours?" she replied, glaring at him. "You're taking this knight-in-shining-armor routine a little far, don't you think?"

"What are you talking about? Alex, we're *obligated* to this woman. I don't give a rat's ass if she's a client or not. We came into her life and we told her about this and now we owe her. Why is this so hard for you to understand?"

"You flew all the way out to Iowa to warn her, Nick. Our obligations to her should end right there."

"She can help us. She has the Swiss account, remember?" He slowly shook his head at her. "All the crap I'm dealing with, and you gotta pull this little . . . jealousy act."

She stepped into the kitchen and got right in his face. "Jealousy? Your ego cannot be so out of whack that you actually believe that. Are you getting off on having both of us under your thumb?"

Nick turned from her and took a seat. He purposely waited ten seconds, counting them down silently, before speaking.

"We're both tired, Alex. Stressed out, scared, saying things we don't mean. The only two things I'm concerned with right now are you and me. You and me. Can we just agree on doing whatever it'll take to come out of this alive?"

The anger faded from her face. She leaned against the kitchen counter and frowned at the floor.

"I'm sorry. I'm acting really stupid."

"I'm sorry too. I know you're not jealous."

She smiled self-consciously at him. He smiled back, and it was as good as forgotten.

"Hey," Alex said, entering the bedroom, "I want to show you something." She returned with the tiny tape recorder. "Remember this?" She pressed Play.

". . . *Yeah, Jacobs—it's Demello . . . I need you to gimme a call today . . . it's important. . . .*"

"I remember," said Nick. "What about it?"

She reached down and took the phone book. She flipped through the pages, then placed her finger on a line for him. He read it aloud.

" 'Demello and Blount, Private Investigators.' " He looked up at her quickly. "That's our boys."

"It's got to be," agreed Alex. "I called the licensing board and verified it. James Demello—licensed PI in the state of New York. But you know what I find strange? Look at their address. Tell me why an elderly millionaire would go all the way down to an ugly part of East Harlem to hire a PI. There's plenty in Albany he could've called."

"Maybe he didn't want to hire anyone too close by."

Alex shrugged. "I called their office about ten times. No answer. Not even a machine. I'm checking it out tomorrow."

"Just be careful," he warned. "How bad is it down there?"

"No worse then my old neighborhood."

"Bring your gun. I'm going to book our flight. You have a place in Albany for passports, right?"

"Yes, but they're not cheap."

"Just as long as they're quick. Once we're gone, you're running the show here in the States, Alex. I know you'll come up with something good."

"I'm glad one of us is sure."

Nick turned away, then paused. "I just remembered something else I need you to do here. Can you run a credit transaction report for Michael Dean Collier every, say, two hours?"

"That often?"

"Yes. Every two hours, on the hour."

Her eyes went wide with realization. "They're checking credit reports?"

"I know they're checking Nick Merchant and Alex Moreno. We need to make sure they're not checking Mr. Collier and Ms. Ramos. You need to stay on that two-hour timetable, okay?"

"If you think it's important."

"Important enough to save our lives."

They stared at each other, silently considering the impact of those words. Up until Jacobs, it had been nothing but fun and games. Things were now so horrible it barely seemed real.

Nick didn't expect Alex's next move. In three quick steps, she was in front of him, hugging him around the waist. He wrapped his arms around her and closed his eyes, stroking her hair. Standing there in the dim light, he doubted if he was any less frightened than she was.

CHAPTER 21

SAN FRANCISCO'S FINEST went to work early Sunday morning. In the Richmond and Sunset districts, they spread the word at cafés, supermarkets, and churches. In the Mission District, the cops on sidewalk beat handed out and posted composites. In the fugitive's former home in the Marina, officers walked among the morning throngs on Chestnut and Union streets passing out fliers and speaking with pedestrians. The story making its way through precinct locker rooms was that the commissioner was following instructions from FBI Director Arthur Gordon himself.

Doug had noticed the fliers when he'd left for the office at 6 A.M. It was frightening how quickly it was all unraveling. He could barely believe it. His best friend—wanted for attempted murder! He was glad Bill Merchant wasn't around to see this.

He settled into his office and tried in vain to focus. He had a busy day in front of him, each minute tightly allocated. His secretary, Darlene, had grudgingly agreed to put in a half day to help him play catch-up, and he hoped the two of them could make a dent in the small mountain of papers now teetering on his desk. He clicked on the computer and reached for his coffee mug. He needed to write up the Branson living trust from 8:00 to 11:00. Prepare the petition for the Hanson heirs from 11:00 to 12:00. Meet with an heir and her attorney in Martinez at 1:00. Shoot back to Oakland at 2:30 to meet with the administrator of the Magruder estate. Fight his way back over the bridge to San Francisco and tear downtown for an early dinner with Kimberly for her thirtieth-birthday celebration, although she was treating it more like a wake. Nothing a few rum and Cokes wouldn't fix, at least for one night.

His intercom cracked to life.

"Two gentlemen to see you, Doug . . ."

On a Sunday? thought Doug. "Tell 'em to come back tomorrow."

"They say they're . . ."

"No time for that today, Darlene. Tomorrow please."

His door swung open. Two clean-cut, middle-aged men in drab blue and gray suits stepped inside followed by his frazzled looking secretary. Doug frowned and gave them both the once-over.

"You heard of knocking?"

"Tom Healy," said one of the men, flashing a badge. "FBI. My partner, John Zepeda. You have a minute?"

Doug recovered after a moment. "I'm a little busy, to tell you the truth."

"We'd appreciate it if you found the time," said Agent Zepeda. He and his partner pulled up chairs and sat in front of Doug's desk. Doug tossed his pen down and sat.

"I'm pretty booked today, guys."

"We've been assigned to the Merchant investigation," said Healy, oblivious. "Like to ask you some questions."

"You're welcome to try. I may choose not to answer."

"Do you know where Nick Merchant is?"

"No idea. Out of the country probably."

"Really. Do you have something you'd like to share with us?"

"No, I don't, but I've known Nick Merchant forever. I know him well enough to know he's not sticking around to face a bunch of trumped-up charges. It's a bullshit charge, guys."

"An innocent man usually sticks around to make sure his name is cleared."

"Not if the deck's stacked against him," replied Doug.

"Have you been in contact with him?" asked Agent Zepeda.

"Not recently, no."

"What's not recently? A week, a day? An hour?"

"A few days."

Agent Zepeda nodded as if he were expecting those very answers.

He looked around the office and spoke to a wall. "Some very danger-ous people would like to meet him, you know."

"Makes me wonder why you're not chasing those people."

"We're still trying to figure out who it is we're chasing. A little coop-eration on your part may help save your friend's life."

"I feel pretty damn sure he would insist on saving his own life. That's the way he is." Doug crossed his arms on his chest and looked at the clock. "Listen, guys, what do you want from me? I'm not hiding him in my closet, okay? I told you I don't know where he is, and that's the truth."

The agents were professional. Cool, unemotional—robots with ties.

"We believe you," said Agent Healy. "But keep something in mind. FBI brass really wants a break in this. If you think you can hide behind client privilege while you aid and abet, you better think again. Tread very, very carefully, counselor. You're being watched."

Doug studied both their faces, then forced himself to speak softly. "Look, I don't want any trouble. I admit I'm a good friend of Nick Merchant's, but that doesn't mean I'm aiding and abetting. I honestly don't know where he is. I'm not covering things up here."

Agent Healy nodded thoughtfully.

"There's a probate hearing this Wednesday for Mr. Jacobs. You may want to think good and hard about whether you want to represent Merchant and Associates."

"You guys are working off yesterday's information. Merchant and Associates doesn't even have a client anymore."

"That could change, couldn't it?"

Doug folded his hands on his desk. He cleared the nervousness from his throat. "So what happens if I *do* represent Merchant and Associates?"

"You'll be getting more attention than you could ever begin to imag-ine. It won't be the kind of attention you'll like, either. Do yourself a favor: think about it."

Doug stared at them hard. When he spoke his voice was steady and cold. "I've got a very full schedule today. If there's nothing else, I'd like to get on with it."

The two agents stood after an uncomfortable few seconds and placed cards on the surface of his desk. Doug closed the door behind them and slouched back into his seat. Something was troubling about this little encounter. He had noticed what looked like smirks as they were leaving, almost as if he had been the butt of some private joke he still didn't get.

Ten in the morning in Brooklyn Heights. Kragen was relaxing at his kitchen table and reading about the latest travails of the Jets. They were headed for the bottom of the division again, and their latest savior was a rookie third-string quarterback, an under-sized Ivy Leaguer with a weak arm and fast feet. It was enough to make him consider becoming a Giants fan. The phone was a welcome relief.

"About time," he said to the caller. "What do you got?"

"We got a name. The car was rented by a Michael Collier. That's C-o-l-l-i-e-r. Paid cash. The girl who helped him said he was about six feet, one-ninety, two hundred pounds, full head of black hair."

"That's our man. He write anything else on the papers?"

"Just an address in Des Moines—1612 Edison Street. We checked it already—no such street."

"Surprise, surprise. Give me an hour to run the name. We'll get him."

Lawrence Castleton and Richard Borg sat like zombies in the conference room of General Inquiry and tried to suppress their anger. The coffeemaker was gurgling in the corner, ignored. Their stomachs were in no condition for caffeine. Castleton squirmed in his chair and cleared his throat noisily. A cue to their guest to get on with it.

"The FBI appreciates your cooperation in the Jacobs matter, gentle-men," said their guest, adjusting his glasses. "You've saved us a great deal of embarrassment."

Castleton frowned. As if he cared what they did and didn't appreciate.

"Who in your firm was privy to the Jacobs matter?"

Borg leaned back. He usually was his boss's spokesman, but now he just didn't give a damn. Let the old man answer for once.

"Myself," Castleton finally said. "My chief investigator. And two of our field people."

The guest nodded. He walked casually to the large window facing Wilshire. "You may be curious to know how our investigation into Nick Merchant is proceeding."

Borg couldn't hold back any further. "We're more curious as to why he was even allowed to proceed on the Jacobs matter in the first place. The FBI didn't seem to mind too much that he was involved—"

"That's right," piped in Castleton. "And this is after you threw your weight around with us. We've cooperated with the Bureau's wishes. Why's a criminal like Merchant given favors?"

The visitor turned back to them. "We're not cutting him any slack now, are we?"

Castleton grunted and jabbed a finger at him. "Nick Merchant was given a free hand to track the Jacobs heirs while my company was ordered off the investigation. I demand an explanation."

"I'll need to consult with my supervisor on that," came the reply. "I can tell you that we're now looking for Merchant in fifty states, and I guarantee you he will not profit from the Jacobs estate. Is there anything you know that may help us find him or Alex Moreno?"

"What could we possibly know?" asked Borg.

"We're an honest company trying to go about our business," added Castleton. "We stay away from crooks like Merchant." He leaned forward, full of fight now. "I intend to consult with our attorneys to see what our legal recourse is here. I'm not taking any more of the Bureau's intimidation tactics. You go ahead and tell your friend Mr. Arminger that for me."

The stranger nodded. He had no intention of doing that. He didn't even know who Mr. Arminger was.

The conference room door noiselessly opened, and a short, stocky man unrecognized by Lawrence Castleton and Richard Borg stepped inside.

"Who the hell are—"

Castleton fell silent as he noticed the large handgun in the newcomer's hand. He swiveled violently in his chair, back to their surprise guest. He too now held a similar weapon.

"What is this?" whispered Borg.

The two men raised their weapons and took out Castleton first, the bullets entering his chest and back almost simultaneously. Borg was too shocked to even beg for his life as the weapons were then trained on him. The bullet from the right entered his head, the one in front tore through his chest. Both heir hunters were dead by the time their bodies slumped to the carpet. Without a word, the killers exited quietly to the hall, closing the conference room door behind them. They walked by the stunned receptionist and hurried around the corner to their car.

*    *    *

Kragen tapped his finger patiently on his kitchen table and held the phone. He wasn't going to let the skinny man upset him. The little prick wasn't worth it.

"Why are you calling me?" demanded Cimko.

"Need a little guidance. I think we got ourselves an alias here on your man, but there's just one small problem. . . ."

"What is it?"

Kragen grabbed the slip of paper and leaned back in his chair. "The name's Michael Collier. The problem is there's fifty-nine Michael Colliers coming up on our computer."

"What am I supposed to do about that?"

"I'm getting to that, sweetheart—"

"Don't call me sweetheart."

"Sure thing. Two of these fifty-nine Michael Colliers have San Francisco addresses—"

"So check those out first, Kragen. What's there to think about?"

"One of 'em just flew to Switzerland."

Five seconds of silence.

"If your question is should you follow him," said Cimko softly, "my answer is yes. Immediately."

"You got it. The only thing is it might take a day to get hold of firearms over there."

"Improvise, dammit. Get the job done any way you can and be quick about it."

"You're picking up the tab on the flight, right?"

"Yes, I'm picking up the tab on the flight. Book the damn thing."

"We're on our way, sweetheart."

## CHAPTER 22

A T FIVE MINUTES to takeoff, Nick grabbed his briefcase and emerged from a bathroom stall near international departures at Philadelphia International Airport. For half an hour he had holed up in there—thirty long, nervous minutes. Airports were generally the most watched locations on earth when the law was looking to nab a fugitive. He could only hope his choice of Philadelphia's air hub would throw the FBI off his track.

He checked himself in the bathroom mirror. His beard was barely two days old, but dark, giving him an older, more serious look. An appropriate effect, he thought. He hated facial hair and the accompanying itchiness, but now the unfamiliar look was a comfort. Each passing day, another millimeter of growth, another bit of distance from his usual appearance.

Outside, the line at Gate 72 had dwindled to nothing. He walked quickly through the airport concourse, half expecting rough hands to grab him at any moment. Thirty yards. Twenty. Ten. He reached the boarding tunnel and hurried through it. He threw a quick, nervous look behind himself. All clear. Safe and sound—until the next flight.

In the cabin, the crush of boarders had found seats, and he made his way down the center aisle. A quick wave of a hand caught his eye. He slid into the row, sitting in the middle seat to the left of Jessica's window seat. He allowed himself to relax a bit as the plane soon taxied into position on the runway. Powerful engines began to accelerate, and the plane sped down the runway, finally lifting off and arcing upward to the sky.

"You feel okay?" she asked.

"I feel wonderful," replied Nick, forcing a smile. "Why do you ask?"

"You look pale."

"Something I ate, I guess. I'm fine."

She nodded, obviously not buying it. The skeptical look on her eyes made Nick wonder what thought she wasn't sharing.

He turned to the books Alex had checked out of the Schenectady library. One was a traveler's guide to Switzerland, the other a handbook on Swiss banking. He had a good amount of brushing up to do during the long hours of flight time ahead.

The classifications of the Swiss banks were detailed and rather confusing. The three prominent banks in Switzerland were Union Bank of Switzerland, the Swiss Bank Corporation, and the Swiss Credit Bank. Jessica's bank box was held at Hahn and Konauer, a bank Nick could only assume was one of the two dozen or so private banking institutions. The address he had was on the Place Bel-Air, Geneva's principal financial boulevard, according to his traveler's guide.

Two interesting facts stood out as he read. One, most of the private banks as a rule refused to handle accounts of less than one hundred thousand dollars. Two, unlike the incorporated and cantonal banks, the private banks were not required by Swiss banking codes to publish their balance sheets. Estimates from the previous year placed each of their holdings in the realm of 250 to 750 million Swiss francs. The Swiss banking authorities readily admitted the true figures could be far beyond the estimates.

He removed his portfolio and glanced at Jessica. Her head was tilted to him, eyes closed. He looked beyond her out the window. The endless spread of the North Atlantic, a cold black carpet as far as the eye could see. This would be the first time he had traveled abroad not looking for a client—a strange feeling.

He pulled a few of the Jacobs banking documents. Of the dozens of letters taken from the Jacobs home, Alex had spotted a clear pattern. Ninety percent of them belonged to four particular Swiss banks—two in Zurich, two in Geneva. He read the names: Droz &

Cie. Burg and Blaus. Alban-Witz. Gubelin & Cie. He closed his eyes and could almost see their dark iron and concrete vaults, gloomy accommodations for decades-old secrets held captive in cold metal drawers. The Von Rohr lockbox held one of those secrets. Or perhaps it held nothing, a little dust and stale air. He prayed that wasn't the case.

He lowered his seat back and closed the shade.

The flight attendant came by an hour later and asked them if they wanted drinks. Nick declined the urge for a cocktail and checked his watch. They were still several hours away. He dropped his head back. He was tired of reading, tired of sitting. He was tired of running. Geneva would be the first time in days he would be taking the offensive. He needed to regain a feeling of control. It was the only way to have any hope at all.

Jessica had gotten a cocktail, something strong from the looks of it. He noticed her hands as she held the glass. Smooth tan skin. Pink fingernails, short and neatly manicured.

"I've been wanting to ask you," she suddenly said, her eyes on her drink. "Do you think they have any way of . . . tracking us?"

Nick glanced at her. She had tried to ask the question matter-of-factly, but her voice had betrayed her. He could hear the fear there, the same fear that flickered in her eyes.

"I hope not," he said softly. It was an inadequate answer, but all he could offer. For all he knew, they could be seated a row away from them.

"Are you concerned they may find us?" she asked.

"We should be okay. I've been pretty careful the last day or so."

Nick sensed she wanted to hear more reassuring answers, but sugarcoating things wouldn't do either of them a bit of good. He studied her and felt sorry that she had been dragged into it. And more than a little guilty. She seemed so small and weak at that moment, just a normal, fragile person who suddenly knew she was in hopelessly over her head. He didn't feel much different himself.

She looked up at him and forced a weak smile. "Did you ever meet my brother?"

He let a breath out slowly. Here was a question he hadn't expected. "I never did, no. My partner went and met with him the other day." He couldn't look at her. "I understand he was a real nice guy. He was . . . pretty happy, from what I hear."

The smile quickly died on her lips. "I thought it was all a joke. I didn't really buy any of your story that day you came to my door."

"Most people don't believe it."

She nodded. "Do you like what you do?"

"Private investigation?"

"Connecting people with inheritances."

Nick leaned his head back and thought about that one. A week ago his answer would have been a resounding yes. Now it seemed ridiculous to even ponder the question.

"I did once," was all he could manage.

Several minutes passed as both of them were lost in private thoughts. Nick's focus centered on Rose. And Matt Von Rohr. He closed his eyes and wished he could turn back the clock. He thought back to his conversation with Alex by the Hudson River. He had done a wonderful job of justifying the break-in of Gerald Jacobs's home. His words had swayed Alex rather quickly. *We're not hurting anyone. We're just taking a little look around.* He shook his head. Considering where they were now, perhaps he should have given a hell of a lot more thought to that rationale.

He reached up and directed a stream of cool air in his direction. The close quarters of the cabin were starting to make him feel claustrophobic, like an animal in a slowly compressing cage.

Jessica suddenly leaned over and touched his arm.

"Listen," she whispered, cognizant of the close quarters of the cabin. "I don't really care about finding out answers to all this. If you can find a way to get me this inheritance, I'll sign your contract. I don't care what it takes—just find a way. I know the kind of things you're capable of, and it won't bother me. Just do what you need to do."

Nick thought for a moment, then turned to her. "What do you mean by that? What I'm *capable* of?"

"You know what I mean. You'll do whatever it takes to get this money, and that's fine if it gets us out of this alive."

Nick wasn't sure how to take these comments. He leaned over to her. "You don't know me," he said softly. "You don't know what I'm capable of or what I'm not capable of."

"I think I know you enough," she said, placing her drink aside and reaching to the floor. She brought the newspaper to her lap. It was a current edition of the *San Francisco Chronicle,* and it was neatly folded into a tight square. Nick felt his mouth go dry as he read the headline.


Outside, the sky was clearing, and glimpses of France were now visible below, dark blotches of brown and green through a haze of scattered clouds. The flight attendants were making their rounds and collecting empty breakfast plates. Jessica waited until they had privacy again before speaking.

"I knew something wasn't right when we left out of Philadelphia instead of JFK," she said calmly. "When I first saw that headline in the terminal, I walked outside and flagged a taxi. But something stopped me from getting in." She lowered her voice to barely a whisper. "You're right—I don't know you. But I do know what happened to my brother, and I know what happened out at my home yesterday."

"Jessica—"

She silenced him with a finger to her lips.

"In light of all that, I'm going to give you a chance to offer your side. I want the truth, okay? Personally I couldn't care less if you're a thief—I've seen so much crookedness among lawyers that I've gone numb to it. What I need to know is whether or not you'd actually shoot a cop."

Nick stared at her and tried desperately to formulate his response. He was angry with himself for allowing himself to be blindsided. He knew he should have come clean right from the start.

"Okay—the truth." He lowered his voice appropriately. "I'm guilty of all counts—*except* for the attempted murder charge. This all started when my partner and I paid a county official ten thousand dollars to see the Jacobs file before any other heir finders could get to it. I don't apologize to anyone for that. That's how it is in this business. Right or wrong, that's how it works." He took a breath. "The burglary charge: technically, yes—I committed burglary. In reality it was nothing of the sort. I admit illegally entering Holtzmann's home, but all I wanted to do was find clues about the old man's family, and that's exactly what I found. I know that doesn't justify it in the eyes of the law, or the eyes of anyone for that matter, but—"

"Where does the cop fit into this story?" she asked.

"I had *nothing* to do with that. You wouldn't be sitting here right now if you believed that. There was someone else in that house, Jessica. I saw him. For Christ's sake, I was hiding under a damn grand piano when he walked in, gun out. Someone must have been watching the house when I went in. They must have come in to take me out."

"So what happened?"

"I'm not entirely sure what happened. Right when I'm running away through the backyard, a police car pulls up to the house. The person who came in looking for me must have shot the cop when he realized he was going to get caught inside. That's my guess anyway."

Her eyes were skeptical. "So you're innocent. That's asking me to believe a lot."

"I just told you I'm *not* innocent. But I didn't shoot anyone."

"You've been framed then—by the FBI, of all people."

"That's exactly what I'm saying. The only reason I've been accused of this is because they wanted me off this investigation and I wouldn't get off. Kill a cop? Come on. I used to *be* a cop. My *father* was a cop. Don't look at me like this is so far-fetched, either, not after everything else that's happened. You know what happened to Matt, you know what happened to my secretary, and you know what almost happened to the two of us."

She rolled her head back and stared at the ceiling. He reached into his coat pocket and found something he had been saving for just that moment.

"I'd like to show you something now, if I may. As a matter of fact, I'll read it for you: 'Mysterious Apartment Explosion Kills Two.' One guess whose apartment that was. My secretary walked into the middle of it with a key *I* had given her. Yeah, I get to live the rest of my life knowing I sent her there." He took a moment to calm himself, to make sure his voice wasn't getting too loud. "You were right next to me running through that field, Jessica. Call me dishonest, call me a thief, but I'm no murderer. You would've turned around and ran at the airport if you really thought that."

She closed her eyes. "I don't know what to think anymore."

"You have to believe me."

"Well, you've got me there," she said. "There's no one else to believe in."

The private investigator's office was on 100th Street. It was housed in a dirty gray building that was tattooed with spray paint and mildew, and almost all of its first-floor windows were cracked and covered with gray electrical tape. The building looked more like a tenement than a place of business.

Alex studied the address and again felt confused. With so many private investigators to choose from in New York, she had difficulty imagining why a millionaire would enlist the services of one in such a sorry part of East Harlem. But then again, there was nothing about Gerald Jacobs that wasn't bizarre.

The yellow pages ad for Demello and Blount, Private Investigators, offered a wide spectrum of investigative services, everything from promiscuous involvement to domestic deceit to decoy services, whatever that was. The old standbys of surveillance and missing persons were "specialties." Asset recovery was even mentioned. A jack-of-all-trades, Alex thought—offering every service under the investigative sun, probably excelling in none. "State licensed," the ad proudly proclaimed, as if this were something unique and confidence inspiring.

Their suite was located on the second floor. She knocked on the thick wooden door, waited a moment, and entered cautiously.

"Hel-lo?" she ventured.

She looked around. The office was threadbare—a couch, a chair, two dented file cabinets. Several stacks of full cardboard boxes were propped up against a wall. A telephone and computer sat on a cluttered desk. High-tech private investigation.

"Anybody here?" she asked.

She approached a door, opened it, and surveyed the second bare room. A large desk sat in the back. A wastebasket lay on its side in the middle of the floor, a pile of crumpled-up papers spilling from its mouth.

She returned to the front room and immediately felt uneasy. The office was too still, its isolation a bit unnerving. She was glad she had brought the pistol. She stepped toward a leaning stack of boxes and looked inside. A coffeemaker, a tape gun, an answering machine wrapped up in its own cord. Someone was either moving in or hitting the road.

She lifted the top box off the stack, placing it on the ground. The box beneath it was a jumble of papers—bills, company invoices, surveillance reports. She randomly picked through a few of them. Seeing little of interest, she approached the file cabinet. Empty drawers gaped at her.

She cupped her chin in her hand and thought. The entire building was dead quiet. The only sound was the heater hissing weakly from the other room. She slowly turned her head. A heater? She pulled the gun free. It was seventy-five degrees outside.

She stepped to the doorway cautiously. The hissing was faint, irregular. She entered the room slowly. It seemed to be coming from directly behind the desk, a place she felt fairly certain there was no heater. She drew nearer, squinting in anticipation. She extended the gun with both hands and stepped around the desk.

"Oh God."

The man was lying on his back. He was wearing a button-down shirt and black jeans, and what was left of his face pointed to the ceiling. His nose had been crushed, his jaw hung open and slightly askew. The entire face was a swollen, bloody pulp. Alex felt herself tremble as she heard his breath leave his throat. She slowly knelt down to him.

"Can you hear me?" she asked.

One eyelid slowly opened halfway. The whiteness of the eye stood out like an island in a sea of red.

"Listen to me," Alex said, touching his hand. "I'm calling you an ambulance. Just hold on. Help will be here very soon."

She started to stand, but the man gripped her hand with just enough strength to hold her there. The eye remained half open, focusing on nothing.

"Are you Demello?" Alex asked.

The voice was barely audible. "Part . . . part . . ."

"His partner," she repeated. "You're Blount. Where's Demello?"

The eye closed. "Dead . . ."

"Who killed him?"

"Old man . . ."

"Old man? Jacobs?"

"They . . . killed . . . him too. . . ."

Blood was dripping steadily from his nose and one of his ears. A checkered pattern was visible on half his face—the imprint of someone's heavy boot.

"Lie still," said Alex, removing her phone.

"Pictures . . ."

Alex paused, then tilted her head to him.

"They want . . . pic . . . tures . . ."

Alex removed one of the Jacobs pictures she had brought along. She placed it in front of his face.

"These pictures?"

"Yes . . ."

"Do you know who these people are?"

"Jacobs . . ."

"Yes. And the others? Do you know the others?"

His throat made a gurgling sound and he coughed weakly.

"State . . . Street . . ."

She leaned toward him. "State Street?"

"Swan . . ."

Alex's eyes widened. "Are you talking about Albany?"

"Yes . . . near . . . the park . . ."

She stood and dialed 911.

"Yes, I need an ambulance at 198 East 100th Street. I have a man here bleeding to death. . . . He's in unit 206 . . . Yes, 206. You need to hurry—he's in very bad shape. . . . A friend . . ."

She bent down to him, touching his hand again.

"Help is on the way," she said. "You need to just hold on."

His eye slowly rolled over to her. Alex swallowed a knot in her throat. The paramedics would be able to do very little once they arrived. She reached out her hand and traced a small cross on his forehead. She then wiped the doorknobs and file cabinets clean and left.

CHAPTER 23

THE TAXI WOUND endlessly through the mountains, and as the road finally began its descent the sparkling surface of Lake Geneva eased into view. With the snow-tipped mountains and the shimmering crystal of the lake as borders, Geneva appeared more resort town than busy metropolis. Tiny white-sailed boats dotted the surface of the lake like hundreds of swans at rest.

Nick didn't notice the surrounding beauty. He was studying a map of the city and planning the day's agenda. The layout of the city seemed bizarre, a maze of twisted side streets feeding from a dozen main thoroughfares. He wasn't surprised—foreign cities were always that way. Paris, Sydney, Copenhagen, Naples—they had all been geographically perplexing to him. He would find his way around somehow.

He glanced over at Jessica. She was leaning forward in her seat, appreciating the sights in spite of herself. Despite the revelations of the flight, he felt the air had been cleared. Her defenses, strangely enough, seemed a bit lowered, and he was hopeful they would get along better now. They had to. Their agenda the next twenty-four hours required it.

The taxi moved along the northern edge of Lake Geneva and entered the city center. For a bustling financial center, it was hardly what Nick had expected. No glass and chrome towers in sight, just beautifully restored old buildings, Gothic structures with wooden shutters and sharply pointed spires. Fashionably dressed pedestrians filled colorful outdoor cafes lining spotless streets. This was a financial center utterly different from New York City and San Francisco; a business mecca of quiet confidence, of hidden fortunes in underground vaults, of forgotten secrets. Nick was eager to get started.

He consulted his tourist guide. He had used Michael Collier's line of credit to book them a room at the Beau Rivage, one of the finer hotels in Geneva and a minute's cab ride from the banks on the Place Bel-Air. Nick scanned the inside of the hotel approvingly as they registered. With its dark wood paneling and tasteful furnishings, it reflected Old World elegance, understated and comfortable. The staff seemed unobtrusive but attentive.

Their room was as nice as he had expected for the money. It was elaborately decorated with a fireplace and a sweeping view of the lakefront. The snow-flecked peaks of the Alps were visible from the window. Jessica lingered by the sill and seemed to be quietly admiring the view.

"It's three o'clock," Nick said, finding the phone directory. "We have plenty of time to get to your bank before closing time. First I need to fax something from the hotel lobby, though."

"What are you sending?"

"I've arranged for a local PI to do address checks on some people we may be visiting later today if we have time. I need to get him the list of names I want checked."

He walked behind her and gazed down at the water. The lake was dark blue and had lost its glare beneath a suddenly overcast sky.

"The hotel is wonderful," she said, turning back to the room.

"Compared to what we're used to. Too bad we're not here to enjoy the sights. You ready?"

Her nod was a bit hesitant.

"Let's just move along quickly," Nick said, approaching her. "I prefer if we stick to the side streets, where there's less foot traffic. The less people we come across, the better. We're probably safe here, but no sense in taking crazy risks."

He held the door for her and silently considered the absurdity of his statement. The entire trip was a crazy risk. What was even scarier was the utter lack of a contingency plan. If they walked away from Geneva empty-handed, he couldn't see anywhere else left to turn.


The weather was not unlike a typical summer day in western San Francisco. A gray-white sky, so thick and choked with clouds that it took an extra moment just to find the sun. The air was a pleasant seventy degrees, but it felt colder because of the breeze coming down from the mountains.

They caught a taxi and were taken over the river to the south side of the lake. Jessica was questioning their latest driver about every monument they passed, and he was more than happy to play tour guide as they crossed the final bridge over the Rhone River. They reached the Rue de Rhone and went east along the river until reaching the Place Bel-Air. Nick paid the driver, and then they were just another two faces among the crowd on the boulevard. The cobblestone street was teeming with pedestrians browsing back and forth between the boutiques and outdoor cafes, and the two of them passed through the crowds, quickly finding the safety of an adjoining side street.

The bank of Hahn and Konauer was actually behind the Place Bel-Air, about three hundred yards from the river. It was a small yet secure looking two-story building sandwiched between an art store and a bakery. The first-floor windows were tinted and allowed no view inside. A gold-plated doorbell button was inlaid into the door frame. If not for the bronze address number, Nick would have seen no indication at all that this was indeed their bank.

"Here we are," he said. "I think."

Jessica backed up several steps into the street and surveyed the building. It looked as if it could house any of a hundred different businesses, and a bank wouldn't even be on the list. Nick stepped forward and pressed the doorbell. He glanced at her and could see his own tension mirrored in her face.

After a moment, the door swung inward with a shrill buzz. Nick stepped to the side and let Jessica enter first. A man in slacks and a white button-down was waiting. Nick noticed the pistol at his side.

"May I help you?" he asked, his French accent thick.

Nick answered, "We'd like to view the contents of a security box held here."

The man studied the two of them briefly before turning to a desk behind him. He picked up a phone and continued to watch them.

Nick glanced around. This still looked nothing like a bank. It was one room with a desk and a narrow carpeted corridor leading to another door. The walls were white and completely bare. The property looked vacant.

The guard replaced the phone. "Do you have the certificate to the box?"

Jessica handed the letter of authorization to him. He scrutinized it closely, holding it up to the light to check for watermarks. He handed it back to her with a frown.

"Come with me."

He led them down a corridor to a heavy metal door and slid a card through a sensor. Through the door a carpeted stairway ascended to what Nick assumed was the main floor, a larger room equipped with four heavy oak desks sporting computer monitors. Several impressive paintings hung on the walls, and some large potted plants added a touch of life.

They were directed to a black leather couch and barely had time to sit before a young woman in a fashionable business suit emerged from a rear office. Nick guessed she was no older than her mid-twenties.

"Hello," she said, extending her hand to them. "I am Bernadine Konauer, acting director." She looked them both over. "You wish to view the contents of a vault box?"

"Yes, we do," replied Jessica, extending the letter and her identification.

"But I've a question first," said Nick, guiding Jessica's hand down.

The woman gave him a curious look, as if he had just breached some unspoken rule of etiquette. "A question?"

"Right." He took the paper from Jessica and handed it to the banker. "This certificate was signed by Eric Konauer—"

"My father, yes. He is cofounder of the bank."

"I'd like to ask him some questions regarding the account."

"My father is out of the country," she replied, somewhat sharply. "What exactly would you like to know?" She read the owner's name from the certificate. "Monica Von Rohr is the owner. Her personal account information would be confidential."

"Can you tell us when the account was opened?"

"That I can allow," she said, taking several steps toward a desk.

"One other thing, Ms. Konauer," said Nick, removing a small piece of paper from his wallet. "We've come to Geneva on behalf of my uncle who's just passed away in the United States. We're aware that he very recently had a number of accounts with your bank. We'd like to gain ownership through right of inheritance. The only problem here is that we don't know if the accounts still exist. Could you please check these account numbers and tell me?"

"If these accounts aren't under your name, I can tell you very little. We maintain full customer confidentiality."

"And I respect that," replied Nick patiently. "But please try and see our problem. We're about to open a very time-consuming court procedure back in the United States that we wouldn't even have to bother with if we knew that the accounts were gone. All we want to know is if they still exist. I have the numbers here with me."

She took the paper, her frown widening. "Eight accounts your uncle had with us."

"Yes, he did. Uncle Ludwig always felt his money was safe here."

She studied Nick's face to detect sarcasm but found only a smile. She was suspicious, and Nick knew he needed to be careful. This wasn't like the American banks, where a customer tantrum would ensure a sympathetic talk with the manager. Getting upset here might get them thrown out, and that couldn't be allowed to happen.

"Give me a moment," she finally said, turning back to the desk.

Nick clasped his hands together and waited. From the assortment taken from Jacob's garage, he and Alex had actually counted nineteen accounts with Hahn and Konauer. He hoped these eight would provide an indicative sampling of the total.

Jessica had returned to the couch. Nick gave her a look of reassurance as he listened to Bernadine Konauer's fingers skim over the keyboard. He wished he had brought more account numbers.

He took a seat on the edge of the couch, clasping his hands together. Konauer was frowning at the monitor screen as her fingers pecked at the keys. Nick licked a finger and rubbed out a scuff on the tip of his shoe. He glanced back up as Konauer suddenly muttered something to herself. The banker's eyes were wide, an expression of surprise spreading on her face.

"Find anything?" Nick asked, rising from the couch.

"I'll need to access your uncle's records from my office," Konauer stammered, walking to a rear suite and abruptly shutting the door behind her.

Nick turned and gave Jessica a puzzled look. "Did I miss something?"

"She seemed a little . . . funny," commented Jessica.

"More than a little," said Nick, walking around to view the desk Konauer had just vacated. She had cleared the monitor screen. He was tempted to tap in some numbers himself but didn't want to push his luck.

Jessica stood. "Is something wrong?"

Nick strode around the office and glanced down the stairs. From what he could see, Konauer and the guard were the only employees present. He took a slow breath and told himself to relax. He was in Geneva, not San Francisco. The Swiss were known for unconventional banking. Relax.

He returned to the couch and motioned for Jessica to sit.

Ten minutes passed slowly.

The sudden buzzing at the front door was so loud Nick felt it through the soles of his shoes. Konauer's door instantly opened, and the banker took a single hesitant step out into view. Coming up the stairs, the dull thud of footsteps on carpet.

The policeman was short and rather slight, but there was a confidence in his stride. He said a quick word in French to Konauer, who responded with a nod.

"I am inspector Philippe Bourdier," he said, approaching Nick. "And you are?"

"Michael Collier," replied Nick.

"Your name?" asked the policeman, turning to Jessica.

"Jessica Von Rohr."

The policeman gestured to Konauer's suite. "May we speak in private?"

Nick paused, then arched an eyebrow at Jessica. Now this, he knew, was *not* normal, even for the Swiss. He noticed the armed guard who had gained them entrance downstairs was now standing watchfully at the top of the stairs.

He followed Jessica inside the office. The inspector shut the door and waited for them to take seats before speaking.

"You are here on behalf of your uncle?" he said to Nick.

"That's correct."

"Your mother is the named owner of an account here?" he asked Jessica.

"Yes, she is," confirmed Jessica. "She's deceased."

"Is this the only account she held with this bank?"

Nick had tired of the interrogation. "Is there a problem here?"

"Yes," replied Bourdier succinctly. He crossed his arms on his chest and began to pace slowly in front of them. "I have been notified by the bank proprietor of your inquiries into these accounts. The accounts to which you make a claim appear on a list the police have built over the last several months."

"What kind of list?"

"A list of marked accounts." He stopped pacing and faced them. "Your bank accounts, as well as a number of other accounts, are being used as evidence in a vast fraud investigation now being conducted by the Swiss police."

The policeman purposely paused to read both of their faces, looking for a telltale twitch or quiver of guilt. Nick kept his face calm, knowing well the techniques of police interviews.

"Fraud," he replied thoughtfully. "Have you spoken with the bank owner?"

"Monsieur Konauer has left the country under—shall I say—suspicious circumstances."

"You should probably speak with his daughter, then."

"She has been cooperative," Bourdier replied ambiguously.

"We just want to see the contents of a bank box," said Jessica. "We don't know about any fraud."

Bourdier leaned against the wall and crossed his arms on his chest. "The accounts you've asked about have all been illegally emptied. Every one of them." He looked casually at his fingernails. "Are either of you familiar with someone named Otto Kranzhoffer?"

Nick swallowed. Bourdier was laying a trap now, and he wasn't about to place his head in its jaws.

"No, I'm not," he replied, rather innocently.

The inspector looked to Jessica.

"I've never heard of him," she said.

Bourdier locked eyes with Nick. He let the room simmer for a moment before pushing away from the wall and opening the office door.

"Please wait in the lobby."

Nick nodded at Jessica, and they stepped outside. Bourdier motioned both Konauer and the guard over, and the three of them entered the suite to speak in private.

Nick immediately moved for Jessica. Their opportunity wouldn't last long.

"Come on," he whispered, taking her hand and pulling her along.

They quickly padded down the stairs. Nick was relieved to see that another guard hadn't assumed front door duty. He pushed the door bar and looked out into sunlight. Another police officer, probably Bourdier's partner, was happily chatting with a citizen.

"Walk," said Nick, tugging Jessica along in the opposite direction. "Casually."

They reached the end of the alley in seconds. Nick whisked her around the corner and looked about the avenue. Plenty of people to lose themselves in, but luckily a cab was parked just down the street. They ran up to it and slid in.

"The Beau Rivage, please."

The taxi moved through light traffic. They passed by the alley and had a perfect view as Bourdier and the security guard burst from the bank and sprinted to the corner of the boulevard. The second police-man joined in behind them, and the three of them fanned out in oppo-site directions down the street.

Nick frowned, his suspicions confirmed. He had heard a warning bell in the back of his mind as he had listened to the inspector, a signal telling him to get out. The Swiss police weren't the ones they needed to speak with. By tomorrow morning he hoped to acquaint himself per-sonally with one Otto Kranzhoffer.


Alex sat in the small studio apartment, shades drawn and lights dim. The situation was worsening. Bad news seemed to be snowballing, dragging her and Nick along with it.

The perky news anchor was annoying her. The woman was deliv-ering the morning news so glibly she seemed to be speaking directly to her, almost mocking her. Alex knew that was crazy, but she couldn't shake the impression. To make matters worse, the woman's shiny blond hair and perfect teeth were reminding her of Jessica Von Rohr.

The pretty blonde was droning on mercilessly, describing the current status of the ongoing search for fugitive Nicholas Merchant. The suspect was described as armed and extremely dangerous. A phone number to a police hot line was shown at the end of the story.

Alex angrily grabbed the remote and silenced the television. For several minutes she just sat and rubbed her eyes. Had it really been only *seven days* ago since they had found out about Gerald Jacobs? It seemed like a month—one terrible, disastrous month.

She reached for the morning edition of the *Albany Times Union*. The small headline still delivered a nasty jolt as she read it again.

FAMED PRIVATE INVESTIGATORS SLAIN IN LOS ANGELES . . .

She was genuinely frightened now, and more than a little paranoid. She couldn't possibly be out driving around, not if she wanted to feel safe. She was afraid to pick up lunch, for God's sake. She questioned whether she would be able to keep food down anyway.

Doug had called after she had left the Bronx and told her what had happened in Los Angeles. She had found the story on the second page of the *Times*. The brazenness of it was shocking. Apparently the killers had strolled right into the main office and done it. She had considered Lawrence Castleton nothing more than an unscrupulous bully these last four years, but there was no way that he or any other heir finder deserved to go out like that.

She walked to the window and pulled aside the curtain slightly. It was seven in the morning—one in the afternoon in Switzerland. Nick was safe and sound in Geneva—she hoped. He said he would try to sign Jessica Von Rohr at some point. This was looming larger in her mind every passing minute. They would be back sometime within the next day or two. If Jessica wasn't a client by then, it would be time to say goodbye, adios, sayonara. She rubbed her forehead. Four years of heir finding and look where she was now.

The phone made her jump. She stared at it like it was a bomb. This wouldn't be Nick. Or Doug. They knew to call the cellular.

The fax connected and clicked to life. She slowly approached it. She was expecting two documents, one of which would be another key addition to the Holtzmann file.

With any luck, the German courier's work would bolster their case. The old man at the Institute for Historical Review had said that Rudolf Hess had died in 1987 in Spandau prison. That being the case, Hess's death certificate would be on file with the department of health in the city of Spandau unless it had been removed for reasons of notoriety—a distinct possibility. But if Hess's was there, Holtzmann's should be too.

She considered the Jacobs/Holtzmann cover-up as she waited for the fax. If certain individuals were powerful enough to construct a fraud of this enormity, surely they would have had the common sense to cover their tracks and fabricate a false death certificate. If they had done so, the existence of the certificate wouldn't support any cover-up theories. But what if they hadn't been so thorough? The mere absence of a death certificate wouldn't prove anything, but as one of a handful of a growing number of other coincidental facts, the impact of the total would surely be strengthened.

The paper was curling through the fax. The courier had done his job quickly. The first sheet—a cover page with a hastily scribbled message. The second sheet—the death certificate of Rudolf Hess. She read the handwritten note.

*Unable to obtain death certificate for Ludwig Wilhelm Holtzmann. Health official says record "nonexistent." Please verify Spandau as Holtzmann's place of death.*

She was right, then—they had been sloppy. It was unbelievable how careless they had been in covering their tracks. It would have been relatively easy for them to get away with it. If they had only swept up after the old man's death, they would have been home free. The crumbs they had left were being detected now, scooped up and analyzed by people who were trained to take crumbs and blow them up under microscopes. She would make sure those mistakes exploded in their faces.

She sat back at the small kitchen table with a pad of paper. It was time to construct a chronology, a timetable of everything they had uncovered about Jacobs/Holtzmann. She suspected several hundred newspapers would be interested in hearing the story.

Alex spent an hour writing up the report. It was neither orderly nor neat, but for now she didn't care. All she wanted was to get it all down on paper; the final organizing of the information could take place later, when Nick was back. He would undoubtedly have more to add.

When she was done, she read everything, adding details here and there. It was an astounding story, but there were still too many gaps, so much unexplained. It was intimidating trying to put it together and much more complex than she was prepared to deal with.

She cast the papers aside. Without the entire story, the report lacked impact. The words were flat. Not real enough. It needed something more, something that would jar the recipients from their seats. Yes—whoever got the story needed to meet the partners of Merchant and Associates face-to-face. And she knew just exactly how that would happen.

She found her car keys and said a quick prayer. Back roads—she would take the back roads. She would drive safely and pray every mile of the way that the cops wouldn't see her. She wasn't wanted, but there was little doubt they knew exactly who she was. The last thing in the world she wanted to do was set foot outside the safe confines of the apartment, but it couldn't be avoided. Nick was depending on her.

She walked to the closet. The pistol was loaded. She placed it under her belt and stepped outside into the sunlight.

Three minutes after Alex left, the phone rang. The fax came to life with a whirl.

The credit transaction report for Michael Dean Collier was the seventh one she had received. Like the others, it was a standard printout, showing Mr. Collier's latest purchases, including his most recent flight and travel accommodations. But there was a crucial piece of new information. The current printout showed that a report had been requested and faxed to an unlisted telephone number in Brooklyn Heights, New York.

## CHAPTER 24

THE PASSENGERS IN the rear of the taxi were silent as the driver found the bridge to the north end of the lake. Nick sat slouched, his eyes on the frigid waters. Jessica had been silent since they had left the bank. The driver hummed along to a happy tune on the radio, oblivious to the both of them. The sun was sinking quickly to the horizon.

Nick checked his watch. Ten after five.

"It's too late to get anything else done today," he said. "We need to get back to the hotel. Maybe we can order up something to eat."

She rolled her head to him slowly, her face expressionless. "I don't think I'm very hungry right now."

He nodded and turned back to the lake. He wasn't particularly famished either, but it would at least waste some time until eight the next morning. They had over twelve hours to kill.

"I need a drink," she suddenly said. "Badly. You interested?"

"Read my mind."

"One rule. We don't talk about my mother or Ludwig Holtzmann until tomorrow. I'm sick and tired of thinking about this."

"Gladly. It's probably safest if we limit ourselves to the room, though."

She shivered noticeably. "You couldn't drag me out of there."

*      *      *

The driver let them off behind the hotel. They entered from the rear, and quickly but cautiously made their way up to their room.

Nick took the phone. "Red or white?"

"Red, please," Jessica replied, taking a seat on one of the double beds.

Nick ordered two bottles and hung up. He wasn't terribly fond of wine, but it packed more of a kick than beer did.

He entered the bathroom and looked himself over in the mirror, wincing a bit as he did. He looked bad. Bags under the eyes, sleep-deprived pallor, scraggly beard growth—he wondered how he would look in a week. He hoped he would be around to find out.

He shaved and took a quick shower, dabbing a towel to his face as he emerged from the bathroom. Jessica was curled up on her side, resting comfortably. She looked up at him and attempted a tired smile. She was very good-looking, the kind of woman who drew hungry stares from men and envious looks from women. Despite their personality clashes, Nick couldn't deny her allure.

"Could you pour me a glass?" she asked, gesturing to a table where two bottles of wine and glasses stood. Nick placed the towel aside and uncorked one of the bottles, filling both glasses. He handed her one and took a seat on the adjoining bed.

She took a long, slow sip, seeming to savor it. Nick gulped a mouthful and frowned. To him, it had a sweet, vinegary taste, but perhaps it would loosen him up a bit. He needed to limit himself to no more than two or three glasses. He had not forgotten what alcohol had almost done to him the other night.

They drank in silence for several minutes, listening to the sounds of the street outside their window. Nick finished a second glass and felt calmer. He looked down at the foot of the bed and noticed his bath towel bunched up on the edge of the mattress. He smiled to himself. Alex would wring his neck if he pulled that stunt at her place, which reminded him—he would need to call her very soon. He got to his feet and hung the towel in the bathroom.

Jessica was dozing on her side when he came out. It was the best option for both of them at this point. He reclined on the other bed. He could only pray that tomorrow would yield better results than their trip to the bank had.

"I spoke with a friend of mine in Colorado," she suddenly said. "As soon as we get back home, I'm flying to Denver. I'm staying with her for a while until all this cools off."

Nick turned on his side to face her. "Smart move," he replied. "I wouldn't go near Des Moines for a while."

"I was actually thinking of going to San Francisco. I have a friend there too. I've never been to California."

"You'd probably like it."

"I'm sure I would," she said. "I'm used to the city. I practiced in Manhattan for a while."

"Really," said Nick, not altogether surprised. Her background check revealed that she had earned her law degree in the state of New York. "That must have been rough—moving from Des Moines to New York City."

"It was at first. I made some good friends who helped me adjust, though."

"What did you do there?"

She opened her eyes. "I had a job in a Wall Street firm doing corporate securities work and billing twenty-five hundred hours a year. Seventy-plus hours a week. But I made good money, and that's what I'd always wanted." She sat up and reached for her glass. "That's what it's about, right? Money?"

Nick shrugged. Up until he had found the Jacobs case, he might have agreed. "My partner Alex was an attorney for a couple of years before she hooked up with me. She couldn't hack it. Didn't like her work, didn't like being bossed around. Hated everything about it, actually."

"Not everyone has what it takes to be a successful attorney."

"Alex has exactly what it takes," Nick said emphatically. "Her heart was never in it, that's all. It just so happens she loves private investigation, and she's very damn good at it too. She's probably the most capable investigator I've ever met, and I've met a hell of a lot of PI's."

Jessica refilled her glass, then asked, "How did you ever get into this heir-finding thing anyway?"

Nick hesitated. This was a question he normally shied away from, but the wine was making him comfortable. He poured himself a modest refill. Last one, he warned himself.

"My father was a cop for years, but he always wanted to start up a PI firm, only he didn't want to stake out apartments and click pictures of cheating spouses. One day he read an article about a one-man firm in Chicago that specialized in asset recovery, specifically through heir finding. He researched the industry, found a niche, and set up shop twelve years ago. I was in college at the time in Texas and didn't really know what I wanted to do. I came back to San Francisco after I graduated and became a cop, working with him on the side."

"So eventually he hired you full-time."

"Actually, no. He never got the business to the level where it could support two full-time investigators. It was only after he died and I took over that I found out just how much business there really was."

"Sounds like your father started a pretty good thing."

Nick nodded and rose to his feet, approaching the window. The water was oil black, the moon's glare dancing across its surface like a flame. The massive chateaus and villas dotting the shore on the opposite side of the lake stood like solitary castles in the night.

"He found a good niche," Nick said softly. "He didn't live to see the business reach its full potential. I tried to investigate his death after I quit the force, but nothing ever came of it."

"Investigate it?"

He stared into the dregs at the bottom of his glass. "He was murdered. The police never caught the killer. I didn't either."

She looked down. "I'm sorry to hear that."

He spoke after a few seconds. "It seemed like the right decision for me to take over. I felt like I *had* to keep the business alive. It was my way of keeping my dad alive." He paused, then started up again quickly. "The timing was perfect for Alex. She was hating life with a New York City law firm and really looking for a change. I taught her the ropes over the course of a few months and she set up a similar operation based out of her home in Albany."

"And that's worked out okay?"

He smiled. "It's worked out wonderfully. We're partners, yet we're independent of each other most of the time. She's really done great with the East Coast wing. I'm very proud of that girl."

"You two must do very well. You probably live in a mansion."

Nick shook his head. "I live—correction, *lived*—in a one-bedroom apartment not much bigger than this room. That was before it got blown to bits, of course." He turned to her. "You might laugh, but what I do isn't about money, believe it or not. If I could find heirs and make a cop's salary, I'd do it. It's the work itself that grabs me. It's fascinating. To be able to go to a stranger's home and tell him things about his own mother or father or brother or sister that he didn't know himself—that's just an incredibly powerful thing. I've never experienced anything quite like it." His face quickly turned somber. "I doubt I ever will again."

Jessica sat up and cradled her glass with both hands. "Can you I ask you something personal?"

"Why not?" he asked, barely hearing the question. All the talk about his father was starting to weigh on his mind. He wanted to lose himself in sleep for a few hours. He dumped the remainder of his glass out on the landing outside the window.

"You and your partner," Jessica said. "Are you . . . together?"

"Not at the moment," Nick replied, wondering why he hadn't just said no. "Why?"

"Just curious," she said, with a shrug. "I thought I picked up on some . . . undertones when we were in that apartment. Some sort of vibes— mostly from her, I guess."

"We're not together," said Nick flatly.

"I didn't think so," she said, placing her glass aside. "You two seem very different."

Nick's response came quickly.

"Funny you should say that, because when I think about it, we're actually about as similar as two people can be." He turned away from her. "Excuse me."

He entered the bathroom and shut the door. The wine had left a film in his mouth, and he cupped his hands under the faucet, using the cold water to gargle. He did that three times but still tasted a faint sourness.

He grabbed the towel and rubbed his hands dry. Something was bothering him about Jessica's last few observations. She was quick with her opinions, but she was off the mark regarding his relationship with Alex. The fact was, they were good for each other. It was a rare occurrence when he didn't talk to his partner at least three times a week, and he didn't mind the staggering phone bills. Somehow he had never considered any of their conversations strictly business. He enjoyed them too much to think that way.

The room was dark when he came back out. Jessica had clicked off the light next to her bed and pulled the covers over herself. Good, he thought. He would try to sleep as well, and with a little luck he might actually nod off for an hour or two.

His cell phone rang the second he reclined on the bed.

"Nick, it's me."

The urgency in his partner's voice instantly brought Nick to his feet. "What is it, Alex?"

"Thank God you answered," she said, breathless. "We got a fax—someone's been checking Michael Collier's credit transactions. They've got your alias, Nick—"

"Wait a second. What exactly does it say?"

"It says some company in Brooklyn Heights called Hamilton Leasing Agency has requested and been sent a copy."

"Hamilton Leasing Agency?" said Nick. "Could it be some kind of mistake—?"

"It's a bogus company, Nick. I called information, then I had Doug run the name. There *is* no Hamilton Leasing Agency."

Nick stepped to the window, purposefully avoiding eye contact with Jessica. The streets outside were dark but still full of pedestrians.

"Does it give a time when they ordered it?"

"It says yesterday. The—"

"*Yesterday?* You were supposed to be checking these every two hours—"

"There's a time gap!" Alex said, her voice desperate. "There's a lag of anywhere from twelve to twenty-four hours from when someone requests a report and when the request's actually logged. I just found this out, Nick!"

Nick was trying to show a facade of calm in front of Jessica, but his mind was in overdrive. Whoever had requested the report was now en route to them. Or already there.

"Okay then. I'll take care of it."

"Nick, they know you're there. *They know where you're staying.*"

"We'll be fine," he replied. "I'll do what I have to. Call you later, okay?"

"Be careful—"

He clicked the phone off and finally looked at Jessica. She was sitting up, her face worried.

"What's wrong?" she asked sharply. "What is it?"

He grabbed his suitcase and flipped it open. "We need to find new lodgings—just a precaution." He gave her an unconvincing little smile. "Get your bag, okay? We've got five minutes to pack."

The calm and cool act didn't work. Jessica latched on to his arm tightly.

"What exactly did she say, Nick?"

He saw by her eyes that she would not accept anything but the truth. He licked his lips.

"They know we're here," he said.


Regnier was in a heavy black coat and was standing at the far desk of the Beau Rivage. The girl at the counter was eyeing him nervously. The three bills were neatly laid out on the sleek marble surface between them.

"Very important," he said, flashing a cruel smile. He placed another fifty-franc note down with the other three.

She bit her lip and glanced down at the money. Her eyes darted down the lobby, then back to the bills. Her hand slipped out and drew the money toward her.

"Room 412," she said, turning and walking away.

Regnier put his hands deep in his pockets and walked through the lobby. He met his comrade outside. They spoke briefly, then split up and found their positions.


Nick and Jessica passed through a laundry room on the first floor, ignoring the curious looks of a half dozen maids. Nick pressed the rear door open as quietly as possible, scanning the back alleyway carefully. He motioned to Jessica and then they were out on the street, walking casually but briskly toward the boulevard.

They stopped under the shadow of a jewelry store canopy. The stars were gone, and a light rain was falling. Nick was staring down the street, his eyes on the illuminated sign of the Beau Rivage.

"Are you sure we've got everything?" Jessica asked.

Nick checked their surroundings before answering. He couldn't think of anything essential they might have left in their room. His travel bag had been haphazardly stuffed full of clothing and notepads.

"Let's get a move on," he said, taking her arm. "Come on . . ."

They hurried across the Quai du Mont-Blanc. The boulevard was an overwhelming commotion of noise and lights. Nick frowned. They were far safer catching a cab away from the city center, on a quiet street with sparse foot traffic. He scanned their surroundings a final time before directing Jessica down a poorly lit side street and heading south.

They walked quickly. The street was quiet and lined with little shops and trinket stores, all of which were dark and closed for the day. Pedestrians were few. A beggar sat on the sidewalk and muttered to himself. Nick raised the collar of his jacket and quickened his pace. Jessica had to hurry just to keep up with him.

"Where are we going?" she asked.

"We'll catch a cab a couple of blocks from here," he said. "Then we'll find a place to stay somewhere on the outskirts of town. Cash transactions from here on out."

He was not slowing his stride as he spoke. She stepped along quickly to keep pace.

"Walk any faster and I'll have to run," she said, trotting along at his heels.

"You're doing fine." Nick scanned two pedestrians as they passed by. He looked over at Jessica. "Come on, lady. I thought you were a jogger."

"Funny, I don't remember telling you that."

"You must have."

He slowed as they reached the corner. Another narrow street, devoid of much foot traffic. Nick scanned it and kept walking.

"I meant to ask you," Jessica said. "What's your take on all that business at the bank?"

"Still trying to figure that out," replied Nick. "I think I'll know more tomorrow."

She took three quick steps and pulled even with him. "Sounds like this Kranzhoffer stole my inheritance."

"*Your* inheritance? Jessica, these weren't clean accounts."

"My mother wouldn't have been involved in any fraud."

"I really don't want to talk about this right now. All I want to do is find a place where we can hide out. You should—"

Nick suddenly caught movement in his peripheral vision. They were no longer alone on the street. The man was tall and as big as a professional wrestler, and he was walking straight for them, his hand extended. Instantly Nick had Jessica step behind him.

"Light?" the man asked.

Nick studied him, studied the cigarette between his fingers. He placed his hand on Jessica's shoulder and moved them along again. "Sorry," he replied.

They were three or four steps away when the man spoke again. "Merchant!"

Nick's head turned involuntarily. In the dim light, he saw the stranger smile.

"And Blondie too," said the man, reaching into his coat and pulling out a gigantic, saw-toothed knife. "Remember our night in the park? Nowhere to run now, Nick . . ."

The street was empty and cold. Water flowed from a roof drainage pipe and trickled along the street in tiny rivulets.

The man stepped forward, the knife partially extended. Nick could barely breathe. He kept his eyes on the glimmering steel blade as he felt his heart kick into high gear. He had disarmed knife-wielding punks back on SFPD, but those had been nothing more than emaciated dopers, too strung out to pose much of a threat. This man was no blurry-eyed drug addict.

"Only hurts for a second, Nick," said the stranger, smiling. "I promise you . . ."

He shot the knife forward, making Nick flinch violently. The stranger chuckled as they circled each other. Nick held his eyes on the blade and kept himself fluid, ready to move. He could feel the ground, hard and slick beneath his feet.

The thug swiped a wild horizontal arc that made Nick draw back on his heels, and then he charged. Nick caught his wrist with one hand and threw a sharp uppercut to his attacker's chin. When his foot slipped he knew he was going down, but his grip on the wrist was tight, and he pulled the man down with him. A thick forearm leaned into Nick's throat, and then he was on his back, choking for breath and struggling to hold back the descending knife with his left hand. His vision started to waver as the sound of his own gagging filled his ears.

Out of the shadows, something swung through the air. Nick heard a solid whack, and all at once the stranger's grip loosened. Nick punched out viciously and caught him squarely in the throat as another sharp blow from behind struck his attacker in the back of the head. Nick slammed his knuckles solidly into his nose, and the man's eyes rolled in their sockets like loose marbles. He pitched forward with a groan, landing face-first on the pavement.

Nick squirmed free. Jessica dropped the brick and knelt down to him.

"Are you okay?" she asked. "Are you hurt?"

Nick stood and rubbed at his throat as his vision came back into focus.

He slowly nodded, coughing. He stooped down to the body on the ground, taking the knife. A quick search of the man's jacket and pants pockets turned up no ID. He stood and placed the knife in his coat.

"Jesus. We need to get out of here."

"What about him?" she asked, bringing her hands together to stop them from shaking.

"Let the rats have him. Let's get moving before his friends come looking for him." He pointed down the alley. "Quick—there's our ride."

They jogged down the alley and waved down the taxi. Nick held the door as she stepped in.

"Take us to the west side of town," Nick instructed the cabbie. "And make it quick, please. We need to find some lodgings."

The driver nodded and entered the street.

"Maybe we should get out of Geneva," Jessica suggested, a quavering still audible in her voice.

"We'll be fine if we can just get inside. They can't kick down every door in town."

She hugged herself and shivered noticeably.

"You all right?" he asked.

"Sure," she replied. "Someone just tried to kill us, and we can't set foot outside for fear of getting murdered in broad daylight. I'm wonderful."

Nick threw a quick glance at the driver, then looked over at her, placing a finger to his lips. He moved closer to her and spoke in a whisper.

"We'll be okay. We'll find a little inn we can check into on the edge of town and get some sleep. We're going to be up early tomorrow. I'm going to go see that PI in the morning, and then we'll pay Mr. Chagnon a visit. Once we—"

He stopped. Jessica was shaking her head back and forth.

"What?" he asked.

"After what just happened to us? No, no—I'm not stepping outside again until we leave the country."

A pang of irritation rippled through Nick. "Look," he said evenly. "If you want to sit it out when I go to the PI's office, that's fine, but I'm definitely going to need you afterward. Having you at Chagnon's could help me a lot."

"I did my part at the bank. You don't need me for anything else. I'm not risking my life so you can solve some big mystery."

"This *big mystery* may help me clear my name."

Her stare was adamant. "I'm not going anywhere." She looked up at him. "I'm sorry. It's all up to you now."

Nick almost exploded, but he was exhausted, tired to the point of defeat. He sat back on his side of the backseat and leaned his head back. He would try again in the morning. If need be, he would set off on his own. For now all he wanted was the nothingness of sleep.

He closed his eyes. He had never felt so wrung out before in his life. He wasn't sure how much longer he would even be able to run.

CHAPTER 25

THE STREETS OF Geneva came alive with the sunrise. Blue and white streetcars clanged and rumbled noisily along their steel tracks like giant toy trains as businesspeople hurried to work along the cobbled streets. The tightly packed little souvenir shops were open for business, and the cafes were filled with coffee drinkers shading themselves under colorful oversized table umbrellas.

Nick had gotten up early and showered, not bothering to wake Jessica as he left. The taxi was waiting for him outside. He instructed the driver to take him to the southern side of the lake, to the early morning bustle of Place Bel-Air. Nick sat low in the backseat, his eyes scanning the busy streets as they moved through traffic. The driver reached the address in twenty minutes' time and stopped the cab. Nick paid him, checked his surroundings, and stepped quickly to the curb.

He had managed to steal approximately five hours of sleep the previous night, but it felt closer to two. He had been troubled by dreams, none of which he could remember in detail, but they had been unsettling enough to prevent him from feeling completely rested. He would catch up on his sleep later—have all the time in the world to rest—when the Jacobs ordeal was over. For some reason, that thought wasn't comforting in the least.

The private investigator's office was just off the square, on a side street called Rue de la Cité. Arne Muend was one of three private detectives listed in the Geneva phone directory, and his proximity to the banks on Place Bel-Air made him Nick's rather arbitrary choice. The tiny ad offered spousal surveillance and background checks, among other services. Nick smiled grimly. Cheating husbands and wives knew no national boundaries.

He checked his notes for the address. The road was narrower and emptier than the Place Bel-Air and full of shuttered wooden buildings with colorful trim. A cluster of little stores—an art gallery, an antique shop, a travel agency, even a pet store—vied for the eye's attention.

Nick pressed the appropriate doorbell and waited. When the gate buzzed, he pushed his way in. Someone was waiting at the top of a flight of stairs.

Arne Muend was a fortyish man with wavy brown hair and a thick waxed mustache. He wore a checkered blazer and sat at a desk beneath a huge wall-mounted elk's head. He greeted Nick with a smile and a powerful handshake.

"Good to meet you," said Muend, gesturing to a chair in front of his desk. "I've made some very interesting finds for you."

Nick sat and looked over the tiny office. The elk's head stared down at him with dull glass eyes.

"I've a fondness for Americans," Muend said in a loud German accent. "I consider myself a bit of an American. I lived in your state of Colorado for nearly two years. The mountains—once you're near them, it's impossible to be away. May I ask what city you are from?"

"Phoenix."

"I know it. Flat and hot—not much else to it, eh?"

"Not much else," replied Nick, glancing at his watch.

Muend folded his hands on his stomach and smiled again.

"Before we begin, something I'm naturally a bit curious about," he said. "Switzerland is a long way to travel to see a private detective."

"I'm here visiting with some old friends," Nick replied. "Doing a favor for them. A confidential favor, actually."

"And it will stay that way. This goes without saying. You will hear many things said of the Swiss around the world, my friend. If you choose to believe any one thing, let it be that we have a keen respect for privacy." He tapped the side of his nose and winked. "We are exceptionally good at keeping our mouths shut. No matter what the circumstances."

"That's why I'm here."

"Of course." He removed a folder from a desk drawer. "Unfortunately we need to discuss payment first. Let me see—yes, five names. My fondness for Americans prevents me from charging you any more than two hundred and thirty francs. That rounds to one hundred and fifty American dollars."

Nick removed a roll of bills and peeled off a hundred and a fifty. Muend placed the bills in his coat pocket and nodded cordially.

"This was surprising," Muend said, leaning forward on his desk. "When I received your request yesterday, I immediately recognized half the names on the list. Anyone in Switzerland who reads the newspaper would have . . ."

Nick nodded. This sounded promising so far. "What can you tell me?"

"Let's start with the only nonbanker of the group, shall we?" He removed a piece of paper. "Otto Kranzhoffer."

Nick nodded, anxious for this. He hoped it would help him make sense of their encounter with the Swiss inspector the previous day.

Muend continued. "Swiss immigration records show that Herr Kranzhoffer arrived in Switzerland in 1961 from Austria. Since 1967 he had lived here in Geneva, on the Rue de Malatrex actually . . ."

"Nearby?" asked Nick.

"A short walk."

"Good. I'll take that address."

"You may want me to finish first," replied Muend, lowering the paper. "Herr Kranzhoffer died last February. Heart attack."

"Christ," muttered Nick, rubbing his forehead. He let out a long breath. "Any details on that? Do you know for certain it was a heart attack?"

"His chauffeur found him at home. The autopsy was very conclusive."

"Chauffeur. Was he wealthy?"

"Was he wealthy?" asked Muend, seemingly amused by the question. "As a king, my friend. But no one knew until after he was gone."

"I don't understand."

"One week after his death, a legal request was filed with the public court of Geneva. A man claiming to be his son stepped forward and tried to make a claim on the estate. His name was Erich Eckart. Do you know this name?"

Nick shook his head slowly. "Should I?"

"Not likely that you would," replied Muend. "To make the story short, Eckart presented documentation showing Otto Kranzhoffer to actually be someone by the name of Hans Eckart. The court found the paperwork to be proper and true. Before it could render a ruling, however, city officials by custom were required to enter Herr Kranzhoffer's home on the Rue de Malatrex and appraise the property. Shortly after this they did so. What they found inside was beyond what anyone could have imagined."

"What was it?"

"An astounding collection of valuables. Vases of pure gold, close to a dozen classical paintings, gold bars—every possible bit of Nazi plunder you could imagine."

"Maybe he was a collector," Nick said, although the suggestion sounded hollow. "How do you know it was Nazi plunder?"

"The surveyors reported what they had seen, and experts were brought in. Within several weeks, the authenticity of seven original medieval paintings which had vanished during the war had been confirmed. In addition to this, over four hundred kilograms of pure gold bars were found in his cellar. Oh, it was incredible, my friend—front page news in *Le Matin*. A day later, the historians came forward with more information. Hans Eckart was verified to be a Nazi war criminal who had vanished in 1945. Naturally, after this information was revealed, Erich Eckart's request for inheritancy rights was promptly refused."

Nick rubbed his chin and frowned distantly. Eckart and Holtzmann—two criminals who clung to each other in life and who would almost certainly be spending their eternities together.

"So what about the others?" he asked.

"Ah yes," Muend said, finding another paper. "The others. Here's where things get interesting. As I said earlier, the four other names you selected are known to many Swiss, especially those in the newspaper business. And the police stations. These are bankers—did you know that?"

"I did."

"May I ask you one final question?"

"I suppose."

"Might these four bankers be the old friends you spoke of?"

"They might be," said Nick, after a pause.

"I feared that. I'm sorry to say that your friends are all gone. Let me go down the list chronologically." He cleared his throat and read. "Henry Blaus, managing director of Burg and Blaus of Geneva. Murdered in Paris in November 1997. Found stabbed in an alleyway. No one arrested for the crime. The Parisian authorities have closed the case. Just like our French friends, eh? Quick to give up.

"Oscar Roullon, director, Droz and Cie of Geneva." He looked up at Nick and winked. "Here's where the tactics changed. He was found at the bottom of a ravine in March of 1998. A fall—seemingly. Apparently Herr Roullon was an avid hiker, but odd, wouldn't you think—a seventy-two-year-old man choosing to venture out by himself into a region he had never visited before? This is the story from his widow."

Nick spoke quickly. "What's this you say about 'tactics'?"

"First the final two names." He looked back at the paper. "Charles Chagnon, president of Alban-Witz, a very prestigious private bank here in Geneva. Located very close by, actually. Herr Chagnon drowned in a boating accident on our lovely Lac Léman. Classified as—wouldn't you know—an accident. June of 1998. This brings us to the final one of your friends . . .

"Amil Gubelin, director, Gubelin and Cie of Lausanne. Herr Gubelin vanished in July of 1998. The police have been unable to trace his whereabouts. The newspapers speculate that he fled the country in fear for his life. Who could blame him, I say. I think he saw what was coming. The authorities are of course connecting it to the *Die Bankmörder*."

"The what?"

"*Die Bankmörder*—the banking murders. A name created by the Zurich newspaper *Tages Anzeiger*. Understand something: bankers in this country are held in a certain esteem. If one is murdered, this is front-page news. But one murdered, two killed in peculiar accidents, and one vanished in the span of a year and a half? Can you imagine? It's outrageous."

"What have the police found? They must be piecing some of it together."

Muend gave a short derisive laugh. "You would think so, eh? The only group in Switzerland that is more secretive than the bankers is the police. They've released almost no information of their investigations.

The *Tages Anzeiger* has even gone so far to say that they are part of it. Once the police heard that, forget it—they closed up tighter than a clam. But I tell you, they would be quick to congratulate themselves if they had indeed found the murderers or some important leads. My opinion is that they have no information to release. Nothing at all."

Nick felt overwhelmed with what he was hearing. He chewed a fingernail as he thought.

"Back to Chagnon. You said he died in a boating accident, correct?"

"Correct. June of 1998."

"Now, who is *Victor* Chagnon?"

Muend found the paper. "His only son."

"He's taken over as bank director, then."

Muend shook his head. "When his father died, he left the bank. I understand he's hired private security guards and become somewhat of a recluse. He hasn't been seen in public for quite some time."

"I need his address."

Muend handed him the paper and pointed at the address.

"Herr Chagnon has an estate on the southern edge of the lake. It's an exclusive community with no public roads. You may have to shout through a gate to get anyone's attention. Be careful, though."

"Why?"

"You'll need to be," said Muend, nodding his head grimly. "These people are very different from us, my friend. But you may have one thing in your favor. In Geneva, you have a better chance of getting answers from a recluse than you do from a banker."


Nick checked the street before stepping out into the open. He neared the corner of Place Bel-Air and Rue de la Cité cautiously, stopping behind a large metal dumpster. He scanned the boulevard. People were everywhere. He stepped back into the doorway of a small gift shop and pulled out his phone. Jessica needed a wake-up call if she wasn't already up. He would try to convince her to accompany him to Victor Chagnon's one final time, and now that she had had a night's sleep he suspected he might have more success. He flipped open the phone, and as he was set to punch buttons he spotted them.

They were on a corner across the street, just three pedestrians in the crowd. He recognized his ponytailed assailant instantly—he was just standing there, in broad daylight, speaking to two smaller cohorts. Nick quickly backed into the gift shop and found a spot behind a display window to watch them. Ponytail was talking, and he didn't look pleased. The big man took a step away from his companions and pointed down the street, then gestured the other way. He threw his arms in the air in a clear gesture of frustration. His mouth was moving quickly, giving harsh instructions.

Nick took a step back from the window. It was sobering to see them, but better for him to spot them than the other way around. It was a grim reminder not to let his guard down, even for a second. He doubted if they were the only three hired hoods looking for him on the streets of Geneva.

A sudden noise from behind gave Nick a start. An overweight Swiss woman smiled at him nervously from behind a cash register. He returned an awkward smile and looked around the cramped little store. Delicate little collectibles filled wooden tables and shelves. Displays were filled with porcelain bells and figurines, tiny clocks and little wood-framed watercolors. He picked up a small music box and opened it as he kept his eyes on the trio across the street. He listened to the tinny sound and automatically thought of Rose. His jaw clenched hard enough to hurt. He had never returned from a foreign excursion without bringing his secretary some sort of little trinket. This would be the first time.

He closed the cover of the box and glared at his three pursuers in the distance. He couldn't tolerate standing there any longer, cowering in the shadows. Hurriedly he scanned the interior of the small shop. He found what he was looking for beneath a display of clocks. It was a four-piece fireplace set, but one part in particular grabbed his attention. He reached for the pointed black poker. It was an ideal length and weight— the perfect billy club. He wanted nothing more than to make immediate use of it, but not to stir coals.

Outside, a cab had pulled to the curb next to his pursuers. Ponytail threw out a few more brusque words to his two lackeys before hopping into the taxi and speeding off. The two remaining men said a final word to each other and separated, walking in opposite directions down Place Bel-Air.

Nick stood, torn by conflicting impulses. Part of him wanted to chase one of them down, beat the living hell out of him. But his logical side told him to stay back, not to do something foolhardy. For once he wished the logical part of his brain wasn't so damn persuasive.

He placed the poker aside. As he was heading for the door, some-thing made him pause. He walked back to the display table and took one of the little watercolors, bringing it to the counter. He paid cash, slipping it into his pocket before cautiously stepping out to the street and ducking into a taxi.

At midnight Doug grabbed his coat, switched off the lights, and locked up the office. He was exhausted and irritable, but his work was done. Every couple of weeks, he would put in one of the necessary late nights and play catch-up. This night had been for the benefit of a demanding but rather wealthy client living in Pacific Heights who tended to shout when neglected. Six extra hours of work on his pending divorce hearing would hopefully lessen the chances of catching heat from him in the morning.

Doug entered the Jag and sped out of the lot into the street. Powell Street was bathed in the orangy-white glare of streetlights. The tops of skyscrapers were lost in a flowing haze of fog. On the streets, the bums had hunkered down for the evening on their carefully primped little nooks of concrete.

He drove up Geary and made a left on Polk to take the freeway home. The tarnished white palace of City Hall lay ahead, bathing in the searing white heat of its own searchlights. In front of it, Civic Center Plaza with its scattered encampments of the less fortunate.

Doug braked at a yellow light and thought of Nick for the hundredth time that day. He wasn't quite sure where his friend was at that moment. His phone had been frighteningly quiet. He just hoped and prayed Nick was still alive.

Doug was too lost in his thoughts to notice the police car that had been tailing him for several blocks. The red and blues were flashing suddenly, and a quick bleep of the siren made the cops' intentions clear. A floodlight bathed the back of Doug's neck in a blinding glare. He swore and made a right on Grove Street, pulling to the curb. With all the junkies and drunks near Civic Center, they had to bug an honest cit-izen like him.

He found his license and registration as he heard the cop's heavy boots stepping toward his door. A flashlight beam skimmed over the front and backseat before the officer spoke.

"License and registration, please."

Doug handed them over. "What's the problem?"

The cop didn't even look at him. He glanced at the license and then turned back to his car. "It'll just be a minute," he said, disappearing back into the glare.

Doug slouched back and listened to the police car's radio crackle. God, he was drained. All he wanted to do was collapse next to Kimberly and pass out. He had received three calls from SFPD that day and returned none of them. Did this harassment have something to do with that? He had nothing to say to them! *No, I don't know where Nick Merchant is. No, I haven't spoken to him. No, I won't come down and speak with the detectives.* Jesus Christ already! This Jacobs thing had been an absolute nightmare.

The cop walked slowly back to the side of the car after about five minutes. "I'll need you to step out of the car, sir," he said.

Doug thought he might have heard him wrong. "Excuse me?"

"Could you please step out of the car?"

"What the hell for?"

The cop's hand settled on his holster. "Step out of the car now, sir."

Doug unlatched his seatbelt and slowly stepped to the pavement. He glanced at the police car, then back at the cop. This had gone beyond simple harassment.

"What's the problem?"

"Step to the sidewalk, please."

Doug hesitated, then did as he was told. It was then he noticed that a gray sedan had pulled to the curb behind the cop car. Two shadowed figures in suits were stepping out. Detectives?

One of the men approached the police officer and nodded. The cop said something back and gestured over at Doug. The newcomer approached him, and as he did, Doug remembered the face.

"Agent Healy, FBI. Met you yesterday."

"I didn't realize it would be a daily occurrence. What is this?"

"Agent Zepeda and I would like your permission to search your car."

Doug blinked. *"What?"*

"I'm asking for permission to search your car."

"Get out of my face."

"We've received a tip from a reliable informant that your car may be involved in the transport of narcotics—"

*"Narcotics—"*

"—so with or without your permission, we *will* be searching your car. Give me the keys."

"What informant?" Doug took a step back. "You're not getting my keys."

The two cops, as well as the other FBI agent from his office that morning, were by Agent Healy's side now.

"I'll ask you one last time. Keys."

Doug weighed the situation momentarily before muttering a curse and fishing into his pocket. A hollow, sick feeling was suddenly aching in his stomach.

The two agents ducked into the Jag. They looked under the seats, pulled loose the paneling, emptied the glove box. Doug looked help-lessly over at the cops, who were standing nearby pretending not to pay attention. Several midnight pedestrians had stopped to gawk.

The agents moved on to the trunk. It took four or five seconds before Healy removed the bag, looked at it, then stared over at the attorney. Doug's eyes shot wide. He ran up to them.

"What's that!" he demanded, his fists clenched. "What the fuck is that!"

He could see what it was, or at least what it appeared to be. It was a large, clear cellophane bag. It was filled with a fine white substance he assumed wasn't powdered sugar.

The Agent named Zepeda tore the bag and dipped his finger in, touching it to his tongue. He nodded.

"Put your hands on the hood," said Healy.

"You gotta be kidding me," said Doug, backing away. "You piece of shit . . ."

"Put your hands on the hood!" shouted Zepeda.

"Kiss my ass!"

The cops were immediately back in the fray. The four of them shoved Doug face-first against the hood of the car. They pulled his arms back and applied the cuffs tightly. After patting him down, they half dragged, half carried him back to the unmarked sedan and tossed him in the back, slamming the door on his shouting.

Doug cursed and yelled for several minutes before tiring. His head was spinning. He could never have prepared himself for this. He thought of Kimberly and the girls. Try explaining this to them. See you in the Big House, Daddy—visiting hours every Sunday.

He leaned forward and tried to watch through the fogged windshield and the swirl of flashing lights. The four of them were congregating on the sidewalk. The agent held several white bags now. Another two black-and-whites slowly cruised by and left. More gawkers were gathering on the sidewalk, stealing glances at him like leering apes.

He hunched forward and wiggled his fingers. They were numbing up on him quick. His wrists were rubbed raw from the handcuffs. He waited and felt very frightened.

The cops who had pulled him over finally got in their car after about fifteen minutes and pulled off into traffic. The two federal agents slammed the trunk of the Jaguar, gathered up the bags in their arms, and slowly strolled back to the car. They reentered and swiveled to look at him.

"You can't possibly be this low," said Doug, forcing some restraint into his voice. He scanned both their faces. "You can't be. Listen, whatever Nick Merchant's done, I don't deserve this."

Agent Zepeda seemed unfazed by the argument. "Heard the news about Lawrence Castleton, Spinetti?"

"Yes, I have. I think it's terrible."

"I bet you do," he replied. "We aren't the only ones after Merchant, are we? For his sake, you should hope we find him first."

"I couldn't agree more." Doug leaned forward and tried to look as contrite as possible. "What do you guys want from me? I'm not speaking with the guy, I don't even know where he is. Why bother with me? I'm nothing, I'm nobody."

"Those cuffs tight enough?" asked Healy. "What do you think of when they dig into your wrists like that? Do they make you think of your little girls? Or maybe you think of some good-looking young stud hopping on your wife because she didn't feel like waiting fifteen to twenty for your release?"

"Do you know how close you are to seeing it all go down the crapper, counselor?" asked Zepeda loudly.

Doug bowed his head. "I get the picture."

"Are we finally making ourselves clear about how important this Jacobs business is?"

Doug was nodding, his eyes down. He was through arguing. "Yes," he said. "You've made yourself clear."

Agent Healy let the silence torture him a bit longer before speaking.

"There's a court hearing scheduled two days from now in New York State. As it turns out, you have a schedule conflict. A prior engagement. Check your day planner, Spinetti. Find something else to do that day. Go to that fancy club you belong to and practice your putting."

"It's a pretty good deal, Spinetti," said Zepeda. "Skip this hearing and you get your life back. Doesn't take a genius to figure out this one."

Doug considered it in silence. Not much to consider really. "Okay, okay—I understand. I agree to everything. No hearing, no nothing. Can you take these cuffs off now?"

"Sure, we'll take them off," replied Healy. "But you go back on your word and it may not be flour we're finding in your car next time. If you do try to attend this hearing, you'll be stopped. We're very serious about this, counselor. Next time it'll be the real thing."

They walked him out to the sidewalk, removed the cuffs. The thought of decking the two of them flashed through Doug's mind, but sleeping next to Kimberly that night was now priority number one.

"Think about what Agent Zepeda said," said Healy, handing back the keys and driver's license. "Better we find him than the other guys. You read what they did to Castleton. How long do you think he can run from them? One mistake—that's all it's gonna take. One mistake and he's gone."

"It's gonna happen, Spinetti," chimed in Zepeda. "Count on it. At least if *we've* got him, he'll have a fighting chance. I want you to think about that. You can still save your friend's life."

"Talk to you soon," said Healy. He and Zepeda turned and walked back to their car.

Doug could think of several choice responses, but he thought better of sharing them. He returned to the Jag and slumped into the driver's seat. The FBI agents pulled from the curb, Zepeda giving a wave from the passenger window. Doug slowly raised his key but couldn't find the ignition. He lowered his head to the steering wheel and closed his eyes.

CHAPTER 26

FOR DECADES THE sprawling estates on the southern edge of Lake Geneva have been inhabited by the wealthiest of Genevese. Steep and winding private streets lead to the homes, immense mansions shielded by high concrete walls and retractable steel gates. Each street corner is equipped with a security camera directly linked to the network of police stations along the southern bank. Crime in the area is virtually nonexistent.

The Chagnon manor was located on Rue du Lac, an immaculate cul-de-sac with spotless concrete sidewalks and bronze streetlights. Rue du Lac was only accessible after clearance through a security station that blocked the mouth of the street. Two security guards manned the station at all times.

Nick sat in the back of the taxi and stared out at the gate. The driver watched him with concealed amusement in his rearview mirror.

"Oh man," Nick muttered to himself as he pondered the imposing steel barrier. "Good luck."

The driver turned to him. "Your stop," he said, the statement sounding more like a question.

Nick frowned. The driver wasn't the only one who was wondering what the hell they were doing there. What seemed like such a logical plan in the States now seemed doubtful at best, outright ludicrous at worst.

"I need you to wait here," Nick said to the driver. "It won't be any more than a few minutes."

The cab driver shrugged and found a cigarette as Nick stepped out to the road.

He was alone. Jessica had again refused to accompany him. He had tried to convince her of the necessity of her coming along, but she had been adamant. It was his problem to fix, his mystery to solve, and she wasn't going to be the one who lost her life over it. He had been angry, but at the same time he had understood. What real right did he have to get upset with her? He *had* been the one to bring the Jacobs estate into her life, and she had lost a brother and been chased across the globe because of it. Maybe Jessica Von Rohr had done all that could be reasonably expected of a normal person. Either way, he had hung up the phone and left her in the room.

Nick headed up the inclined street to the security station. A frowning guard glared down at him from behind heavily tinted glass and waited. The gate seemed to expand as he neared it. A lack of horizontal crossbars made scaling it virtually impossible. Nick had a passing vision of himself trying to clamber over the top, and he had to smile at how stupid he would look trying

Barely visible through the dark glass, the guard leaned forward and waited for him. An intercom buzzed.

Nick stopped in front of the booth. He glanced back at his taxi, then nodded a greeting to the guard.

"I've come here to see Victor Chagnon," he said. "I'm a private investigator from the United States. I have important news for him."

A second guard Nick hadn't noticed appeared at the window. The two of them stared at Nick with disinterest.

"I am not a reporter," continued Nick. "Or a policeman. All I want—"

A suspended speaker crackled to life.

*"Monsieur Chagnon doesn't see anyone but family."*

"Monsieur Chagnon would surely like to hear me out," replied Nick. "This has to do with the murder of his father."

The guards looked at each other. Nick held his ground. It was a risky statement, one that would undoubtedly get him tossed back out very quickly if he couldn't back it up inside. But he had to get in.

He heard the speaker click off as one of the guards reached for a phone. Nick glanced back down the street. The cabbie was looking back at him, finishing his smoke. He kicked a pebble and waited, feeling small and very exposed standing there in the street. He tried to bolster himself by mentally reviewing Alex's conversation with Chagnon, but he suddenly felt considerably less confident over his chances to meet with Chagnon. He wondered why he had felt so certain before.

It took the security guard nearly three minutes to hang up the phone.

"He doesn't wish to see you," the man said. "Leave now."

Nick stepped forward and placed a hand up against the glass. "I have to see him," he said.

"Leave now or you'll be placed under arrest."

Nick stood there, defiant. He reached into his shirt pocket and found a business card. "I've written my phone number on the back of the card," he said, placing it into a sliding tray in the front of the station. "Tell Mr. Chagnon if he wants to find out more about his father's murder to call me. Tell him I know all about Holtzmann and Taylor. If he has any shred of courage left in himself, he'll call me."

He slapped the plastic cover of the tray shut loudly. The guards did not draw it in. Without so much as another glance, Nick turned back to the waiting taxi.

"That's it," he said, slamming the door shut. "Let's get out of here."

Nick watched the gate shrink as they drove off. This wasn't the end of it. He would take the phone number Muend had given him, and he would call every five minutes until he got Chagnon on the line. He would do that for twenty-four hours straight. If that didn't work, he would consider his last-ditch options. If he could just figure out what exactly those were.

Nick gripped the phone and silently cursed. Twentieth ring and no sign of life. He had called Victor Chagnon a dozen times in two hours and gotten nowhere. He dropped the phone to the cradle and rubbed his eyes.

"Nothing?" Jessica asked.

"Muend wasn't too sure if the number was correct," replied Nick. "I think it's bad."

"So now what?"

"Grab your skis," he replied bitterly. "Let's hit the slopes."

Nick let himself fall back to the mattress, his thoughts black. He felt a piece of paper being placed into his outstretched hand.

"We need to talk about that whenever you get a chance," Jessica said.

Nick sat up. She had slipped him one of his blank inheritance contracts.

"What about it?" he asked.

"You don't want me to sign it?"

Nick held the paper, looking at it blankly, then suddenly crumpled it up. He tossed it to her, rolling it to her feet in a tight ball.

"You don't want to make your claim anymore?" she asked.

"I have a few slightly more pressing concerns at the moment."

"Well, I intend to make *my* claim," she said. "Do you still want to represent me in court?"

"I can't jeopardize my attorney or anyone else by having them make an appearance at this hearing. If whoever's behind this wants to stop the hearing, what will they do? They'll stake out the courthouse and try to make a final hit right there."

"How could they? The streets are probably packed outside, and the inside is full of metal detectors and bailiffs."

"Metal detectors and bailiffs aren't enough. You're more likely to get killed on the street than inside anyway. It's not worth the risk."

"It *is* worth the risk." She sat next to him. "This is enough money to live comfortably for the rest of your life. This is what you broke into that damn house for, what you risked everything for. You deserve this money—"

"No one deserves this money."

"Probably not, but isn't it a good thing to get it away from these crooked bankers? They've been sitting on these assets for over *fifty* years now. At least you'd get it out of their hands, right?"

Nick fell back to the mattress. He stared at the ceiling and pondered her words. A week ago, her argument might have made a lot more sense. Now it didn't sit right.

"I'll figure all this out later," he finally said.

"There's nothing to figure out, Nick. The hearing's tomorrow and I'm signing it. If you don't want to be a part of it, I'll understand. I can write up my own contract and make a claim all by myself."

Nick was about to respond when his phone suddenly rang. He reached for it, hope against hope.

"Hello. Hello?"

"My name is Victor Chagnon."

Nick exhaled in relief. He quickly walked away from Jessica, sitting on the opposite bed.

"Thank you for calling me back, Mr. Chagnon. My name is Nick Merchant. I've been trying to speak with you. My associate called you the other day regarding Ludwig Holtzmann—"

"That's what I thought," the voice said. "Listen closely. Go to Lyon Park on the western edge of Geneva at exactly ten o'clock. Enter from the north side of the park and follow the signs along the Touillon path. Come alone. You will walk for five minutes and come upon a bench. Sit there and wait."

"I'll be there. Do you—"

"Come alone."

The click of the line silenced him. He put the phone away and clenched his fist.

"Chagnon's going to meet with me. I need to find out where Lyon Park is."

Nick found the map of Geneva and laid it out on the bed.

"When are you meeting?" asked Jessica.

"One hour," replied Nick, glancing at his watch. He ran his finger across the map. "Maybe we won't be flying home empty-handed after all."

"Just so long as you fly home, *period*. Why do you think you can trust this person?"

"Common enemies," replied Nick. He jabbed at the map. "Here it is—all the way on the other side of town. Nice and desolate, I assume."

Jessica grabbed his arm. She said, "And you're not concerned about meeting with some stranger in a desolate park? How do you know he's not going to put a bullet in you?"

"I *don't* know, but I'm a lot more scared of what will happen if I *don't* meet with him. Once he hears what I have to say, he should see I pose no threat. Remember that conversation my partner had with him a couple of days ago? This guy hates Taylor."

She shook her head, hardly convinced. She sat on the bed and brought a pillow up to her chest. "If you're wrong, you'll be all alone there. No gun, no nothing." She shivered. "I don't think you should go. Why take the risk?"

"Everything I've done for the past week has been a risk," said Nick, finding a notepad and pen. "How's this any different?"

He began scribbling an addition to his trip log, acting as if Jessica's words hadn't stayed with him. If he was wrong about Chagnon, the chase was going to come to a rapid—and very final—end. But that was already the case for two unfortunate people by the names of Rose Penn and Matt Von Rohr. It was a risk he had to take. Whether he wanted to or not.

Beneath an oppressive gray sky, the seasons were changing in Geneva. The colors and life of summer were fading, a collage of decaying foliage and greenery. The air hung warm and dry, trying unsuccessfully to breathe life into the last remnants of summer. Nature had begun its solemn slide into the bleakness of winter.

Nick had walked for nearly five minutes, encountering only two pedestrians along the wooded path. The young man and woman seemed to be enjoying the ambience of the changing seasons, a state of mind Nick found impossible to duplicate. He was feeling guilty about Alex. He had chosen not to let her know about this latest development, but his secrecy was not meant solely to assuage her fears. The nervousness and doubts she would undoubtedly have expressed over the meeting would only have fueled his own reservations, which at the moment were nagging at him yet again.

He considered the proper approach with Chagnon. He needed to be concise, yet there was so much he needed to include. He shook his head at the thought of it all. No matter how eloquent he was, there was no guarantee Chagnon would buy a shred of his story. He could scarcely believe it himself, and he had witnessed it all firsthand.

He rounded a corner and abruptly stopped. A bench, forty yards from him—first one off the southbound path. He paused and glanced about cautiously. Somehow, just striding up and taking a seat didn't seem very prudent, but he saw little alternative. He stood for a moment longer, then stepped out into the open. He walked quickly, tensed to react at the first sign of anything unusual. He wondered if he was being watched. Reaching the bench, he looked around, then forced himself to sit down. Leaning forward with his elbows on his knees, he took a careful look about. There was no sign of anyone else, just the quiet serenity of the park. It seemed an unthreatening, neutral place to meet.

Nick leaned against the back of the bench. He felt as calm as he could possibly feel under the circumstances. Chagnon would want to hear him out. The banker had nothing to risk by listening. But just because he would listen didn't mean they were going to be exchanging gifts. From what Muend had told him, Chagnon was on edge, a virtual recluse hiding from professional killers who had already done away with his father. Nick frowned. Every word out of his mouth needed to be spoken carefully. He wouldn't grovel, but if playing to the man's ego would get him the information he sought, then he wouldn't hesitate.

Ten minutes passed. It was nearly a quarter after the hour and no one was in sight. No sound except the occasional lonely cry of a bird. Nick rubbed his legs and felt his anxiety building again. From what little he knew, Chagnon didn't seem like the kind of person who would normally be late. Had something gone wrong, perhaps scared him off? How skittish was this man?

Something snapped behind him, instantly bringing him to his feet. There was movement deep in the brush—something big—and what sounded like the steady hum of an engine. He backed up several steps, ready to move if need be. He squinted through the foliage. There was a large black car coming, following a dirt path so rough and overgrown he hadn't even noticed it.

Despite his wariness, Nick again felt comforted. Chagnon was probably going to take him to another location, and that was fine as long as they got the time they needed to talk face-to-face. The more he thought about it, the more confident he felt. Chagnon would *have* to be impressed by his story. Maybe they could even work together somehow.

The car emerged from the brush, dusty and leaf-laden. Nick could see the driver but little else. A side door flew open, and an average-sized man in a gray sport coat emerged from the car. Nick stood still, waiting for some indication of the agenda. He took a step forward and heard a voice.

"Raise your hands."

Another man had stepped from the trees behind him, a pistol held at arm's length. Nick paused, not having expected to see guns drawn.

"I don't have a weapon," he said, lifting his arms.

The man from the car descended on him quickly. He patted at Nick's clothes, then ran a handheld metal detector over him.

"I'm not armed," Nick repeated.

The two of them drew back and studied him. The armed man had

lowered his weapon, but the barrel still pointed directly at Nick's stomach. Nick began to drop his arms slowly.

"Up," said the man, flicking the barrel of the gun upward.

Nick quickly obliged. The two of them were gruff and angry looking.
Apparently they had been given the job of screening him.

"I don't mean Mr. Chagnon any harm," Nick said softly. "I just want
to talk."

The gunman frowned, his eyes narrowing distrustfully. He made a
short sweeping motion with the gun in the direction of the car.

"In the front."

Nick did as he was told as the two of them entered from opposite
rear doors. He glanced at the driver, an older man who didn't acknowl-
edge him. The car instantly did a tight U-turn and moved up the path it
had arrived on.

Nick tried to concentrate on his script as he watched the branches
scrape against the side windows. He could understand their caution, but
somehow he hadn't expected to be brought to Chagnon at the point of a
gun. Armed bodyguards certainly weren't a surprise, but they were making him feel more like a prisoner of war than a courier of valuable news.

The car did not drive for long. It was difficult for Nick to gauge
exactly how far they had traveled, but it was easily within walking distance from their meeting point. The second the vehicle stopped, he
heard the rear doors open.

"Step out."

Nick forced his door open against some bushes and slid out. They
were under a canopy of low-hanging branches, thick enough to block
out any direct sunlight. Again the gun was trained on Nick. The other
man walked to the edge of an embankment and looked back at him.

"Go," said the gunman, using the pistol as a pointer. "Follow him."

"I don't have a weapon," said Nick, a bit angry now. "I don't think
you need the gun."

The barrel was redirected at Nick's face.

"Walk."

Nick walked. The sooner he made it to wherever they were taking
him, the quicker he could get away from the goons. Chagnon surely had
to be more reasonable than his hired help.

The path was steep, with loose, dry dirt that broke away easily. The
ground gave twice under Nick's feet, forcing him to a knee. Behind him
the gunman followed, maintaining a safe distance. Nick reached the

bottom of the hill, trotting down the last few steps. Thirty yards in front, two men waited.

Nick immediately guessed which one was Chagnon. He was a gray-haired, bearded man of about fifty seated on a fallen tree trunk. He wore a white button-down shirt and black slacks, but seemed somehow disheveled, three to four weeks beyond a good haircut. A burly body-guard stood at the ready near him.

The older man instantly stood at the sight of the newcomers. Nick drew to within twenty feet of him and stopped.

"Mr. Chagnon?"

The man's stare didn't show a trace of warmth. He snapped his fingers at his bodyguard. A brief, rapid conversation was exchanged in French.

Nick was about to speak when someone shoved him firmly in the back. He took a few momentum-driven steps, then looked at Chagnon, confused. Before he could speak, he was blindsided again. He stumbled to regain his balance.

"Hold on here," he said.

One of the three bodyguards kicked him hard in the stomach, doubling him over. A fist slammed his cheek. Nick staggered sideways and looked about wildly.

"Wait a second," he said. "You need to listen to me—"

He dodged another fist thrown at his face but fell to his knees as another hit him in the back of the neck. A powerful kick smashed him in the kidneys, then another sent him to the dirt. Dazed, he felt a knee pressed into his back. His head was twisted roughly around, a gun barrel stuck to his temple. The older man was suddenly stooped on a knee, barely three feet from him.

"Please," Nick blurted out. "Let me explain . . ."

"I'm Victor Chagnon," the man said. "Tell me who you are. Keep in mind your life may depend on your answer."

The weight on his back was pressing the side of Nick's face into the soft soil. He swallowed, tasting dirt, and began talking, much faster then he had originally intended.

"My name is Merchant—Nick Merchant. I'm a private investigator who knows about Holtzmann. Ludwig Holtzmann. I'm just trying to share information that may help us both."

Chagnon's face was tired, his eyes bleary. But he was listening. Nick stammered on before he could speak.

"I've learned that Holtzmann was involved somehow with your father. All I'm—"

"Do you think I'm a fool?" said Chagnon. "Do you want to die there in the dirt? I know all about Holtzmann. And I know who you work for."

Nick was breathing fast. With a man on his back and a gun to his head, he couldn't put his thoughts together. Being beaten nearly senseless hadn't helped. But their viciousness couldn't be this random. He had to figure out who they were mistaking him for, and quick.

Chagnon stood and strolled out of sight. Nick's cheek was pressed to the ground so tightly that he couldn't watch where the banker went. He felt paralyzed. His story was coming out fragmented, bits and pieces that weren't adding up. He licked his lower lip and forced himself to slow down.

"Let me tell you how I know about all this, Mr. Chagnon. I got involved with Holtzmann when an old man by the name of Gerald Jacobs died recently in New York. Jacobs had an estate worth millions of dollars. What I was trying to do—"

"Enough," said Chagnon, walking back into Nick's line of sight. His face was flushed with anger. "I know who sent you, and I don't want to hear any more. You need to listen to me now, if you want to live."

Nick fell silent. He was desperate to get his story out, but if Chagnon's plan included keeping him alive . . .

"Why were the others killed?" asked Chagnon. "Every one of Holtzmann's accounts were released, every requirement was met. Everything agreed upon was done. Why is Taylor doing this?"

Nick's eyes darted about the ground. He wasn't sure what the safest answer was, especially now that he had run his mouth off about Taylor and Holtzmann. If he denied any knowledge, he would only infuriate Chagnon further. But playing along could get him killed just as quickly.

"Answer me!" shouted Chagnon.

"Because he didn't trust them," Nick exclaimed. "He needed to insure their silence."

"Their *silence*?" Chagnon asked. "What reason would we—would *I*—have to talk of our dealings with Holtzmann? By talking we would have only indicted ourselves!" He shook his head, his cheeks purple with rage. "Taylor knew. He knew if he came for us that we would have nowhere to run. Where could we go—to the police? They would have imprisoned us for life!"

Nick felt a chill as the pieces came together. Chagnon had his hands in it then, as all the murdered bankers did. Once Taylor had milked the accounts, the bankers had become a liability, so the arrangement was voided, the accessories targeted. The conspirators had turned upon themselves. He was dealing with another criminal then, a crook at the end of his rope, someone no better than Taylor and Holtzmann. And probably no less dangerous.

"We let our greed take over," said Chagnon, reaching into his coat. "It killed the rest, but I won't let it kill me." He removed a thick manila envelope and tossed it near Nick's face. "Let him free," he said to his henchmen.

The pressure on Nick's back was removed. Painfully he got to his feet, brushing the dirt from his cheek.

"Pick it up," said Chagnon.

Nick stooped for the envelope and brought it up with unsteady hands.

"That's right—look at it."

Nick opened the envelope with some difficulty and removed a collection of photographs. He looked at them one by one. Surveillance photos—very similar to the ones he had found in Jacobs's home. He brought one close to his face. There was one man in the group he definitely recognized.

"Someone you're familiar with, I see," said Chagnon. "Take these to him—wherever he is. Tell him I have many copies. If anything happens to me, these will go to your media. Your *Washington Post* and your *New York Times*. Tell Taylor it won't be so easy for him after all."

Nick folded the envelope and placed it in his pocket. He was going to walk away from this, then, and not empty-handed either. Serving as their messenger—a false one—would save his life. He felt dazed. Surrounded by half a dozen men who probably wanted nothing more than to shoot him in the head and he was going to walk away.

"Take these to him," said Chagnon. "Tell him everything I've told you."

Nick gripped the envelope with both hands. He slowly nodded. "I will."

"Now get out of here," whispered Chagnon viciously. "If I see you again, you're dead."

Nick scanned the circle of men surrounding him. No weapons were drawn. They were done with him. He jogged to a clearing, looked back once, then ran as quickly as he could through the park.

## CHAPTER 27

THEY ARRIVED AT the airport one hour early and found a dark
corner of the airport lounge to wait in. At five minutes before
departure they would ease out of the bar separately, hurry through the
concourse, find the gate, and walk down the boarding tunnel. It was a
short, simple little gauntlet, and if luck was on their side, it probably
wouldn't get either of them killed.

Nick sat with his back to the corner and waited. He was facing
Jessica, but his eyes were trained to the walkway beyond her.
The Geneva airport was thankfully busy, the concourse bustling
with travelers. When boarding time arrived, they would be two of
hundreds of travelers passing through. Excellent odds, but the fact that
there even *were* odds was terrifying. He had to assume their pursuers had taken the airport into account. Somewhere, then, they
would be part of the crowd, casually checking faces as they
moved, making themselves as inconspicuous as possible as they walked
back and forth, hoping for that one chance encounter with their targets.

Jessica sat and watched him scan the crowds. Someone from the
bar came by, and she ordered them sodas and an order of appetizers,
strictly for the purpose of making them appear relaxed and unwor-
ried. Neither of them touched the food. She watched him, he

watched the walkways, and for half an hour they sat and said almost nothing.

The boarding call for Flight 103 to Montreal came in English and French. Nick leaned forward and placed his hand on hers.

"It's time," he said softly. "I lead. Give me about a thirty-second head start, then walk to the gate at a normal pace. Stay on the right side of the walkway, right next to the wall so I'll know where to look for you. When you get to the boarding tunnel, just hustle down it."

"Why don't both of us just—"

He shook his head.

"Because they're looking for *me*. You're safer and a lot less conspicuous on your own. If you see a line to board, wait a few minutes in the bathroom until it clears. I'll be watching out for you. Just move quickly and stay to the right at all times."

He rose, but she did not release his hand.

"I'll be waiting for you," he said. "I'm not boarding until I see you."

He touched her shoulder reassuringly and eased his hand from hers. The table behind them was a collection of empty beer bottles and dirty paper plates. He took one of the longnecks and exited out to the walkway.

He strode quickly through the crowd, feeling as skittish as a rabbit. The departure gate was only sixty yards away, but it seemed to be retreating from him—a cruel mirage. He picked up his pace. A man's shout made him jerk his head to his left. A Swiss family was greeting an arriving traveler and being awfully loud about it. He turned away and focused back on their gate. He could see a line now, and a pretty sizable one at that. What the hell was the delay?

He reached the gate, still clutching the beer bottle. People were everywhere—happy faces, tired faces, bored faces. There were far too many people to keep track of. He quickly took a seat against the wall. The line of travelers was slowly filing into the boarding tunnel but not nearly as quickly as he wanted. He put the bottle on the ground and rubbed his hands. The walkway he had come from was packed. He couldn't see her. Ten seconds passed. Twenty. He stood. He couldn't see anyone but strangers.

Finally he caught a glimpse of her. She was by the bathroom, searching for the gate. God, was it him or was she standing out like a cat in a kennel?

*Get inside!*

As if hearing him, she pushed her way into the rest room. Nick let a breath out slowly. He wiped his hands together furiously. Another minute or so and they would be safe in the cabin. He leaned forward, his eyes on the bathroom door she had entered. He gave an anxious glance at the boarding line. People were still taking their sweet time boarding the plane. He wanted to run up and start shoving people in.

He turned back in the direction of the women's rest room, just catching the sight of a man suddenly ducking inside.

Nick didn't have time to think about it. He grabbed the bottle and was up in a charge. He jostled his way through the crowd and sprinted for the door. People stared as he nearly ran a woman over. He reached the restroom door and threw it open.

The stranger was at one of the stall doors, kicking it powerfully. Several women were screaming and running for the exit. Nick lunged for him. The man tried to turn, but he wasn't fast enough. Nick swung the bottle like a blackjack and shattered it viciously against the side of his head, sending him to the floor. The man struggled to get up but Nick was powered by sheer violent adrenaline. He kicked the attacker under the chin, putting everything he had into it. The man flipped over on his back and didn't move.

"Jessica? Jessica!"

The stall door creaked open. She was near the back, her face white.

"You all right?"

She nodded hesitantly. Nick grabbed for her hand and pulled her out. A cluster of curious people had gathered outside. People were pointing. A small group of airport security guards was rushing through the terminal toward them. Nick ignored the crowd and kept them moving forward to the boarding tunnel. A Swiss in a green uniform grabbed his elbow.

"What are you doing in there?" he demanded.

"A man just attacked me," said Jessica.

"Get in there and arrest him," said Nick, jerking his arm free.

The security guard looked thoroughly confused. The crowd seemed to encircle them. It looked as if every traveler in the terminal had gathered around to gawk.

"Stay here," the guard said.

"Our flight's leaving," snapped Nick, walking again. "He's in there. Go get him."

The man glanced over his shoulder as two of his comrades entered the rest room. When he turned back to the young couple, they were already gone, out of sight down the boarding tunnel.

The Lear rolled to a stop on the private airfield at nine in the morning. The doors flew open and a half-dozen suits and ties streamed down the stairs and into the waiting limousines. Director Gordon fell into the backseat and immediately read Edmund Arminger's dour expression.

"Let me guess," said Gordon. "Nothing new?"

Arminger's silence spoke volumes. Gordon shook his head and gave a short rueful laugh.

"I'll have half a dozen of my agents in place for the hearing tomorrow," Arminger said. "We've got a verbal commitment from the attorney not to participate."

Gordon sat up and nodded. This was something positive at last. "What's this Spinetti character have to say about Merchant's whereabouts?"

"Claims he has no idea where he is."

"Naturally," replied Gordon. "Here's my thought: if Merchant has gotten a replacement attorney, then it indicates to me he's still in town. If no one shows on his behalf, then he's left the country. I suspect that's probably the case. With his client dead, he doesn't even have a claim on the estate."

Arminger shook his head adamantly. "Remember, he may be traveling with the girl. He's a cool one, Arthur. Very crafty and very calculating. He may have convinced her to sign, and if so, he'll have to be nearby."

Gordon waved his hand. "It doesn't change what we need to do. We seize all court records as they're filed and erase the court docket. This hearing never happened."

They sat silently and watched the woodlands tear by on the interstate.

"Have the police found anything on those murders in Los Angeles?"

"Not yet," replied Arminger. "They've got a composite description of the gunman. They've called FBI headquarters in L.A."

Gordon looked at him. "Why would they do that?"

"There've been leaks. The media's all over this. Some loudmouth attorneys with General Inquiry are throwing fits. The L.A. police chief is making a lot of noise about this, Arthur." He reached for a folder between the seats. "Something else. I have copies of the petition Merchant's attorney filed. I think you may want to look at it."

"I was hoping to ease my headache, actually. Give me a summary."

Arminger kept his arm extended. "You'll want to read this yourself. It may be wrong, but it's interesting reading."

Gordon took it and flipped it open. "Does it have anything to say about Jacobs's family?"

"More than you may want to know."


Nick relaxed only when the plane lifted from Swiss soil. He was ready to make good use of the hours looming ahead. Their time in the air would be used to plan, to play out scenarios. In the case of Gerald Raymond Jacobs, it was an opportunity to begin to make sense of it all.

Nick's last week was laid out before him on a scattering of torn white and yellow pages. Was it really only a week ago that Alex had found out about the case? He could barely believe his life could have seen so much devastation in just five days. It had been nothing more than a routine investigation, just another lonely old man dying at home, leaving the earth with the remnants of his life behind him like a slug's trail. But then they had made the decision to enter the house. From there things had spiraled hopelessly out of control.

He leafed through his notes. The fragmented bits of information were no longer swirling about independently of each other; they were now coming together and taking shape. Ludwig Holtzmann's death in 1997 had been staged, an elaborate hoax conducted for the sole purpose of pillaging a staggering Swiss treasure trove. This was clear enough now. But what wasn't clear was the *reach* of the theft. Nick suspected any number of individuals had their hands in the till. Swiss bankers. Holtzmann, of course. FBI officials? American government officials? It was maddening. The facts he now knew were only raising further questions.

Nick glanced over at Jessica. She had slipped into an uneasy doze. He looked beyond her to the window and thought of Alex.

Why hadn't they just backed off?

He knew what most people would assume—it was all about the money. The figures found in the Jacobs file were blinding. But there was another truth, a truth that went beyond the money. It was an incredible thrill to find heirs, and he *needed* that thrill. That need was inside of him, a quirky and powerful gene handed down to him by his father. For better or worse, that's what made him who he was, and there could be no other way.

He looked back at Jessica. She was intent on claiming her portion of the inheritance, and she would do so with or without Merchant and Associates. He reached for the phone encased in the seat in front of him and pulled it loose. Not representing her would be a concession to the enemy at this point. He would deal with the rights and wrongs of it later, but for now he intended to see it through to the end. But only if his friends were in agreement.

"It's me, Doug. Sorry to wake you."

"Where the hell are you?"

"En route to New York."

"You all right? Are you with the heir? What's going on?"

"We're fine. Listen, Jessica Von Rohr has agreed to become our client. We'll need you after all, man. You feel safe enough to be in court?"

Nick heard him take a long, slow breath.

"Yeah. I guess so."

"It's okay to think about it, Doug. It could be very dangerous, showing at this hearing. You know I don't expect you to go. I have no problem if you choose not to—I mean that. It's up to you."

Five long seconds passed.

"I have to do it."

Nick squinted and held the phone. Something wasn't right here. "You okay, pal?"

"I'm fine. Why?"

"You sound out of it."

"I haven't slept. Don't worry about it. I'm fine."

"You're sure then that you want to make this appearance?"

"I just said so, didn't I? I'm positive, Nick."

"Very important then—book a flight into Albany and *pay cash*. That's crucial. No credit cards. Got that?"

"I got it."

"Good. That's about it then. Don't forget all our documentation."

"I'll call you when I get in. Make sure your damn phone's on."

Nick replaced the phone. Doug sounded like a zombie, an irritable one at that. Nerves most likely, and that was fully understandable after the week they had all had. He wondered if there was something else on his friend's mind.

"You didn't have to twist his arm too hard."

Jessica was looking at him with heavy, red eyes.

"I'm sure the fee he'll earn had something to do with his courage," replied Nick.

"You've changed your mind then. I thought it was dirty money."

"I don't intend to do anything but return it once I get my feet back on the ground."

"Return it, huh? Those bankers will certainly be grateful."

"Not to them. To the heirs. That's what I do, remember?"

She straightened up in her seat. "I want you to think about something. Is it possible that maybe you *deserve* some of this money after what you've been through? You plan on bringing all of this out, right? That has to be worth something."

Nick shrugged and turned to the window. "Something about that argument doesn't work."

"I think it does. Think about it. You're helping straighten out something that should have been straightened out fifty years ago. This money's been sitting there since the forties."

"Yeah, I'm a real hero. A real noble guy." He shook his head in frustration. "All I want is my life back."

"Won't this money help you *get* it back?"

Nick leaned back and closed his eyes. Her words weren't swaying him. He felt that the grim truth was finally starting to sink in: the life he had was gone. He wasn't sure any amount of money would ever bring it back.


Kragen stalked around the fifteen-foot dining room table and muttered to himself. Bad news—he was sick and tired of bad news. San Francisco, Des Moines, and now Geneva—these were three inexcusable foul-ups. It was embarrassing and, even worse, very costly.

Malloy sat fiddling with a pen between his fingers. He was feeling smug. If nothing else, he was the one person who couldn't be accused of incompetence. His only stumble had occurred in Hudson, and no one else knew about that but him and Nick Merchant.

"So this PI didn't cough up anything then?" asked Kragen, still stalking around.

Malloy shook his head. "Just a few teeth."

"And you went through the office?"

"Wasn't much to go through. The place was already half cleared out. Nothing there."

Kragen plopped down into a chair. "Our client's very concerned about this," he said.

"What's in these pictures? Space aliens?"

Kragen didn't answer, although he could only guess that it was something damn incriminating. As far as he was concerned, these mythical photos were now a lost cause. He would not dwell on them any further.

"Merchant and the girl must be en route back to the States by now. Our associates in Europe aren't as efficient as I thought."

"Crazy," commented Malloy, feeling increasingly superior. "Even Regnier's blowing it."

"Regnier can't do everything, Malloy. It's not like he was the only one over there."

Malloy frowned smugly. "So now what?"

"We wait. We know Merchant was using the name of Michael Collier, but he's abandoned that by now. I'm waiting to get confirmation on a report of a sighting of Moreno just a few hours ago in Albany. We may soon have her alias." He clenched his fists. "This has all got to happen tomorrow, Malloy. The reason I called you here is to let you know that there's some kind of a court hearing scheduled at three-thirty P.M. at the Columbia County courthouse. I've been told that we can expect Merchant and Associates to be represented."

"By who?"

"By someone. I'm not risking mistakes this time, Malloy. This one's reserved for you and Regnier. You two will need to keep an eye on both the front entrance and the back. I want you to find positions and be set by nine A.M. tomorrow morning. It's up to you who watches the front plaza and who watches the rear."

"Gotcha."

"I've been told that the two most likely targets are the Von Rohr girl and the attorney. For some reason, the girl may be obligated to attend. Or so I've been told."

"So we need to move on 'em *before* the hearing?" asked Malloy.

"Preferably," replied Kragen. "But if not, nobody walks. Before or after, you two have to take care of them."

"No problem. What about Merchant, though? We written him off?"

Kragen crossed his arms on his chest and smiled widely. "Don't worry about him. We've got ourselves a nice little plan for him. I've just been informed that there's something in the works right now that should put a quick end to that merry little chase."

"What plan?"

"It'll be a few hours before I get the full details. As I understand it, though, come tomorrow our friend Nick Merchant will be served up to us on a platter."

The large two-story home on Franklin Street was completely still. The three female occupants slept peacefully upstairs. The man of the house had been awake all night.

Doug sat motionless in his den, his head in his hands. His ears were ringing faintly, and his eyes hurt. He had never felt so tired in his entire life.

Dawn's first rays were filtering into the study, faintly illuminating the surface of his desk. He looked up numbly and caught three pairs of eyes staring at him. He reached out and brought them to him. The three most important people in his life were captured there, in a small gold-framed photograph. It was his favorite—a professional studio shot with Kimberly in the foreground, Carey and Nicole on opposite sides behind her, hands placed on their mother's shoulders. He grasped the picture and studied it for a long time.

He finally stood and stared out the back window. He was actually *seeing* the backyard for once. It was a large, beautiful yard, behind a large, beautiful house. They had been living there for three years now, and he was finally noticing how wonderful everything was. At thirty-six years of age, he was exactly where he hoped to be in his life, and strangely, he felt as if he were realizing that fact only now.

He stuck his hands deep in his pockets and looked back down at the desk. Behind the picture of his family, in a smaller, wooden frame, was a picture of three other people. It was an older snapshot, taken before his little girls were born. The three men in the picture were shoulder to shoulder in a dimly lit bar, their smiles wide. Doug was in the middle, with Bill Merchant to his left, Nick to his right. He remembered neither the place nor the exact date, but he did remember the occasion. The three of them were celebrating his hiring as Merchant and Associates' company counsel. Although he had never told them so, he had always been grateful for that. Bill Merchant wasn't around to accept his thanks anymore, but his son was still alive.

He reached for the phone, his hand barely steady. He would have to live with his decision. He only hoped that if something went wrong, he might someday be forgiven.

The airline representative came on the line. Doug hesitated, then charged a one-way ticket to JFK International.

CHAPTER 28

DUSK COULDN'T COME quickly enough for Nick. The three-and-a-half hour trip was nerve-wracking, and he looked forward to the reassuring darkness of night. He drove at a steady speed in the right lane, one eye on the road, one to the rearview mirror. The highway patrol was out there somewhere, lurking like a silent predator among the headlights behind him. A chance encounter with them needed to be avoided at all costs.

Nick pulled over in a town called Coopersville and found a small shopping mall. He parked in a shadowed area beneath some trees and waited in near darkness as Jessica went inside. He clicked the radio on and dropped his seat back. Forty-five minutes later she returned. She put the two full shopping bags of clothes in the backseat and then they were on the highway again.

They reached Albany just after 6 P.M. Jessica approached the front desk of the Manor Inn. The woman behind the counter was too grouchy to do anything but scowl and slap down registration papers. Jessica signed in under the name of Kathy Beck, requested an extra key, and found room number ten.

Nick dropped their bags to the carpet and collapsed on the bed. He had been awake for nearly twenty-four hours straight now, and he felt it. But he had far too much to do before he could even think about sleep.

Jessica stepped from the bathroom, having changed into jeans and a sweater.

"You're sure you want to do this, then," he said to her.

"We've talked about it enough, I'd say."

They sat on the bed. The contract was of the form he had used since the company's inception, a simply worded legal agreement between client and owner assigning a percentage to Merchant and Associates for its time and effort in finding the assets of one Gerald Raymond Jacobs, a.k.a. Ludwig Wilhelm Holtzmann. Doug Spinetti had drafted the original contract in Bill Merchant's living room twelve years ago, two days before the founder had signed his first client. Nick remembered that day well, the beginning of such exciting times. So alive, so promising. Father, son, and attorney had gone out and gotten roaring drunk that night in celebration of the new enterprise. It was a long time ago, taking place in a world that no longer existed for any of them.

"Nick?"

He turned to her, looking without really seeing.

"Are you okay?" she asked, laughing at his blank look.

"Yeah," he said softly, feeling somber from the memories. "This contract's really simple. It basically says—"

"I don't think you need to explain every phrase and clause, Nick. I am a lawyer, remember?" She smiled and put her hand on his shoulder. "Just give me a pen, okay?"

He reached into his coat and handed her one. She gave a cursory look over the document and signed her name on the line marked *Client*.

"There's no percentage filled in."

"It doesn't really matter. Put anything under forty."

She printed in *35* and handed it to him. Nick glanced over the contract and felt only hollow. There was supposed to be such a celebration for this one. The dream contract. He shook his head and placed it aside, in the middle of the wrinkled paper and scraps accumulated over the past week.

"I'm catching a flight to Denver tomorrow," she said, rising to her feet. "Cab's picking me up in the morning to take me to the airport. . . ."

Nick didn't know what to say. He began gathering up what he needed for the rest of his agenda that evening.

"I'll let you get some sleep, then," he said, finding the car keys. He fidgeted with them for a moment, then looked up at her. "I want you to know that I am truly sorry for everything that's happened."

She nodded at him, accepting this. "Me too," she said. "Before you go, there was something I wanted to ask you about in this contract."

She sat next to him, closely enough for her leg to touch his. He looked at her. She was reading over the agreement, her silky blond hair blocking her profile. Nick wasn't too tired to notice how nicely her jeans hugged her legs. For the first time since Iowa, he noticed what an attractive woman she was.

She placed the contract aside and leaned back on the bed, casting her hair aside with a slight head toss.

"Never mind. I suppose everything's okay after all."

"That's . . . great," replied Nick, after a pause.

She smiled at him. "Where are you staying tonight, Nick?"

With some effort, he turned away from her. "Haven't really thought about it. Somewhere nearby."

She rose to her feet and approached the blinds, taking a careful peek out. She lingered there a moment, legs and waist displayed in full glory. Perfect thighs and calves. Smooth, tight waist. She turned back to him and suddenly clicked off the lights, leaving only the indirect beam of the bathroom light streaming in.

"You don't think there's any way we could have been followed, do you?"

Nick felt magnetized to the bed. The room was small and cozy, an oasis against the cold, dark streets. It was safe there, and comfortable, and the bed would be warm.

She settled on the bed next to him. Nick caught a trace of a fragrance that smelled very, very appealing.

"Why don't you stay for a while," she said softly. "I don't want to be alone tonight. I would feel better if someone were here with me."

Nick looked at her and realized he felt the same way. He had felt that way since his apartment had been reduced to rubble, since a deputy director of the Federal Bureau of Investigation had told him he would soon be wanted for attempted murder. He had felt like that the entire time in Geneva, but somehow that someone hadn't been there for him. But tonight that would change. He knew where he needed to be.

He rose to his feet.

"They have no way of tracing you here. You'll be fine." He held out his hand to her. "Take care of yourself."

She drew back, looking disappointed. "You sure, Nick?"

"Sorry."

They shook hands. Nick removed his keys and walked to the doorway. He paused as the door swung open, then shut it without looking back.

Nick scanned the parking lot of the Towne Villa apartments and walked quickly to unit 204. The door opened only seconds after he knocked.

Alex was wearing an oversized T-shirt, just like the night they had started the Jacobs investigation. In the faint light of the apartment she looked just like a twenty-one year old coed.

"For once you ring my bell at a decent hour."

Nick stepped forward and hugged her. Alex was startled for a moment, then hugged him back.

"What's *this* all about?" she asked, laughing.

"It's been a long trip," he replied. He released her and held her at arm's length. "Just happy to see a friendly face."

She let out a slight gasp as her smile vanished. "Oh my God, Nick—what happened?" she asked, touching the right side of his face lightly.

It took him a moment to remember. Chagnon's crew had left their mark on his cheek.

"Slept on it wrong," he said, smiling to hear the genuine concern in her voice. "Let's get inside."

Nick could just barely see his way into the kitchen. Alex had the blinds nearly closed, and the final bit of daylight cast a dull striped illumination over the carpet. They sat in the dark at the kitchen table. The laptop was there, as well as the small laser printer.

"I want to know what happened to your face, Nick."

"I'll tell you in a little while. I'm fine—that's all that counts. How are *you* doing?"

She shrugged. "I just got off the phone with my mother. I've got her at a friend's apartment in Flushing."

"Good. Does she know about the charges?"

"Unfortunately."

"What's she have to say about it?"

Alex shook her head helplessly. "She doesn't know what to say. It's too much for her. Her entire world is work, prayer, and television, Nick. At least she's still got prayer. I couldn't pry that rosary out of her hand if I wanted to."

"A few prayers might come in handy."

"Probably would."

He brought his hand to hers, and she squeezed it. Alex broke the silence after a moment.

"I've got to make sure she's safe, Nick. I've made arrangements at an airfield for a flight out to Canada tomorrow."

"Good. I think it's a smart move."

"I've decided I'm going too."

Nick stared at her.

"I have to," she continued. "I can't just sit around here waiting to get arrested. I know you think we're going to be free and clear after we get this report or whatever it is together, but I'm not taking any chances. I'm not risking prison, Nick. No way."

Nick slowly nodded. "You don't have to explain anything to me, Alex. Do what you think is best. Hell, I'll probably skip the country for a while myself until all this blows over."

"I'm glad to hear you say that, because you're coming with me. I lined up a six o'clock flight for us."

"Where?"

"A little airfield upstate. Friend of a friend has a six-passenger Cessna. Five thousand dollars, but more than worth it, I'd say. He'll take us right over the border to Canada."

"Where's this airfield?"

"Simple—just take 87 north to the first dirt road after the Fernwood exit. The road winds for about a mile or so. It's a little strip of concrete in the middle of nowhere. We ask for Bob. He should be the only one there. Five thousand dollars a head—a bargain if you ask me."

"Yeah, I guess so . . ." he said softly, looking down at the table.

They both fell silent. Alex took a trembling breath.

"How did this happen, Nick? How? A week ago we were set. We were having the time of our lives. Everything's ruined now. Forever. What's going to be left for us?"

"It won't be so bad, girl. Things will cool off, and then we'll rebuild. Yeah, we'll have to lay low for a while, but at least we'll have the money to do it." He wrapped his fingers around hers. "Jessica Von Rohr signed. Thirty-five percent. Doug's flying in tomorrow, early afternoon. Half of it's yours. You deserve every damn penny."

She looked down at their hands and showed little reaction. "This money's dirty, Nick."

"Yes, it is, but unfortunately we need it right now. I'm going to be sinking a chunk of it into a couple of high-priced lawyers who are to begin working on my defense. On *our* defense. We going to clear ourselves, Alex. The report we put together tonight will be a huge step in the right direction. Once we get ourselves out of this mess, we'll figure out something to do about this money."

"Like what?"

"I don't know. Maybe with a little work, we can find some heirs. I don't see why not. It's no different than what we've done with regular bank accounts here in the States."

Alex's silence was skeptical.

"I met with that PI I was telling you about, Nick."

"The one who worked with Jacobs?"

She told him about her visit to the PI office in the Bronx. Nick leaned forward in his chair, hanging on every word.

"So this person wasn't Demello, then."

"It was his partner, last name of Blount. He said Demello's dead."

Nick frowned and rubbed at his eyes. "Why does nothing about this story shock me?"

"We knew it was Jacobs in those pictures," said Alex. "But it's the State and Swan part that really grabs me."

"What's the significance there?"

"State and Swan Street are right where all the government buildings are in Albany. Empire State Plaza, the capitol building. The thing is, I'm not sure if he meant that area specifically. He said the pictures were taken at a park *near* there. I think that's what he said, anyway."

"He couldn't be more specific?"

"Nick, this poor man was literally dying there on the floor. I had to call him an ambulance, and I wasn't about to stick around and wait for them to show up."

Nick nodded and rose to his feet. He looked through the shades down to the quiet, empty street.

"It's another thing to add to the mix. You and I are gonna put this all together right now. We're going to assemble our documents, write up a summary of everything we've learned, and mail it off to the *Post* and the *Times*. I—"

"What exactly do we know? I'm not even sure if *I* know."

"Yes, you do," he said. "Alex, think about this. Think how huge this is. We're talking about a cover-up involving a war criminal, we're talking about robbery on an unprecedented scale, we're talking about multiple murders, possible FBI complicity, and God only knows what else. The newspapers are going to go absolutely wild over this." He approached her. "We were perfect scapegoats for them. We happened along and they jumped all over us. Well, this is gonna be our first shot back. Our first step toward exonerating ourselves. When we mail these packets off to the newspapers, some very deserving people are going to get fried. The mailer's going to lay it all out—everything we've learned in this past week. I don't know who exactly will get nailed, but I have a feeling there's more than one of them. The media will figure out the specifics. There's about a million reporters and journalists who'll take this and run."

Alex nodded, looking a bit more heartened now. She stood.

"I've got something that might help us."

She went to the bedroom and returned with a small camcorder.

"All *right*," said Nick, taking it from her. "Where did you get it?"

"Debra Ramos rented it," she said, with a wink. "I think it'll drive our point home a little better, don't you?"

"You bet it will." He held it to his eye. "Hope you know how to work it."

"Point and shoot." She turned and clicked on the laptop. "Let's get this done."


Nick had decided during the flight home from Geneva what the form and content of the packet would be; it was now simply a matter of assembling it. Exhibits would include the FBI document taken from Claudia Dorsch, the letter from Holtzmann to Claudia explaining his "obligations" to the Americans, and a sampling of the letters of authorization found in Gerald Jacobs's garage.

The written summary would give it a cohesiveness. It would explain everything the partners had done in regard to the Jacobs case—except the break-in of the Jacobs home. Although it was true that they were guilty of bribery and technically burglary as well, they would admit to nothing. The readers would draw their own conclusions as to how the partners had obtained the crucial documentation included in the mailer.

The video account would follow. It would begin chronologically. They would explain who they were, what they did, how they initially became involved with Gerald Raymond Jacobs. The account would take them from San Francisco to upstate New York; from Germany to

Iowa; from Geneva and back to upstate New York. They would intro-
duce the viewer to Rose Penn and a dead killer-for-hire by the name of
William Brecker; to Lawrence Castleton and Richard Borg; to Matthew
Von Rohr; to Victor Chagnon and the proprietors of Hahn and
Konauer, Gubelin & Cie, and all the other dead bankers surrounding an
eighty-seven-year-old millionaire recluse from the little town of
Hudson, New York.

"Is this really enough, though?" asked Alex.

"Are you kidding?" replied Nick. "There's too much to just ignore
here. My God, the *Post* will have an absolute field day with this. They'll
have two dozen reporters looking under every rock to get to the truth.
Sure, it's not everything, it doesn't have all the answers, but it's an
incredible jump start."

They gave them the rest of it then: the photographs taken by Jacobs's
PI's (two more of the dead); the status of the Swiss bank accounts; the
identities of the secondary holders that Alex had found; the result of
the efforts to obtain the death certificate of Ludwig Holtzmann; and of
course the complete details of the intensive efforts made to murder
both the partners and the heirs to the estate. No detail here was
insignificant, no facet ignored. It would land in the newsmen's laps
partly assembled; from that point it would be up to them to use the
resources at their disposal to make the picture whole and clear.

The final segment of the deposition was Nick's personal statement
addressing the criminal charges pending against him. He unequivocally
denied the attempted-murder charge levied against him, pointing
instead to the at-large murderers-for-hire who conspired in the deaths
of Rose Penn, Matthew Von Rohr, Lawrence Castleton, and the others
named in the statement above. He would not be turning himself in to
the authorities, because it was his desire and intention to clear himself
by his own means and methods of any charges related to the shooting
of a City of Hudson police officer.

Nick splashed cold water on his face. It was nearly 5 A.M. They had
printed eight copies of the document and were satisfied with the video.

Any touch-ups or additions could be made after three or four hours of sleep. He stood in the bathroom doorway and wiped his face with a towel. Alex was examining the first printing. She looked up and shrugged at Nick.

"It's all in there."

"All of it," agreed Nick. "You think everything's clear? Phrased right?"

Alex thought for a moment. "Maybe we say a little *too* much in this paragraph. I don't think we should admit to anything illegal. Whoever reads this and sees your name at the bottom will be skeptical right off the bat. The fact you're wanted is bad enough—we don't need to say anything more to discredit ourselves. Let the report speak for itself."

Nick nodded thoughtfully. "Makes sense. For a minute you sounded like a lawyer there, you know."

"Yuck," she said, making a face. "Speaking of lawyers, where's your little blond friend?"

"At a motel. She's hitting the road."

"Not giving her a ride, Nickie?" she asked, with a smirk. "The loyal chauffeur?"

"You never stop, do you?"

She chuckled to herself. "Remember that argument we had a couple of days ago? When I told you I wasn't jealous?"

"Yeah?"

"Well . . ." She broke into an embarrassed smile. "Maybe that was just a teensy lie. I might have been a little bit jealous."

"A-*ha*," said Nick.

"It's just that . . ." She paused, looked down at her hands. "What we have means a lot to me, Nick. You do too. We've been through a lot the last four years. The last *fifteen* years. It's pretty much been the happiest time of my life."

"Mine too," said Nick, smiling warmly.

"I guess I . . . just didn't want you to forget that *I'm* your partner. I don't want that to change."

"Like it ever would, you dummy."

They smiled at each other and enjoyed the silence for a good five seconds.

"Have you spoken with any of Rose's relatives?" she asked.

Nick instantly sobered. The thought had crossed his mind—numerous times. "I don't know what I could possibly say. Everything I can think of sounds horribly inadequate. Do you think I should call them?"

"I don't know. Under normal conditions, yes. But now I really don't know."

Nick looked down at the carpet. "I still can't believe it about Rose, Alex. Of all people to be caught in the middle . . ."

"My stomach hurts whenever I think about it," she said. She turned to the bedroom. "I'm going to bed. I don't want to think about any of this for a while."

Nick didn't either. He entered the bathroom, taking a change of clothes with him. He took a long, hot shower and put on a pair of shorts and a flannel shirt.

The apartment was dark when he stepped out. He walked into the living room and groped in the dark for his suitcase, laying some clothes out. He found his jacket and paused as he lifted it. There was something in the inside pocket. He reached in and pulled out the framed little watercolor he had bought in Geneva. The thin plate of glass over the painting hadn't survived the day's excitement. A spidery fissure ran the length of it. He looked it over and walked over to the bedroom doorway.

"Hey."

"Hey," replied Alex.

"Living room floor's a little hard." He approached her and lay down on the futon next to her. "Scoot over—I got something for you."

He placed the watercolor in her hand.

"What is it?" she asked, clicking on a flashlight next to her.

"A memento of the worst trip of my life."

Her face registered shock, then broke into a wide smile. "I can't believe you," she said, her eyes gleaming. "I love it."

She propped it up on its stand next to the mattress. They both looked at it for a few seconds before she clicked the light off.

"I hear Geneva's beautiful," she said. "I wish I could have seen it."

"Next time you will," said Nick. "Who knows—we'll probably need to find an heir there someday."

"Maybe we could go even if we don't have to find an heir, Nick."

The evening was warm, and the window was cracked open a bit. A light breeze rustled the shades against the glass. Outside, nothing stirred except leaves blowing slowly down the black streets.

For the first time in nearly a week, the partners slept well.

CHAPTER 29

B Y DAYBREAK IT was raining. The skies over Albany were gray and angry. A sporadic wind threw gust after gust of raindrops against the window like handfuls of pebbles against the glass.

Nick woke before eight but didn't rise for another ten minutes. He lay next to Alex, telling himself that it was nearly over, and the thought gave him strength. Just a few hours more, and they could put the fear behind them for good. He looked over at her. She was on her side, her eyes closed. He heard her question again. *What's going to be left for us?* He wasn't entirely sure, but maybe they were strong enough to build something new, something with a hopeful future. Maybe it could even turn out to be something pretty damn good.

He stayed there for a few minutes, watching her sleep, before stepping out to the kitchen.

He was at the laptop when she emerged from the shower. The final additions to the Jacobs mailer had been made. The packet would be thorough, eloquent, and make for very compelling reading. He had prepared a mental list of the recipients. *The Washington Post* and *The New York Times* would start the ball rolling, and he would follow those up with the Washington, DC, and Albany offices of the FBI, the Senate majority leader, and the attorney general. He was even considering mailing one off to the White House. The *Post* and *Times* would probably suffice to get the story out, but why take any chances? He would let everybody have a taste of it.

From the motel, they drove to North Pearl Street in Albany. Nick dropped Alex off around the corner of a copy store and waited in the car as she went in and ran off the attachments. He watched the morning pedestrians through the tinted glass and felt safe. The only way the cops would notice him was if he stood out, and he was going to be as inconspicuous as a fire hydrant. For once in a storied career of speeding tickets and late yellow lights, Nick Merchant was going to be the model driver. He would show courtesy unheard of on the Albany roadways.

She returned to the car in ten minutes. She had made copies and purchased envelopes and postage. Nick started the car and headed back in the direction of the motel.

John Malloy eyed the stately gray Columbia County courthouse and nodded to himself. They had decided rather arbitrarily that he would watch the back entrance while Regnier watched the front. It made no difference to him. He now saw that the task would prove equally difficult from either angle.

His reconnaissance had begun at 6 A.M. that morning. The courthouse was on the corner of Court and East Allen, probably the busiest intersection in Hudson. Normally the existence of a crowd was only beneficial to his assignment, but in this case he saw no advantage gained. His chief difficulty lay in the surrounding landscape. From the rear of the building, he saw no elevated vantage point. Directly behind the courthouse was a small park offering scant cover. He had photographs of Moreno, the Von Rohr woman, and Spinetti, but picking them out of the crowd in a four- or five-second window of opportunity would be nearly impossible. They weren't going to be wearing name tags.

He walked along the sidewalk, his hands in his pockets. He stopped at a hot dog stand directly in front of the courthouse and bought a footlong with mustard. He devoured it in half a dozen bites and returned to the car. His mind was made up. Making the hit inside would eliminate the use of gun or knife, but that was fine. Anyone as intimately familiar with the crucial arteries as he was could do a job with a pencil, a comb, anything handy, really. He made his decision. He would do it inside.

He checked his watch. It was 9:30 A.M. The hearing was at three-thirty that afternoon in courtroom number two. He could think of no surer spot to find them than the hallway directly outside.

It took them fifteen minutes to pack and label the envelopes. As a personal touch, Nick added the Israeli consulate general to his final mailing list, bringing the total to eight recipients.

He glanced at his watch. Doug's flight was due to arrive at 1 P.M. It was now 10 A.M.

"Not yet," he said, as Alex stripped off the adhesive from one of the envelopes.

"Why not?"

"I want to run one last errand before we seal them up. Ready?"

"Don't you think we've pushed our luck enough with all this driving around? How about I go do this errand by myself? The police aren't looking for me."

"Somebody a lot nastier is, though. We both go. We'll be fine as long as I drive okay." He grabbed his keys and waited by the door. "Trust me—we'll be fine."

The rain let up on them when they were on the road. The blanket of gray in the sky was shredded with streaks of sunlight. Blue sky reflected off the puddles in the street like a million little mirror fragments. The trees along the sidewalks glistened wet-green under the sun's glare.

Nick kept both hands on the wheel as his stomach did cartwheels. A sheen of sweat had formed on his forehead. He wanted rain, buckets and buckets of it. The sunlight seemed to be fading the tint of the windows. He felt as if he were on display to the world. He drove like a little old lady, avoiding congested streets and the main thoroughfares. If he had the bad luck to get into a fender bender, there would be no sticking around to exchange licenses.

Alex watched him closely as he gripped the wheel. A police car was coming toward them the opposite way on Sheridan Avenue.

"Cops."

"Just be cool," she said. "Nothing to worry about."

The patrol car was moving at a crawl. Nick wiped the back of his hand over his forehead. He didn't dare glance at them as they passed by.

"Didn't even look," Alex said, patting his leg. "Where are we going anyway?"

"We're here," he replied.

The sun had slipped back behind a mass of clouds. He made a right on Lark Street and then a left on Washington Avenue. They passed the State Education Building. Nick had never been to this part of Albany before, but there it was, between Washington and State Street, looming like a monolith in the center of Empire State Plaza. He was almost certain that he was looking at the state capitol building.

"What is this, Nick?" Alex asked. "What are we doing here?"

The sign by the sidewalk declared it in gold-faced letters: NEW YORK STATE CAPITOL BUILDING. Nick turned into a ten-minute loading zone on the street in front of the building.

"You said . . ." He pinched the bridge of his nose and tried to remember. "You said that that PI you found in the Bronx told you that he took the Holtzmann pictures at State and Swan. No—at a park *near* State and Swan. Where are those pictures anyway?"

"Right here." She reached to the floor and found them. "We only brought a few of them."

She handed him the half dozen photographs.

"These are the best ones we have of this Taylor person," he said, sorting through them slowly. "See how Jacobs labeled the backs? Victor Chagnon had his own photos too."

She took one of the pictures and examined it. The man had glasses, thick black hair, and a long, thin face.

"So you think he might work around here," she said.

Nick nodded. "Someone here might recognize him."

"He could work *anywhere*, Nick. You can't assume that he—" She stopped herself and looked beyond him. An elderly security guard was ambling up toward them. "Uh-oh. I think it's time to get moving."

Nick was staring at one of the pictures, oblivious.

"Nick, someone's coming."

He looked up at the approaching guard. "This guy might be able to help us," he said, opening the door.

"*What are you doing?* There's too many people around here."

He hesitated and scanned the crowd. There were *way* too many people, but he was too close to back away now.

He stepped out of the car and walked briskly to the sidewalk. The
guard put his hands on his hips like a grouchy old grandfather as Nick
hurried up to him.

"You're gonna have to leave," he said, waving a finger. "No parking
there."

"We're leaving right now," Nick replied. "I wanted to ask you something first." He showed him one of the pictures. "Do you recognize this
person?"

The guard squinted his gray eyes at the photograph. "I might. I've
worked here for thirty-two years, y'know." He studied the face in the
picture. "Yes, sir . . ."

"Yes sir what? Do you know him?"

The old-timer frowned at Nick, then snatched the picture away with
surprising speed. "What're you—a reporter? What's this all about?"

Alex quickly gave two quick honks on the horn. Nick waved his arm
back at her without looking. A police car was moving down Swan Street
toward them.

"Does this man work here?" Nick asked. "That's all I want to know."

"Yes, he does," the guard replied testily. "You're gonna have to get
that car out of here now. No one is supposed to be stopping there." He
gave a little wave in the direction of the slowly moving police car.

"I'll move it, I'll move it. I'd appreciate it if you'd just give me this
man's name."

"I'm getting the cops over here."

Nick grabbed the picture back from him and hustled back to the car.
Alex's face was like a ghost as he fell back into the passenger seat. The
cop had stopped thirty yards down from them and was harassing a dou-
ble-parked delivery van.

"He's here!" he said. He was euphoric. "He knew him!"

He started the car and reversed into the street. The ancient security
guard was trudging back to his post in the front of the building.

"What did he say?" asked Alex.

"He knew the face. He said he works here."

He made a right on State Street and then another right on Swan.
They were behind the capitol building now. Nick was slapping his palm
on the steering wheel.

"Why don't I—"

"Bad idea," she said. "I know what you're thinking and it's nuts. If you're actually thinking of sneaking around inside that building and flashing those pictures—"

"I can't run off now."

"Nick, you're *wanted*. Let *me* go in and ask around."

He stopped in a red zone and threw the gear into park. "There's another guard," he said, reaching for the door handle. "Lemme just give him a try."

Alex grabbed his arm. She didn't say a word, but her eyes were pleading.

"One more shot," he said softly. "Then we're gone. I promise."

He stepped to the curb and walked quickly to the guard. This man was black and about fifty years old.

"How are you?" Nick asked casually, drawing a nod and a suspicious frown. "Hoping you can help me." He brought the picture up. "This gentleman here works here at the capitol. You recognize him?"

The guard studied Nick harder than he did the photograph. "Maybe so."

"You know his name?"

He reached a large hand up and took the picture. Nick held his breath.

"Kinda looks like Mr. Cimko."

"What was that?" asked Nick.

A shrill whistle tore through the air. Nick looked up quickly. The elderly security guard from the front was hurrying toward them from the back of the building now, blowing a whistle. "What was that name you just said?" asked Nick.

The guard was looking back at his rapidly approaching coworker. "What the heck's goin' on here?"

Nick wheeled and walked quickly back to the car as the whistle continued to sound. Alex had taken the wheel. She pulled into traffic, and Nick directed her to make a left down Elk Street.

"I got him," he said, checking the rearview. "I *got* him."

"Who?"

"That guard recognized him too. He said his name is Semka or Semko—something real close to that." He pointed her down Dove Street. "Once we get back to the motel, I'll get the wheels turning."

"What exactly did he say?"

"He said he recognizes him," Nick repeated. "He said his name was Semko, or something like that."

"And he works there?"

"That's what he said."

Alex frowned. "Those old guys were a hundred years old. They probably wear reading glasses an inch and a half thick."

"No way. The second one said it very emphatically. How would he recognize him if he didn't work there? I could tell he knew."

"What can we do back at the apartment?"

"Bust it open, baby. We'll send a courier to hit up a library and look up all the Semkas or Semkos in a government employees directory. Once we verify the name, I'll call the Department of Motor Vehicles and try to finagle a driver's license photo out of them. Once we get that, we just compare it to the Jacobs pictures."

"What if we *can't* verify the name?"

He took a breath. "Then I guess I go back to that building."

"No, you don't, Nick. A couple thousand people must work in there. We're already including the photos in the mailer. Let some hotshot reporter figure it out."

"Are you kidding? After everything these people have put us through? After Rose and Matt? No, no, no—I want them to know that we were the ones who brought this out. I'm seeing this all the way to the end." He shook his head. "Jesus Christ, can you believe that guard and his whistle? Somebody please give that old guy a promotion."

She was not amused by this. She rubbed her forehead and pulled the car to the side of the road.

"Look," he said. "Hopefully I'll be able to do this through DMV. I don't think I'll have to go back there."

"If anybody goes, it's me," she said. "There's no argument on that, Nick."

Her expression was angry, combative. Nick smiled at the realization of how much he had missed that look.

"I would never argue with you, Alex. Look, you said yourself we've taken enough chances. Let's get some runner to get to a library and look this up for us. It's the safest way."

Alex held the photograph and frowned.

"It's the best plan," he said.

"It's *your* plan, Nick. I can get to the library and find out exactly who this guy is in about two seconds. You think some fifteen-dollar-an-hour runner is really going to care about this?"

"No, they're not, but I don't want to expose either of us any further."

"I can handle it. No one's going to find me in a *library*, for Godsakes."

Nick nodded, not comfortable with it. "Just be careful."

Alex turned back to the photos, focusing on Taylor and the cold black eyes behind the metal-framed glasses. She was going to enjoy this. It was time to turn the tables on Mr. Taylor, drop the curtain right on his head, and she was going to savor every last moment of that.

Back at the motel, Nick called for a taxi.

"I don't care if you're not wanted," he said. "You need to watch yourself."

Alex was sitting on a kitchen chair. "Relax," she said. "I'll be fine. When are we supposed to hear from Doug?"

"Any time," replied Nick, glancing at his watch. "His flight's landing just about now."

A car horn sounded outside. Nick pulled aside a window blind and spotted the cab.

"There's your ride. You're coming straight back here after, understand?"

"Yes, boss."

Alex gathered up what she needed and opened the door. She turned back to Nick and winked. Nick watched her enter the cab. He continued to watch until the car was out of sight.

"Please be careful," he said aloud.

He made a final addition to the Holtzmann dossier.

> *Addendum: We believe the persons shown in this picture are Ludwig Wilhelm Holtzmann and the as yet unidentified individual named "Taylor." A source in Albany believes "Taylor" works at the state capitol building in Albany. . . .*

He read it and frowned. Not conclusive, but enough. If Alex couldn't come through, the newspapers would have the pictures and the address.

If it took publishing the pictures to crack the story, they certainly wouldn't hesitate to do so.

The entire letter was reread a final time. Then one by one he removed the adhesive strips from the envelopes and sealed them. The single videotape would be included as part of one of the two FBI mailers. He would make sure those arrived in their Manhattan and Albany offices that very day.

The shades were closed and the lights were on. He was sitting on the edge of the bed thinking about his father when his phone rang. His attorney, he guessed.

"Where are you?"

Doug's voice was choppy and mingled with the sound of his car humming along the road. "Albany. Where else?"

"You brought everything?"

"Yeah, yeah. How many times you gonna ask me?"

"Probably four or five more. Lighten up, you'll have about half a million dollars in your pocket in few hours."

Normally a comment like that would get some sort of rise out of Doug. Nothing.

"You been watching your tail, Doug?"

"I'm clear."

"You're sure?"

"Yes, I'm fucking sure. Lay off, will you?"

Nick felt the blood rush to his face. "Hey, what the hell's your problem? I'm not enjoying this any more than you are."

He heard Doug exhale into the receiver.

"I'm sorry. I haven't slept. Nick, I . . ." He paused. "I just want to get this over with."

"You ain't the only one, buddy. Listen, meet me at 200 Willett Street, okay? I'm driving a gray Ford Aerostar."

"You're driving a what? Wait a second—what's your room number?"

"There is no room number. Just drive there and wait on the street."

"What's going on?"

"Just a little precaution. I'm going to let you sit there by yourself and have a smoke for a while I reconnoiter the area."

"For Christ's sake, nobody's following me, Nick."

"The only reason I'm alive to talk to you right now is because I've been careful, Doug. Quit fighting me, all right? What kind of car are you in?"

"Blue Taurus. How long will I be waiting?"

"I don't know. Probably no more than fifteen minutes. If you see anything behind you that looks even remotely suspicious—"

"I'll call you. Where's Alex?"

"Taking care of a little last-minute research."

"What about Jessica Von Rohr?"

"What about her?"

"Is she coming with you?"

"She's gone, man. I'll see you in a while."

Alex paid the cabbie and walked quickly through the campus of Albany State University. She had more than enough time for what she needed to do. She stopped and asked a student for directions and was directed to the east end of campus.

The library was a bustle of students getting back into the flow of another semester. She moved through the crowds and found the elevator bay. Government Publications was on the third floor, west side. She strode down the rows of books and felt like a law student all over again— not a great feeling. It took her only a minute to find her bearings.

She spotted the New York State Controller's directory and paused. It was worth a shot. She found the current year's volume and took a seat at a table. The biographical index was in back. She ran her finger down the *S*'s and checked for *Semko* and *Semka*. Then *Simko* and *Simka*. After that she moved on to *Senko* and *Senka*, *Symko* and *Symka*. Nothing. The *C*'s were checked in a similar fashion. Same result.

She found the New York Serial Set. An Ernest Semko was listed as working for the State Controller's office but as a mail room clerk. The other variations of the name revealed nothing.

She returned the book and checked her watch. It was one forty-five—less than two hours before the hearing.

She scanned the labels of books and drummed her fingers on her chin. She tried to recall exactly what Nick had said. Had he just heard the guard wrong? Semko. Semka. Phonetically it could only be spelled so many ways.

She took the current year's Congressional Listing and found the index. She checked the *S*'s and then moved on to the *C*'s.

When she saw the name, a fluttering ran through her stomach. This was the closest yet. Philip Anthony Cimko, page S-249. She quickly turned the pages and sensed this would be something well worth reading.


Two hundred Willett was not actually a building, but a wooded playground on the edge of Washington Park frequented by young mothers and their small children. Between the neatly manicured trees and bushes was a small clearing with swings, slides, and a sandbox. Nick knew it better than any part of Albany, other than his partner's house. He and Alex had used the park as their private sanctuary a number of times, their oasis when an investigation was stalled or the walls in Alex's house seemed to be sliding inward. Lunch outside on one of the green wooden benches beneath the trees was often all it took to break down the mental walls blocking one of their searches.

Nick drove through Albany, only blocks from Alex's home. If the police or his other pursuers were keeping a list of likely places in Albany to find him, he would guess that a children's playground would have to be near the bottom. What business would Nicholas Merchant— the fugitive cop-killer—have in a place like that? He smiled. Well, maybe he just wanted to ride the swings.

Just then the phone rang, the sound muffled in his coat pocket.

"Nick, I got him! I got him!" Alex said.

"What?" He pulled the car over to the curb. "Where are you?"

"Never mind that. I got Cimko, Nick!"

"Are you at the apartment?"

"I will be shortly. Shut up for a second and listen to me. I think I've figured out who this Cimko person is. It all makes sense now."

"Who is it?"

"I've got it all photocopied," she replied. He could hear her shuffling papers. "'Philip Anthony Cimko—State Capitol Building, One Clinton Avenue, Albany. Regional Director for Republican senator Thomas Newland of New York . . .'"

Nick stared through the windshield. "Newland? What could he—"

"Wait—it gets better. Listen to some of the dear senator's committees: Commission on Security and Cooperation in Europe, Committee on Appropriations, Committee on Veterans' Affairs, and twelve others.

But here's the really interesting one: Senator Newland is the head of a special Banking Committee he formed four years ago which—I'm quoting here—'has led an inquiry into the current status of assets and accounts of European Jews and others held by Swiss banks deposited in the 1930s and 1940s. The Banking Committee will seek to aid Swiss banks in an independent and impartial audit of all accounts under question through an unprecedented cooperative agreement with a number of Swiss banks, both private and cantonal. . . .'"

Nick studied the dashboard and tried to replay the information in his head. A bevy of half-formed questions were swirling in his mind, refusing to come together.

"I don't know about this," was all he could manage.

"I know it's wild, but is it within the realm of possibility? Nick, if I'm right here . . ." She didn't finish her thought. "I think our mailer's complete now. If we're wrong, we're wrong, but this is where those photos will come in handy."

"Why would a senator be involved in this?" Nick asked. "Why?"

"What do you mean, *why*? Why *wouldn't* he? Everyone knows Newland is the party's candidate in the next election. I think a man like that would have a hundred different uses for a few extra million dollars, don't you? Who knows who he's paying off?"

Nick was slowly shaking his head back and forth. "I don't know about this."

"I don't either," Alex replied. "But *now* we've done our part. Now we can sit back and watch it all come together once you get that mailer out. And if those pictures do turn out to be this guy Cimko, God help Senator Newland."

He was nodding now. She was right. It was time to pass the baton. "Are you going to the apartment now?"

"Yes, and I'll have all these documents for you when I get there."

"Just be careful."

"You think you need to tell me that?"

When she hung up, he reached for the envelope and quickly, almost feverishly, reached for the photographs. He had doled out almost all of the Jacobs pictures to the eight mailers, keeping a few for his own records. He cursed as he pulled them out. He only had three of them left.

But they were the right three.

He was in the background, less prominent than the others, behind several younger men in suits. His face was shaded a bit and at a quick glance very easy to miss. Nick brought the picture to within inches of his face, his eyes slits of concentration. There was no doubt in his mind. There was no doubt at all.

His arm fell to his lap as he closed his eyes and swore softly. He had never wanted to be a part of this. But they had dragged him into the middle of it, tried to murder him, and damn them, they had succeeded with Rose and Matt Von Rohr and who knew how many others.

He opened his eyes and looked at Senator Thomas Newland's face once again.

Nick cast the photos aside and felt physically sickened. The partners' assumptions had been wrong from the very beginning. All along, they had focused on the most prominently featured man, Taylor, or Cimko, or whatever his name was. Jacobs, clearly unaware as well, had made the same mistake. They had all been wrong. The boss—the master-mind—had been there all along, lurking in the background.

He looked at the picture once again and a soft, involuntary groan escaped his lips. He dropped the photo and rubbed his eyes. If he had only recognized Newland that morning, perhaps he wouldn't have gone to Germany. Perhaps he would have elected instead to burn every scrap of paper he had found in Jacobs's home. Burned them all and flown home. In hindsight he realized that might have been the best move of his life.

He took to the road fifteen minutes later. From Spring Street, he made a left on Willett. He could see the park dead ahead, a blue sedan under the shade of trees. He circled around, scanning the streets as he went. Two older ladies walking briskly. A mother pushing a stroller. A work-er in a hard hat and fluorescent orange vest was up a telephone pole while another one chomped on a cigar stub and watched from below. He glanced up through the windshield. Clouds and broken blue sky. He felt reassured. Doug was a champion attorney, but asking him to be able to recognize when he was being followed by professionals was beyond him.

He circled the streets a final time and pulled up behind him. Doug stepped out of the car. His face was ash gray as he walked up to Nick's driver-side window.

"You okay?" asked Nick. "Usually *I'm* the one who looks terrible."

"I'm all right. Little bit nervous."

"You'll make it. We all will. Doug, I've got something really shocking to show you."

"What is it?"

"Follow me back to the apartment and I'll show you everything."

Doug nodded and turned back to his car. Nick wrapped his hands around the steering wheel and frowned. *We'll make it,* he thought. *We all will.*

Doug sat down in front of the wheel and slammed the door. The second he did, it all came undone.

It was a gray sedan with two men inside, and it screeched around the corner in front of them. Nick's eyes shot to the rearview mirror. Two more sedans appeared from around the corner in back. Cars suddenly seemed to be coming from everywhere. Nick's confusion vanished in one sickening instant of realization. Blind instinct told him what to do. He kicked open the door and ran.

Later he would remember it as being just like a dream.

Everything around him was moving at normal speed while he was stuck in some horrible slow motion. His path opened up for him. Women were grabbing their children as he tore through half a dozen toddlers in the little playground. He slammed his shin hard hopping a concrete step but didn't feel a thing. He was running on the wet grass as voices, harsh and commanding, seemed to be coming from every direction. Every tree, every bush, seemed to hatch forth one of them. A large man in a blue suit was charging hard from the right, yelling something. Nick felt one of them lunge for his legs, and he swung his fist back wildly, grazing the top of his attacker's head. But the dive had served its purpose. The failed tackle had caused him to stumble, slowing him enough so that the pack could gain a crucial three or four steps, and then they piled on hard, throwing him to the ground on his stomach. He could feel the weight of half a dozen men pressing on him and the wet grass against his cheek as puddles on the cold ground soaked through his clothes. They turned him over after his hands were cuffed, and he was vaguely aware of young mothers holding their children and watching. A dark-haired man in an overcoat was looking down at him then, and when he spoke, the satisfaction in his voice was as palpable and cruel as the cold, hard shackles binding his wrists.

"Nicholas Merchant, by order of FBI Director Arthur Gordon, you are under arrest."

CHAPTER 30

THE DRIVER STOPPED at the intersection of East Allen and
Court and flicked his eyes to the mirror for what must have been
the hundredth time of the ride. Knowing that this would be one of his
last opportunities, he decided he would give a long, appraising look to
the pretty young passenger in the backseat of his cab.

Alex was too stunned to even notice the leers she was receiving. She
was having enough difficulty coming to grips with the disastrous events
of the last thirty minutes. She had just received the shock of her life.

Her call to Nick had been answered, but not by her partner. The FBI
had finally gotten him. The agent who had answered Nick's phone had
even shouted her name once. Panic-stricken, she had called Doug to let
him know. A federal agent had greeted her on Doug's line as well.

Distraught, she cupped her face in her hands. It was over, then. Both
Nick and Doug had been arrested. No happy endings, no riding off into
the sunset. Simply—cruelly—over.

She looked up after a moment, oblivious to the gawking of the driver.
She could still leave the country. Nick wouldn't blame her for hopping
on that plane and fleeing the country. He would be happy to see her do
it. But this was not an option. If she ever wanted to face herself again,
she needed to do one last thing.

Angry, she pulled herself together. Nick had been convinced that their portion of the estate could help clear him. She had her doubts, but if he truly believed that, then she would do everything in her power to make it happen.

The driver slowed the cab to the curb. Alex studied the outside of the Columbia County courthouse with a renewed feeling of dread. She had hoped that she would be able to simply step out of the taxi and duck into the building in a few quick steps, but apparently nothing about this day was going to be easy. Reaching the front stairs entailed walking fifty yards through a front courtyard of thin trees and little other cover. Moving at a brisk pace would easily mean a good twenty seconds of complete exposure. But there was no getting around it.

"Courthouse," said the cabbie, as if she couldn't see that for herself. He swiveled around to face her. "You okay, lady?"

She shook herself into motion and found her wallet. Stalling would make her neither safer nor less nervous. She handed the driver her fare and pushed the door open.


It was the taxi that got Regnier's attention first, then the dark hair of the passenger. He lowered his binoculars and reached for his rifle.

He was on the roof of the Hudson post office directly across from the courthouse. It was the best vantage point to be had. He watched the woman through the scope as he flicked the safety off. Just another brunette, but this one was special. Dark-featured, a little bit heavy, very attractive—he felt reasonably confident that it was her. She was halfway to the entrance. He closed one eye and brought the crosshairs to the side of her head. Held it.

But there was an ounce of doubt. He jerked the gun down. A wrong choice would bring a swarm of cops and undoubtedly chase off the real target. He couldn't place the entire assignment in jeopardy. He watched as the small figure hurried up the stairs and disappeared inside.

He frowned and rose to his feet. It was too risky this way. It was time then for a much more direct approach.


The lobby of the courthouse was packed. Alex took little comfort in that. Safety in numbers only applied if everybody was on the same team, and she felt hardly certain of that. Every casual glance that happened upon her felt like a loaded glare.

She hurried through the crowd and found a stairway, scanning each face as she climbed the steps. She told herself she was safe. They couldn't dare try anything with so many people around. She wondered why her knees felt so weak if that were the case. Maybe a crowd was exactly what they wanted.

On the second floor, she was faced with three doors—one on each side, one straight ahead. This was nerve-wracking. Behind door number one awaits . . . what? The hall was empty except for two clean-cut men in navy suits. One suddenly took a step toward her.

"Alex Moreno?"

She held her breath and took a step back.

"Nothing to be concerned about, ma'am," said the man, producing a badge. "David Foulke, Federal Bureau of Investigation. Possible to have a word with you?"

"If it's a quick word. I need to be somewhere."

The agent gave a knowing little smile and gestured to a bench in the hallway.

"I'll stand, thanks."

He placed the badge back within his jacket. The other agent had moved away from them, positioning himself at the top of the stairway.

"I'm sure you're aware of the manhunt currently being conducted for Nicholas Merchant."

"I'm aware, yes. What about it?"

"Any idea where he may be?"

"How would I know?"

The arrogant grin was back. "Why don't you stop with the Little Orphan Annie routine, Miss Moreno. Some very reliable sources inform us you're his partner."

"Really. And what do your very reliable sources have to say about the murder of Rose Penn and Matt Von Rohr?" The sound of her own question triggered her anger. "What kind of progress is the FBI making in its search for their killers? Or are you trying to pin those on Nick Merchant too?"

"We're not involved in either Miss Penn's or the Von Rohr brothers' murder investigations. What we're trying to do is—"

"What did you say?" she asked quickly. "Brothers?"

"I said we're not involved in Miss Penn's or the Von Rohrs' murder investigations at the moment, but—"

"Tim Von Rohr is dead too?" Alex asked, looking shocked.

Foulke nodded gravely. "Yes, he is, Miss Moreno. You weren't aware of that?"

"Where did it happen?"

Foulke looked slightly uncomfortable now. "California. I thought you—"

"What happened to him?"

"He was slain in San Quentin Prison."

Alex shuddered a bit and looked around. The mystery of Tim's whereabouts had been solved with all the subtlety and warmth of a bucket of ice water in the face. The few remaining survivors of Gerald Jacobs had dwindled to one.

"I have nothing more to say to you," she said, stepping past him.

She pushed her way through the double doors of courtroom number two before he could reply.

Court was in session. Alex walked to the second to back row and found an empty seat. She needed to pull herself together, to focus. She had witnessed enough of Doug in court to know what to do. The procedure was actually quite simple. First she would establish the genealogy with the vital documents they had gathered—the obituaries, the birth and death certificates. From there, she would reconstruct the family tree. All she would have to do then was simply prove the identity of the heir. In this case, Jessica Von Rohr's birth certificate in conjunction with her driver's license issued by the State of Iowa would do the trick.

Barring any tricks from the feds, she would win them their fee. For all the good it would do her partner, she would earn Merchant and Associates the biggest fee they had ever hoped to see.

Alex rubbed her face and thought of Nick. She wondered where they had taken him. What was their plan for him? She felt nauseous, almost dizzy enough to pass out. She fanned herself with her papers. She noticed one of the bailiffs keeping a watchful eye on her. What she didn't notice was the man named John Malloy as he settled into a seat to the right of her and pretended to focus on the court proceedings in front of him.

They took the fugitive to FBI headquarters in Albany. He was seated between two agents in the backseat of a Lincoln Town Car, hunched forward with his hands shackled behind him. The car lurched over the sidewalk and descended down to the parking garage. No one spoke.

Nick was numb. After all the chances taken, the risks and dangers withstood, this was how it ended. He couldn't have predicted a finale like this in his wildest nightmares. Murdered perhaps, arrested even, but betrayed by Doug? He could not allow himself to believe that. His best friend could not have sentenced him to the next twenty-five years of his life in prison.

He was pulled from the car and escorted through the basement, a powerful hand on each of his elbows. Half a dozen agents walked around him like a boxer's entourage. They stopped and silently waited in a dimly lit entryway, then filed into the elevator.

Upstairs a small crowd of men in dress shirts and ties greeted the group. One of them made a smug comment. Nick could feel the eyes on him as he walked, head partially down.

The FBI's Albany office had three small holding rooms at the end of the second floor. They led him wordlessly down a corridor, undid the handcuffs, and motioned him into the last cell. When the door was shut, he was alone.

Nick glanced around the tiny room. It was perhaps seven by ten feet, with a cot affixed to the wall and nothing else. The walls were a glossy pink. He frowned. So he had become their latest psychological experiment, their lab rat. Holding cells painted pink supposedly did wonders on agitated cons, and he would now do his part to help bolster that claim. What did they think—he was going to scratch and shout and pound his fists on the door until they were bloody? Well, he was sorry to disappoint them. The show was over.

He sat on the cot and looked himself over. He was still wet with mud and grass, and his leg was pulsing with pain. He rolled up his pants leg. Blood was congealing around an ugly red gash on his shin. He had no recollection whatsoever of slamming it.

He tilted his head back and stared at the ceiling. The sickly bright pink was giving him a headache already. He closed his eyes and thought of Doug, and his stomach ached. He couldn't believe it. His attorney had been acting strange, a behavior he had attributed to court nerves. Had he been given another incentive? A sweet little deal perhaps? At any rate, it didn't make a difference now. The Jacobs fiasco was over, and for all intents and purposes so was he. He just hoped Alex would have the good sense to get out of the country. Unfortunately she would have to do it without money, because without Doug there would now be no hearing and thus no inheritance.

*     *     *

They came for him after thirty minutes. The booking was standard procedure, not any different from his own days back on the force. His fingerprints were taken, as was his picture, both a front shot and a profile. His pockets were emptied, their contents taken away. He was given a wet cloth to wipe the ink from his hands. The agent seated in front of him watched him in silence as he cleaned his fingertips.

They led him back down the hallway to a small interrogation room. He sat as requested at the end of the rectangular table. Then they left him alone again.

Nick watched the dust particles float through the air. In a strange way, it was almost a relief. At least now he knew he would be alive to attempt his defense. His thoughts now could be directed solely to that end. He thought of Alex. He prayed she was safe. The image of her being on a plane out of the country was a huge comfort.

After ten minutes, the door opened, and a man in coat and tie entered. Nick knew this was no simple field agent. His visitor was on the smaller side, with slicked black hair and a pale complexion—a ghost in a tie. Something about him seemed vaguely familiar.

Deputy Director Arminger took a seat to the side of him and folded his hands together. He was close enough for Nick to catch the staleness of his breath. Nick looked at the surface of the table and waited.

"So," Arminger said softly. "This wasn't part of the script, was it?"

Nick looked at him, impassive. Bad enough to be arrested—he had to hear gloating on top of it. He turned away and focused on a picture of the President on the opposite wall.

"Where's Alex Moreno?"

"I have no idea."

"I think you have a very clear idea where your partner is."

"Why don't you go ask Doug Spinetti?"

Arminger leaned back in his chair, a bemused smile on his lips. The comment seemed to have him at a momentary loss for words.

"You're about all he could come up with," he finally said. "He did the right thing. He may have saved your life."

"Saved and ruined it all at the same time," replied Nick. His elbows were on the table, his head in his hands. "What are friends for, I guess."

This earned another humorless little smile. Arminger had a folder in front of him on the table. He leafed through it casually, as if he were browsing through the Sunday paper.

"Where have you been staying this past week?"

"I'd like to speak with a lawyer."

"You'll get your chance. I'd like to ask you a few questions first."

"You're welcome to try."

"It may be to your benefit to cooperate. Miss Moreno might benefit from it as well."

Nick stared at his fingernails and thought for a moment. "What's she have to do with this?"

"She *is* your partner. Or should I say accessory. I assume she's been helping you evade us this entire time?"

"I'm not sure I know what you mean."

"We know you've been traveling with Jessica Von Rohr. We also know you've signed her to one of your inheritance agreements. Did you do this before or after the murder of her brother Matthew?"

Nick did not like the overtones of the question. He decided it was best to say nothing.

"Fine then," said Arminger, leaning forward to him. "Let me try you another question. Do you know a certain Swiss private detective by the name of Arne Muend?"

Nick's eyes flicked involuntarily over the table.

"I'll take that flinch as a yes. In any event, he knows you. How about Victor Chagnon? Does that name sound familiar?"

Nick said nothing.

"Answer the question, Merchant."

"I want to speak with an attorney."

"I heard you the first time. What business did you have speaking with a Swiss PI, Merchant?"

"It's all explained in the report."

"What report?"

"The one you'll be getting in just a little while. I sent a couple to you guys, one here, the other to Manhattan. I think you'll want to take a look at it. I have a feeling you're not going to like it very much. You'll have a whole slew of new questions once you read it, believe me."

Arminger blinked several times, then pushed himself away from the table and stood.

"My main purpose in speaking with you was an attempt to determine what charges we'll be bringing Miss Moreno in on. It's interesting,

Merchant—this little partnership of yours. The sudden deaths of the two Von Rohr brothers triples the value of Jessica Von Rohr's inheritance. Then—with your help—she disappears. That's going to be an interesting avenue for the prosecution to pursue. And a very difficult charge for you to refute."

Nick didn't even look at him. Apparently Timothy was dead as well. Jessica was the final heir, then, the only one they hadn't murdered. Yet.

Arminger lingered for a moment, waiting for a response, but finally stalked out.

"Get him out of my sight," he muttered to an agent waiting outside.

Two agents led Nick back to the holding cell, shutting the door behind him.


When Arminger returned to his makeshift office, someone was there waiting. Senator Thomas Newland smiled and took a step toward him.

CHAPTER 31

AT EXACTLY 3:35, one of the armed bailiffs of Columbia County courtroom number two approached the bench and leaned toward the Honorable Judge Darius Pritchard. After a minute's discussion, the bailiff positioned himself in front of the crowd.

"Ladies and gentlemen, I'm going to have to ask anyone not involved with case number 612375 to kindly exit the courtroom. I repeat: anyone not a part of the Jacobs estate hearing will have to vacate the courtroom."

A few hushed comments and confused looks were shared among the public, and then as one they stood and began filing out. Alex straightened up in her seat. This was a first for her. She had never heard of the public being excluded from a court hearing. The FBI's doing, no doubt.

She stood and made her way to the side walkway. A man was blocking the end of her row, his hands deep in his pockets. He looked at her with dull brown eyes when she drew within a few feet of him.

"Excuse me," she said.

Malloy smiled warmly and flicked his eyes to the bailiffs quickly. One of them was at the door holding it for the departing public. The other was on the opposite side of the bench, watching them. He looked back at her, smiled again, and stepped aside.

"Sorry about that," he said softly.

She nodded and moved by. He watched the back of her head as she walked to the front and took a seat at one of the long wooden benches facing the judge. He paused, then grabbed his briefcase and exited the courtroom, ignoring the bailiff as he passed into the hall.

Alex looked around the now nearly empty courtroom and felt a shudder of fear. She was alone, exposed and waiting for anyone who might come charging in. Yes, metal detectors guarded the entrance of the building, but they would hardly scare off the people looking for her. They were accustomed to being creative.

She scanned the room. To the right side of her, a fiftyish man in a sport coat had taken a seat at the opposing attorney's table. This she assumed was the public administrator of the county. The man caught her stare and gave a quick, businesslike nod. Alex noticed that two men in suits were seated in the first row behind him. Feds—they were everywhere now. They were staring back at her like she was an unwelcome guest.

She turned her attention back to the bench. Judge Pritchard was a stern, silver-haired old man, a wizened figure with a imposing frown. He leaned forward from his perch, his elbows splayed outward on his desk.

"Now that the fortunate few are assembled," he growled, "we'll proceed with the next case—the hearing for the Jacobs estate distribution." He looked down at the surface of his desk and muttered, "For reasons unknown to me, this is a closed proceeding. I'm certain we all feel quite privileged to be in attendance." He looked at the man to Alex's left. "I see the public administrator representing the interests of Columbia County is in attendance. Mr. Brumfield . . ."

"Good afternoon, your honor."

The judge nodded in formal cordiality. He turned to Alex. "And you are . . . ?"

Alex cleared the nervousness from her throat. "Your honor, my name is Alex Moreno." She read off her long-dormant state bar number. "I will be serving as attorney on behalf of the petitioners, Merchant and Associates."

Judge Pritchard frowned and scanned a paper in front of him. "Where is Douglas Spinetti?"

"I'll be filling in for him, your honor. I realize it's a sudden change and I apologize, but it seems Mr. Spinetti will not be able to attend."

"And why is that?"

"I'm not exactly sure why," she replied. "But with your permission, I'll be taking his place."

The judge turned to the public administrator. "Do you have any objection to this change, Mr. Brumfield?"

"Not at all, your honor," replied Brumfield.

"Fine then." He nodded to Alex. "You may serve as counsel, Miss Moreno."

"Thank you, your honor."

Pritchard grunted and turned his attention to the documents before him. He surveyed the petition closely as Alex stood and remained silent, her hands crossed in front of her waist. His eyes ran across the documents carefully, no word ignored, no phrasing unanalyzed. Alex stood quietly, feeling almost like a grammar school student in front of the principal. One of the bailiffs sneezed, and she was grateful. After what seemed an eternity, the judge looked down the bridge of his long, bony nose at her.

"Your research shows that there are three heirs to this estate, counselor?"

She hesitated. A catch seemed to be stuck in her throat. The judge stared at her.

"Counselor?"

"Your honor, there are no longer three heirs. Unfortunately, Merchant and Associates' client, Matthew Von Rohr . . ." She paused. It was difficult to say. "Merchant and Associates' client is now deceased. I understand Timothy Von Rohr is also recently deceased. Jessica Von Rohr is now claiming one hundred percent inheritance rights on the Jacobs estate."

Pritchard frowned. This flip-flopping of claimants was unusual to him. He looked as if he would comment, but he instead shook his head and looked back down at his papers.

"I've received correspondence regarding Timothy Von Rohr," he said, a bit softer. "His death certificate is now on file with the county."

Alex nodded and looked down at the table. Her mind could not rid itself of Nick. She tried not to think about him. Impossible.

"Do you have a certified copy of Matthew Von Rohr's death certificate?"

"Yes," she said, finding it. The bailiff relayed it to the bench.

The judge scrutinized the petition.

"This is quite a sum, counselor," he said, giving a dry, humorless smile. "Your vital documents which establish right of inheritance?"

She produced a manila folder and handed it to the bailiff. The judge perused the Von Rohr birth records, the family tree that Nick had con-structed, the Jacobs death certificate. Alex saw him hesitate and study the FBI document Nick had taken from Claudia Dorsch in Germany. He suddenly raised it and waved it at her.

"A question, Miss Moreno: Where did you get this document? Given the enormity of the estate, I believe it's within my scope to ask."

Alex didn't expect the question, but she had her answer quickly.

"Your honor, that document was given to a company researcher by a friend of the deceased. The researcher flew to Germany and met her personally six days ago. The situation was explained to her, how Holtzmann had passed away, and how the company wanted to make sure that his estate was properly divided up among his blood relatives. He was astounded when she pulled out that document, but realizing its potential impact in court, he convinced her to let him have it." She spoke smoothly, confident that she had delivered some version of the truth.

"I've looked over the FBI memorandum," replied Pritchard. "The authenticity of the documents has been verified." He leaned forward, clearing his throat roughly. "The temptation to fabricate a document in dealing with a case this size might be an option for some. Don't think that I'm saying that you're involved in a fraudulent presentation of the facts, but I'm certain you're keenly aware that involvement in any such activity would constitute perjury."

"I am aware of that, your honor," replied Alex, finding this warning a bit odd.

Pritchard turned to Brumfield, the public administrator. "Does the county have anything to add to this, Mr. Brumfield?"

Brumfield tapped his papers together on the tabletop in front of him. "Your honor, the county sees no reason to contest this claim. As far as we can see, there's little to dispute. We do have some additional good news for the petitioners, however. The county has managed to locate some bank accounts which were not included in the original estate appraisement." He waved a paper to the bailiff. "This addendum to the file includes them. The decedent apparently had another six hundred thousand dollars in various local banks, jointly held with his sister, Monica Von Rohr. . . ."

Alex looked down at the varnished table. Six hundred thousand. Over half a million dollars more and she felt nothing.

"Miss Moreno?"

She had missed the judge's question. "Yes? I'm sorry . . ."

"Have you anything else to add?"

She was seeing his lips move, but barely hearing the question. She felt light-headed and wanted to get outside and breathe fresh air. She looked up at the judge and slowly shook her head.

"Give me a moment, then," said Pritchard, rising to his feet.

He gave a nod to the two FBI agents, and the three of them disappeared into his chambers. The public administrator smiled at Alex awkwardly, but she was oblivious. She sat back in her chair. She thought of Nick's words from the previous night: *It won't be so bad. Things will cool off, and then we'll rebuild.* She looked up at the ceiling and closed her eyes. Nick was wrong. He wouldn't be rebuilding anything from inside a prison cell.

Feeling nauseous, she thought back to Lloyd Koenig and wished she could turn back time, just take back that ten thousand dollars and reclaim their lives.

In the hall outside, the public waited patiently for the hearing to end. Regnier and Malloy moved about the crowd and waited with them.

Two agents came for him again and brought him to the same antiseptic interrogation room. He waited in silence, the only sound the slow clicking of a wall clock. It was four o'clock. He and Alex were supposed to be on a plane in two hours. He tried to comfort himself with images of her flying away to freedom, but it didn't help. He was certain she would not go without him, and for once he wished she wasn't so hardheaded. There was no reason for her to put herself at risk any further.

The deputy director joined him after several minutes. Something was different about him this time. His jacket was off, his tie loosened, his sleeves rolled up. Nick could see dark perspiration rings under his arms and a less arrogant look in his eyes.

Arminger pulled a chair forward and sat. "What was it?" he asked, his face scornful. "What was it that kept you on this? Did you want to be a hero? Did you need twenty-two million so fucking badly?"

Nick couldn't help but look at him. The voice had changed, lost some of its previous bravado.

"What was it, Merchant?"

"I told you what it was a few days ago," Nick replied. "My friend was killed, and I was almost murdered. It wasn't about money after that."

"What was it, then? Some sort of heroic pursuit of the truth? Do you expect anyone to believe you were motivated by anything but greed?"

Nick looked down, realizing the pointlessness of the debate. Arminger picked out one of the surveillance photos Nick had found in Gerald Jacobs's bedroom.

"We found these pictures in your car. What exactly are they?"

"You'll find out soon enough. There's a pretty complete explanation in the packet I mailed to you, along with a few more of those shots. It should be arriving here any time."

Arminger stood and paced around the table, studying the photographs.

"These are . . . interesting, I'll admit."

"You noticed who's in them, then," said Nick. "In the back."

"I see him," snapped Arminger, straining for a measure of control in his voice. "Does it mean anything?"

"Not at this point, I suppose. It will once you read the report."

"What's this damn report? Don't keep me in suspense, Merchant. Out with it."

Nick shook his head and couldn't help but smile. "You'd never believe me. It's still hard for me to believe. I'll tell you, though, it doesn't show the FBI in a very nice light. And it all happened in your jurisdiction too. But I guess you'll justify it by saying you were only doing what you were told to do. Hell of a defense. Following orders! That's taking a page right out of Ludwig Holtzmann's book, isn't it?"

"What are you talking about?"

Nick was relentless now. "Maybe the ignorance defense will work better. Yeah—that'll play well. Number two man in America's top crime-fighting outfit claims he didn't know what was going on. That'll do wonders for your public image, not to mention your career prospects."

"What the hell are you talking about?" demanded Arminger.

"I'm talking about Newland and his committee. I'm talking about an old man named Gerald Jacobs and all the garbage that was supposed to have been buried with him. Oh yes, Mr. Arminger—check the mail. It's going to be worth reading."

"And how did you put this so-called report together? With what you stole out of Jacobs's home?"

Nick swiveled in his chair, glaring at him. "Does it matter how I put it together? Answer me something—did the FBI place me on their Most

Wanted list for breaking and entering and an attempted murder? It never dawned on you that something slightly more serious than a burglary might be going on? Are common burglars now the FBI's top priority?"

"No, they're not," replied Arminger, an angry smile forming on his lips. "But I'll tell you who is, Merchant. The scum who try to murder cops. International fugitives. There's a house in Hudson that was burglarized. And there's a police officer who's still in the hospital because of it."

"I don't know a damn thing about that cop."

"But you surely must have seen who did it," said Arminger, sarcastic now. "Your fingerprints *were* all over the inside of that house, Merchant. Did you ever consider gloves in your plan? Probably wouldn't have been a bad idea."

"I want an attorney."

"He better be the best fucking attorney on the face of the earth."

Nick stared at him, his lips thin and tight, holding back a torrent of anger.

"You're finished," Arminger said. He stepped out to the hallway and gestured. Three agents immediately entered the room. "Bring him back to the cell and get him ready for transportation to the city. I want handcuffs and leg manacles from here on out."

Arminger watched them lead Nick out, then he took the three photographs and stepped out to the hallway.


Gordon was the only one waiting for the deputy director inside his temporary office.

"You should have heard him," said Arminger, still agitated. "I don't know what he was trying to do in there."

Gordon was watching him closely. "What did he say?"

Arminger pulled up a chair and sat. "Said he mailed us something. Something to do with the senator, his committee, and Jacobs. Said it would . . . make us look bad." He slid the photos in front of Gordon. "These are the photographs we found in his car."

Gordon looked the pictures over very carefully. "What exactly did he say about the senator?"

"Nothing that made any sense," replied Arminger, slowly gathering himself. "None of it's relevant anyway. We're dealing with a thief, a liar, and a goddamn attempted murderer. Where do we want to hold him?"

Gordon's face was distant, his hands joined together in front of his chin. The pictures were flat on the tabletop, facing him.

"Arthur?"

"I wonder when this mail will get here."

They were both silent. The deputy director suddenly rose to his feet.

"I'm having Merchant brought to the city. We'll hold him there until we have time to—"

Gordon was shaking his head slowly back and forth.

"We're not keeping him here, are we?" Arminger asked. He studied his chief. "What *are* we doing, Arthur?"

"The senator and I had a long discussion while you were in there with Merchant. We came to a decision. Neither of us is particularly happy about it, but we agreed it's probably the wisest thing at this point."

"What decision is *this*?"

Gordon leaned forward, his hands now pressed to his temples. He let out a long, tired breath.

"I think it's best if you sit for this."

## CHAPTER 32

THE SILENCE WAS broken by the footsteps of two federal agents as they exited from the judge's chambers and stepped over the dull marble floor of Columbia County's courtroom number two. They retook their seats quietly as the judge emerged a few seconds later.

Alex rose and watched Judge Pritchard smooth his robe out from under him and retake his seat. He folded his hands in front of himself thoughtfully before he spoke to her.

"Let me preface my ruling by telling you that never in my thirty-odd years of practicing have I ever seen a case as large as this one, or, I might add, as dangerous. I don't know the intricacies here, Miss Moreno, or your connection to Nicholas Merchant, but I'm sure you're aware that this situation will not only be examined by this court, but by federal law enforcement officials as well. I'm very certain that this estate will be studied and picked over for many years by the heir-finding industry. Estates this size are almost never without claimants, and there are heir-finding outfits which will seek to verify and validate the work done by Merchant and Associates. That said, my ruling . . ."

The federal agents were watching the judge intently. Even the public administrator seemed riveted.

"Your documents are in order and, I believe, legitimate. I find no reason not to approve this petition. The estate is to be divided per the terms of the contract written up by Merchant and Associates and signed by Miss Von Rohr, the sole heir. The proceeds will be wire-transferred per the instructions in the petition." He tapped his gavel. "This hearing is concluded. Bailiffs, I'll have the public back in here now. . . ."

Alex gathered her papers together, feeling numb. She had assumed she would receive a favorable ruling, but she felt no joy in the decision. The more she thought about the money, the more repulsed she felt. No doubt Nick could use some of it to mount his defense, and perhaps he even deserved a portion after all the grief these criminals had put him through.

The public was filling the courtroom quickly now. She wanted to get out of there, into fresh air where she could think. She jockeyed her way through the crowd and emerged into the corridor outside.

Regnier saw her immediately. Finally he was certain. He took stock of the crowd. There were probably fifty people milling around the courtroom entrance. Women mostly, a few men in suits. The bailiffs were inside. He slipped his hand under his coat and grasped the handle of his weapon as he moved forward. He would position himself near her and wait for the optimal split second. If necessary he would casually follow her outside. In the ensuing confusion surrounding her death, he would slip through the crowd and be gone.

Alex took the stairway to the first floor and saw the phones near the bathroom. Very few people were around. She entered the booth and closed the folding door behind her. As pointless as it was, she needed to try Nick a final time. The line clicked and connected. She let it ring a dozen times and got no answer. She hung up and tried again, punching in the numbers carefully. It rang another ten times before she gave up.

She stepped outside and rubbed her forehead. She felt foolish. Nick was gone, and sacrificing her life in a futile attempt to talk to him wouldn't do either of them the least bit of good. She headed back toward the stairway and the safety of the crowd upstairs. Whether it was safer than being alone she didn't know, but it felt that way. She would call a cab and get out of there, away from the city of Hudson forever.

Regnier had been watching her every step from just down the hallway. She was ten feet from him and seemingly oblivious to his presence. He made his move when she was two steps up the stairway, creeping up behind her and pulling the makeshift blade free.

Alex was caught completely unaware. A sharp crack tore the air, and by the time she had turned, Regnier was lunging forward into the front of her legs. The force of his weight pushed her down hard to the stairs. She tried to kick free, but his weight was on top of her. She saw his eyes, wide and blank, and she screamed. A thread of saliva ran down his chin as Regnier tried to say something, and then his head fell forward, landing facedown on her stomach. Something was skipping down the marble stairs, making a clicking sound. A man's shout came from the top of the stairwell.

Guns and badges were suddenly surrounding them. A broad-backed man with a crew cut pushed aside the dead man's body and freed her.

"FBI Agent Greenwell, Miss Moreno," said a balding agent with swept-back blond hair. His badge was a foot from her face. "You're okay."

"What happened?" she asked.

"This man just came at you with some sort of homemade knife. You're okay. Can we take you out of here?"

Alex stared up at him, confused. People had gathered around them and were gasping and shouting back and forth. She looked away from the crowd and down at the body at the foot of the stairs. She could see more blood now—a slowly spreading puddle on the floor—and a small sharpened object. The bailiffs were standing around looking confused. Alex looked down at herself and saw that her blouse was spotted with a large circle of the dead man's blood.

"Miss Moreno?"

"Yes, what?"

Another agent was flashing a badge at her now. "We're taking you out of here."

She nodded remotely. They led her to a rear exit. Six of them were crowding around her now, and she still didn't feel the slightest bit safe. They walked outside quickly. Half a dozen police cars had blocked off East Allen, and the gawkers were everywhere. Alex walked in the middle of the small group and felt dizzy. She still didn't feel entirely sure of what had just happened.

A limousine was waiting. An agent opened the back door and ushered her in. Another entered from the other side and sat next to her. The doors were closed, and then the limo was moving.

"Good to meet you, Miss Moreno," said the man. He was in a navy blue suit, white shirt, red-diamond-patterned tie. He wore glasses and was balder than a cue ball. "John MacDowell, FB—"

"FBI, right," she said, angry now. "If I see one more badge, I'll throw up. Are you the one who's finally going to tell me what's going on?"

He nodded and looked to the front. The partition between them and the driver was darkened and impenetrable to the eye.

"A man just tried to kill you, ma'am. We don't know his name or who may have been accompanying him. You've been under surveillance by a number of our agents since your arrival here this afternoon. Apparently we weren't the only ones who were watching you." He adjusted his glasses. "We first noticed the man outside. When he entered the building, we had two agents watching him. He was shadowing you and moving very cautiously. We needed him to try something before we could act. When he reached for the weapon, we moved. You're very fortunate."

"You don't know who he was?"

"Unfortunately not. Obviously it's related to the Jacobs probate. We've connected two murders to it so far and suspect as many as five more."

"Why am I under surveillance?"

He crossed his hands on his stomach. "We needed to speak with you after the hearing."

"Fine. Why don't you start by giving me some answers first. I want to hear about your leads in these murder investigations, specifically those focusing on Rose Penn and the Von Rohr brothers."

"I personally have no involvement in those, Miss—"

"Then you can let me out of this car right now, Agent whatever-your-name-is. I don't have anything to add to your investigation. Everything I know is in the probate file. I'd like to be dropped off at a taxi—"

"That's not going to happen, ma'am," said the agent, adjusting his cuff links. "I've been instructed to bring you to FBI headquarters in Albany."

She recovered after a moment. Her eyes narrowed. "Am I under arrest?"

"Consider it protective custody. You're about to meet some very important people, Miss Moreno."

At ten minutes to five, four agents came for him. Nick was handcuffed and taken to the elevators. The five of them descended to the lower parking garage and met with another group of agents. They led him to two heavy looking prisoner transport vehicles and made him wait there. Two tinted-glass limousines quickly pulled up in front of them. One of the agents walked behind Nick and removed the cuffs. Nick scanned their faces.

"Where are we going?"

"Manhattan office," replied an agent, opening the back door. "Get in the car."

Nick slid in. Someone was there waiting for him.

"Nicholas Merchant," the stranger said with notable satisfaction. "I'm pleased to finally meet you."

Nick instantly recognized the face. He had seen it before in the newspaper, on television, in magazines. With his cotton-candy white hair and wrinkled-leather face, Arthur Gordon looked more like a grandfather than the director of the FBI. Nick could only stare at him.

"Been quite a week, hasn't it, Nicholas?" said Gordon as the limo moved up the ramp leading outside. "You're lucky to be alive."

"I don't feel very lucky under the circumstances," said Nick, still slightly dumbfounded by his company.

"We have quite a bit to discuss. Do you mind answering a few questions?"

Nick shrugged his approval and waited.

"I appreciate it. There are several things I'd like to go over regarding this Jacobs business." He took a deep breath. "First of all, let me ask you: Deputy Director Arminger showed me the photographs you were carrying when you were arrested. What exactly is the significance of those?"

Nick paused but saw no real reason not to answer him. "They're part of a report I've put together which proves who Gerald Jacobs really was. I assume you already knew this, being that you placed him in your protection program. Or did Newland lie to the FBI all along? I wouldn't be surprised if that was the case."

"How did you manage to assemble this report of yours?"

"Research. Does it really matter how it all came together, sir?"

"Unfortunately it does matter, Nicholas. Now tell me—I read your court petition the other day. Who exactly is Ludwig Holtzmann?"

*"What?"* asked Nick, confused. "You have to know who he is—you *placed* him." Nick studied Gordon's expression. "Oh my God— Newland did lie, then. Of course! You never would have touched this if you had known."

"What makes you think Jacobs's true name is Ludwig Holtzmann?"

"I don't *think* it, sir—I *know* it. You need to read my report."

"When might I see this report?"

"Today. I sent a copy to FBI headquarters in Albany, same-day delivery."

"And is the FBI the only organization privileged enough to receive this?"

"No, they're not. *The New York Times* and *The Washington Post* will get their copies. There are half a dozen other people on my mailing list too."

"Perhaps if this is so shocking we should have been the only ones to get a copy."

"Perhaps that might have happened if you people weren't so busy trying to arrest me for a crime I didn't commit."

Gordon frowned and turned to the scenery outside his window. Nick looked back through the rear windshield. Two agents were following them in a gray Cavalier, and an unknown number were behind them. They were on Highway 87 heading . . . north? Nick leaned forward and caught a road sign. If the destination was Manhattan, they were taking an awfully strange route.

"Another point," continued Gordon. "It's not very relevant, I suppose, but it astounds me that you didn't simply back off. I don't see any amount of money being worth all this trouble."

"I had no choice, sir. You may not buy that, but it's true. My secretary was murdered the night my home was blown to bits. People have been trying to kill me left and right ever since. From your vantage point, it may have seemed like a simple decision, but you weren't the one being tracked and chased by men with guns."

"What confuses me, then, is why you never went to the police. Or us."

"The police? Come on, Mr. Gordon—what could they have done? I needed to find out what was going on, and you people certainly weren't going to tell me anything. I had no choice but to stake out on my own."

"That's where you're wrong. You did have choices and you made some very poor ones. Starting with that break-in up in Hudson."

Nick shook his head in frustration. "That may be true, sir, but what about the FBI's poor choices? You people put all this time and effort into hunting me down when there's been a pack of murderers running around killing completely innocent people. But I realize I must have been convenient for you in the end. A nobody, just an insignificant nothing PI who was unlucky enough to stumble onto this. Well, it's going to be very hard sticking this entire Holtzmann mess on me. If that's your intention, I can't see anyone buying it."

"That's not our intention. We've begun a quiet investigation into the Von Rohr murders, as well as the double slaying in Los Angeles. I suspect we'll link even more victims to this as the investigation progresses. We will piece this together, I assure you."

"I think my research will point you in the right direction. Or does the FBI plan on just disregarding it?"

"I'll give it a look," Gordon admitted. "If this wonderful report of yours ever surfaces."

Nick looked out and caught a road sign flying by. SARATOGA SPRINGS NEXT EXIT. They were twenty miles north of Albany now and not getting any closer to Manhattan.

"Where are you taking me?" he asked.

"We're almost there. Another ten minutes."

They sat in silence then. The prior week replayed in Nick's head. He thought of Rose, of Alex, of Doug. He thought of all the choices made, right and wrong. The decision to bribe Lloyd Koenig, to enter Jacobs's house, to send Rose to his apartment. Above all others, the decision to carry on what his father had begun. Every choice he had made in life had somehow led to this end. His father must have been shaking his head at that moment, looking down from some shunned corner of heaven where everyone was an heir and the bars never stopped serving.

After a long period of silence, Nick finally spoke. "So what did you give Doug Spinetti?"

Gordon tilted his head and frowned. "I don't understand your question."

"What did you give him? To turn me in. Did you bribe him, threaten him, what? I can't help but be curious."

Gordon brought his hand to his chin. "What did Director Arminger tell you?"

"He said Doug led you to me."

Gordon looked slightly surprised by this. He finally turned to the road and shook his head slowly back and forth. "Deputy Director Arminger is a pain in the ass. He's the only—" He stopped himself, not wishing to reveal any more genuine feelings. "Spinetti didn't have a damn thing to do with this. Not directly anyway. If anything, it was the opposite. Your attorney charged a flight ticket to JFK but never showed for the flight. Clearly his goal was to draw us to JFK in hopes he could pass through Albany airport undetected. Not much of a plan, but probably all he could think of under such short notice. Naturally we had coverage at all the local airports. We didn't take him in Albany because we had our eyes on a bigger target."

"So you tailed him, then. Followed him to me . . ."

Gordon nodded. "Suffice it to say we discovered some of his past travel preferences. Avis rental cars seemed to be the company of choice. A special car was reserved for him and the rest was simple." He looked at Nick. "Forget what the deputy director may have said. Spinetti didn't betray you. He had no idea he was leading us to you."

"Has he been arrested?"

"He's being detained at the moment. Director Arminger is looking to charge him with an entire list of crimes, including conspiracy and aiding and abetting. He's very enthusiastic about that." He turned back to Nick. "I have a different plan. I intend to have him released shortly. I don't see a point in pursuing a case there."

Nick leaned his head back and let out a slow breath as a weight lifted from his shoulders. His sense of relief was almost as great as the shame he felt for doubting his friend. Doug had made the right choice. He had remained true until the very end.


They took the Glens Falls exit and headed west. The turnoff wound through thick forestland, and Nick could now see that four other cars—one in front, three in back—were in the convoy. Gordon sat silently, content to watch the scenery. There was little to see—forestland, an abandoned gas station, a few dirt roads disappearing into the hills. Nick sat back and waited.

After several minutes, the caravan took a gravel road up a slight hill that opened into a small circular lot surrounded by trees. One by one, the cars eased to a stop. Gordon turned to Nick.

"Listen closely—I'll make this quick. If we take you back to the city and lock you up, you'll face a long list of very serious charges. If we choose to do that, Nicholas, I feel confident you will serve at least twenty years in a penitentiary. Frankly, after the headaches you've caused us, I wouldn't mind that in the least. Not one little bit, my friend. You're not half the victim you make yourself out to be, and these half-baked stories of yours don't win you any points in my book. Due to some very unusual circumstances, however, you're getting one final option, and you better be damn thankful for that. Now step out of the car."

Gordon grabbed the door handle but felt a hand close powerfully on his arm.

"I'd like to say something now, sir," said Nick, his cheeks feeling as if they were on fire. "I never wanted to be a part of this. You talk to me about choices I should have made—well, let me tell you about the ones I didn't make. I didn't choose to have my home destroyed, I didn't choose to see my friend and a client who trusted me murdered, and I didn't choose to have you people in my life. You say I'm no victim, but I'm no criminal either. And speaking of criminals, maybe the FBI should take a long, hard look at itself before it starts pointing fingers, because I wasn't the one who closed my eyes to this and hid this Jacobs bastard in the first place. Take a good hard look, Mr. Gordon. I'm not sure you'll like what you see."

He removed his hand but not the stare. Gordon looked as if he was about to reply, but instead he simply nodded slowly, almost as if he accepted this. He turned and opened his door.

"Step out of the car, please."

Nick did as he was told. The other agents were out now as well, standing around looking sheepish. Deputy Arminger stood by himself and scowled. Nick looked at each of them slowly. Something was afoot here, and he was clueless.

"Nick!"

He couldn't believe it was her. Alex was halfway out of the back of the other limo. She ran to him, and he caught her in a tight embrace. He stared over her shoulder at Gordon.

"What the hell is this?"

Gordon gave a nod to one of the agents, who removed a wallet.

"Give us a minute alone," he commanded his troops.

The agents distanced themselves. Arminger was the only one who didn't flinch.

"Alone," repeated Gordon, his cheeks flushing.

Slowly, Arminger backed away. He gave Nick a final glare before turning and walking off with his men. Nick nodded at Alex and followed the director. When they were alone, Gordon spoke quietly.

"There's two thousand dollars inside your wallet, along with your fraudulent birth certificate. A driver will take you over the border to Canada. Once you get there, you'll have two options. You can cross back over into the States, in which case you'll promptly be arrested to face every last one of the charges I just told you about. Your second option is to keep moving. Go somewhere far away and keep your mouth shut. If you ever set foot here again, I'll know about it, and I'll see to it that you are put away for the rest of your life. Am I making myself clear?"

Nick managed a slow nod.

"Do you have any questions before I send you off?" Gordon asked.

Nick looked down at his wallet. He had dozens of questions, a hundred probably, but he wasn't about to risk any one of them. He shook his head slowly.

"Your driver's waiting for you."

Nick turned to walk, but Gordon suddenly grabbed his forearm.

"Watch yourself," was all the director said. He released his arm. "I want to speak to the girl for a minute."

Nick approached the waiting car and slid into the backseat. The driver half turned to him as he started the engine. He was fiftyish with a fat crooked nose and deep wrinkles around his dark eyes. His cheeks were ruddy and newly shaven. He nodded and gave a slight smile, but Nick didn't notice. He had swiveled to watch through the rear window as Gordon led Alex into the backseat of the limo he had ridden in. The doors closed. Were they taking her away? Maybe it was better for her if they did.

Less than a minute later, she was out. She walked quickly toward the car, then ran the last thirty yards. When she sat in the back next to him, her face was paler than he had ever seen it.

"Let's go, driver," she said.

"What did he say?" Nick whispered to her, but she shook her head. It would have to wait.

The driver reversed direction and gassed it. Gordon and a dozen agents stood like statues and watched solemnly. Arminger leaned over the hood of one of the limos, refusing to even look. The gravel spit and ground beneath the tires as they accelerated out of the lot and found the road.

When the car was out of sight, Director Gordon climbed into the back of the limo. His deputy director slid in from the other side before he could react.

"This is insane," said Arminger. "I can't believe this."

Gordon looked exhausted and suddenly very old. He didn't feel like talking to anyone at that moment. Especially his current company.

"I'm not happy about it," he said. "Newland and I agreed, though. With Merchant gone, this problem disappears."

"He tried to *murder* a police officer," exclaimed Arminger, incredulously.

"And luckily for him, he failed. The officer will live, and the senator's committee will no longer be jeopardized."

"How do you figure that? What assurance do we have that he'll keep his mouth shut once he's in Canada?"

"Very little. But he would definitely talk if he was put on trial in Hudson."

"Who exactly was driving that car?"

"It's an agent with the New York State Department of Justice. I told Newland he would have to assume all responsibility for releasing him. Now step out of the car. I'm riding alone."

"What did you tell the girl?"

"That doesn't concern you," snapped Gordon. "Step out of the car."

"But how is—"

"Get out of the damn car!"

Arminger reluctantly exited, slamming the door behind him. Gordon instructed the driver to head south, back to Albany. The driver started the engine, then paused. Gordon leaned forward, staring through the windshield. A car was speeding up the road, flashing its headlights and heading straight for them.

CHAPTER 33

Sun merged into horizon, shooting laser beams of light over the highway. The shadows of the countryside stretched across the endless expanse of pavement. The forestland on both sides of the road was turning black with the end of the day.

They had driven for five minutes in complete silence. Nick was studying the back of the driver's neck as he struggled to bring a semblance of sense to it all. It was impossible. What had just happened didn't add up. He could not believe in any way, shape, or form that they were being set free. And that was what was now frightening him.

He sneaked a sideways look at Alex. She was staring ahead, refusing to look back at him. Her hands were wrapped together, her knuckles white. She gave him a quick glance and mouthed something he couldn't understand, and at that moment he could see it clearly in her eyes. She was scared, so afraid she could barely turn her head to him. She was keeping something to herself, something he had perhaps missed, and whatever it was was terrifying her.

Nick turned to the driver. "Where are we going?" he asked.

The dark eyes rose to the rearview mirror.

"Where are you taking us?" he repeated.

"Good evening to you too," Kragen said amiably. "I'm taking you to the Canadian border. Didn't they tell you?"

"Not everything," replied Nick. "Who are you anyway?"

"Nobody important, although I suppose you could say I'm your best friend tonight. I'm with the New York State Department of Justice. You've got nothing to be concerned about. In just a little while, you'll be on your way. There's a car waiting for you over the border, then it'll be up to you to lose yourself." He glanced back at the mirror. "I don't know who you know, friend, but they've got serious pull. This thing's been a real headache for everybody."

"Who exactly do you work for?"

"We don't need to bother with that. Just sit back and enjoy the ride. You'll be on your way in just a little while."

Nick watched the woods stream by and considered the situation. If they truly were being sent on their way, why didn't the FBI take them to the border? Perhaps this transfer was their way of washing their hands of it. But did the feds have the power to do a switch like this? Most incredible of all, did whoever wanted him released actually trust him to keep his mouth shut once he was gone? If they wanted that assurance unequivocally, there was really only one way they could get it.

He glanced back through the windshield again. Rush hour traffic was lessening. Was it paranoia or was the dark blue car one hundred yards behind following them?

There was ten minutes of tense silence before a phone in the front seat began to ring. Kragen pulled it from his coat pocket.

"Yes . . . right . . . north of Glens Falls . . . good . . . appreciate it." He hung up.

"Who was that?" demanded Nick.

"Supervisor. Just making sure we're on track here."

Nick sensed this was a lie. It had been too careful a conversation, with quick, one-word responses. Completely unrevealing. The driver's hands were wrapped tightly around the wheel. Nick noticed his rough, powerful fingers. He noticed something else as well. The little finger of the right hand was missing.


Arminger ejected the tape and quickly reached for the sheaf of papers. Gordon was simply sitting back, a stunned look on his face. He felt as if he might get sick right there on the leather seats of the limousine.

"Holtzmann," said Arminger, flipping through pages. "Ludwig Holtzmann. I don't see any mention of Martin Schmidt."

"Maybe because there is no Martin Schmidt," said Gordon, his head back. "Dear God, I knew it. I knew it in the Oval Office. Goddamnit—something wasn't right."

"So you actually believe all of this?"

"I believe enough of it." Gordon grabbed his phone. "I want every police car and highway patrolman from here to Canada alerted. We have to stop that car!"

The road signs flew by like green tombstones: WARRENSBURG, CHESTERTOWN, POTTERSVILLE, SEVERANCE. The rays of the fallen sun were withdrawing in defeat.

Nick was concentrating on the back of the driver's head when it suddenly came together for him. Gordon's words surged through him like electricity. He could feel the hair stand on the back of his neck as his breathing picked up. Was he crazy, or did the director's parting words suddenly make sense?

Traffic had thinned on the highway. Nick checked his watch. It was five-thirty. The flight was scheduled for six and they were now nearly an hour north of the airfield. Something had to be done now.

"I need you to pull over," he said.

Nick saw the driver's eyebrows rise in the rearview mirror.

"What's that?"

"Nature's calling. Pull over."

"What? Merchant, I've got my—"

"Look, we're still a long ways from the border," Nick said. "I can't possibly wait. Pull the damn car over. I'm not going anywhere."

Kragen thought for a second, then clicked the turn signal and pulled slowly onto the gravel lip lining the freeway. Nick could see the edge of the road dip down a slope and lead to a cluster of trees twenty feet beyond.

"Just make it quick," Kragen grumbled. "We're on a timetable here."

Nick nodded to Alex and ducked out of the car quickly. The slope was gravelly and loose, perfect for a nicely choreographed slip. He reached the bottom of the hill and slid down nicely to a knee, grabbing and placing a golfball-sized rock into his coat pocket. He threw a look back as he approached the trees. Kragen had stepped halfway out of the car and was watching him closely, his hands in his coat pockets. Nick positioned himself behind a tree, pissing air. Nightfall was almost on them now, and the sooner the better for what he was about to do.

"Let's move it, Merchant!"

Nick emerged from the trees and stole a look down the highway behind them. Any pursuers seemed to have vanished. He stepped back up the slope and reentered the car. He waited for Kragen to slip the key back into the ignition as his fingers found the rock. It was at that moment that Alex tapped the side of his calf lightly with her foot. She was stooped forward a bit, her hands low in her lap. She held a small snub-nosed revolver.

Nick forgot the rock and inched closer to her as the car accelerated back onto the highway.

"You said we'll have a car waiting for us?" he asked, reaching his hand to hers.

"That's right," said Kragen.

"How long until we're there?" The gun was now in his hand.

"About an hour and a half, I'd say."

Nick hesitated, then leaned forward and pushed the gun into his neck. "Pull over."

Kragen stiffened in his seat and kept his eyes on the road. "You lost your mind?"

"Yes. Get to the side of the road now."

Kragen eased the car to the edge of the freeway.

"What are you doing, Merchant? Think about this for a second."

"I already have. Shut up and hand me the keys, then reach slowly into your jacket and give me the phone. Slowly . . ."

Nick kept the barrel pressed to his neck as the phone was handed back to him. He passed it and the keys to Alex.

"Raise your hands to your shoulders and slide over to the passenger door," he ordered. Kragen shuffled over. "Now step out of the car. Slowly."

Nick followed him out to the gravel border of the freeway. He kept the gun low.

"Down the slope. Move or you're catching a bullet."

"Stop and think, Merchant," said Kragen, stepping down the embankment. "You've just been given a free pass. I'm your ticket out. You don't want to do this."

Nick said nothing until they were down out of view of traffic.

"Do you have a gun?" asked Nick. "Open your coat slowly."

The shoulder holster was full. Nick reached over and snatched the gun. It was a large semiautomatic—a foreign make.

"Standard issue for you DOJ boys? I doubt it." He put away the revolver and waved the barrel of Kragen's gun toward the trees. "Move."

"Merchant, if you get back in the car right now, I might—"

"You can walk or you can drag a leg behind you. I mean it."

"Sure you know how to use that?" Kragen asked, and he lunged for him.

Nick squeezed the trigger quickly enough, but it was locked rigid. Kragen caught his arm with a swift chop, separating Nick's hand from the weapon. Nick dodged a grazing punch and tackled Kragen to the ground. They rolled once and suddenly Kragen had the weight advantage and was jabbing at Nick's face with rapid-fire punches. Nick caught him squarely in the face with a solid right, throwing him off. Kragen's footing gave on the gravel as he tried to charge, and this gave Nick the time he needed to rip the revolver free and fire off a wild shot. Instantly, Kragen's hands were in the air. Nick stood panting for a moment, gun extended, before walking up to him.

"You're a damn fool, Merchant."

"Get on the ground," ordered Nick. "On the ground!"

Kragen did as he was told. Nick bent to a knee, grabbed a handful of his hair, and stuck the barrel to the center of his forehead.

"I'm gonna kill you right now," he whispered, "unless I get answers. The way I feel right now, I may kill you anyway—"

The shout came from behind him. Alex hurried down the embankment and ran up to them.

"Nick, *wait*! You don't know for sure who he is! Wait!"

Her words were barely registering. Nick's eyes were locked on Kragen's. He was shaking his head slowly, thinking of a dead woman by the name of Rose. "I know . . . who he is. . . ."

"We can't be sure." She grabbed his shoulder. "Check his ID."

Nick shook his head slightly. His teeth ground as his finger tightened on the trigger. For the first time in his life, he wanted to kill a man, spread his brains out onto the dirt. He took a deep, trembling breath before jumping to his feet and pushing Kragen hard with his foot.

"Roll on your stomach, hands over your head. C'mon—move!"

Kragen slowly did so. Nick stuck the barrel of the pistol against his neck as he slapped at his back pockets, feeling for a wallet.

"I want ID," Nick demanded. "Where is it?"

"I'm not carrying any," mumbled Kragen, his face to the dirt.

Nick grabbed him roughly by the back of his shirt and yanked him to his feet. He stepped back and raised the pistol to his face, pulling the hammer back with his thumb.

"See the trees?" he asked, flicking his head in the direction of the woods. "Last chance."

Kragen quickly turned and started walking. Nick waited for him to move forty yards into the brush before taking Alex's arm. They turned and ran back to the car.

Kragen stopped and watched from the cover of the trees as the investigators pulled back onto the road. He quickly removed a tiny transmitter from a side pocket in his jacket and punched in an activation code. A green diode began to flash. He watched it momentarily, then ran back to the side of the freeway and waited.

The stars were out now. The black outlines of trees pointed like daggers into the night sky. Nick's eyes were dividing time between the road ahead and the rearview mirror. He was heading south at seventy-five miles an hour. He couldn't stop talking.

"He *knew*," he said. "That's why he tried to tip me off, that's why he gave you the pistol. He knew they might try this."

"Tip you off?" Alex asked. "What do you mean?"

"Gordon told me something strange before he sent me off. I wasn't sure of the point he was making until later. It was a warning. He was trying to tell me that they might try and kill us. He must have given you the gun because he didn't feel comfortable putting it in my hands. What did he tell you?"

Alex was rubbing her forehead. A road sign announcing the approach of Pottersville zoomed by.

"He told me to take it and get it to you if necessary. I asked him what was going on, but he just shook his head. He was acting so strange, Nick."

Nick nodded quickly as he changed lanes and accelerated past another car. "He knew," he said again. "Once we were dead and our bodies disposed of, no one would have ever been able to prove that we hadn't disappeared out of the country. No one would ever have known what really happened to us."

They passed the turnoff to Highway 9. They were half an hour from the airfield.

"Something else," said Nick. "Did you notice the driver's hand?"

"What about it?"

"The little finger on his right hand. It was gone. Maybe I'm nuts but when I saw that, it was like a switch got triggered. A damn buzzer went off in my head."

"I don't understand."

"I don't either. But something stunk about that guy. Even Gordon knew, Alex."

"Why didn't he stop him, then?"

Nick shook his head helplessly. He had no answer. The speedometer climbed beyond seventy-five as he pressed the accelerator to the floor.

Malloy was confused. His tracking screen now showed two blips, and they were separating quickly. Something had gone wrong. He held the wheel and tried to zero in on his boss's signal. It was close, so close he was practically right on top of him.

Slowing the car to forty miles an hour, he scanned the deserted highway. His high beams suddenly illuminated a solitary figure waving his arm back and forth by the side of the road. Malloy skidded to a halt in the gravel, then floored it in reverse. Kragen emerged from the cloud of dust, ripped the door open, and slid in.

"The feds gave 'em a gun!" he shouted.

"What?" Malloy leaned toward him. "What happened to you?"

"Gimme the damn phone!"

Malloy handed it to him. Kragen punched in a number and held it to his ear, cursing under his breath as he waited.

"Yeah."

"You reading that blip?"

"Yeah. Where are you?"

"Don't worry about where I am—just follow that fucking blip. They're running for it. Get everybody moving now!"

"We're gone."

Kragen threw the phone aside and reached for the tracking screen.

"Gas it, Malloy. We're not that far back."

Malloy grabbed the gearshift, then hesitated. A pair of headlights suddenly beamed through the haze behind them.

"Who the hell's this?" asked Malloy, reaching for his gun. He watched as the car's door flew open. A figure raced up to them out of the dust cloud. Philip Cimko's face was a twisted blend of fear and anger.

"You idiots!" he shouted.

Malloy looked at Kragen, confused. "You know this guy?"

Kragen frowned and the two of them stepped out of the car.

"You let them go!" screamed Cimko, all restraint discarded. "You *had* them!"

Kragen's lips were tight, barely holding back a boiling fury. He grabbed the back door of the car and flung it open. He approached the ranting Cimko, silently daring him to speak again, to say one more word. Philip Cimko did not disappoint.

"Incompetent fucking *idiots*!"

Kragen could take no more. His hands shot forward viciously, locking on the smaller man. He twisted Cimko's arm behind his back and bent him down to the car.

"Get him in the car! Help me, Malloy!"

"Hey!" shouted Cimko. "Stop!"

Malloy eagerly joined in, and the two of them shoved him face-first into the backseat. Kragen fell in next to him as Malloy retook the wheel.

"We'll see who's incompetent, you little shit!" He looked to Malloy. "Gas it!"

Tires kicked dirt and pebbles as they made a wild U-turn and re-entered the highway. Cimko frantically grabbed the door handle but the vehicle was already moving too quickly for him to bail out safely. He shouted for them to let him out as the speedometer climbed to sixty-five. Kragen smiled to hear the fear in the little man's voice. He ignored his pleading and leaned over the tiny fluorescent screen. The signal was clear and strong. They weren't any more than ten or fifteen minutes ahead of them, heading south. When they caught up to them, he would personally bring this assignment to a close.

For minutes they sat in silence, the only noise being the thump of the wheels on the road. Alex's voice gave Nick a start.

"I didn't tell you," she said quietly. "They approved it."

For a second, he had no idea what she was talking about.

"The judge okayed it," she said, seeing the confusion in his eyes. "They're releasing the Jacobs money."

The car was strangely quiet. Nick shook his head. A week ago he would have been popping champagne corks. Now he just felt numb. All of this—*all of it*—had happened because of money. Rose dead, Doug arrested, he and Alex fleeing the country—everyone had lost something forever because of the Jacobs case.

"They got Tim Von Rohr, Nick. They found him in prison and killed him."

"The FBI told me." He slammed his palm to the dashboard savagely. "They killed everyone, then. Everyone but us and Jessica!"

"Not only that," continued Alex. "They found six hundred thousand dollars more. A joint bank account held by Holtzmann and Monica Von Rohr."

Nick held the wheel and said nothing. Jessica had been wrong all along—her mother *had* succumbed to her brother's terrible greed. He wondered how Jessica would have reacted to this. He wondered if she would have even cared.

They passed Warrensburg. The sign read GLENS FALLS 7 MILES. The turnoff was only minutes away now. Nick was now doing eighty miles an hour.

"We're over an hour late," Alex said. "There's no way this guy stuck around for us."

"He better have."

"Do you think this car might be rigged, Nick?"

Nick's face was grim. He found Kragen's gun and handed it to her.

"That's why this guy better be there."

Nick wasn't certain he had taken the right dirt road. The turnoff wound through the forest like a snake. The trees were thick and black, like some nightmare landscape from a child's fairy tale. Nick almost began to worry after a minute of nothing but trees, but then their surroundings cleared and a strip of concrete, glimmering light gray under a half-moon, was visible before them. The scene was desolate and cold, like an abandoned lunar outpost. Two solitary structures stood alone on the edge of the airfield, one the size of a small home, the other more like a

shed. He could see two beat-up cars in a dirt lot behind the larger building. A light was on.

"What time is it?" Alex asked.

"Seven-thirty. What time was he supposed to wait until?"

"He wasn't. But there's a light on."

Dust kicked up behind them as they pulled into the lot next to the
two junkers. Nick couldn't remember the name Alex had told him to
ask for. He grabbed his pistol as a figure suddenly stepped from the
building. They watched him as he drew nearer. The man stopped about
ten feet away from them.

"Well, hey there. Is that Alex finally?"

"Who's that?"

"It's your damn pilot, that's who. You're over an hour late, y'know. I
was getting ready to shut off the lights and head home."

Nick let out a loud breath of relief. They stepped out of the car and
hurried up to him.

"What's your name?" Nick asked.

"Call me Bob."

"We need to get going now, Bob. Are you ready?"

"I've *been* ready. What kept you two?"

"I'll tell you when we're in the air. Let's just get going first."

"You got it, buddy."

They followed him through the building, which was really nothing
more than a dusty, oversized toolshed. Several hanging fixtures cast
faint light over wooden workbenches and rusting metal aircraft parts.
Bob grabbed a ring of keys hanging next to a girlie calendar and led
them back outside. He gestured to a small four-windowed Cessna that
sat about forty yards down the single strip of asphalt.

"There she is," he announced, like he was showing off his newborn
child. "She's gotta idle for five minutes before we can lift off. Engine
needs to build up some heat."

"Okay. Let's just please hurry."

They watched him enter the plane. The engine started in a low
whine, then leveled to a steady hum. Nick let himself relax slightly.
Without a word, he pulled Alex to him and closed his eyes. This was the
end, then. He wasn't sure when they would be back, but it was a secondary concern now. The future was a blank, but at least they *had* a
future.

"Nick . . ."

"Yes," he said, his eyes still shut.

"Nick, what's that?"

Nick looked over and felt his stomach plunge as if in free fall. Through the trees—was he imagining it? No—he could see the flash and glimmer of headlights. Whoever they were, they were coming fast.

Nick looked around wildly for cover. The shed was a concrete bunker with a single door. The larger building offered few places to hide. He saw one option.

"Come on!" he shouted, taking her hand and pulling her to the surrounding trees.

He was pulling Alex along so quickly she almost tripped. They reached the brush the moment the car broke into the clearing. It barreled toward the lot, then swerved wildly up to the plane. Two figures jumped out with guns in their hands.

"Oh God," Nick whispered. He looked at Alex. "We have to split up."

"Split up? Nick—"

"I'll draw their fire. Try and lose yourself in the woods. You've got your gun, right?"

"Yes, but—"

"Go now, Alex. *Hurry.*"

She looked as if she were going to argue, but then she turned and ran off into the dark woods. Nick clenched his gun and found cover behind a thick tree. The gunmen were outside the plane now. Nick watched in horror as they pulled Bob out by the back of his shirt. Kragen quickly ducked into the plane. Malloy pushed the pilot to the ground, and a gunshot tore the night air.

Nick felt his hopes die. The flight out was about to become a shootout, if it could even be called that. The men had emerged from the toolshed and were scanning the trees with goggles, sweeping the perimeter of the airstrip. Nick raised his gun, ready to fire. Every second he could pin them down was another second for Alex to lose herself in the thick woodlands.

He squeezed off two rapid shots that succeeded only in making them duck. The response came in a furious flurry of shots. Nick shrank against the tree as splinters of bark flew around him. The tree was easily thick enough to serve as a shield, but the gunmen were moving forward now, firing as they advanced. Nick reached around the tree and blindly fired off another shot. He ducked back around and cursed. It had been too long since he had fired a gun. Even if he had been at his best, the pistol was no match for the hardware now raining down on him. He slid low against the tree. Two bullets left. He closed his eyes, and an image of his father, quick as a flashbulb, blinked through his head, and then he stood to fire off his final shots.

What he saw made him pause. A pair of beams, bright enough to hurt the eyes, was suddenly bathing the gunmen in searing white light, freezing them like stage actors. They turned from Nick and raised their weapons—a second too late. The car plowed into them, throwing both of them through the air like rag dolls. They landed in the dirt and rolled pitifully. The driver's-side door flew open.

"Nick?"

Nick blinked, his mouth open. He wasn't sure if he had really witnessed this.

"Nick!" came Alex's voice again, frightened now.

He stepped out from behind the tree and ran out of the woods to her.

"Oh my God—*Nick!*"

They met and hugged in relief. The gunmen were on the ground and very still. The front grill of the car was cracked and twisted, and steam was billowing from the radiator.

"I made a run for it," she panted, her hand on her chest. "They pinned you down and I ran for it." She looked down at the two crumpled figures. "I think I killed them . . ."

Nick gave them a glance and frowned. He saw little chance in any human surviving an impact like that, not that he really cared. He walked up to them and sent their weapons skittering over the dirt with his foot. Then he remembered.

"Oh my God—the pilot!"

He ran to the plane. Bob was on his stomach, his eyes closed. A small trickle of blood was flowing from the side of his head.

"Oh God," said Nick, stooping to him.

The eyes suddenly opened.

"Those guys gone?"

Nick stepped back, startled. "You're . . . alive."

The pilot pulled himself up and dabbed at a mark on his forehead. "Son of a bitch pistol-whipped me," he said with a frown. "Blew out my damn eardrum with that shot. Said I was dead if I moved. What the hell were they after?"

"Don't worry about them. Can we get off the ground now?"

"No, we can't. I didn't agree to any of this, buddy."

"Bob, please—I'll make this worth your while. I promise you that."

"I don't want any part of this, pal. What the hell's this all about?"

"Look," said Nick. "More of these men are coming. If they find you here, they'll shoot you. I'm not lying, Bob. They'll kill all three of us. We need to leave now."

Bob glanced back at the road, chewed on his lower lip, then quickly reentered the plane.

"Get your friend and let's get the hell outta here before I change my mind."

Nick helped Alex up the stairs. Alex's eyes flew wide.

"Look!" she said, ducking low and pointing back toward the cars.

Nick didn't see anything at first, but then movement caught his eye. A figure had slunk out of the gunmen's car and was loping across the dirt lot toward the woods. Nick quickly realized the trees weren't his goal. Directly in his path were the dead men's guns.

Nick took two steps forward and raised the pistol. He held the gun steady and closed one eye, aiming low. He squeezed the trigger once, and the man did a clumsy hop and rolled to the ground.

Nick started toward him, gun extended. The man was on his back like an upended tortoise. His glasses hung crooked on his face, and tears were welling up in his eyes. He was shivering and clutching his leg. Nick patted him down quickly and found no weapon. He stared down at him and lowered his pistol, slowly shaking his head. There was no threat here, just a broken coward lying in the dirt. A familiar coward.

"Cimko," he said, disgust in his voice.

Philip Cimko didn't say a word, just lay there quivering like a scared child.

"Oh my God," said Alex, running up from behind. *"Him?"*

Nick nodded as he glared down at the wounded man. "Our mailers are on the way, Alex. Everything's taken care of."

He took the two dead men's weapons and turned to leave. He stopped himself. Alex wasn't budging. Her stare, like ice, was riveted to Cimko. The little man's eyes were shut now and failing to hold back the tears.

"We're walking away, Nick? After Rose? After everything he's done to us and the Von Rohrs?"

Nick's face was grim. He knew what she was considering, and he wasn't shocked. He looked down at the man and knew he wouldn't lose much sleep over it.

"Let's go, girl," he said, gently moving her along. "Pilot's waiting."

Alex was sitting by a window watching the field grow smaller, as the plane gained altitude. She suddenly jabbed her finger against the glass.

"Look!"

Nick placed his face to the circular window and saw them. Down on the ground, two more pairs of headlights had emerged from the road and were speeding onto the now deserted airfield. The cars stopped and men with guns were pouring out. Whoever they were, Nick was glad to miss them. They had arrived a minute too late.

He looked at Alex. She gave him a tired, beautiful smile. For once in their lives, neither of them could think of anything to say to each other.

The pilot had his headphones on. A radio was on softly and giving up-to-the-minute weather reports. The plane dipped and stabilized as he pointed the nose to the north.

Gordon waited alone at the gate. He was tired and a bit numb from it all, but more than anything he was angry. He was angrier than he had ever been in his entire life. He waited patiently beneath the speaker, looking old and worn down in the shadow of the immense home. His appearance was undoubtedly causing confusion, but this was to be expected, for he had never been here before. After a moment, the gate buzzed, and he pushed it open and followed the curving stone path to the front entrance. He stopped at the double oak doors and waited again. Three seconds passed, and a door swung open.

"Mr. Gordon," said Senator Newland, smiling but showing an uncertain glint in his eyes. "This is a bit of a surprise."

Gordon's stare was frigid. "We need to talk. It won't take more than a minute."

Newland nodded stiffly and stepped out of the doorway. Gordon entered and took a quick glance around the interior of the home. He assumed the senator's wife was around somewhere, but that didn't matter to him in the least. As far as he was concerned, she was more than welcome to listen in. She of all people was entitled to know, if she didn't know already.

"How can I help you?" asked Newland.

"Where's your VCR?" asked Gordon, not looking at him. "Is this your study?"

Senator Newland followed Gordon into the large study. Two senatorial aids stood motionless, their arms clutching thick bundles of papers. Their eyes darted nervously from the director back to their boss. Gordon looked about the study and waited as the senator sent them on their way. The room was the size of a small library, with a large television set in the wall opposite the rows of books.

"Can I offer you something to drink?" asked Newland, reentering the room.

"No. This won't take long."

"What can I help you with?"

"To begin with," continued Gordon, "I'd like to ask you a question. The day we met in the Oval Office—did you drop the truth about Jacobs on the President that day? Or did he find out from Merchant's report?"

A moment of surprised silence hung in the air. The tiny smile looked strained this time.

"Mr. Gordon, I am *not* following your question here."

"Of course you're not," replied Gordon condescendingly. "I expected you to say that. It doesn't matter—I already know the answer. It's clear I've been lied to all along, just as the President was lied to three years ago. Marshall never would have sent Jacobs to the Bureau if he had known who the old man really was. No—only one person knew the truth. Isn't that right, Senator?"

Newland folded his arms on his chest. "Mr. Gordon, if you have an issue with something the President's done, you probably would be best off going directly to him. Is there something you had specifically for me?"

"You bet your lying ass there is." He reached into his coat and removed a videotape. "May I?"

Newland eyed the tape warily. "What is that?"

Gordon took the liberty of clicking on the television and inserting the tape.

"I suppose you could call it a testimony of sorts. You may be interested in seeing it." He pressed Play. "I'll give Merchant one thing:

seems he was a damn good investigator. I don't know how he put all this together, but it's a solid piece of work. Of course, you may not agree."

Newland's eyes were narrowed. "And why do you think I would have the least bit of interest in hearing—"

A voice blared loudly from the television speakers. The sight of the fugitive made Newland pause, and only perverse curiosity made him stop and listen. Gordon decided he would sit now, but he had no intention of watching the video; he had already seen it twice. The only thing he was interested in seeing now was the reaction on the senator's face.

Newland stood silently, his face grim, and listened. Listened as Nicholas Merchant introduced himself, his business associates. Listened as he explained his findings in the Jacobs investigation. Listened as he held and explained a very clear set of color photographs. As he listened, Gordon waited, his eyes on the senator's profile.

Halfway through the monologue, Newland abruptly stopped the tape.

"May I ask where this piece of drivel came from?"

"This piece of drivel, as you call it, arrived at FBI headquarters just a short time ago. Along with a carefully put together packet of exhibits."

Newland was blinking rapidly. "Exhibits? What exhibits?"

Gordon walked up to the senator very, very closely.

"Photographs, FBI documents, bank documents. In other words, very damning exhibits, *Mr.* Newland. As I understand it, Merchant had the foresight to make half a dozen copies of this packet, as well as the videotape."

Newland swallowed. "And you have these? You're holding them at FBI headquarters?"

Gordon slowly shook his head. "Merchant says he mailed them. To the *Post* and the *Times*, for starters. I can't recall the other destinations, but there were at least half a dozen more. The President's already gotten his copy."

"The President?"

"That's right. I can tell you right now—I have *never* seen him this furious. He told me he doesn't give a damn what the fallout may be— he said he'll see you fry for this. That was a quote, Senator. He's getting a copy to the attorney general right now, and when that happens, my friend, I'm happy to say you'll be up to your eyeballs in shit."

Newland made a barely audible noise, like a groan from deep within himself. His hand reached out to steady himself against the wall. Gordon turned and made for the doorway. Suddenly he stopped and turned around.

"I imagine we'll be getting to know each other quite well these next few months, Newland. After the week I've had, I look forward to that."

He showed himself out and made his way back to the waiting limo.

THE LITTLE CESSNA was a surprisingly smooth ride. Alex was doing her best to calm Bob. She sat next to him and asked him about the intricacies of aerial navigation as she periodically dabbed at the gash on his forehead. After a while, the bleeding stopped and she put the towel aside and questioned him about the scattering of knobs and dials on the front console. He gradually succumbed to her attention, happy to demonstrate his knowledge to such a beautiful young woman. Eventually he even forgot about the lump on his head.

Nick sat in the back, feeling drained. His eyes were closed, but he was wide awake. He was listening to the conversation up front, and it was soothing to hear. Alex was dealing with the end of it in her own way, and he wouldn't intrude. When she was ready to talk, he would be there for her.

After a while, she stepped back and took a seat next to him.

"You okay?" he asked.

"I'm okay," she replied. "We're safe and I know my mother's okay."

"You got her out on the earlier flight, then?"

She nodded, then leaned her head on his shoulder, taking a slow breath. "Nine days ago, Nick. Nine days ago we found out about that estate. It feels like it was six months ago, but at least it's finally over."

"For us it's over. For some other people it's just beginning. Wherever we are, we'll hear about the fallout, I guarantee that."

Her smile indicated that she liked the thought of this.

"What happened with the FBI, Nick? How could they just let you go?"

He shook his head. "I don't know. Eventually it will all be traced back to Newland and his flunkies. Blame will fall where it should."

"Newland's wealthy, Nick. He'll fight it."

"He'll lose. He's already lost. He's ruined politically, legally—you name it. He'll be spending a long, long time in prison, Alex. The rest of his life, if there's any justice at all."

The plane shook momentarily in the headwinds. Bob had clicked the radio on to a county music station. Alex spoke after a minute.

"When will we be back, Nick? Will we *ever* be back?"

"Yes," he replied, putting his arm around her. "We'll have to lay low and see what comes out of this, but we'll get by. It won't be easy, but I think we'll be okay."

"I'm scared."

"Try not to be."

"I can't help it. Tomorrow scares me. And the day after that. Are we going to have to worry for the rest of our lives?"

"No," he said firmly. "No one will ever be able to find us. If everything unfolds like I think it will, they won't even have a reason to look for us anymore."

"Where are we going?"

"Anywhere we want."

"And when we get there? Then what? Drift around like two lost souls, too scared to go back home and too scared to find a new one?"

"It won't be that way. You know, maybe getting away for a while isn't such a bad thing for me. I've had ghosts hanging over me that I've wanted to do away with for a while now. This may be the way to do it." He looked at her. "Don't worry, Alex. You and I are survivors. We'll get by just fine."

She didn't reply. A bright fingernail of a half-moon reflected through the glass on her face—that beautiful face. He was thankful he didn't have to do this by himself. Things would be easier with Alex nearby. They always were.

He rubbed her shoulder and the memory of his father floated through his mind. He wondered what he would have thought if he had been around to see this. Would he be happy, ashamed, pleased, disgusted? Probably none of those, he realized. His father would have seen the good and the bad. He would have seen that they had gone too far trying to solve Jacobs, and that in doing so, they had let loose a monster. But he would also have seen that they had put their lives on the line to try to make things right again. And he would have felt good about that part of it.

"Maybe even proud," murmured Nick.

Alex looked at him. "What did you say?"

Nick shook his head. "I was wondering what my father would be thinking if he could see all this."

"He'd be sad that Merchant and Associates is dead. We'll never find heirs again, Nick."

Nick looked out the window. Below, the scattered lights of civilization twinkled like stars. He tried to fight back a smile.

"What's so funny?"

"You know, I was thinking of shutting down Merchant and Associates anyway, even before all this happened."

"You *what*?"

"*Merchant and Associates* sounds so dull. I was thinking something along the lines of, say, *Merchant and Moreno*. Sound okay?"

Her smile was huge.

"Sounds perfect."

He squeezed her hand, and the two of them looked out the window together, toward the horizon.

Chris Larsgaard, a real-life heir hunter with more than a decade of experience on the job, lives in San Francisco. *The Heir Hunter* is his first novel.